A DARK DIRTY WAR

Siobhan Dunmoore Book 7

Eric Thomson

A Dark and Dirty War
First paperback printing July 2021
This edition June 2023

Published in Canada
By Sanddiver Books Inc.
ISBN: 978-1-989314-40-1

Sanddiver
Books Inc

— One —

The ear-splitting shriek of *Salamanca*'s battle stations siren shattered the flag combat information center's quiet yet expectant atmosphere. Although Siobhan Dunmoore, sitting in the throne-like command chair, was expecting the sudden change in the Reconquista class cruiser's condition, she nonetheless felt a familiar rush of adrenaline shoot through her body.

"Here goes nothing," Gregor Pushkin, sitting at the operations director console in front of the holographic tactical projection, muttered. Then, in a louder voice, "Ship's sensors report three unknown contacts lit up just under seven hundred thousand klicks off our starboard bow. Based on size and detectable power emissions, the combat systems officer estimates that they're warships in the same class as Commonwealth Navy cruisers. No transponders, no markings, and no clear indications of who built them, but they seem human. Since the sensors didn't detect a transition from hyperspace, they were likely running silent and waiting in ambush, using the distressed civilian vessel as bait."

Dunmoore nodded once, a sphinx-like expression on her lean face.

"So far, so good."

The sound of a panicked male voice came through CIC's speakers tuned to the emergency sublight frequency.

"*Salamanca*, this is *Hideki Maru* again. The damned bastards are back, and they're pinging me with targeting sensors. My threat board is glowing red. You need to make it here fast. I repeat, my ship is being painted by targeting sensors."

Pirates had attacked and disabled *Hideki Maru*, an Edo-class mixed passenger and cargo ship with two hundred and sixty humans aboard the previous day, though her captain claimed they drove off the attackers. Since the Edo-class vessels were built for the volatile frontiers and well-armed, the assertion seemed plausible. *Salamanca*, the first of the Series Ten Reconquista cruisers, an evolution of the Shrehari War design and outfitted as a flagship, had been on a routine patrol along the Commonwealth's outer edges when she received the signal. She'd immediately jumped through hyperspace to render assistance.

Dunmoore swiveled her command chair to port and studied the bank of displays covering the bulkhead. Instead of telemetry and various status readouts, most showed live feeds from multiple parts of the ship, notably its bridge, the CIC, and the main engineering compartment, where members of her team sat at unused workstations, observing the crew.

"Gunnery is targeting the three tangos," Pushkin reported, "and helm is changing course for an intercept."

"*Hideki Maru*, this is *Salamanca*. We're on our way at best sublight speed. Stand by."

Dunmoore recognized the voice as that of Captain Piotr Rydzewski, the cruiser's commanding officer, freshly promoted into the job after three years as first officer in one of *Salamanca*'s older sister ships. He'd come out of the Shrehari War as a junior lieutenant commander and was moving up the ranks at a decent enough clip, even though he'd never held a starship command before this one.

"Unknown vessels," Rydzewski continued, "this is the Commonwealth Navy ship *Salamanca*, cruiser. The civilian ship you are targeting is under my protection. Withdraw at once. If you open fire, we will do so as well."

"That'll be fun," Pushkin said, sotto voce, even though he and Dunmoore were alone in the flag CIC. "We could handle odds of three to one back in the day. These postwar captains? Not so much, I think."

"Be nice, Gregor." She gave him a wry smile. "They don't enjoy the benefit of several years commanding starships in combat like us. I'm sure Captain Rydzewski is perfectly capable of handling the situation. Otherwise, he wouldn't be commanding the Fleet's newest warship. Besides, the Series Ten are more than twice as capable as the original Series One Reconquistas. He might surprise even a jaded old space dog like you."

Pushkin let out a soft snort.

"I suppose you'd know, seeing as how he was one of your students at the War College. But there's a wide gulf between theory and practice."

"Says the man who never attended and is now too senior for a year ashore in a classroom."

"You mean overage in grade. But since I don't nurture any ambitions of becoming a flag officer, let alone a staffer in some large, probably dysfunctional peacetime headquarters, it's just as well the Navy didn't waste money on furthering my professional education." A pause. "The tangos are now targeting *Salamanca*, and from the emission signature, they're powering weapons. The sparks are about to fly."

"You're enjoying this more than is decent, Gregor."

"And you aren't? Face it, this is the closest we come to reliving the glory days of Task Force Luckner."

Dunmoore made a face at him. "Don't remind me."

Rydzewski repeated his message to the unidentified ships, forestalling Pushkin's reply. Instead, the latter said, eyes on the image of *Salamanca*'s captain, "They won't answer, Skipper. There's no percentage in speaking with the Navy when you have the edge."

"I'm sure Piotr is aware of that, but he's duty-bound to try everything short of opening fire until the very last minute. The Admiralty no longer tolerates the shoot first, ask questions later doctrine. Targeting ships with fire control sensors may be impolite, but it isn't explicitly illegal, and he only has *Hideki Maru*'s word that they're hostile. For all he knows, there's a much different game being played over there."

"Did anyone ever mention how devious you've become since the war ended?"

"Almost five years of intellectual sparring with up and comers determined to count coup on the infamous Siobhan Dunmoore, head of the Unconventional Warfare Department, will do that."

"Did any of your students ever succeed?"

She glanced at him over her shoulder, one eyebrow cocked. "What do you think?"

"Since I heard no War College graduate boast about winning a debate with you — and they would, believe me — I guess that's a no."

A nod. "Apparently, I was known as Dunmoore the Destroyer among those who witnessed me tearing apart ill-prepared students, not that I was ever supposed to find out. Unfortunately, those whose lack of hard work resulted in unpleasant consequences used a different nickname, one that could see them disciplined for insulting a senior officer, and no, I won't repeat it even if we're alone in here."

Pushkin grinned at her.

"Then I'll ask the chief. If he doesn't know, he'll dig up friends who can find out."

"He's more likely to tell you some things are best left alone."

"Probably." Pushkin turned his gaze back on the holographic tactical display where the blue icon representing *Salamanca* was closing with the tangos, marked in red, and *Hideki Maru* in green. "We're entering extreme engagement range. Our shields are up, guns are powering, missile launchers are ready. Still no transponder signal or reply from the unknown ships."

He paused.

"Correction. Incoming message from one of the tangos, text only, no voice or video. To the Commonwealth Navy ship *Salamanca*, withdraw, and we'll spare the lives of *Hideki Maru*'s crew and passengers. Keep coming at us, and our first salvo will kill everyone aboard her. Their deaths will be on your conscience." Pushkin looked up at Dunmoore. "Nasty."

"What can I say? Piotr will probably face this sort of thing during his command tour." She shrugged. "The Shrehari War's unresolved issues have been festering for years, Gregor. Surplus ships, surplus spacers, and surplus anger on both sides is a dangerous mixture. Especially when our government would rather maintain the pre-war arrangements between Earth and the sovereign star systems instead of acknowledging the latter's greater stake in charting humanity's future."

Pushkin made a face.

"Much as I didn't enjoy the war, at least you knew where you stood. But the politicking since it ended isn't particularly peaceful either."

"It hasn't been peaceful, period. While you and I were riding desks, the known galaxy took on the sort of deadly edge we never experienced while fighting Brakal and his like."

Pushkin turned his attention back on the holographic tactical projection, alerted by a low-pitched signal, and let out a soft whistle.

"Two more tangos unmasked aft of our current position and are painting us with targeting sensors. So it just became a five against one proposition. Missile launches from all tangos — twenty apiece for one hundred birds in the first salvo. That'll leave a mark."

A hundred small missile icons appeared in the tactical projection, every single one of them headed for the cruiser.

Dunmoore glanced back at the display showing *Salamanca*'s CIC. Captain Rydzewski, a solidly built, square-faced man in his late thirties with dark blond hair and deep-set blue eyes, was leaning forward, staring at his tactical display. She could see his jaw clench as if he were fighting back a coiled spring ready to explode. Astonishment had wiped away his earlier calm confidence, replaced by something that could be the realization he now faced a no-win scenario.

Three against one for a Series Ten Reconquista cruiser might still be feasible. Five against one, not so much, especially with hostiles both forward and aft. He could still accelerate and risk making an emergency jump, even though his drives hadn't yet fully cycled. A new ship like *Salamanca* would take the added strain. But it meant condemning *Hideki Maru*'s crew and passengers to a ghastly fate — if the freighter was a victim and not in on a scheme to ambush the Fleet's newest warship.

"*Salamanca* has fired a full spread of missiles at the tangos, ten per, and is now diverting resources to shields and anti-missile defenses." A few moments passed, then, "Engaging enemy birds."

Red missile icons vanished one after the other from the tactical display. But Dunmoore knew it wouldn't be enough.

Her eyes were drawn to the screen showing the bridge, and she caught sight of Chief Guthren's lips moving. Though she couldn't hear his words, Dunmoore would bet anything he was muttering the time-honored words used by spacers throughout the ages and by wet navy sailors before them.

For what we are about to receive, may the Almighty make us truly grateful.

Silent explosions tore at the cruiser's shields, transforming them from a sedate, rippling green to a deep, menacing purple in a matter of moments as competing energies warred with each other. The tangos fired again, sending another one hundred missiles to further erode *Salamanca*'s defenses and strike her hull. But they wouldn't escape unscathed. The cruiser's ordnance, more powerful, modern, and effective than anything fielded by the Commonwealth's enemies, gave her attackers problems of their own.

But it came too late.

"The starboard bow shield has just collapsed after its generator burned out." A pause. "Helm is rotating the ship on her long axis to hide the vulnerable zone from direct fire." Another pause. "Central port side shield is gone as well. Missile strike on the hull."

A new alarm siren rang out, sending damage control parties into action under the second officer's orders.

"Oh. Here it goes. Another shield just failed." Pushkin shook his head. "Looks like the generator wasn't up to spec and burned out faster than it should. Port side main guns took a hit. One of the capacitors triggered cascading damage through that part of the system. Engineering isolated the event but not before it affected the power node."

By now, Dunmoore could sense growing concern, if not yet panic, in the CIC, the bridge, and main engineering. Once failures began cascading, a starship's life could be counted in minutes, if not seconds.

"More hits on the hull. Starboard hyperdrive nacelle is damaged. We will not be jumping out of this situation. All damage control teams are in action. The second officer is triaging as fast as he can. Both forward missile launchers are offline. Hull is punctured in seven — no, eight different spots. Engineering is venting antimatter fuel."

Dunmoore nodded. If the ship was ridding itself of the highly volatile substance that powered its hyperdrives, it meant either Captain Rydzewski or his chief engineer had decided the end was nigh. Her assumption was confirmed moments later when a new klaxon rang out, followed by Rydzewski's voice.

"All hands, abandon ship. I repeat, all hands, abandon ship."

— TWO —

Captain Siobhan Dunmoore tapped the arm of her command chair and released control of *Salamanca*'s main computer back to its crew. Then, she called up the public address system.

"This is RED One Leader, endex. I repeat, this is RED One Leader, endex. The ship will resume cruising stations as per the captain's orders. RED One will assemble in the flag conference room in ten minutes. Dunmoore, out."

Pushkin slowly stood and stretched, then rotated his shoulders with a sigh of relief.

"You really pushed the no-win this time, Skipper. I almost believed it myself. Judging by the faces in the CIC and on the bridge, many of them were as well. It'll be a bit before the adrenaline levels around here drop."

She imitated her deputy team leader and operations officer, then made a face.

"Piotr Rydzewski was getting a little full of himself during the last few tactical evaluations. He displayed the same bad habit during simulations at the War College. I can't recall who, but someone told me he seriously discussed sabotaging the no-win scenarios with his classmates when I used them to cure him and a few others of their overconfidence."

"And did he?"

Dunmoore shook her head.

"No one managed during my time there, though my informants tell me one or two tried. Not Piotr, though. I think he may have decided it wasn't worth the risk."

"What would you have done if you'd caught a student changing the code?"

"Assigned one or two extra command essays on top of extra no-win simulations." Dunmoore nodded at the door connecting the flag CIC with the conference room. "Do you think the coffee urn survived *Salamanca*'s brush with oblivion?"

"If the galley hasn't ejected it into space as retaliation for our turning the ship into a chaotic mess. Although if pastries magically materialized, I'd be careful lest they contain a substance that might send us running to the heads with comical expressions on our faces."

Dunmoore let out a quick snort. "They wouldn't dare."

Pushkin gave her a wink. "Then I'll let you take the first few bites."

Upon entering the conference room, Dunmoore and Pushkin found not only a coffee urn on a sideboard, merrily chugging, but a platter of sandwiches, vegetables, and fruit — a belated lunch now that *Salamanca* was no longer at battle stations.

They were both enjoying a cup when the members of Readiness Evaluation Division Team One filtered in. Four experienced lieutenant commanders, each assisted by an equally experienced chief petty officer second class, they were subject matter experts in their fields — combat systems, propulsion engineering, systems engineering, navigation and communications, and security. Last to arrive was Chief Petty Officer First Class Kurt Guthren, RED One's security specialist and Dunmoore's unofficial coxswain.

The team members had more than just subject matter expertise in common. None of them expected any further promotions and were likely in their final assignments before retiring. It meant they couldn't be pressured into going easy on ships under readiness evaluation, or ignoring faults, no matter how minor.

Dunmoore and her fellow RED team leaders, veteran captains who'd commanded starships during the Shrehari War, remembered only too well the losses incurred because ships and crews weren't fully prepared for the worst situations, especially during the war's early years. The same held true for all of the Readiness Evaluation Division's officers and chief petty officers. RED teams weren't particularly welcome aboard warships, but most understood they performed a vital function.

Once they were seated around the table with food and drink before them, Chief Guthren said, "Hearing the 'all hands abandon ship' order never gets old, Captain."

Pushkin chuckled. "Mainly because it means the next word on the public address system is endex, right?"

Guthren grinned at him. "In part. But also because you can witness the crew's unfiltered reaction at knowing they failed. The first officer was a true study in repressed anger."

"Alright." Dunmoore held up a hand. "Let's discuss your observations and what each of you will tell the relevant department heads during their respective hot washes."

One by one, the lieutenant commanders, aided by their chiefs, laid out their findings and recommendations, adding them to *Salamanca*'s detailed readiness report. It would be read with great interest by the flag officers commanding the cruiser's assigned battle group and fleet, the rear admiral commanding the Readiness Evaluation Division, and ultimately the Navy's Chief of Operations.

Failure to meet the exacting standards in one or more areas meant further work-up training and a new evaluation cycle. Rarely, though it had happened during Dunmoore's tenure with the division, a ship experienced issues grave enough that captains were relieved of duty. But not this time.

"So we're agreed?" Dunmoore let her eyes roam around the table once Chief Guthren, the last to report, fell silent. "*Salamanca* is in every respect ready?"

The team members nodded in turn as her eyes briefly rested on them.

"Thank you." Dunmoore stood. "I'll debrief Captain Rydzewski while you speak with the department heads. Once that's done, you may consider yourselves off duty until we dock."

Dunmoore found *Salamanca*'s commanding officer in his day cabin. He looked at her ruefully as she settled in a chair across from him.

"That was nasty even for you, Siobhan."

"Remember when I took you down a peg at the College?"

He nodded. "I guess I did it again, right?"

"Yes. You're blessed with a superb crew, Piotr, and the finest ship in the Fleet. Failure was never an option, and everyone aboard knew it. That's why success after success in our evaluations made you a little overconfident. But as you know, I have the ideal remedy. Remember it whenever you feel a little full of yourself."

"I will."

"That being said, congratulations. You passed with flying colors. My report will declare you ready for duty in every respect. You'll receive a copy when I send it up our respective chains of command. Since nothing is perfect, there are a few areas where improvements will help tighten things, but overall, you command an efficient, well-run ship, my friend, and I wish you joy of her. Give your people a Bravo Zulu from me and RED One. We're the toughest of the bunch and take the most important assignments."

"Wilco." He studied her for a few seconds. "If you don't mind me asking since this was my first readiness evaluation as skipper, do you always end the sequence with a nasty no-win like that? I haven't heard much on the grapevine about your habits."

"It depends on the captain and crew. I always end an evaluation cruise with something that will push them beyond their limits after passing everything else. The no-win doesn't come up often, so consider it a compliment. And in case you're wondering, they're never the same scenarios. The next one I run will differ from yours, and the captain under evaluation won't know whether it's just another test or my version of the final exam."

Rydzewski sat back and nodded.

"I'll take it in the spirit you intended. Did you ever face a no-win, or is that question still as taboo as it was at the War College?"

"A few. I lost the corvette *Shenzen* at Antae Carina in '63 to a Shrehari task force, making me one of the few surviving wartime captains who gave the command to abandon ship. Then there was the time I fought Brakal in the Cimmeria system during my first cruise as *Stingray*'s captain. We shouldn't have survived, except my chief engineer and one of her ratings sacrificed their lives to restart our sublight drives." Dunmoore shook her head. "So many dead. And that's why I put you and your crew through the wringer."

"Understood. I may not have enjoyed the experience, but we've come out of it stronger and more confident." He raised a hand before she could speak. "And no more overconfidence. Promised. Another question, if I may?"

"Sure."

"Where do you sit during what you call the final exam in a ship without a flag CIC?"

She smiled.

"Wherever I can access every part of the ship's systems while being invisible to the captain and first officer. If there's an auxiliary bridge, I'll kick the chief engineer out. If not, sometimes I take over the captain's day cabin for that final evolution. I'm a big believer in the Navy's interpretation of the observer effect, remember? The mere presence of an observer changes the behavior of those being observed."

"Yet your people were watching us."

"True, but they can blend in with your crew and make themselves inconspicuous. Another post captain like me, not so much."

Rydzewski let out a rueful chuckle.

"Especially one with the name Siobhan Dunmoore. What happens to you and your team now?"

"You drop us off at Starbase 30 from where we'll take a ship either home to Caledonia or to our next tasking. I'll know once I pick up my orders from the base commander."

Rydzewski cocked an eyebrow. "Caledonia and not Earth?"

"The RED teams are dispersed around the Commonwealth. It reduces travel time. Besides, Caledonia has enough shipyards to keep us busy with new crews. But when the Navy plans to put something like the first of the Series Ten Reconquistas through its paces, HQ assigns RED One. My team is what you might call *primus inter pares*, the first among equals."

"With you as its leader, that doesn't surprise me. Am I right in remembering Commander Pushkin and Chief Guthren served under your orders in *Stingray?*"

"As the first officer and coxswain, respectively. Chief Guthren followed me to *Iolanthe* while Gregor was promoted and took *Jan Sobieski*, which ended up becoming one of my frigates when I was Task Force Luckner's commander. In fact, I used her as my flagship for the attack on the Shrehari home system. So, you could say he, Chief Guthren, and I lived through a lot together, which is why I finagled their appointment to RED One."

Dunmoore caught the expression in Rydzewski's eyes and knew he was diplomatically avoiding any mention that Pushkin and Guthren were probably in their last years of service anyway, just like she was. Her ultimate turn in front of the commodores' promotion board was coming up, and if they didn't place her file above the cut-off line, she'd be facing retirement as well.

The captains' boards had published their results before RED One joined *Salamanca,* and Pushkin already knew his name wasn't on the list. It had been his last turn as well, meaning this was likely his terminal assignment before separation from the Navy.

Exemplary wartime service as a starship captain didn't count for much anymore, now that the memories were fading and officers too junior for command during the war occupied the most coveted senior positions, those leading to a flag officer's stars. It wasn't fair, but as Dunmoore knew, it happened after every conflict.

Not for the first time, she wondered whether the three of them should set up their own private military corporation once they marched into retirement at what were still relatively young ages. Dunmoore, Pushkin, and Guthren, Spacers of Fortune — it had a certain ring. A depressing one, certainly, but such was life.

"Always good to have old comrades you can rely on as part of any team." He gave her an uncertain smile.

"The friends we make and, more importantly, keep are the only certainty in this life." Dunmoore stood. "I won't take up any more of your time. You have a million things to set right after we threw *Salamanca* into a tailspin. As of now, RED One personnel are mere passengers who'll do their best to stay out of everyone's way. But, thankfully, the trip to Starbase 30 won't take long."

"No. We should see you ashore in two days."

— Three —

Siobhan Dunmoore remembered docking at Starbase 30 almost a decade earlier, just before she embarked on the most momentous mission in her career. It seemed unchanged to her eyes as *Salamanca* made her final approach. For a moment, she was back in *Iolanthe*, commanding Task Force Luckner and wearing a commodore's star on her collar, though the storied Q ship was built as a lone hunter, not the leader of a formation which changed the course of history.

She didn't turn when the door opened with barely a whisper, though it pulled her out of the moment.

"Reliving old glories?"

"Those were the days, Gregor. Life in this old Navy hasn't been the same since we faced Brakal across the armistice table on Aquilonia Station. Starbase 30 isn't even home to 3rd Fleet HQ anymore. A few years ago, it relocated to the surface, leaving the admiral commanding the local battle group as the senior officer aboard." Dunmoore glanced over her shoulder. "But in a little twist of fate, that is now Rear Admiral Oliver Harmel, who had *Terra* back then. Remember him?"

Pushkin joined her by the command chair, dropped his bags, and nodded.

"Sure. Nice guy. Made that massive space control ship run like a finely tuned machine even with a surfeit of top brass getting in the way. He must have the patience of a saint."

"Oliver and I commiserated many an evening watch on our way to Caledonia because both of us knew we'd never command another starship again. We'd had our turn."

"Except Harmel parlayed his flag captain posting into a pair of stars and his own battle group." Though Pushkin tried to keep an even tone, Dunmoore caught a hint of bitterness underlying his words.

"And I parlayed an extensive tour at the War College into command of RED One — that's what you meant to say, right? But like I told Zeke when my orders arrived, no admirals in their right mind would take a former commodore whose broad pennant flew over the war's most famous task force as their flag captain. Don't worry. I'm not jealous of Oliver. He's solid, competent, and yes, a genuinely nice guy who earned command of the Fleet's flagship where he was noticed for the things a peacetime Navy wants in a senior officer. I'll be making my manners with him when we dock and not only because he'll pass on our orders." She gave Pushkin a wry smile. "Who knows? If I set up a private military corporation after retiring, I might need a few reliable contacts who can steer work my way."

"I think you'll have more luck with that Mikhail Forenza chap. Based on what you told me about him, his lot are the ones who might employ shady operations the government can disavow."

"Perhaps, though I've not come across him in so long that I don't even know if he's still working for the Colonial Office's Intelligence Service. Or whether he's even among the living. Besides, I'd need someone with deep pockets to help create a PMC before I can chase contracts, and that's a whole different challenge." A shrug. "I doubt I'd make a good mercenary in any case. Maybe I can find a job as a civilian starship captain. The big shipping companies will have absorbed the postwar surplus of trained officers by now."

"Keep developing the PMC idea, Skipper. You wouldn't last long working for outfits whose biggest concern is cutting costs."

Dunmoore let out a soft snort. "Probably not."

They watched the rest of the docking maneuver in silence until the public address system lit up with the first officer's voice, calling the crew to harbor stations.

"I suppose we should head for the main airlock." Dunmoore climbed to her feet and picked up her luggage.

They found the rest of the team, along with Captain Rydzewski and his coxswain, waiting for them.

Rydzewski stuck out his hand and grinned.

"Always a pleasure being put through the wringer by my old *sensei*."

As they shook, Dunmoore smiled back. "Take good care of your ship and her crew, Piotr. They deserve nothing but the best."

With that, RED One disembarked, another job finished to Dunmoore's exacting standards, and headed for the base's transient officers' and chief petty officers' quarters. She dropped her gear in the sitting room of a suite usually assigned to visitors with stars on their collars — no doubt Oliver Harmel showing her the utmost courtesy — and headed for the latter's office, where she was expected.

Harmel's flag lieutenant jumped to her feet when Dunmoore appeared in the antechamber and gestured at the door behind her.

"Welcome, sir. Please go ahead. The admiral is waiting for you."

Before Dunmoore took more than two steps, a dark-complexioned, heavy-set, bald man in his late fifties with intelligent eyes beneath thick brows popped through the open doorway, smiling broadly.

"Siobhan! What a delight to see you again after all this time. Come in, come in." His booming voice was as deep as ever.

He ushered her into the office once occupied by the Flag Officer Commanding 3rd Fleet and gestured at a settee group in one corner.

"Please make yourself comfortable. Can I offer you coffee, tea, or perhaps something a bit stronger?"

"Thank you, sir, but I'm good."

Harmel sat across from her and leaned forward.

"You've not changed a bit since we last met."

"Other than a few more strands of gray in my hair and additional wrinkles around my eyes, you mean?" She grinned at him. "You, on the other hand, look like a true flag officer. Congratulations on the promotion and the appointment."

"Thanks. I never thought I'd make it this far." Harmel's expression changed, and he almost seemed chagrined. "Unfortunately, I'm the bearer of bad news."

"I didn't make the cut-off on the most recent commodore's promotion list." Dunmoore was happy her tone remained flat and without a shred of emotion.

Harmel shook his head.

"Sadly, no. And if I'm not mistaken, that was the last time you were under consideration."

"It was." She shrugged. "Such is life. I'm sure the Fleet will squeeze a few more years out of me as RED One's team leader. Do you have the list? I'm curious about who made it."

"Certainly. I also received the other flag officer lists if you're interested. Shall I forward them to your quarters?"

"Please. And by the way, thanks for giving me the VIP suite. I appreciate the gesture."

"You outranked me once and would still outrank me if there was any justice in this universe." He sat back. "And now, deliberately changing the subject, how did *Salamanca* do? I'd give up any chances at a third star to see her assigned as my flagship."

"She did extremely well. So well, in fact, I ran her through the nastiest no-win scenario as the last test."

"Please tell me everything. Believe it or not, your job is more fun than mine most days. All I'm busy with is approving patrol schedules and various bits of administrivia."

**

"How's the admiral?" Pushkin asked when Dunmoore joined him in the almost empty wardroom for a drink before supper. Her other officers hadn't shown up yet, but she knew without checking that Guthren and his colleagues were in the chiefs' and petty officers' mess next door.

"Prospering, and still a nice guy. He delivered the news I didn't make the commodore's list personally. And then, just to torture myself, I asked for a copy of the list so I could see which undeserving bugger took my slot."

When Pushkin gave her a look of astonishment, she let out a grim chuckle.

"I also perused the various admirals' promotion lists, so yes, I'm a tad bitter at the moment. Several of my less brilliant students at the War College are now wearing a commodore's star, officers whose only saving grace is the ability to do precisely what their superiors expect, no more, no less. You know, the type I wouldn't employ as captain in Task Force Luckner."

She raised the whiskey tumbler she'd picked up at the bar on her way in and took a healthy sip.

"Too bad it's not Thursday. The toast of the day would be more than appropriate."

"To hell with it not being Thursday." Pushkin hoisted his glass. "A bloody war or a sickly season."

She imitated him, and both downed their drinks. Pushkin turned toward the bar, caught the bar tender's eye, and raised two fingers. Fresh servings appeared within moments.

"But on to more easily digestible news. Officers of our acquaintance, people we actually like and respect, made the flag officers' promotion lists too, so it's not completely depressing."

Pushkin cocked a questioning eyebrow. "Such as?"

"Kathryn Kowalski, after spending a mere two years as a commodore, is now a rear admiral and one of Fleet HQ's rising stars in the Naval Operations branch."

"Wow." He let out a low whistle. "I wish I knew how she did it after finishing the war as a relatively junior commander."

"Yes, but Kathryn served as the first officer of a Reconquista class cruiser, where she evidently shone because she was promoted to post captain two years after the armistice. Then, she spent the next two years in command of another Reconquista, followed by another two years as flag captain, then off to Earth and Fleet HQ where she evidently found a path to glory."

"Well done, her. She'll finish with four stars, if not five at this rate."

"I wouldn't be surprised if that's her ultimate goal. Ezekiel Holt received his first star, almost in the nick of time. I think he had two more chances after this one. He's another of our friends who made an assignment to Fleet HQ pay off, but in counterintelligence."

Pushkin took another sip. "I guess during peacetime, it's not what you know but who you know."

"Things weren't that different during the war. If you'll recall, I could also count on friends in high places back then. They helped get me *Stingray* and *Iolanthe*."

"Because you were the perfect captain for the job."

Her face briefly took on a dismissive expression.

"Perhaps, but without them, someone else would have commanded both."

"Screwing *Stingray* up even further and ensuring the war would continue for another ten years because there's no one with your genius for doing what's necessary in the most unusual and effective way possible."

Dunmoore shrugged off the compliment and stared at the amber liquid in her glass.

"Any other acquaintances with new stars on their uniforms?"

"A few." She rattled off half a dozen names.

"Can't say any of them don't deserve it." He saw movement by the entrance. "Here's the rest of the crew. Time to plaster our best smiles on and chat about other matters, such as whether we go home or directly to our next job."

She looked up and gave him a tight smile.

"Saved by RED One. Oh, and we are going home on the next available ship. Admiral Harmel gave me our orders."

**

Rear Admiral Kathryn Kowalski, the newly appointed Director of Operations for the Rim Sector and Protectorate Zone under the Chief of Naval Operations, looked up from her workstation as Commander Ahmad, one of the desk officers, rapped his knuckles on her office door jamb.

"Come on in."

"Sir, we may face a problem that could involve the Protectorate Zone, something 3rd Fleet just kicked up to us."

Kowalski, a tall, slender blond in her early forties with intense blue eyes, instinctively knew that what started as another ordinary day, had just taken a sharp turn to starboard. Only the most intractable — read political — issues filtered up to Naval Operations at Fleet HQ on Earth.

— Four —

Kowalski made a go-on motion with her hand.

"The Marengo system subspace array, as well as one of our interstellar arrays, picked up a distress signal on the emergency band from the civilian luxury liner *Athena* approximately thirty-six hours ago. Apparently, the ship was on a cruise of the outer colonies when pirates hijacked it. The captain managed to send a message before the pirates seized his bridge. He claims insiders took over just as three ships that didn't quite seem built by human hands intercepted him at the Marengo system's heliopause. Images accompanied the distress signal, and I concur with the assessment on the ships, though I've passed the images to the intelligence desk. Using both arrays for triangulation, the senior officer in the system determined the approximate position where the incident occurred. He then dispatched one of the frigates on station to pursue and hopefully figure what course *Athena* and the pirates took, though with orders to make sure they didn't violate the Treaty."

"Why did 3rd Fleet pass it on instead of taking action and merely informing the operations center?"

Ahmad grimaced.

"Several reasons, sir, and I can't blame them. First, according to the manifest, most passengers aboard *Athena* have high-level political or commercial connections and were on a junket to convince the colonies they're better off under direct Earth rule. Among the names are those of the SecGen's eldest daughter, the brother of ComCorp's current president and CEO, along with relatives of star system senators and other high-level officials. A veritable who's who of the Commonwealth upper crust. Then there's the matter of insiders and a clean intercept, meaning the hijackers compromised the junket well before *Athena* reached Marengo's heliopause. They clearly knew what course she was on, which makes it a national security issue. Finally, there's the matter of presumed pirate ships not being of an identifiable type so close to the Protectorate and the Shrehari Empire. We've known for years pirates and other assorted criminals use the Treaty of Ulufan provisions forbidding naval and military forces of both parties from violating the Protectorate's neutrality to escape our patrols."

Kowalski grimaced.

"One of the diplomats' more boneheaded moves, theirs and ours, though I suspect the bastards are still operating naval ships disguised as corsairs to keep tabs on bad actors and smack them as needed."

"And we're not, sir?" Ahmad grinned. "Our Q ships vanish for weeks at a time in that area."

"Did you ever hear the expression ask me no questions, and I will tell you no lies?"

Ahmad's smile broadened. "Understood, Admiral."

"You're preparing a note for the CNO?"

"The moment we're done here. We received more details from 3rd Fleet, which I'll include in the note."

"Good. I'll pass the word up the chain of command. Be ready to brief him, and possibly even the Grand Admiral, before the day is out. This can become a clusterfrack in no time."

Ahmad nodded once and vanished back into the bullpen, where teams of officers and chief petty officers stood watch twenty-four hours a day. Meanwhile, Kowalski asked for a link with her direct superior, the deputy chief of naval operations, to warn him of impending trouble.

Both she and Ahmad found themselves in Grand Admiral Sampaio's conference room ninety minutes later, briefing the supreme commander of humanity's Armed Forces. Sitting with him were Admiral Zebulon Lowell, the Chief of Naval Operations, and Admiral Jado Doxiadis, the Chief of Naval Intelligence.

Sampaio took on a thoughtful expression when Ahmad fell silent and sat back in his leather chair.

"This is extremely troubling news and can trigger the worst political crisis since the war. I don't doubt a large faction in the Senate and our own ranks will accuse Shrehari revanchists of waging a dirty war against us despite Brakal ordering his forces to stand down after he seized power. And in turn, the Shrehari government will accuse us of fomenting a crisis to rekindle hostilities over the status of the Protectorate Zone. Brakal is nothing if not a stickler for keeping his and the Empire's commitments as a matter of honor. That could easily put us on the slippery slope to a new interstellar conflict, something which certain parties in both the Commonwealth and the Empire would welcome."

Admiral Doxiadis nodded.

"A disastrous outcome, especially since it could just be another case of common piracy, this time aimed at ransoming members of wealthy and powerful families. Criminal organizations in that part of the galaxy are becoming bolder with every passing year, thanks to our and the Shrehari's postwar drawdown, leaving us overstretched. More worrisome yet, we're seeing disenchanted Commonwealth Armed Forces veterans entering that ugly universe by creating their own mercenary outfits, whose members are intimately familiar with our tactics, techniques, and procedures."

"I'm open to suggestions," Sampaio said. "I need a plan I can present the SecGen before he goes ballistic when I brief him on this in," he glanced at the antique clock on a sideboard, "two hours."

"If I may, sir." Kowalski raised her hand. "We have no choice but to pursue with every means at our disposal. Anything less will precipitate the crisis you fear. I suggest we take it as a given that *Athena* is on her way to a destination in the Protectorate Zone, which naval forces cannot enter because of the Treaty."

"Agreed," the Chief of Naval Intelligence interjected. "Please continue, Admiral Kowalski."

"We must create a mission element capable of finding and rescuing our people, and it must be under the command of an officer who is best suited for such a task. One who knows what's now the Protectorate Zone from wartime missions. More importantly, one to whom the Shrehari ambassador and perhaps even *Kho'sahra* Brakal won't automatically object when we seek the Empire's consent to temporarily suspend the Treaty of Ulufan's relevant provisions so we can retrieve our citizens."

Admiral Lowell gave Kowalski a suspicious glance. "And who would that be, pray tell?"

"Siobhan Dunmoore, sir. Give her a small task force and let her loose. If anyone can find these pirates in the Protectorate and retrieve their victims, she's it because she took *Iolanthe* deep into that part of space before. Of equal importance, we know Brakal respects her and considers her honorable beyond reproach. Their conversation at the armistice talks on Aquilonia and his subsequent comments to our ambassador on Shrehari Prime is proof enough."

"Hasn't Dunmoore filled shore billets since the war?" Lowell asked, frowning.

"Not quite, sir. She leads the Fleet's premier readiness evaluation team and has probably racked up more time aboard warships than most officers of her rank over the years. She certainly knows more about commanding them than any of the current crop, and she wrote the book on unconventional operations. Give her *Salamanca*, the Reconquista class cruiser configured as flagship, which she just certified, and three or four frigates from 3rd Fleet that aren't currently on patrol. Dunmoore's on Starbase 30 with her team at the moment, waiting for transport to Caledonia, and could be redirected with a simple subspace message. Her people can fill the flag billets, meaning a dedicated task force could be underway the moment 3rd Fleet releases a handful of ships."

"Isn't *Salamanca* destined for another formation?"

"Yes, sir. She'll replace the Series One Reconquista *Corregidor* as the flagship of Battle Group 31, so the latter can go into refit, but there's no urgency."

Sampaio nodded slowly. "You really thought this through, and quickly at that. Well done. I can see why someone as young as you now fills an operations director billet as a two-star. Are there any objections?"

The CNO turned to his superior. "I'm not overly enthusiastic at the idea, sir. Dunmoore was a wartime commodore who never regained her star after she reverted to post captain during the drawdown. The most recent promotion board didn't rate her as suitable either, and it was the last time her file would be considered."

"With due respect, sir," Kowalski said, "Dunmoore is the most suitable officer for this job, the one with the best chance of success. But if she fails, then she will become the ideal scapegoat."

"We'll get our share of the blame; you can be sure of that if only for appointing someone the Fleet no longer considers flag officer material," Lowell replied in a warning tone.

"Yes, sir. Understood. But we'll be blamed only if the rescue mission fails. And once the public affairs people massage the story, then it'll be obvious that if the officer who raided the Shrehari home system can't succeed, no one else stands a chance."

Grand Admiral Sampaio let out a soft snort of amusement.

"I admire your persistence, Admiral Kowalski. May I ask why you're so adamant?"

"Because I served under Siobhan Dunmoore's command in *Stingray*, sir, and know firsthand how she thinks and operates. Everyone who's served under her since told me the same thing

— she'll finish any job, so long as we let her run free of peacetime restrictions. Besides, for all intents and purposes, *Athena*'s targeted hijacking is just as much an act of war as the Shrehari invasion was. This war is merely darker and dirtier, one which can't and won't end with an armistice and a Treaty with questionable provisions."

Sampaio tapped his fingertips against the tabletop.

"Agreed, and that means we have a plan. Admiral Kowalski can draw up the necessary orders and make it happen within the hour. If 3rd Fleet raises objections, make sure they understand this comes from me directly, and I won't brook any nonsense. When I see the SecGen, I want to tell him the rescue mission is underway."

"Aye, aye, sir." Kowalski and Ahmad stood. "With your permission?"

"Dismissed, and thank you."

When both were gone, Sampaio gave Lowell a sardonic look.

"Kowalski was an inspired choice as one of the operations directors, even if you didn't like her pushing for Siobhan Dunmoore's appointment. And yes, I know she didn't clear it with you first. That's obvious. But don't be overly hard on her. Time was of the essence, and she took a calculated risk, something I daresay her fellow operations directors wouldn't contemplate. I realize Dunmoore's not on everyone's most favored list. However, she was successful beyond every expectation during the war, and I understand those who served under her command are fiercely loyal."

"Commodore Holt certainly is," Admiral Doxiadis said. "And he's just as smart as Kowalski, who may well sit in your chair one day, sir. She, along with Holt, is one of the few around here who understands how to play the Great Game."

**

The suite's communicator softly chimed for attention, and Dunmoore, engrossed in one of her historical treatises, reached out absently to stroke the screen.

"Admiral Harmel for Captain Dunmoore, sir."

She sat up, the First Migration War instantly forgotten, drowned by the hope their transport to Caledonia was arriving early, and this was Harmel's goodbye.

"Dunmoore here."

"I'll transfer you."

The video link lit up with Harmel's smiling face.

"You'll never believe this, Siobhan, but I received orders for you from the Chief of Naval Operations himself. Remember telling me how you enjoyed the view from *Salamanca*'s flag CIC?"

An intrigued Dunmoore nodded. "Yes."

"You'll be spending more time in that command chair than anyone expected, and on an actual mission, not a readiness evaluation. Although you don't get a flag or even a broad pennant, she's temporarily yours, nonetheless. You've been appointed as commander of a revived Task Force Luckner to retrieve a hijacked luxury liner filled with the most politically connected and influential people in the Commonwealth. Based on the mission parameters, I'm not sure if I should congratulate you or offer my sympathies, but at least the Fleet is giving you one more hurrah.

"Your team will go with you and fill the staff billets. If there's anything you or your people need in terms of clothing or gear, let my aide know, and we'll make sure it's issued. The orders themselves are top secret special access, so you'll need to pick them up from me in person. But since there's a lot of urgency in this matter, I'll stay in my office for the next few hours while you put things in motion. I warned *Salamanca*'s captain that he should expect your return as task force commander. The other four ships joining you — three Voivode class frigates and one Argo class corvette — are mustering and replenishing along with *Salamanca* as we speak. They come from my battle group, by the way, since they're available. It means you could sail within the next six hours."

Dunmoore didn't reply for what seemed like an eternity, then she said, "Pinch me because this doesn't seem real. Task Force Luckner rides again?"

"Should I ask the supply depot to run off a few hundred copies of the old shoulder patch?"

— Five —

"Folks, the Fleet, in its mercy, gave us a stay of execution," Dunmoore said once the last of RED One's members assembled in her suite's day room an hour later. She'd fetched the classified mission orders from Harmel's office shortly after his call and read them twice before summoning her people.

"A former first officer of mine — not Commander Pushkin, by the way — once said something to the effect that those of us who thrive under wartime conditions should, when peace breaks out, be placed in stasis pods with the notation *decant in case of conflict.* Well, we old warhorses have just been decanted. Grand Admiral Sampaio activated a new Task Force Luckner for a specific and urgent mission. As its commander, I now report directly to the CNO. We will rejoin *Salamanca*, designated as the task force lead ship, and take four other units under our command. They are the Argo class corvette *Sackville* and three Voivode class frigates — *Charles Martel, Arthur Currie,* and *Jan Sobieski.*" Dunmoore smiled at Pushkin. "Yes, Gregor, your former ship. All five were ordered to replenish from Starbase 30's stocks as fast as possible and take on a full wartime load of ammunition and missiles."

Chief Guthren let out a low whistle.

"I can't wait to hear what the CNO wants from us, sir."

"In a moment. As of now, Commander Pushkin is the task force operations officer. Since I stay at my substantive rank, there will not be a flag captain. So *Salamanca*'s captain will be the task force second-in-command. However, Chief Guthren will be Luckner's command chief petty officer. The rest of RED One will act as command staff and stand watch in the flag CIC. And now the mission, which is classified top secret special access, not to be discussed with our starship crews, not even the captains, until we're underway." Dunmoore pulled out the orders and read them verbatim.

"Won't the Shrehari howl blue bloody murder when five obvious human naval ships enter the Protectorate Zone?" Lieutenant Commander Jasmine Zakaria, the combat systems specialist, asked.

She, like the other RED One officers, were old wartime acquaintances and had been handpicked by Dunmoore when the latter formed her team.

"It seems to me this is more of a Q ship mission."

Dunmoore nodded.

"Without a doubt. But since the hijacking might involve the Shrehari, that's almost a certainty, though I suspect high-level negotiations are happening right now with their ambassador on Earth. The Treaty of Ulufan contains provisions allowing for military incursions into the Zone if both parties agree beforehand. Besides, it's a given both they and we routinely patrol that part of space in undercover ships despite the Treaty. And yes, I'd rather be sailing in *Iolanthe* alongside three or four Savoyard class Q ships, but she and the Savoyards are no doubt on their own classified missions. Recalling them would take much too long. That means we go with what we have. Now, preparations."

Dunmoore turned to Pushkin.

"Obtain a copy of Battle Group 30's standard operating instructions. Four of our five ships will be used to them, and I don't enjoy the luxury of issuing my own."

"Aye, aye, Commodore."

She scowled at him. "Not even in jest, Gregor."

"Sorry." His tone and expression were anything but contrite.

"We don't know how long this will take. So if there are any personal items you think you might need, you can take a few hours to visit the base's stores and commissary — after we shift our dunnage back aboard *Salamanca*. And that will be the moment I'm done here. I've already spoken with Captain Rydzewski, and the cabins we used during the evaluation cruise are ready and waiting for us. Once we've digested the battle group SOIs, we can discuss crewing the flag CIC and distributing the watchkeeping duties. Finally, I'll be hosting a command conference with the five captains at sixteen hundred hours in *Salamanca*'s flag conference room. Gregor, Chief, you're both in on that."

"Sir."

"Any questions or comments?"

"Oo-rah, sir." A broad grin split Chief Guthren's square face. "Dona Quixote rides again, and not before time."

Zakaria let out a burst of laughter.

"Oh my God, I'd forgotten about that nickname." Her smile disappeared as quickly as it had come on. "Hearing it again after all this time makes me feel old."

The others around the table nodded in sympathy. One of the chiefs said, "You and everyone else in this room, Commander."

Dunmoore gave Guthren an exasperated look.

"I'd rather we didn't get overly enthusiastic. If it hasn't occurred to everyone yet, we weren't just chosen because we're available, have the requisite experience for this sort of mission, and are in the right spot. Can you guess what the fourth reason might be?"

"Should things go sideways, and we fail wholly or even in part, we're completely expendable," Pushkin said without hesitation.

"Correct. The political implications of anything other than complete success are such that we will be figuratively tossed out the airlock if our superiors deem it necessary."

"On the other hand, those with nothing left to lose can take chances from which most of our colleagues would recoil, Skipper."

"We in this room, certainly. But our five starship captains and their crews will not agree with the sentiment. They weren't in decision-making positions during the war and won't have developed our ability to evaluate and, more importantly, tolerate risks. However, dealing with them is my job, not yours. Anything else? No? I'll see you aboard *Salamanca* in an hour or so. Dismissed."

The ten snapped to attention before exiting the suite in silence while Dunmoore contemplated the twist of fate that gave her one last chance at command in space, and she wondered who revived the Task Force Luckner name. Though the orders weren't signed by the original drafter, she couldn't help but wonder whether an unexpected friend in high places arranged things in her favor.

**

Captain Rydzewski surprised Dunmoore by receiving her at the airlock with full honors due to a formation commander. Upon the words 'Luckner arriving,' the bosun piped her aboard in the time-honored fashion.

They exchanged salutes, then Rydzewski said, "Welcome back, sir. The ship is in the process of taking on stores and ammunition as ordered by the Flag Officer Commanding, Battle Group 30. I received the SOIs from Commander Pushkin and will ensure everyone understands them by the time we sail."

"Excellent. Since you outrank Gregor, you're my second-in-command, but he'll handle the staff duties of a flag captain and run my CIC."

"Understood, sir. That was what I expected."

"I'm having personal stores sent to the ship later this afternoon since I didn't bring enough for what could be a lengthy mission."

"We'll make sure the deliveries reach your quarters. I've assigned you the flag officer's suite this time, incidentally, since you'll need more space and privacy now that you command an entire task force." He gestured at the passageway beyond the airlock. "Shall we?"

As Rydzewski led her back to the accommodations deck, he asked, "When will we find out what emergency precipitated the creation of an ad hoc task force with orders to sail as quickly as possible, sir?"

"Once we're away from here. HQ classified this operation as top secret special access, meaning we cannot risk anyone speaking out of turn even if it's a seemingly harmless comment made to another service member on the station. It's the normal protocol for a mission of this type. Back when I had *Iolanthe* and then the original Task Force Luckner, only a few select people knew about an upcoming mission until we'd already sailed."

"My curiosity has rarely been this intense, sir. But I'll contain myself. I understand you called a command conference for sixteen hundred?"

"It will be more of a meet and greet than a discussion of the mission beyond what already came down from Admiral Harmel. Do you know any of the other captains?"

"Not personally, no. My space-going assignments since the war were in the 2nd Fleet, and they were no doubt a few years behind me at the Academy and the War College. Didn't any of them pass through your class?"

"Not that I can recall. Keep in mind this is my fourth year as RED One team leader, so they probably attended the College after I left."

A mischievous smile lit up Rydzewski's narrow face. "But I'm sure they know about you."

"That's what I'm afraid of."

They stopped at the door marked 'Flag Officer Commanding' on the upper accommodation deck, which opened when she touched the call screen embedded in the bulkhead beside it. Dunmoore took a deep breath and stepped across the threshold.

Though she'd visited the suite out of idle curiosity two weeks earlier, taking it as hers felt strange, but it also felt right.

"If you've no further need for me at the moment, sir..."

"Thank you, Piotr. You may return to your duties. I know how much work is involved when you take on a wartime load. I'll see you at sixteen hundred, or I should say eight bells in the afternoon watch now that I'm no longer a landlubber."

She gave him a tight smile.

"You'll get back into the swing of things quickly enough."

He briefly came to attention, nodded formally, then turned on his heels and vanished into the passageway. The door closed silently behind him.

Dunmoore carried her luggage into the sleeping cabin, where she found the emergency breathing gear she'd borrowed from the ship's stores during the evaluation waiting on the bed. Her needs were simple, and therefore she carried little more than spare shipboard uniforms, exercise gear, a set of civilian clothes, along with underclothes and toiletries.

New battledress uniforms and boots, spare underclothes, and a pressure suit would arrive shortly from the station's logistic section, where they were being fabricated based on the measurements in her file. She'd also ordered food, drink, and other items from the commissary because she planned on hosting her captains and staff as she did while commanding the wartime Task Force Luckner. There was nothing like a small gathering around the dining table, with a glass of wine in hand, to discover an officer's true personality, the one they hid behind naval formality.

With her personal effects stowed away, she settled at the day cabin's workstation and saw everything was set up for her and the command staff. Messages waited in her queue, including copies of the five captains' service record summaries. She'd been right — the frigate commanders attended War College after her departure, while the lieutenant commander in the corvette hadn't gone yet.

The oldest of the four, with the longest service, was still a relatively junior lieutenant at the end of the war. As a result, none of them had seen much action during the long stalemate when most of the Commonwealth and Shrehari navies played hide-and-seek.

All had exemplary records and could reasonably expect further promotions. But they seemed typical of the new breed of commanding officers — Academy graduates with suitable assignments at the proper times in their careers, no recorded missteps, and no experience in conducting operations like the one they now faced. What she wouldn't give for a few Q ship rogues like the ones who'd run amok behind Shrehari lines a decade earlier and kept the Empire's forces off balance.

She set the personnel files aside and began working through her orders and the intelligence reports that accompanied them so she could come up with the outline of a plan before they left Starbase 30. Dunmoore was so engrossed that the chime caught her by surprise.

"Enter."

The door slid aside, admitting Chief Guthren followed by one of *Salamanca*'s ratings towing an antigrav sled loaded with boxes bearing both the commissary and the station's logistics section markings.

"Your items are here, sir. Where would you like this?"

"The clothing store stuff in the sleeping cabin, the rest in the day cabin pantry over there."

Dunmoore stood and stretched, figuring she might as well stop to unpack. The first Task Force Luckner Redux command conference would begin in just over fifteen minutes.

— Six —

"The task force commander." Chief Guthren's voice stilled the room as the assembled captains, and Commander Pushkin came to attention behind their chairs.

"At ease, everyone. Please sit." Dunmoore dropped into the chair at the head of the table, one she'd used often during the readiness evaluation. "I'm Siobhan Dunmoore. You've already met the task force operations officer, Commander Gregor Pushkin, who will carry out a flag captain's staff duties, and Chief Petty Officer Kurt Guthren, the task force command chief. As you're probably aware, I just subjected Captain Rydzewski and his ship to one of the most strenuous readiness evaluations in recent memory, so I know him and his crew as well as he does. I never met the rest of you, but I perused your service records earlier today and am familiar with what you've accomplished. I realize curiosity about an unexpected mission and change of formation must be eating at you. But as I explained to Captain Rydzewski, this is one of those times when I can only reveal our orders after we set sail, so there is little or no chance of word getting out."

As she spoke, the four newcomers studied her with wary eyes and expressionless faces.

"Normally, I'd host a meet and greet so we can get acquainted in a less formal setting. However, we must be away the moment our ships are ready, and since this is probably the first war load you and your people are taking on since the armistice, I'm sure everyone is busy as can be. So, what I'd like is for you to give me a thumbnail sketch of your ship's status — stores, systems, crew, and anything else Commander Pushkin and I should know. We will, of course, read the reports I've requested. But since I'm already quite familiar with *Salamanca*'s status, Captain Rydzewski can put on his task force second-in-command hat and listen."

Dunmoore turned to Commander Davina Kardas of *Jan Sobieski* and the most senior of the three frigate captains. A lean, sharp-faced, dark-complexioned woman in her late thirties, with short black hair and intelligent brown eyes, she'd graduated from both the Academy and the War College near the top of her class.

"Please go ahead, Commander Kardas."

"Yes, sir. When I left to come here, we were almost done topping up food stocks and other consumables. Ammunition loading will be done by the end of the dog watch and missiles before the night watch starts. All but five of my crew billets are filled. Thankfully, none of the empty ones are vital. We completed our last readiness evaluation fourteen months ago, with RED Three giving us good marks. I still have mostly the same officers and crew who earned that pass. I'm sure Commander Pushkin will find her unchanged from his day, and that's the only major issue." Kardas allowed herself a quick grimace. "*Jan Sobieski* is the oldest of the Voivodes and overdue for a tour in dry dock. Everything works, but a lot of it is getting worn out. She saw hard service during the war and hasn't been given much tender loving care since. Over a decade of continuous service in space will take its toll, sir."

Kardas' words didn't surprise Dunmoore. A penny-pinching government was forcing the Fleet to reduce time in drydock for anything other than life extension refits. And the reason was simple. Fleet engineering facilities, not civilian shipyards whose corporate owners donated generously to political causes, did everything but life extension. More importantly, keeping the latter in contracts for new builds was a lucrative business, and to hell with the crews of worn out starships.

"Understood. Thank you."

"Please don't misunderstand me, sir. We will carry out the mission to the best of our abilities. I just want to make sure you understand she's no longer the *Jan Sobieski* that served in the original Task Force Luckner."

Dunmoore gave her a rueful smile.

"Age has a way of changing us all, Captain." She gestured at Commander Shamir Bryce of the frigate *Charles Martel*, a stocky, broad-shouldered man of roughly Kardas' age but with straw-blond hair and steely gray eyes. "Your turn."

"Sir, *Charles Martel* will carry a full war load before the end of the evening watch as well, and like every other Series One Voivode, she's overdue for a refit. We have no major issues other than running through spare parts at an ever greater rate. But I'm short fifteen crew, including a few vital ones like an assistant combat systems officer, an engineering chief, and two senior bosun's mates. Nevertheless, we're just as ready and able. We learned to work around the crew shortages. I can't claim a recent readiness evaluation like Davina. However, you won't find fault with us."

There was no false bravado in Bryce's words or tone, and she nodded. "Thank you, Captain."

Her gaze landed on Evanne Sani, *Arthur Currie*'s captain, a slender, auburn-haired, olive-skinned officer in her early thirties whose dark eyes were devoid of emotions.

"And you?"

"My ship is a Series Three build, sir, so we're not yet due for a refit and have no issues beyond normal wear and tear, though I'm short six crew, all of them junior ranks billets. We will complete stores and ammunition loading by midnight, like everyone else. But we'll need a top-up on our antimatter fuel reserves before leaving the system."

"Every ship in the task force will refuel on the way out, so that's baked into the deployment plan. Thank you."

She turned to the most junior commissioned officer at the table, Lieutenant Commander Faraz Qiao, *Sackville*'s commanding officer. He'd graduated from the Academy at the top of his class in the final year of the war. Although based on his service record, Dunmoore suspected it wasn't why he was given command of a corvette at such a young age. Compact, raven-haired, with eyes that seemed hewn from shards of basalt, he wore an expression half-detached, half attempting to hide bemusement at his change of circumstances.

"And last but not least, tell me about *Sackville*, Captain."

"As you're probably aware, she's one of the last few pre-war Argo class corvettes left in active service. She received a life extension refit shortly after the war, along with the others of her class not immediately mothballed. Sackville is in decent shape for a ship her age, though I wouldn't put her in the line of battle or make emergency jumps unless it's essential. I'm four crew members short, and we'll be fully provisioned by midnight tonight as well."

"Excellent." She looked around the table. "I'm not a complicated commanding officer, as Gregor Pushkin can tell you from personal experience — he served as both my first officer and one of my captains. This is why we will use the Battle Group 30 standard operating instructions rather than the ones I developed during my first tour as task force commander. But I tend heavily toward the unconventional, something both Gregor and Captain Rydzewski know only too well. The fact they chose me for this mission should tell you it will be far from ordinary and could conceivably present the sort of risk to ships and crews generally unheard of outside a full-blown war.

"If time permits, I will discuss my intentions at command conferences such as this one while we plan operations. I expect candor from my captains if they believe I'm on the wrong path, forgot a vital element, or missed something important. Finally, always remember Gregor Pushkin is my voice. When he makes a request or gives direction, you may be sure it comes from me. Feel free to ask him about how I operate. Are there any questions that don't pertain to the specifics of our mission? Let's do this in my preferred way — reverse order of rank and seniority. Chief Guthren?"

"Nothing, sir."

"Commander Qiao?"

"I'm good, Captain."

"Commander Sani?"

"No questions, sir."

"Commander Kardas?"

"Nothing from me as well, sir."

"Commander Pushkin?"

"No questions, sir."

"And finally, Captain Rydzewski?"

"Will you need people for the flag CIC beyond those who came with you from RED One, sir?"

Dunmoore shook her head.

"No, but thanks for reminding me to mention them. I drafted my ten evaluation team members as command staff. Along with Gregor Pushkin, normally RED One's deputy team leader, and Chief Guthren, I also have four lieutenant commanders, highly experienced officers, and four equally experienced chief petty officers. Everyone of them saw plenty of wartime service. When we're not at battle stations, one officer and one chief will stand watch in my CIC. I'll make sure you receive a list of names after this meeting so you know who they are. It was a pleasure meeting you. Keep in mind this may well be the last time we meet in person for a while. I'm not a fan of captains shuttling over to the flagship when my business can be conducted via holo-link." She stood, imitated by others, and walked through the door leading to the flag CIC, where Guthren joined her moments later.

"I'll tell you what, Skipper. The way they listened, you might as well be wearing your old star. But I don't sense that they're overjoyed at an unexpected covert mission under the command of the infamous Siobhan Dunmoore, who tweaked the Empire's nose and ended the war."

She snorted.

"Then remained stuck at the rank of captain until her chances ran out because of a grievous career-ending mistake along the way. So I'm sure they're wondering why me and why them."

"We're all wondering that, sir. You included. Someone at Fleet HQ evidently pulled a few hidden strings."

"Or they figure it's hopeless, but the Fleet must be seen doing something, and sending the officer who carried out the raid on the Shrehari home system would be politically expedient."

The conference room door opened again, admitting Gregor Pushkin. When it shut behind him, he shook his head.

"That's not a bunch of happy captains, sir. I'll wager next month's pay they're trying to figure out why the fickle finger of fate assigned them to an ad hoc task force commanded by one of the most superannuated captains in the Fleet and a former commodore to boot. One with the reputation of pulling off stunts that make most officers cringe in fear of career consequences."

"Funny, but the chief and I were just discussing the same thing. Do you think we'll encounter problems?"

Pushkin made a face.

"Propose something like the Shrehari home system raid we carried out to those five, and you won't receive the same enthusiasm as from your captains back then."

"Meaning?"

"Without a war to focus their minds, they'll be either consciously or subconsciously worried about mistakes that could kill off any further chances of promotion. In other words, we might find we're dealing with one or more risk-averse captains. I was watching them while they listened to you, and they didn't seem comfortable with your characterization of this mission."

Guthren let out a soft grunt.

"You can't entirely blame them, Mister Pushkin. Scratch your hull nowadays, and it's an even chance a stuck-up careerist with stars on the collar will call for a board of inquiry or some other administrative garbage. You'd blow your top if you knew the things I hear on the old chiefs' network. The hard-charging Navy that came out of the Shrehari War is slowly but surely vanishing."

"Then let's make sure we revive a bit of that old spirit, folks," Dunmoore said. "At least for as long as this iteration of Task Force Luckner exists. I want to leave the moment all ships declare themselves ready. Gregor, you can warn the fueling station that we'll swing by sometime between twelve and twenty-four hours from now, with confirmation once we actually break out of orbit."

"Aye, aye, sir."

— Seven —

The insistent chime of the communicator pulled Siobhan Dunmoore from a light sleep, and she sat up in her bed, only half-awake while her brain registered the time — just past two in the morning.

"Dunmoore."

"Flag CIC, sir. Chief O'Hara. I have the watch with Commander Yun. *Salamanca*, the last of the five, just reported readiness to sail, meaning the task force can depart at your command."

The cruiser took longer to prepare than the others, simply because of her larger size, greater armament, and bigger crew, something Dunmoore expected.

"Send out a general signal to the task force that we will undock in thirty minutes, then let Battle Group 30's operations center know. I want airlocks shut in fifteen minutes and a status report in twenty. I'll be in the CIC shortly."

"Aye, aye, sir."

"Dunmoore, out."

She climbed to her feet and pulled on one of the battledress uniforms delivered by the station logistics section less than twelve hours earlier. Since they were sailing into danger with a war load, she'd made it the dress of the day. If nothing else, it might help focus the mind on the fact this wasn't a training mission. After a quick visit to the heads, she stopped for a make-your-own sandwich and coffee in the wardroom. Although it was the middle of the ship's night, her stomach clamored for breakfast.

When the door to the flag CIC slid open, Commander Yun, sitting in the command chair, stood and stepped aside. A wiry, sharp-faced, black-haired man in his fifties, he eyed Dunmoore with intelligent dark eyes as she sat.

"Our ships, as well as battle group operations, acknowledged your orders and reported airlocks shut. The status reports are waiting in your message queue, but they confirm readiness for immediate departure." He paused as a faint smile shone through his usually solemn countenance. "And may I say how pleasant it is to be operational again? I've not worn battledress in so long I can hardly remember how it feels."

"You may because I second the sentiment."

"Make that three," Chief O'Hara, a stocky, balding redhead whose round face was fringed by a white beard, added over his shoulder. "The other RED teams will rage with jealousy when they find out the Fleet drafted us as a task force command crew. RED One to the rescue!"

She took the command chair and called up her messages. Those from her ships were brief and to the point, and the one from station operations reminded her Task Force Luckner would undock and leave under station traffic control. Dunmoore also found a brief note from Rear Admiral Harmel wishing her good hunting. That he'd been awake at this hour to draft it once his people told him about her impending departure spoke volumes.

Gregor Pushkin showed up while she was reading and took the flag captain's workstation in silence. As per her orders, the rest of the command crew remained in their cots, unneeded for this evolution.

"From the operations center, Task Force Luckner will leave under traffic control direction in the following order — *Sackville, Jan Sobieski, Arthur Currie, Salamanca,* and *Charles Martel.*"

Dunmoore nodded. No deviation from the plan. Once it released moorings, each ship would move to a higher orbital altitude until they were free of Starbase 30. Then, under flagship control, they would break out of orbit and adopt a standard diamond formation with *Salamanca* at its center, *Sackville* taking point, and the three frigates forming a staggered triangle around the cruiser. As per Battle Group 30 SOI.

She knew without checking that the captains were either handling or overseeing the departure maneuvers themselves. Not even peacetime commanding officers would sleep soundly in their bunk while the officer of the watch cast-off unsupervised. Yet sitting in her command chair, observing as each ship released moorings in turn, fired forward-facing thrusters to drift aft of the orbiting station before rising above it, seemed anti-climatic after the last time she'd overseen a departure from this same starbase.

Dunmoore remained in the CIC, going through administrative busywork until well into the morning watch to see how her ships synchronized navigation. Then, when they went faster-than-light as a single unit on instructions from the flag CIC for a short five-hour run that would take them to the nearest antimatter refueling station, she returned to her quarters.

There, she stripped off her uniform and slipped back into her bed after setting the alarm to chime an hour before they reached the refueling station. Not since her early days in *Stingray* had Dunmoore experienced this sort of disjointed sleep pattern. Still, needs must when the devil drives, and she never experienced issues nodding off, if even for an hour whenever possible. Should anything untoward happen, the duty officer would summon her.

The transition warning woke her briefly, but she fell back into a light sleep after *Salamanca,* and her companions, dropped out of hyperspace. If any of them reported a problem, the CIC would call, but it didn't. Forty-five minutes before they were due at the refueling station orbiting the larger of the system's three gas giants, Dunmoore was back in the flag CIC after a quick breakfast and cup of coffee. She wanted to see each ship as it carried out the delicate maneuver so she could evaluate their handling skills.

As she slipped into the command chair, Gregor Pushkin turned around and grinned at her. "Coming to see them in action, Skipper? I vaguely recall you putting me through my refueling paces."

"A fine job you did then and ever since."

Lieutenant Commander Olmos, thin, dark-haired, with a sallow complexion, craggy face, and deep-set brown eyes, raised his hand. He had the flag CIC duty along with Chief Petty Officer Hogan — both were RED One's engineering systems specialists.

"We are now under the refueling station's traffic control orders. They've accepted our proposed sequence and will take *Sackville* first."

"Thank you."

Dunmoore sat back and studied the gas giant on the primary display. Like many used by the Fleet as a source of raw material for conversion into antimatter, it was striped with bands of various colors whose edges were roiled by storms big enough to swallow her entire task force.

The refueling station, an octopus-like construct with massive arms aimed at the planet — the collectors — and smaller ones pointing away from it, sparkling in the light of the distant sun. Each of the ten-kilometer-long smaller arms ended at a buoy from which the crew would extrude a magnetic tube that latched onto a starship's magnetic fuel reservoir access point.

In theory, the station could take all five simultaneously thanks to its six buoys but preferred one at a time. And since Dunmoore wanted to see each go through the evolution, she'd accepted the more cautious method when it was mentioned earlier, during the planning phase.

Task Force Luckner assumed position behind the station, at its precise altitude, the ships separated by several dozen kilometers. Then, at traffic control's orders, the corvette briefly fired her thrusters and slowly closed the distance with the target buoy.

"I've seen faster," Pushkin muttered when she finally lined up with the buoy after a few minor corrections.

"We've also seen slower, but at least there was little extraneous maneuvering. She has a steady hand on the helm and a captain who's not forcing said hand by overthinking it."

Guthren, who'd entered the CIC while *Sackville* was making her approach, said, "Good cox'n, sir. I know him by reputation. If he's at the helm, he won't listen to bad maneuvering orders. That doesn't mean Captain Qiao needs correcting, mind you."

"What about the other coxswains?" Pushkin asked.

"Solid people, sir. More so than the current crop of officers, if you ask me. They finished the war as senior petty officers and haven't lost the fighting spirit yet. Half of the lieutenant commanders, ours excepted, and below two-and-a-half stripes, never heard a shot fired in anger. They don't know what it's like."

Chief Hogan, a giant of a man, bald, with a boxer's flattened nose and a gray mouth beard, glanced over his shoulder and nodded.

"What Mister Guthren said, Captain. We saw it in *Salamanca* clearly enough."

Pushkin gave him thumbs up.

"Backbone of the Navy, our chiefs."

As usual, the candor of her people amused Dunmoore. RED One had truly coalesced into a tight-knit team over the last few years. She couldn't think of any other outfit where her chiefs would openly comment on the postwar officer corps in front of their captain. Those discussions usually happened behind closed doors in the chiefs' and petty officers' mess.

By the time all five ships had full antimatter fuel loads aboard two hours later, Dunmoore was satisfied none lacked in ship handling skills. But, of course, she already knew that about *Salamanca*. As they headed for the gas giant's hyperlimit, she called another command conference, this one virtual for the frigate and corvette captains.

Only Rydzewski joined Dunmoore, Pushkin, and Guthren in person. The rest appeared as holograms around the conference table, linked in via laser beam, so no stray radio emissions with details of their mission floated across the star system.

"Now that we're as far from unauthorized ears as we can before leaving this system, it's time for the big reveal. I'm sending you a copy of the orders I received as a reference, but I will now go through them item by item."

When she finished speaking and showing them the visual evidence, the five captains stared at her in disbelief.

"How does something like this even happen?" Rydzewski asked no one in particular, a frown creasing his high forehead.

Even though his question was rhetorical, Dunmoore answered.

"Treason. Negligence. Political infighting. Revanchism by Shrehari or human diehards unhappy with the results of the war. Greed. Simple piracy that caught the wrong ship. We won't know until we find the culprits and save the victims. But calling the situation delicate would be an understatement."

"I can understand the war loads now," Kardas of *Jan Sobieski* said. "But won't the Shrehari scream blue bloody murder at a human naval task force entering the Protectorate Zone?"

Dunmoore shrugged.

"Probably, but solving that is the job of our diplomats. You know, the ones who came up with the Protectorate idea in the first place. We have our orders. If we meet Shrehari Deep Space Fleet ships, we will only open fire in self-defence, and I'm sure the Shrehari commander will operate under the same rules of engagement. They can't afford a new interstellar war over what is, in galactic terms, a minor incident. *Kho'sahra* Brakal's position is still far from entrenched against the old interests."

"What about Shrehari corsairs?" Commander Bryce, *Charles Martel*'s captain, asked.

"Same rules of engagement. If they fire first, we shoot back. Otherwise, we ignore them. Many are probably undercover intelligence gathering ships from their new *Tai Zohl* or the Shrehari equivalent of our Q ships and engaged in keeping piracy to a manageable level. We do it, so why wouldn't they?"

Dunmoore was mildly surprised the first two substantive questions concerned the Shrehari reaction to a Commonwealth Navy task force entering the Protectorate Zone rather than the more germane issue of how they would find the hijackers.

"However, that means both our intelligence gathering and undercover anti-piracy units, or at least those who came within range of an interstellar subspace array in the last few days will also be looking for the hijackers. Therefore, with luck, we'll not be entering the Protectorate Zone entirely blind. That being said, our first stop is Kilia Station."

Dunmoore looked around the table for reactions to a name infamous in Special Operations circles but saw only blank stares.

— Eight —

"I gather you're not familiar with the place." Everyone save Pushkin and Guthren shook their heads. "Which, I suppose, is natural since the Navy mostly ignored it during the war, save for intelligence and Special Operations. Kilia is an anomaly in almost every sense. A hollowed-out asteroid in an otherwise lifeless star system rich in easily extracted ores, it is human-owned and operated, one of those little-known, secretive, privately established colonies operating beyond government control. The Navy found it useful as an intelligence hub during the war, something which I experienced firsthand — the chief and I visited Kilia while we were in *Iolanthe* — and probably still does. But for reasons which baffle me, our diplomats let Kilia's star system become part of the Zone instead of claiming Commonwealth suzerainty. Perhaps there were undisclosed reasons for leaving it beyond the Commonwealth sphere, but I suspect we'll never know."

She nodded at Guthren.

"Based on our observations, it clearly serves as an interface between other unregistered colonies in what is now the Zone and the rest of the Commonwealth, as well as a transshipment point and market for pirates and others engaged in illegal commerce. Come to think about it, I wouldn't be surprised if that's the main reason we didn't claim it as ours during the Treaty negotiations. Considering the amount of untraceable wealth moving through, I can easily think of many well placed individuals and organizations who prefer Kilia remained beyond the Navy's reach forever."

When everyone other than her old companions put on shocked expressions, Dunmoore chuckled.

"I forget how sheltered the regular Navy is. Corruption permeates every part of the Commonwealth, although the Armed Forces mostly keep it at bay after the war cleaned the venal, the incompetent, and the corrupt from our ranks. The number of commanding and flag officers who fell by the wayside when their lack of integrity and professional honor was finally laid bare thanks to the Shrehari invasion is breathtaking. Buy Gregor a drink and ask him about his experiences in the matter when you're bored and in need of a little unwritten history. Sadly, I can't discuss most of the operations we carried out for SOCOM in *Iolanthe*, but we saw things that would make you despair."

Guthren nodded. "Did we ever."

"So Kilia Station will be our first stop. Lieutenant Commander Khanjan, who I've appointed Luckner's navigation officer because that's his specialty in RED One, will prepare the task force plot. We'll drop out of FTL shortly before entering the Zone and query the nearest interstellar subspace array for news. I will inform HQ we're about to violate the Treaty of Ulufan and then wait for a response, so we might loiter a bit. And that, folks, is the plan as it stands. When we reach Kilia Station, I'll decide the next steps based on what we find. Any questions?"

When no one spoke, she stood.

"We will reconvene when we drop out of hyperspace after crossing this system's heliopause. Should anything come to mind between now and then, we can discuss it at that time. Thank you."

Dunmoore swept out of the room as four holograms dissolved into nothing. The moment she was gone, Rydzewski intercepted Pushkin before he could vanish into the CIC.

"I'd like to buy you a drink, Commander. It seems as if my awareness of the Fleet's seamier side is lacking."

"How about a coffee once we're FTL, sir." Pushkin nodded at Guthren. "And if you want a fulsome story, I suggest you offer the chief one as well. He's been with Captain Dunmoore longer than I and saw *Stingray*, the first ship in which we served together, from a distinctly different angle."

"Done. Let me know when you're free, and I'll see the galley delivers a fresh urn and something appropriate to nibble on."

**

"They're armed, fueled, briefed, and on their way out of the star system," Kowalski reported when Admiral Lowell stuck his head through her office door. "If that's what you wanted to know, sir."

"It was, though I'm not sure I'm overly fond of your flippant tone, Kathryn."

She put on a contrite air.

"Sorry, sir."

Lowell, balding, square-faced, in his early sixties, was clearly still a bit miffed at Kowalski for recommending Dunmoore to the Grand Admiral as the rescue task force commander without discussing it first. She figured he saw it as a poor way of repaying him for appointing her as an operations director despite being among the youngest two-stars in the Navy. On the other hand, he knew she had the top job in her sights and both the smarts and political cunning to get there.

"What about the avisos sent to warn our listening posts in the Protectorate?"

"We've not heard back from them yet, but it's still early days even for ships that can almost outrun time itself."

Lowell let out a soft grunt. "Anything on the intelligence channels yet?"

"No, sir. I spoke with Commodore Ezekiel Holt — the CNI's action officer for this matter — an hour ago. But he's heard nothing through intelligence and Special Forces channels, including both the 1st Special Forces Regiment's deployed units and the Q ships. Zeke is in contact with the Colonial Office's Intelligence Service as well. But, so far, they're also coming up blank."

"Or so they say. Those damned Colonial Office cowboys never inspired confidence. But as long as no one speaks with the Special Security Bureau, I'm happy. They're more likely to be involved with the culprits than anything else."

"Oh, I'm sure the SSB is in the thick of things, sir. They always were the SecGen's covert attack dogs rather than a legitimate law enforcement agency. The Commonwealth would be better off without them."

Lowell shrugged. "We'd still need a federal organization to coordinate star system police forces and take care of issues beyond their jurisdiction."

"True. A paramilitary constabulary or gendarmerie with a proper disciplinary framework and an ethos resembling ours would do the trick."

A bark of laughter escaped Lowell's throat.

"Good luck obtaining SecGen and Senate approval for something like that. A real federal police force would reduce the opportunities for graft, tax evasion, interstellar fraud, and the Almighty knows what else."

"True as well, sir. But we're sliding back to the bad old days before the war when the outer star systems were increasingly at odds with Earth and the core systems on how much freedom they should enjoy from the central government. And when the differences become irreconcilable, well, we've seen how that ends twice now. But, unfortunately, a third time would mean the end of the Commonwealth as we know it and trigger a resurgence of Shrehari military adventurism."

"You're quite the pessimist, aren't you?"

"I prefer the term realist, sir. There's always been something wrong with how the Commonwealth functions. But we've muddled our way through since the Second Migration War. However, the Shrehari invasion and ten years of interstellar conflict fundamentally changed that equation. The outer systems have lost faith in Earth's ability to protect them. Yet, any attempt at reform is rebuffed with the help of the core systems, who not only didn't suffer from Shrehari depredations but became wealthy from war profiteering. And do the OutWorlders ever know it."

"I'll stick with pessimist if you don't mind. The situation isn't quite that dire in my eyes."

"Fair enough." Kowalski hesitated for a fraction of a second. Then, "Changing the subject ever so slightly, may I ask what, if anything, you have against Siobhan Dunmoore, sir? At least in the matter of appointing her as the senior officer for the rescue mission."

"You were one of her bridge watchkeepers during the war, weren't you?"

She nodded.

"In *Stingray*, as a two-ringer. I came out of that assignment as a two-and-a-half. Dunmoore was one of the rare fighting captains who had that special touch with her ship, crew, and the enemy."

"I have nothing against Dunmoore as such, Kathryn. And I agree about her special touch. But she hasn't adapted that well to the peacetime Navy. What worked during the war doesn't work nowadays, and I think Dunmoore never wrapped her mind around the differences between the two. She was a terror at the War College and is reckoned the most difficult readiness evaluation team leader nowadays. Many promising officers saw their career hit a bump in the road thanks to Dunmoore's uncompromising view of what a proper warship captain should be. Her often brutal frankness doesn't help either. She makes people uncomfortable."

Kowalski gave him a quizzical look. "Is that why she never made the commodore promotion list despite having worn a star at the end of the war while she led the raid that made the Shrehari ask for an armistice?"

Lowell nodded. "Largely, yes. But there are other factors."

"So, the powers that be sidelined one of our most effective naval tacticians because she makes inadequate people feel uncomfortable about their inadequacy."

The CNO gave Kowalski a stern look.

"That's a bit harsh, don't you think?"

She smiled at him.

"Harsh, but true, sir. I can be just as brutally frank as Siobhan."

"But you're more circumspect than she is and know when such forthrightness is appropriate. If Dunmoore had learned that lesson instead of annoying people with her War College antics, she might be a two-star right now, perhaps even sitting in your chair."

"Antics, sir? I was one of her students, and while she was the toughest instructor there, I wouldn't call what she did antics."

"The term was used by people who wore and, in some cases, still wear stars on their collars regarding her pushing for doctrinal changes. When she left the College, Dunmoore was essentially blacklisted instead of receiving the promotion she was due based on her war record. However, as I said, there are other factors. Dunmoore annoyed rather powerful people in the Special Security Bureau and the Colonial Office. As a result, it's doubtful the SecGen will ever sign off on her promotion to flag rank."

Kowalski's eyes narrowed in thought.

"Should I infer from your statement that the SecGen runs our flag officer promotion lists past the Director General of the SSB and the Colonial Secretary?"

"Among others. A recent development since the end of the war, I'm afraid. Apparently, we pushed out the wrong people during the conflict and promoted politically unsuitable replacements."

"The Fleet rid itself of politically connected incompetents who were largely responsible for our miserable showing when the Shrehari invaded, you mean. Maybe I should tell Siobhan to make sure the folks in *Athena* never come home."

Lowell wagged his index finger and her as he scowled.

"Not even in jest, Kathryn. I'd rather your name didn't join hers on the never to be promoted again list. You face a bright future, while Dunmoore's career as a Navy officer is stalled for good. Once the Readiness Evaluation Division no longer needs or wants her, Dunmoore's retiring. And that's only if she doesn't muck up the rescue operation. If she does..." Lowell made a cutting gesture across his throat. "RED One gets a new leader the moment Task Force Luckner returns."

His scowl deepened. "How you talked me into reviving that illustrious name will forever be a mystery. I'm surprised we haven't heard harsh words from the SecGen's office yet."

"Or perhaps they're happy the task force that ended the war is back and under its old commander for this one, sir. And if nothing else, the names Luckner and Dunmoore might give the Shrehari pause if they decide our entering the Protectorate Zone is objectionable to the point of retaliation."

He let out a soft grunt.

"I'll say this in your favor, Kathryn — I've never seen a flag officer as young as you learn to navigate the murky politics of both Fleet and government so effectively, let alone so quickly."

"Thank you, sir."

— Nine —

Shortly after Task Force Luckner dropped out of hyperspace within easy distance of the last interstellar subspace radio array before the Protectorate Zone, Dunmoore decrypted a message from Fleet HQ. It was mostly an intelligence summary that gave her little if anything to go on. But the missive was signed K.K., and she wondered whether she should thank Rear Admiral Kathryn Kowalski for what would surely be her last command in space before retirement.

Dunmoore always felt pride at seeing officers and noncoms serving in her ships rise on their merits and enjoy successful careers. Kowalski was no different, but a slight twinge of jealousy made itself known, nonetheless. However, should her former communication systems officer be responsible for this appointment, Dunmoore owed her a vote of thanks. She knew navigating the corridors of power where the right moves meant early advancement was not a skill she would ever master.

She touched her desk's embedded screen, posted the decrypted message from Earth in the mission repository, and then opened a link with her staff.

"Flag CIC, this is Dunmoore."

"Zakaria here, Skipper," the husky yet unmistakably feminine voice of her combat systems evaluation officer replied a few seconds later.

"Transmit a copy of the file I've just logged to all ships — it's an intelligence summary from HQ — then execute the next phase in the navigation plan."

"Aye, sir. Transmitting a copy of the file, then executing the next phase in the navigation plan."

"Dunmoore, out."

Moments later, the hyperspace jump warning sounded throughout *Salamanca* and her four consorts, a signal that Dunmoore received nothing from the array that would warrant a command conference. The next time she would speak with her captains, save for Piotr Rydzewski, would be at Kilia's heliopause.

As she remembered from her time in command of the original Task Force Luckner, Dunmoore was now nothing more than a passenger aboard the cruiser, with no real responsibilities during their long hyperspace jump.

She and her staff were isolated from four of the formation's five ships until they dropped out of FTL and experienced enough to avoid riding herd on *Salamanca*. It made for a mini-vacation she never really tolerated with complete equanimity, but she'd learned the importance of packing distractions in her dunnage, mainly in the form of books.

At this rate, Dunmoore could probably sit for the examinations leading to a doctorate in military science without further study. After all, she'd earned a master's degree while teaching at the War College by publishing a long list of doctrinal papers, many of which received a rather chilly reception at Fleet HQ.

Questioning dogma was never well-received in peacetime. It generally took a few bloody defeats before entrenched ideas were tossed out the airlock and replaced with new thinking.

Shortly after shaking off the transition nausea caused by *Salamanca* jumping to hyperspace, Dunmoore called up one of the books she was currently reading, a lesser-known analysis of the late 21st and early 22nd-century Corporatist War. A global conflagration, it was the last fought on Earth's landmasses and oceans even as scientists were building the first faster-than-light starships which would carry humans to other star systems in the most significant migration ever recorded. And that migration not only ended with the second most brutal civil war in history but triggered a second migration which in turn gave birth to the most brutal one.

Considering the general mood in the Commonwealth since the armistice, especially among the colonies with no political representation on Earth, Dunmoore feared a third migration war wasn't out of the question. There was already unrest in some star systems, and the well connected cheerleaders from Earth aboard *Athena* likely didn't help.

**

Captain Roy LeDain's mood had swung between rage and despondency ever since pirates, aided by infiltrators from among his own crew, hijacked the luxury liner *Athena* several days earlier. A wiry, dark-complexioned man in his fifties with short, graying hair and an equally short salt-and-pepper beard, LeDain was pacing around the passenger cabin where he'd been confined ever since, his meals delivered by members of his own crew working for the guest services department.

The hijackers took over running *Athena,* and the fifty crew members — out of a complement of one-hundred-and-fifty — responsible for engineering, environmental systems, navigation, and the like were equally confined. However, the other hundred who served the guests still carried out their jobs, albeit blocked from accessing any part of the ship or its systems not needed for hospitality functions. Those guests, all one-hundred-and-twenty of them, roamed the cruiser-sized liner's passenger sections as they pleased. Armored doors and a segregated entertainment network kept them from accessing anything that might give the pirates trouble.

LeDain couldn't fathom how the infiltrators passed Black Nova Shipping's background checks. Sure, they were replacements for crew members struck by sudden illness or dealing with unexpected personal issues just before departure. But no sane company, especially not one owned by a leading zaibatsu like the Commonwealth Trading Corporation — ComCorp for short — hires a second officer without a thorough vetting.

And yet, that second officer, along with four newly arrived crew members from various departments, relieved him and his watchkeepers at gunpoint when the pirate sloops appeared. LeDain got out an emergency message complete with visuals in the ensuing confusion and hoped someone was listening.

But who they were and what they wanted was a complete mystery, as was their destination. *Athena*, presumably along with the sloops, went FTL a few hours after the hijacking and remained in hyperspace. Since then, the only faces he'd seen were those of the stewards bringing him his meals, and based on their body language, the pirates had ordered them to stay absolutely silent, probably with suitably blood-curdling threats.

Making a starship disappear in the galaxy's vastness was easy. But since they didn't plunder *Athena* and simply vanish, leaving the ship to her fate, or space everyone aboard and steal her, they surely entertained plans for the illustrious passengers, if not the crew. And hiding a ship her size in places where she might dock or at least either land everyone aboard or take on supplies was a somewhat different proposition. Which meant they were likely headed for the Protectorate Zone, that abomination negotiated by diplomats who possessed little more than the intelligence of unicellular organisms.

LeDain spent the war serving aboard various merchant vessels, moving cargo and people to support the Fleet. In that time, he never saw so much as a faint trace of Shrehari ships. And now, ten years after peace broke out, he was effectively a prisoner of war aboard his own liner along with everyone else. But who were their captors, other than human beings — at least the ones who'd taken *Athena* from within and those dispatched by the sloops to take over the other billets rendered vacant by the crew's confinement?

Their ships didn't conform to any known type he recognized. But adding a bit of hull plating here and there, perhaps a module or two, and you no longer saw a familiar silhouette. He stopped pacing and stared at the haggard man looking back at him from the full-length mirror. After this — if he lived to tell the tale — LeDain knew he was finished as a captain.

Black Nova wouldn't look kindly on the man who lost a ship full of VIPs to hijackers, and no one else would hire an officer fired by one of ComCorp's powerful subsidiaries. Especially not when Vitus Amali, ComCorp's vice chair of the board, was among those VIPs, along with the eldest daughter of Charles Lauzier, the Commonwealth Secretary General who governed humanity across the stars.

**

In contrast to Captain LeDain, Sara Lauzier's circumstances remained mostly unchanged. She still enjoyed the luxury of her quarters and the ship's amenities and the obsequious service provided by its guest services personnel. A tall, athletic fifty-year-old with long black hair, haughty patrician features, and cold eyes, she was the junket's informal leader even though she wasn't acting in any official capacity.

Yet, as one of the SecGen's closest advisers for the last ten years and the acknowledged forerunner to become Pacifica's junior senator in the next general election — when her father would retire after two terms — she was the most powerful among *Athena*'s passengers.

That none of the hijackers had bothered to speak with anyone after the announcement over the public address system that *Athena* was under new management irked her fellow prisoners. But she remained calm and collected. The people around her needed a soothing influence — *noblesse oblige*, as her father often said. Coming out of this with a reputation for being unflappable would only help cement her lock on that Senate seat next year.

Still, not knowing who hijacked the liner and where it was headed ate at the passengers, though they thought they could guess the why. Lauzier and every single one of her travel companions was wealthy, powerful, and came from equally rich and influential families, and were worth astronomical sums. Alternately, some of the more cynical ones believed, if this was a political game rather than a money-making operation, the pirates might cause no end of mischief along the frontiers with the Shrehari Empire and the Protectorate Zone. Many influential people on both sides remained unhappy the war didn't end with a crushing defeat for the enemy. Then there were those who profited from the conflict and unfettered access to a whole chunk of the galaxy unclaimed by either the Commonwealth or the Shrehari.

What Sara Lauzier thought, no one knew, and no one was courageous enough to ask.

"Are you dreaming up an escape plan, Sara?"

Vitus Amali's voice cut through her thoughts, and she looked away from the soothing holographic aquarium dominating one corner of the small lounge she'd staked out for herself and her immediate entourage at the beginning of the cruise. So many of the lesser lights among the passengers were tedious in their attempts at currying favor with the SecGen's daughter and principal adviser, and it wouldn't do if Lauzier showed a glimmer of irritation in an unguarded moment.

Amali, on the other hand, since he was the number two of the most powerful human zaibatsu in history, needed no favors from Lauzier. Ruggedly handsome, with short, sandy hair, a firm jaw, and intensely green eyes, he possessed a ruthless streak not unlike

Lauzier's and a keen eye for his fellow human beings' weaknesses, follies, and foibles. And as fellow upper crust Pacificans with an unquenchable appetite for power, they not only shared a common background but an instinctive understanding that they could help each other. Or so he believed.

He dropped into the seat beside her and took a sip from the whiskey glass in his hand.

"Escape?" She let out an inelegant snort. "From this gilded cage? Not going to happen."

"No." Amali shook his head. "Of course not. I just wish we knew our heading. This uncertainty risks driving several of our fellows around the bend. Carl, for example. He buttonholed me at the bar just now, already half-sloshed, and it's not even seventeen hundred hours yet. Talked nonsense while I served myself. Something about conspiracies to overthrow the established order via our kidnapping."

Lauzier grimaced. Carl Renzo was married to Senator Judy Chu of Arcadia, one of the most feared politicians in the Senate. A wealthy, indolent socialite by inclination and lack of other talents, Renzo could charm the shell off a Nabkhan sand beetle when he wanted. His family fortune had paid for Chu's political rise, and his glad-handing now helped her consolidate power. But Amali's comment didn't surprise Lauzier. Like many whose every whim was satisfied at hyperspeed, Renzo wasn't equipped to handle this sort of adversity.

"He's a big boy, and we're not his keepers."

Amali took another sip and nodded. "Indeed. Any new thoughts about the situation?"

"Other than it was a targeted inside job commissioned by parties unknown?" She shrugged. "No. That they didn't harm us speaks volumes, but I can't tell yet in what language."

—Ten—

When she heard a rap on her open office door, Kathryn Kowalski looked up and smiled.

"What brings you to the operations center, Zeke? Come in and grab a pew."

Commodore Ezekiel Holt, no longer wearing an eye patch thanks to postwar regeneration therapy that also gave him a new leg, dropped into a chair across from Kowalski.

"I was in the neighborhood and thought I'd say hi. Any news?"

She shook her head.

"No. But it's early days yet."

"Well, I have some for you, which is why I made a detour to operations on my way back from a meeting with the Director General of the Colonial Office Intelligence Service."

Kowalski cocked an eyebrow. "Do tell. Well connected, are you?"

"There's considerable back and forth between them and us on various issues, conversations we keep hidden from most people outside Fleet intelligence and counterintelligence."

"And also from politicians and the wider bureaucracy, I hope."

"Of course. Even the Colonial Secretary doesn't know much about what happens." He gave her an amused look. "The colonials operate quite an intelligence gathering network in places we can't or won't go, by the way, including the Protectorate Zone, one the CNI envies. And that's why I'm here. They admit to having agents on Kilia Station and most worlds with a renegade human population, which we already suspected. But they also seeded the area with interstellar subspace relays, which wasn't specifically mentioned as forbidden by the Treaty of Ulufan. So in effect, they can communicate with their people directly rather than rely on avisos to act as mobile arrays."

Surprise lit up Kowalski's features.

"Would they give us access for the duration of this mission so we can speak with Siobhan directly?"

"We've got it, though I'm afraid to think about the quid pro quo they might ask later on."

"What protocols did you negotiate?"

"I didn't so much negotiate anything as acquiesce to their stipulations. Messages to and from Task Force Luckner will pass through me only. They will also provide anything their people pick up about *Athena* and the pirate ships."

"That's wonderful. Not being solely reliant on avisos will considerably cut down on communications delays." She let out a soft sigh. "But we should really think about either partnering with the Colonial Office permanently or covertly seeding the Zone with our own relay constellation. Operating Q ships beyond useful radio range for weeks on end isn't optimal."

"At least Siobhan can use its facilities to call home."

"Sure, but we're still at the mercy of the resident Colonial Office agents who control access to their network." Kowalski made a face. "We really need a change in our way of thinking. It's fine and well that we — the Fleet — follow the Treaty of Ulufan to the letter, but since Kilia should be part of the Commonwealth sphere in the first place... Well, you know what I think about the subject. Any idea how many people our friends have on Kilia?"

Holt's lips twitched with barely suppressed amusement.

"They established a consulate that oversees the section of the Zone that should be ours, those human-colonized star systems closest to the Commonwealth sphere. But it's mostly a cover for the Intelligence Service which ranges much further afield."

Kowalski let out a grunt.

"Good Lord. A well-kept secret, it seems."

"Oh, it gets even better. My friend over there volunteered the name of the intelligence station chief on Kilia because Siobhan and I worked with him twice while we were in *Iolanthe*, a chap by the name Mikhail Forenza." When her eyes widened, he nodded. "Yes, Helen Forenza's brother. He's her complete opposite — competent, brilliant, courageous, and ruthless in pursuit of his duty. There was no love lost between them. Mikhail Forenza gave me the impression he was relieved she's no longer among the living. If Siobhan takes Task Force Luckner to Kilia, he'll give her every bit of help he can without playing spy games. He owes her, if not his life, then, at the very least, his freedom. And no, I can't discuss that particular action even with you, Kathryn, sorry."

"Understood. If you're good with Forenza being in on this, then I'm okay as well. Not that I have a say in the matter. I just worry about Siobhan retrieving the abductees safe and sound."

A sardonic smile tugged at Holt's lips. "Do I detect more than just concern for the latter in your tone?"

Kowalski raised both hands in surrender.

"Guilty as charged. If there was any justice in our beloved peacetime Navy, she'd be sitting in this chair right now, and I'd be out there leading the charge. The mission to find *Athena* could be what finally tips the scales in her favor before it's too late."

"Didn't she miss the promotion cut-off line for the last time the other day?"

"Yes, but the Grand Admiral can promote someone out of sequence in recognition of meritorious service, and the Fleet needs officers like her more than ever."

He gave her a knowing nod.

"So, you engineered Siobhan taking this command instead of simply sending out Battle Group 30 or 31 under their own flag officers." His flat tone made it a statement. "Did you also engineer the hijacking?"

She chuckled.

"You give me too much credit, Zeke. I merely applied one of Siobhan's favorite expressions — victory is a matter of opportunities clearly seen and swiftly seized. And boy did I see and seize this one from my perch as operations director for the Rim and Protectorate."

"Why would keeping her in the Service be a victory? She's one of those best placed in stasis during peacetime with her pod marked 'decant in case of war,' right?" When Kowalski didn't immediately reply, Holt said, "Humor me. I'd like to hear your reasons, even if they might match mine. Both of us fell under her spell long ago."

"You of all people know true peace is becoming more and more of an illusion, not only along every frontier except the one between the Shrehari Empire and us but also within the Commonwealth. That junket around the colonies to convince the local yokels of Earth's benevolence is as much an acknowledgment as any. But these minor conflicts are part of an ongoing, dark and dirty war, Zeke, the sort our current crop of senior and flag officers barely understand, even though they paid close attention in Siobhan's classes.

"We need fighting admirals who aren't afraid of upsetting politicians and zaibatsus if it means pacifying sectors before they erupt in fire and blood, the sort of flag officers that peacetime navies consider excessive risk-takers capable of tarnishing the establishment's reputation. But, unfortunately, a decade later, there are precious few left in the senior ranks beside Siobhan."

Holt nodded.

"I can't fault a single thing you said. But, yes, it's getting worse out there. Though the people around here, both at Fleet HQ and in the Palace of the Stars, refuse to open their eyes."

"For the latter, willful blindness is normal. Acknowledging there are problems means finding and implementing solutions. And the only effective ones wouldn't please those fixated on short-term profits, the people in whose pockets most of our politicians live. Unfortunately, while that malady hasn't quite infected our own higher-ups, their proximity to the Senate, the SecGen's office, and the bureaucracy ensures paralysis whenever the right decision conflicts with political aims. We need to move Fleet HQ off Earth, Zeke. Get it away from Geneva's cesspool to a place where asking for forgiveness rather than permission is the easier option."

"And remove the military from civilian control? That'll go over like a bottle of radioactive champagne at the SecGen's Armed Forces Gala."

Kowalski waved away his objection.

"I'm not proposing we go that far. The Senate would still control budgetary appropriations, and the government would still formulate defense policy. However, Fleet's day-to-day running, especially around operations and procurement, needs to be removed from direct political and bureaucratic influence. Move this HQ out of the core worlds and rebuild it on someplace like Caledonia, where we already own a fair chunk of the planet and are closer to our vital operational areas, and a lot of the current problems become moot."

"It would take a Grand Admiral with more gumption and ruthlessness than any I've seen in my career."

A mysterious smile lit up her face.

"Not so much gumption as deviousness. We've already moved several of our institutions to Caledonia — the Academy, the War College, Officer Candidate School, the various Special Forces and Pathfinder Schools, our main Basic Training School, and the list goes on. All we need to do is quietly move the HQ functions over in bits and pieces until only an empty shell remains here on Earth."

Holt let out an amused chuckle.

"And then ask for forgiveness, no doubt."

She pointed at him.

"Precisely. Give that commodore his second star. He gets it."

**

"Check, and I believe, mate." Dunmoore looked up from the chessboard and gave Pushkin a triumphant smile.

He stared at the board for a few seconds before letting out a disconsolate grunt as he reached out with his index finger and tipped his king over on its side.

"Nicely done, Skipper. At this point, I think we can call each other equal in skill and cunning."

As the loser, he removed the remaining pieces, placed them on Dunmoore's desk, flipped the board around, and tucked them into their slots. That done, he folded the board in half and set it aside.

"Do you think we'll find *Athena* at Kilia Station?"

She shook her head.

"Doubtful. Whoever organized a slick operation like this knows we planted operatives there. Or at least I damn well hope we did. There's no better listening post to spy on doings in this part of the Zone than Kilia. Everything illegal gets laundered there before it's sold in the Commonwealth." She made a disgusted face. "I still can't believe our idiotic diplomats let it become part of the Zone."

"As you said, too much money passes through Kilia. Did you decide on what you'll do once we arrive?"

Dunmoore shrugged.

"There aren't many options since we're in this as overt Navy units. If I still had *Iolanthe*, I'd take the covert route and infiltrate the local spacer-for-hire community. Instead, we'll need to rely on more direct methods."

"Like painting them with the targeting sensors of five warships. They'll understand that if a few well placed nuclear-tipped missiles strike Kilia's outer crust, they're goners."

"The people running it are savvy, Gregor. I've met them in person. They know Commonwealth starship captains won't open fire in a way that could kill ten thousand sentient beings in one go, at least not now that this part of the galaxy is nominally at peace. So no, offering violence while flying the Commonwealth flag won't work. If we could pass as a squadron of mercenaries, perhaps. But there's no way to disguise who we really are. Besides, Kilia has teeth of its own, and I'd rather not get my people killed for the sake of *Athena* and its passengers when there are alternatives."

Pushkin scoffed at her words.

"Even the lowliest of our spacers is worth more than that entire shipload of political grifters."

"Perhaps, but we have a mission to accomplish, Gregor." Dunmoore stood and stretched. "I'm due for a session in the gym."

"As am I. See you there."

— Eleven —

"Once we find Kilia's current position, we'll jump inward and emerge at her hyperlimit in silent running mode. I hope you have sufficient practice — I know *Salamanca* can turn herself into a hole in space. Kilia might be one step above a pirate's nest, but my visits during the war proved there is nothing wrong with her sensors and weapons."

Dunmoore looked around the flag conference table at the holographic frigate and corvette captains. Task Force Luckner had dropped out of FTL at Kilia's heliopause half an hour earlier, and she'd immediately called her command team together so she could check on the status of her other ships and discuss the next steps.

"*Jan Sobieski* can be as good a hole as *Salamanca*, accounting for her greater age, sir," Captain Kardas replied in a confident tone.

"So can *Arthur Currie*," Captain Sani added.

Charles Martel's commanding officer didn't seem quite as confident when he met Dunmoore's eyes.

"As you know, she's due for a refit, so I'm afraid we might show some emissions leakage, but we'll do our best."

"Understood. And *Sackville*?"

"I confess we don't practice as much as we should, but we'll do our best as well." A faint air of embarrassment hung over Lieutenant Commander Qiao.

Dunmoore privately gave him kudos for admitting what she suspected was true of the four. Running silent was a mandatory drill that should be given as much importance as the others, but with memories of the war fading away, only warships on anti-piracy patrol used it in real-time.

"Sir?" Pushkin raised his hand. "If I can offer a suggestion, let's watch each of the ships go silent in turn and check for emissions before heading inward. It'll give us a chance to make any necessary corrections."

"Excellent idea, Gregor. Set up a test run once we're done here, including *Salamanca*, even though we certified her silent running processes a few weeks ago. The others can check her. It'll be good training for their sensor operators."

She briefly glanced at the three frigate captains to see if any of them seemed worried at being tested by the redoubtable Siobhan Dunmoore after calling their ships ready for silent running. But they kept their composures.

"Any questions or comments?" When they shook their heads, she said, "Thank you. Stand by for orders from Commander Pushkin concerning the silent running drills and a navigation plot from Commander Khanjan."

Dunmoore stood, imitated by the others, and left the conference room via the flag CIC. There Attar Khanjan, a lanky fifty-something with jet black hair and a drooping gray mustache, waited at his station for *Salamanca*'s sensor sweep results. Pushkin joined her a few moments later.

"I guess Qiao is the only honest one besides Piotr Rydzewski," he said as he took the operations director station to prepare for the test. "There's no way the frigates are as polished as we were back in the day. And in a few years from now, *Salamanca* will be no better."

"Possibly, perhaps even probably." Dunmoore took the command chair. "Flag officers rarely leave their offices to sail with their commands nowadays. Too much administration and too few formation exercises. Oh, I'm sure they practice silent running, but for an hour or two, not an entire watch, let alone a whole day."

"And they won't have their chief engineers crawling all over the place trying to stem the slightest remaining emissions either."

"Perhaps." After a second or two, Dunmoore let out a snort of derision. "You know what, Gregor? I just realized we've become annoying old grumps with too many war stories and not enough respect for those who came after us. You know, the people we found irritating when we were young, with our entire careers ahead of us. So let's let our captains prove themselves. If they don't meet my standards, we'll help them fix the issues. If they do, then I'll give them a nod of approval."

Pushkin allowed himself a soft grunt.

"A good thing we keep these conversations among us, then." He paused. "Maybe we do sound a little bitter at times."

"There's no maybe about it, Commander," Khanjan said without turning to face them. "But that's par for the course in the Readiness Evaluation teams. We're past our best before date and acutely aware of the fact. My buddies in the Fleet Security Professional Standards Division are the same. That's why we're both chosen as the much-hated and feared inquisitors, capable of destroying careers with one terse report."

"You're a cheerful one today, Attar."

"No more than usual, Oh Great Flag Captain." This time Khanjan glanced over his shoulder and grinned at Pushkin. "But I'm one day closer to retirement and a little inn by the lake on Mykonos."

"What do you know about inn-keeping?"

"Nothing, but since I tucked away a nice little nest egg, I don't need to chase the bottom line. Besides, I'll let my cousin Thomas run the place and spend my days glad-handing the guests. The Decker branch of the family has always produced dour, hard-working settlers with nary a space-faring soul among them, unlike us Khanjans, who are cursed with wanderlust."

**

"Surprisingly good," Pushkin said in a grudging tone once *Salamanca* finished looking for his former ship, *Jan Sobieski*, now running silent a few thousand kilometers from the cruiser. "They might not practice spending days at it, but the old lady is tight as a drum, just like the others. Color me astonished. Unless the bad guys happen to scan her exact location, they won't see a thing."

"I'll venture old *Jan*'s crew, like the rest, spent quality time between the command conference and now plugging any stray emission leaks, so they don't hear sharp words from the Skipper," Lieutenant Commander Olmos replied. "No way wartime hulls waiting for their turn in drydock are that clean without extra doing. But kudos anyhow. It proves they're doing it right."

Dunmoore winked at him. "Then I'd say we achieved our aim, no?"

Pushkin, a broad grin on his square, honest face, wagged a finger at her. "Sneaky, sneaky."

"She is that," Guthren said. "I seem to recall a worn out frigate that wouldn't move without underhanded incentives."

"Touché, Chief. And thanks for reminding me of my failings." Pushkin gave him a mock scowl.

"You came through fast enough once you understood the Skipper wasn't another Helen Forenza, sir. Never you worry. By the time we got athwart Brakal's hawse, our *Stingray* was the best of the lot."

Dunmoore raised both hands. "All right, enough strolling down memory lane. Gregor, running *Salamanca* through the sequence first as the standard to beat was an excellent idea."

"I seem to recall a certain commodore who insisted the flagship should always show the lead."

"And so she did. I'm glad you remembered. Attar, please get the captains on the net."

"Aye, aye, sir."

When five faces filled the command chair's virtual display, she smiled.

"Well done, everybody. Task Force Luckner can become a hole in space at will. So long as no one has eyes on a particular section of hyperlimit when we drop out of FTL, we'll escape notice until I decide we light up. Keep in mind this will probably take much longer than the test we just ran. I trust you've entered the navigation plot provided by Commander Khanjan?"

A chorus of 'Yes, sir,' answered her.

"If there are no last questions, I'll give the execute in a few minutes." She paused for a moment, but no one spoke. "Going once, going twice, and done... Thank you. We will speak next when I order up systems at Kilia's hyperlimit. Dunmoore, out."

Lieutenant Commander Khanjan glanced over his shoulder.

"Ships linked in and synced, Skipper. We're ready for FTL. Just give the word."

"And that word is given."

Within moments, a klaxon sounded throughout *Salamanca*, followed by the voice of the officer of the watch warning the crew they would jump to hyperspace in three minutes. Dunmoore, like everyone else in the flag CIC, braced herself as the timer counted down the last seconds. Then the universe turned her guts into a psychedelic pretzel. The sensation vanished just as rapidly as it came on, and she stood.

"I'll be in my quarters."

**

"Emissions are tight across the task force, sir." Chief Petty Officer Second Class Harvey Cox, the other half of RED One's combat systems evaluation duo, glanced at Dunmoore over his shoulder shortly after Task Force Luckner dropped out of FTL at the hyperlimit.

A squat, thick-set man in his late fifties, with close-cropped gray hair and a bushy mustache beneath a prominent nose, he could reduce most combat systems officers to quivering masses of protoplasm during evaluations. "We should be invisible to Kilia, provided they weren't looking right at this spot just now."

"Put a live view of the station on the primary display, please."

"Sir."

When it shimmered into view, Kilia Station appeared just as unprepossessing as before. Built inside a potato-shaped asteroid forty kilometers long and eight kilometers wide, spinning on its long axis, Dunmoore could still see little of the habitat itself. But they'd added ten long docking arms sticking out like spokes from a hub where before all ships could do was enter orbit and launch shuttles. But the opening to the main shuttle dock was still there — a gaping maw in the rocky surface.

Using the data collected by *Iolanthe* during her wartime visits, Chief Cox marked the dozen known gun emplacements, eight missile launchers, and twenty-four shield generators. However, they were still camouflaged by low domes which blended seamlessly into the surrounding rock, and Dunmoore wondered whether the weaponry had ever been used.

"If they added more ordnance," Cox said, "we won't find out until we go live. And what's this, I wonder?"

The view shifted and focused on a medium-sized vessel orbiting the asteroid.

Lieutenant Commander Zakaria, fit, muscular, in her late forties with a narrow face and short brown hair, let out a low whistle.

"That's a Shrehari ship and no mistake. I've not seen anything like it since the armistice. The shape is definitely derived from the Imperial Deep Space Fleet's basic design — an elongated wedge with broad, almost wing-like hyperdrive nacelle pylons. Too big for a Ptar, too small for a Tol. A new class of ship, perhaps?"

"But no imperial dragon markings. Whatever those hull decorations represent, they're not military," Cox replied.

Pushkin nodded.

"Agreed, but that doesn't mean the thing isn't in imperial service. I'll wager a bottle of Glen Arcturus that's either their equivalent of a Q ship or something operated by their new intelligence branch, the *Tai Zohl*. Let's check the other visitor, Chief." He glanced at Dunmoore, who'd remained silent, and saw her study the image with what seemed like a wistful expression on her face. "You okay, Skipper?"

"I'm fine," she replied after a moment. "This place holds a few memories of my days in *Iolanthe*. We carried out one of our more outrageous capers here, right, Mister Guthren."

"You said it, sir." Guthren turned to Pushkin. "The captain created an instant mercenary fleet around the Furious Fairy and bluffed her way through. You could say it was *Iolanthe*'s first turn as flagship. Let me tell you about it when we're back home and can talk shop on my bungalow's back deck."

"Sir." Chief Cox raised his hand and pointed at the primary display. "Take a gander at that sloop on the docking arm. Doesn't she resemble the hijackers?"

The images transmitted by *Athena*'s captain during the seizure appeared on a side screen. Everyone in the flag CIC studied both intently, then one by one, they nodded.

"If it's not a hijacker," Lieutenant Commander Zakaria said, "then it came from the same shipyard. Sloop, vaguely human design with particularities we can't yet explain."

"No other ships that we can see, though, sir. We've watched the asteroid for one full rotation by now. So if anyone else is in the vicinity, they're keeping quiet."

Dunmoore leaned forward.

"Please check the leading and trailing Lagrangian points, Chief. Using them to hide was one of my favorite tactics back in the day, and it cost many a Shrehari their lives."

"Aye, aye, Captain."

She sat back while Cox relayed her request to the cruiser's CIC, which controlled the sensors themselves. Looking for ships running silent at a Lagrangian always took time, especially in passive mode, but with luck, the combat systems AI might find something occluding the background stars.

— Twelve —

Rear Admiral Kowalski glanced at her communicator when it chimed — Ezekiel Holt. She touched its control surface.

"What's up, Zeke?"

"The *Athena* hijack story is hitting the newsnets as we speak. Someone somewhere must have talked out of school. We'll be looking for the leaker, but things could become interesting in this city within the next hour. So I thought you might wish to batten the hatches."

"Anything about the rescue operation?"

"Not so far, which makes me think it came from outside the Fleet or the SecGen's office. Did we hear back from the Shrehari ambassador yet? Task Force Luckner will be in the Kilia system by now, and since there is always a Shrehari corsair around, the moment Siobhan's spotted, they'll be tearing up the subspace net."

"I received no news on that front. Perhaps the ambassador is still consulting his government. Subspace radio conversations over that distance take time. However, he knows the name of the task force and the identity of its commanding officer. I confirmed that with the SecGen's liaison office. Hopefully, it'll convince

Kho'sahra Brakal to sanction the incursion. Anything from the Colonial Office?"

"The consulate folks on Kilia Station are expecting Task Force Luckner. Mikhail Forenza will speak with Siobhan the moment she shows up, which will probably be after she keeps the place under observation from the hyperlimit for a day or so while running silent, her usual modus operandi." He glanced to one side. "Hang on. Something's happening downtown. Senator Chu, whose husband is aboard *Athena,* has just released a blistering statement condemning the Special Security Bureau for letting what was clearly an inside job happen. Of course, it's a veiled jab at Lauzier, as usual. I don't think the Director General of the Special Security Bureau needs to pack his personal effects just yet."

Kowalski let out a snort. "I'll read her latest pronouncement in a moment. But, like the rest of them, I'm sure this one is full of colorful language and words that most of the ordinary citizens can barely pronounce, let alone understand."

"Chu never recovered from losing to Lauzier the last time around. On the contrary, she practically accused him of underhanded and corrupt practices in securing a second term. Considering how he handled the postwar years, I can't say she's entirely wrong."

Holt grinned at her.

"After thirty-plus years in the Senate, Chu should know everything about those practices. She's the poster child for senatorial term limits. I don't doubt this newest attack on Lauzier just now is part of her plan to become SecGen after the next election. We've known for a while that she'll do whatever it takes.

For instance, Renzo's presence in *Athena* certainly doesn't impress the colonial yokels. Instead, he's there to build support for his wife among the core star system nomenklatura who make up most of the passengers."

"Ah, the joys of working counterintelligence. You peek into the Commonwealth's darkest, dirtiest corners day in, day out."

"When you put it like that, I think I'd rather sweep the floors at the Academy."

"We use droids for those sorts of jobs."

"My point exactly, Kathryn. This keeping tabs on crooked politicos and bureaucrats isn't for us. We need an internal affairs organization independent of the Fleet, the SSB, the Senate, and the administration. In any case, that was my update for now. Enjoy Senator Chu's latest rant."

"I will. Cheers, Zeke."

**

"We can't detect anything at the Lagrangian points, Skipper," Lieutenant Commander Zakaria reported when Dunmoore returned from the wardroom after a quick meal. "Unless someone is running silent like us, only two ships are visiting Kilia at the moment — the Shrehari corsair and the one of unknown origin that resembles the hijackers."

Dunmoore dropped into the command chair and stared at Kilia's image on the primary display, jaw muscles working.

After a few moments, she said, "Right. There's no point in hanging around any longer. Chief Cazano, open a link with all ships and transmit up systems, followed by prepare to execute navigation plan on flag orders."

The short, slender, auburn-haired chief petty officer second class assigned as RED One's communications specialist nodded once but kept her eyes on the workstation to monitor the local radio traffic.

"Up systems, followed by prepare to execute navigation plan on flag orders, aye."

"How long do you figure before they notice a Navy task force closing in?" Pushkin asked.

Dunmoore gave him a shrug.

"No idea, though I'd put money on the Shrehari corsair spotting us first. I doubt the buggers have grown lax since the war. But, of course, I also doubt they heard from their high command yet about our little visit, so the next half hour could be interesting."

Chief Cazano raised her hand.

"All ships report ready and synced, Skipper."

"Commander Khanjan, you may execute the navigation plan."

"Executing navigation plan, aye, sir. Order to engage is transmitting." Then, a minute or so later, "The task force is accelerating on a new heading."

Though the image of their target on the primary display didn't change, and she didn't sense any difference in the ship's speed or motion, Dunmoore felt that familiar excitement after so long. She was at last heading into the fray again, even though this time it would be without actual combat — provided both Kilia and the Shrehari did nothing profoundly stupid, such as open fire on Commonwealth Navy ships unprovoked.

Just over fifteen minutes later, Chief Cox raised his hand.

"We're being painted by Shrehari sensors from the corsair, Skipper, but no sign they're targeting us. Hang on." A few seconds passed. "They raised shields, although *Salamanca* can't detect weapons powering up."

"A little skittish, are they?" Commander Zakaria glanced over her shoulder at Dunmoore.

"Or prudent. We're probably the first Commonwealth Navy ships they've seen in almost a decade, which means the last time they met humans, it was to exchange missiles and gunfire, not pleasantries. So we'll keep our shields down unless we pick up signs someone is powering weapons."

Zakaria nodded. "Understood."

"Sir." Chief Cazano raised a hand. "The Shrehari are hailing us. They're demanding to speak with the human admiral who dares dishonor himself by violating the Treaty of Ulufan."

"Sure enough, they didn't get word from home about us yet. Is their hail in Anglic or Shrehari?"

"Anglic, but it sounds like something from a translation AI."

Dunmoore nodded. Automatic translation of non-human speech into one of the human languages had never been perfected by any species in this part of the galaxy.

"Let's see if we can set up a video link."

"I'm trying, sir." A minute passed, then another, before Cazano turned to Dunmoore. "They accepted on condition we use their translation AI. I can feed the output from ours in text form to your command chair heads-up display."

"Do it, Chief."

The primary display shed its image of Kilia, replaced by a Shrehari warrior's black within black eyes beneath pronounced skull ridges covered by dark skin. He stared at her with unnerving intensity, then spoke briefly in his language. Moments later, an artificial voice came through the speakers.

"I am Retak, commander of the Imperial Survey Ship *Gar Viq* on a scientific mission. And you are?"

Words floated in front of her face, essentially repeating what Retak said in Shrehari. Dunmoore hoped he didn't expect her to believe his was a science vessel, but there was no point discussing the matter. It was about diplomacy now.

"I am Siobhan Dunmoore, commander of the Commonwealth Navy Task Force Luckner, on a rescue mission sent by my government to retrieve over two hundred of our citizens seized by pirates. Your ambassador on our homeworld has been informed and will have passed the word to your government by now."

Once Retak's AI translated her words a few seconds later, he looked to one side and jerked his massive chin. His mouth moved, but she heard no sound. Then, finally, he turned back toward her.

"You are Dunmoore who attacked the Imperial Home System with Task Force Luckner?" The last word came out badly mangled, but she understood it nonetheless.

"I am, and I also had the honor of meeting *Kho'sahra* Brakal in battle as well as in peace."

The Shrehari stared at her for a few moments, though she couldn't decipher his expression, let alone pick up a hint of his thoughts.

"And you say your government informed mine."

"Yes. It wouldn't unilaterally violate the Treaty of Ulufan by sending a naval task force without warning and without good reason."

Dunmoore held Retak's eyes, wondering whether he understood she knew damn well *Gar Viq* was an undercover military or intelligence unit, and thereby also technically in violation of the Treaty, should anyone dispute its identity. But, of course, the Commonwealth was doing likewise. For example, *Iolanthe* or another of the Navy's Q ships could be stalking this star system right now, wondering why a cruiser, three frigates, and a corvette had appeared out of nowhere.

When he didn't immediately reply, Dunmoore added, "We come in peace and will only offer violence to those who captured our citizens should they not cooperate. But we would be grateful for any help offered by honorable beings who deplore piracy as much as we do. For instance, did you see this ship?"

She called up *Athena*'s image and waited while he studied it.

"No. Pirates took it?"

"Yes, with many notable Commonwealth citizens aboard." She put up a picture of the unknown sloops. "These are the dishonorable pirates who violated Commonwealth space. They resemble the ship currently docked at Kilia. Do you know their place of origin?"

Another pause, then, "They were built on Arkanna, but the design is human."

Dunmoore kept surprise from showing on her face at hearing the name of the reclusive humanoid species whose star systems bordered the Empire on the Protectorate Zone's far side.

Outwardly like human beings, with a few notable differences, their fighting prowess inspired such respect that the Shrehari left them alone.

But why were Arkanna operating ships in this part of the galaxy when it was known that they rarely left their sphere, let alone hijack a human star liner inside the Commonwealth itself? And why didn't Naval Intelligence know the pirate sloops came from Arkanna?

"And that is everything I can tell you, Dunmoore."

"You have my gratitude for your help."

"Good hunting." Retak's image faded away as he cut the link.

Dunmoore exhaled slowly. "That went better than I expected."

"Small mercies, Skipper," Pushkin replied. "Arkanna? How did we not know they were in this part of the Zone aboard ships that bear some resemblance to those built by Commonwealth yards?"

"Perhaps because this is a recent development? I think I'll chat with the station's general manager next and see if I can also speak with that sloop's captain."

"Sir." Chief Cazano raised her hand again. "Incoming transmission from the Colonial Office Consulate on Kilia. They're using Commonwealth government encryption protocols, but the link is on one of the Navy's priority subspace frequencies."

Dunmoore and Pushkin looked at each other. "Curiouser and curiouser. Put them on."

— Thirteen —

A familiar narrow, aristocratic face dominated by piercing blue eyes and topped with carefully sculpted white hair appeared on the primary display.

"Captain Dunmoore, as I live and breathe. Welcome to Kilia." Mikhail Forenza's amused smile held a trace of warmth, if not quite friendship. "I was expecting you. And yes, I will explain everything."

"This is a day rife with surprises, it seems. How have you been?"

"Doing tolerably well." His smile grew warmer, and some of it reached his eyes. "But like another old warhorse of my acquaintance, I've not prospered as much as I had hoped, even though peace hasn't made my work less onerous. On the contrary. Still, being the Colonial Office Intelligence Service station chief on a crossroads like Kilia beats riding a desk back on Earth."

Her eyes widened slightly in surprise.

"I didn't know the Colonial Office opened a consulate here."

"We don't advertise since diplomacy serves as a cover for the consulate's true function as a Commonwealth listening post in what is nominally a neutral zone. So yes, I'm officially the consul, but my actual job is coordinating the Service's intelligence outposts on human-settled worlds in the Protectorate."

A frown creased Dunmoore's forehead as several pieces fell into place.

"Since you're using a subspace channel that doesn't originate on Kilia and you're presumably in touch with those scattered outposts, may I assume you have subspace relays the Navy doesn't know about?"

"Indeed. After the war, the Colonial Office set up its own network when it became clear the Navy wouldn't risk being accused of violating the Treaty by creating its own intelligence nodes in the Zone. Since we're a civilian organization, the Shrehari can hardly point their fingers at us, not when they do the same thing. You noticed the so-called Shrehari science vessel in orbit? It's a bit of a mobile version of our consulate."

"I spoke with its captain just now. He called to tell me I was violating the Treaty but remained polite when I told him about my mission." Another thought struck her. "You said you were expecting us?"

"Yes, my superiors are allowing the Fleet to use our communications network for this operation — via your former first officer who was collaborating with my superiors on other matters before this happened. I'm fully briefed on the events and your orders and am at your disposal."

"Retak said the ship currently docked is Arkanna-made."

Forenza nodded.

"Indeed, and the ships that took *Athena* are of the same construction, but Retak isn't entirely correct in calling them

Arkanna. As so often happens, the situation is rather more complex by several orders of magnitude."

Dunmoore allowed herself a wry grin, remembering the two times her path crossed with Forenza's.

"Don't I know it."

"As you'll recall, after the war, the Navy sold off thousands of surplus starships, mostly civilian hulls pressed into service or taken as prizes, and wartime transports built to supply vastly larger Armed Forces. Some enterprising trader sold a few to the Arkanna, whose own faster-than-light shipbuilding industry is generations behind ours and the Shrehari's. Since their star systems essentially make up an autarky of sorts, they've never been driven to develop long-range vessels. Still, the Arkanna face growing social issues because of population growth. So they not only bought surplus human ships from unscrupulous traders shortly after the war but used them as templates to build their own improved version, the result of which you see docked here."

Dunmoore nodded. "I see, but I'm sure it gets even more complicated."

"Oh, indeed, Captain. The Arkanna are a matriarchal species, and one way they control excess males is by sending them off-world. Building a fleet of long-range FTL ships gave them the perfect means to channel their males' energies and enrich their worlds through trade and conquest. Those ships reached this part of the Zone a few years ago. And here, they met a new player, one which Naval Intelligence is only now recognizing as a potential threat, although the SSB are probably using them for their own ends. Did you ever hear of the Confederacy of the Howling Stars?"

"No." She shook her head.

"I'm not surprised. Our beloved Commonwealth is the greatest accretion of information silos in human history. The SSB doesn't speak with my Service or the Fleet, none of the three speak with any other federal agency, and star system police forces don't speak to the feds, period. Nevertheless, the Colonial Office and Naval Intelligence have begun working together behind the scenes, despite our political and bureaucratic masters, mainly because a few in each took risks and reached out."

"Information is power."

Forenza nodded.

"Precisely. And because people hoard information, we end up with things like the *Athena* hijacking. In any case, the Confederacy of the Howling Stars was founded by disgruntled Fleet veterans after the war and rapidly grew to become a criminal organization offering mercenaries for hire along the Commonwealth's outer edges, especially in the Rim Sector and the Protectorate. A few years ago, the Howlers met the Arkanna, and while it wasn't a match made in heaven, both decided they could help each other prosper.

"The latter offered newly built ships for sale while the former operated hulls worn out by age and war. But they know this part of space and will ally themselves with any like-minded beings who can send business their way. As a result, clear territorial lines were drawn, with the star systems closest to the Commonwealth becoming exclusive Confederacy hunting grounds, while those closest to Arkanna space became theirs. The rest of the Zone is open to both. Thus, the Arkanna-built sloop docked here is crewed by humans belonging to the Confederacy of the Howling

Stars rather than Arkanna. The ones who took *Athena* will almost certainly be as well since the Arkanna do not want to risk a confrontation with either the Commonwealth or their Confederacy allies."

Dunmoore's frown returned. "Why would human mercenaries who operate exclusively in the Zone, especially Fleet veterans, hijack a liner inside the Commonwealth?"

"That's easily answered, Captain. Someone back home hired them. But who, and for what reason? It's a given there's more to come in this matter." A shrug. "All I can tell you is that logic dictates you'll find the paymaster closer to Earth than Kilia."

"Right now, I'll settle for finding *Athena* and those aboard in good health. Then, our common friends can root out whoever is behind this scheme."

"Agreed. I've sent word to our outposts. If your quarry shows up on any human-settled world, they'll let me know. But space is huge, ships are tiny."

She nodded in agreement. "Unless we figure out the end game and determine the optimal intercept point. Where would human mercenaries take a luxury liner filled with high-priced hostages while their employers carry out the next stage of the operation? I'm guessing it won't be deep inside the Zone, far from Commonwealth space."

Forenza shook his head. "No, probably not."

"Then where does that leave me?"

"At the mercy of the Colonial Office's intelligence gathering network, I'm afraid. My people will do their best, but until something surfaces, there's no point in your task force heading off in every direction. The number of star systems within easy reach of the Commonwealth is such that it could take you months to investigate. And that's just the ones with planets suitable for our sort of life."

"What about the captain of that ship? Can we convince him to cooperate?"

An amused chuckle escaped Forenza's throat.

"Unless you plan on using the threat of violence as an incentive, the answer is no."

"Can he be bought off?"

"And face an agonizing death when the rest of his organization catches up with him? Again, no. The only way you'll find out anything is by designating him a pirate and doing what you'd normally do with such beings."

A thoughtful expression crossed Dunmoore's face. "How many aboard?"

"Forty-two. Confederacy traders like *Vuko* run with small crews. If you're thinking of a cutting-out operation to seize it, may I remind you Kilia Station's management also has a vote? This place survived the war by enforcing strict neutrality and allowing agents such as me and my counterparts on the imperial side, along with representatives of many sentient species, to conduct their business. That hasn't changed in the intervening decade. A hostile act on your part will destroy what is a delicate balance and attract the ire of certain people in our government, even if you fire no weapons and cause no damage."

"And a failed rescue attempt will earn me the ire of Secretary General Lauzier, Senator Chu, and Geraldo Amali, among many other powerful people. And generate lousy publicity for the Navy."

Forenza inclined his head by way of acknowledgment.

"I understand, Captain. I'm merely ensuring you're aware seizing a ship docked at Kilia Station without the permission of its management will entail repercussions that can resonate well after you complete your task."

"Trust me, Mister Forenza, I know this. If you'll recall, I already forced Enoc Tarrant — who, unless I'm mistaken, still runs Kilia — to give me what I wanted on one memorable occasion. Or rather, Ezekiel Holt did so on my behalf. However, this time, my task force isn't a single ship surrounded by illusions but the real thing."

"I do remember. It was a well-played ruse, but this time the circumstances are different. By the way, is Holt with you?"

"No. Zeke — Commodore Holt — is now a department head in the Counterintelligence Branch at Fleet HQ. His promotion came through a few weeks ago."

A knowing smile tugged at Forenza's lips.

"Then I think I can guess who's behind my Service's increased cooperation with the Navy to help you carry out this rescue mission. We've been chummy with your counterintelligence for a while."

"So, where does that leave us?"

He shrugged again. "That's entirely up to you, Captain. If it helps, *Vuko* is currently carrying narcotics of a type deemed illegal in the Commonwealth for transshipment to a human free trader whose arrival is imminent. It may not deflect the wrath of those who would cry for your head after you upset the delicate balance here, but as I understand matters, this may well be your last command before retirement."

She gave him a bitter smile.

"There's no may about it. I'm terminal at the rank of captain, and the Fleet doesn't keep senior officers who are terminal around for long. It would rather we didn't hog the finite number of billets available."

Forenza nodded once. "Very well. Would you like the data we collected on *Vuko* and Kilia itself? So much has changed since your last visit."

"Please."

"Would you also enjoy a visit before taking action? Then, as consul, I can arrange a meeting with Enoc Tarrant, and you can see the changes for yourself."

"You know I met with Tarrant under my Q ship captain alias, Shannon O'Donnell, before we sprung you from the internment camp. A man with his sharp wits will recognize me in an instant."

Forenza let out a bark of amused laughter.

"Even better. There's no finer way of unsettling a mind like his than proof you conned him successfully years ago. Let me arrange a parlay between Tarrant and the Commonwealth Navy task force commander who appeared on his doorstep unannounced and unwanted. If anyone on Kilia contacts you, ignore them until you and I speak again. And please don't talk to Retak either."

"You're the resident expert. I shall do as you suggest."

"Excellent. Give me an hour. In the meantime, I suggest you assume the highest orbit possible around Kilia and stay silent. We'll do the talking. It should keep Tarrant's people on edge."

"Quiet and deadly. Got it."

"Forenza, out."

— Fourteen —

"They finally stopped hailing us, Skipper," Chief Cazano announced when Dunmoore re-entered the flag CIC after a hasty meal in the wardroom. "No idea whether it was because of Consul Forenza or they simply became fed up with getting nowhere."

Dunmoore dropped into her command chair and studied the tactical hologram showing Kilia Station with the docked Confederacy ship, her task force, and the Shrehari 'science' vessel, everything in motion like celestial clockwork. That pirate captain could probably tell her where to look for *Athena*, but could she afford the cost of making him speak?

Then, an idea struck her. Enoc Tarrant and his people were solely interested in profit and didn't much care about the sources. Still, they understood the Commonwealth Navy could easily disrupt many of them simply by intercepting and inspecting any ship approaching Kilia. Perhaps he could be convinced his best interests lay in helping Dunmoore find the missing liner. But, of course, a senior Commonwealth Navy officer blackmailing Tarrant could make Forenza's job as Commonwealth Consul and head spy on Kilia more complex, and he might object. Assuming, of course, that Tarrant didn't decide she was bluffing with a pair of deuces.

"Incoming transmission from Consul Forenza."

A faint smile crossed Dunmoore's lips. Speak of the devil...

"On my command chair display."

Moments later, a holographic Forenza appeared in front of her.

"Captain, I've arranged a meeting with Enoc Tarrant. Needless to say, he's rather irritated by your presence because he's correctly deducing the sight of five Commonwealth warships will make customers with questionable cargoes hesitate."

"How nice to hear." Her smile turned into a smirk. "Perhaps he can use his considerable connections in the Zone and help us search for *Athena*. It's the quickest way of ensuring our speedy departure."

"That is something we should discuss beforehand."

She nodded.

"Indeed. I understand your situation and the fact that you'll still be here when I've left with my task force."

"Just so. Let's be clear on one thing. Threatening Tarrant won't get us far. He knows you'll never open fire on Kilia. It would mean the end of your career. Conversely, he'll never open fire on you because it means the end of his reign. What he can do, however, is reject requests for cooperation and use his connections inside the Commonwealth to see you punished."

A snort. "You can't intimidate someone who's out the door when this is over, Consul. I'm the proverbial woman with nothing left to lose. But I wasn't thinking of threats in any case. Coercing Tarrant into cooperation by cutting off his supply of pirates, sketchy traders, and renegades from every species in the

Zone is another matter. As you said, those who fear the Navy won't approach, lest we seize them. And the ones who do, other than the Shrehari, I can threaten with complete impunity. Not that it would take much. I daresay *Salamanca* is the largest fighting ship in the Zone at this point and the most modern. One broadside across a renegade's bow, and they'll know it's either surrender or die. Is this an approach you'd support?"

"If you do it with a smile and merely seek his help in return for a speedy departure. Of course, should he prove false, you'll come back for another chat."

"Then we agree. When is our meeting with Tarrant?"

"In three hours. I've reserved one of the docking arms for your shuttle rather than use the internal bay. Tarrant and his people will be less likely to play silly games that way. Perhaps you could arrive in, say, two hours? I'll show you the consulate, and we can discuss last-minute issues. Is there anyone from your previous meeting with Tarrant in the task force?"

"Yes, my command coxswain, Chief Petty Officer Guthren. I planned on bringing him with me."

"Good. And armed guards. I would suggest four. You and your coxswain should carry sidearms as well."

"Will do."

"In two hours, then. Forenza, out."

Guthren immediately stood. "I'll speak with *Salamanca*'s bosun to arrange the escort and weapons."

"And I'll see that the second officer organizes a shuttle," Pushkin added.

She nodded her thanks. "While you do that, I'll speak with Captain Rydzewski."

Dunmoore found *Salamanca*'s commanding officer in his day cabin and took the chair across from his desk.

"I'm going ashore to meet with Consul Forenza and the guy who runs Kilia, a thug by the name Enoc Tarrant. We met during the war, but Tarrant remembers me as Shannon O'Donnell, captain of the privateer *Persephone*. I'll be taking Chief Guthren, who was with me at the time. He's organizing an armed landing party — four spacers — as an escort. Gregor is speaking with your second officer to organize the shuttle. My goal is convincing Tarrant speedy and willing cooperation in helping find *Athena* will see us gone before shipping around here, and Kilia's profits are unduly disrupted. He has connections and could obtain quicker results than the Colonial Office intelligence network."

Rydzewski nodded. "Understood."

"While I'm away from *Salamanca*, you're in command of the task force. Should Tarrant or anyone else be foolhardy and detain me, you will ignore my presence in Kilia and continue with the mission. In such a circumstance, I am expendable. Should that happen, please work closely with Gregor. We went through something similar during the war."

She held his eyes, knowing he'd likely never experienced a situation where his commanding officer might become a hostage. Besides, the general order covering such an eventuality was rescinded years earlier, a move Dunmoore considered foolishly optimistic. Just because the war was over didn't mean hostile elements wouldn't dare incur the Fleet's wrath if they thought they could get away with it.

"I doubt Tarrant will risk angering the Commonwealth. He didn't strike me as the type, but people change, and there's no knowing what other factions exercise power in Kilia."

"Noted, sir."

"I may call on you for a demonstration of power if Tarrant forces my hand, so be ready."

"Yes, sir." His jaw muscles worked for a moment as if he were chewing on his words. "May I say that I'm not particularly comfortable with you doing this? Flag officers commanding shouldn't lead landing parties. Instead, they should negotiate via comlink and leave the landing to their subordinates."

An amused smile relaxed Dunmoore's features.

"I'm not a flag officer, Piotr, though I understand your sentiments. In any other circumstance, I would proceed with more caution, but here, today, only my physical presence in Tarrant's company can get us results. Remember, I wasn't chosen for this mission merely because I was available but because I know firsthand how things work in this part of the galaxy."

Dunmoore understood part of Rydzewski's worry stemmed from fear he'd be stuck seeing the rescue through to a successful end and either felt inadequate or feared that in case of failure, his promising career would be over.

"Don't worry. I'll be back aboard for the evening meal after hopefully securing Tarrant's help in exchange for our speedy departure."

**

Dunmoore was glad Forenza had arranged a docking arm. Entering the shuttle bay carved into the asteroid would bring back too many memories. Even so, for a fraction of a second when she climbed aboard her craft, she expected four soldiers from E Company, 3rd Battalion, Scandia Regiment as escort rather than bosun's mates.

She'd received invitations to attend the Regiment's anniversary celebrations over the years but could never free herself from her duties in time and make the trip from Caledonia. Besides, just the thought of seeing Lieutenant Colonel Tatiana Salminen, as she was now, and the men and women who'd served faithfully in *Iolanthe* under her command made her wistful for long-vanished glories.

As she settled in beside Guthren after giving the pilot and her escort a nod, the latter said, in a voice pitched for her ears only, "Apropos of nothing whatsoever, I wonder how Karlo Saari is doing."

Dunmoore turned her head and gave him a sardonic look as the aft ramp rose and cut them off from the hangar deck.

"You too, eh?"

Command Sergeant Karlo Saari of the Scandia Regiment led her escort the first time she and Guthren visited Kilia Station.

"Too many memories, sir."

"Last I heard, Karlo was a reserve captain and back as an EMT in his hometown. But you knew that, Chief."

"Those were the good old days, Skipper, when we ran the enemy ragged in this part of the frontier and could threaten guys like Enoc Tarrant without worrying that HQ might take exception."

"You said it."

They fell silent as the shuttle lifted half a meter off the deck, retracted its landing struts, then pivoted and headed for the starboard space doors now slowly opening while red warning strobes flashed. A force field kept the atmosphere from escaping, but the inner airlocks were buttoned up.

The sleek, elegant craft nosed through the shimmering curtain and out into the void, leaving *Salamanca*'s comforting armored hull behind. At that moment, for an inexplicable reason, the blaster at Dunmoore's hip felt unusually heavy and uncomfortable. True, this was the first time she carried a sidearm since the war. But it was more than that, more than the memories.

She abruptly released her seat restraints, stood, and headed for the flight deck. Then, out of politeness, she stuck her head through the open door and asked, "Mind if I join you?"

The petty officer at the controls looked over his shoulder.

"Please do, sir. You can take the weapons operator seat if you like." He gestured at the console to his right. As she settled in, the grizzled veteran indicated the pilot wings on her battledress tunic and grinned. "Want to take the controls?"

"Thanks for the offer, but those," she tapped the wings, "are now just a souvenir of my younger days. I haven't flown anything in a long time. I just want a good look at those docking pylons. They weren't there the last time I visited this place."

"In that case, enjoy the view." He centered their target, Pylon Five, on the flight deck's primary display and zoomed in. The shuttle was level with the docking station, its topside facing the spinning asteroid. "I've matched Kilia's rotation. Now, it's just a question of getting within five hundred meters under our own power. Then Kilia will tractor beam us the rest of the way. Can't say I'm too keen about surrendering control to this lot, but I guess it's that or entering the shuttle bay, which wouldn't be any better."

"I've done the shuttle bay, PO. This is better. Much better. Up here, if things go pear-shaped, you simply blow the docking clamps and shove off. Escaping from down there isn't quite as easy."

"Do you think we might get into trouble?"

She shook her head. "No. But you never can tell when you'll need to make a quick getaway."

"Roger that, sir." He glanced at his console. "And we're within tractor beam range."

Right on cue, the radio came to life. "Shuttle Luckner, this is Kilia Traffic. Activating tractor beam."

A few seconds passed, then, "Luckner confirms. We are under your control."

Dunmoore stared at the petty officer and mouthed, 'Luckner?'

He shrugged. "They wanted a name. Since using the hull number is clumsy and you're the task force commander."

They watched the docking station grow on the primary display, even though the shuttle was approaching broadside rather than head-on. When they were within a few meters, four arms extruded from its surface along with a universal airlock adapter tube. Moments later, four thumps resonated through the hull, followed by a fifth.

"Shuttle Luckner, you are docked. Please confirm airlock integrity from your side."

The petty officer studied his console. "I read pressure on the other side of my hatch."

"In that case, welcome to Kilia. You may disembark. The Commonwealth Consul is on his way. Kilia Traffic, out."

— Fifteen —

Dunmoore unfastened her restraints and stood. "You'll stay with the ship, PO. Let no one other than us aboard. If someone forces the airlock, disconnect."

"Aye, aye, sir."

"Open her up."

She turned and headed back into the passenger compartment, where Guthren and the four bosun's mates waited for her orders. Two stood by the door, grave expressions on their faces, hands hovering over the blasters holstered at the hip.

"Let's go, Chief."

"Sir." He gestured at the leading pair, who stepped cautiously into the universal airlock adapter tube and covered the few meters between the shuttle and the docking station proper at a quick pace. Once they'd checked out the other side, one of them reappeared and gave the all-clear signal.

Shifting from the shuttle's artificial gravity into that created by the asteroid's spin momentarily surprised Dunmoore as she exited. The difference wasn't much, but enough so that it took her a few seconds to adapt. By the time they gathered in front of the elevator connecting the docking station with the habitat, its doors opened, and Mikhail Forenza stepped out.

"Welcome, Captain, Chief." He bowed his head in a formal, almost courtly gesture more befitting a diplomat than a spy.

Dunmoore held out her hand. "A pleasure to meet in person once again after so long."

"Likewise." They shook. Then he offered Guthren his hand. "Glad that you're still by the captain's side, Chief."

"I wouldn't want it any other way, sir."

Forenza gestured at the cargo-sized elevator cab. "Shall we?"

The ride up the pylon was smooth, though Dunmoore felt another minute shift in the gravity as they neared the asteroid's surface. Finally, their cab halted without a bump, and the doors opened again, this time on a huge, hangar-like space with airlocks piercing each of its four shiny, gray walls. A scuffed floor showed evidence of hard use beneath the harsh white lighting.

Forenza led them to the one on their right, which unlocked and swung open at their approach. When Dunmoore gave him a questioning look, he said, "We're under surveillance by the Kilia Operations Center and have been since the docking station. They've upped their security measures in recent years, and I can't say I disapprove."

The airlock opened on a broad corridor like the one she remembered from her first visit, and soon, they passed through another and emerged into the habitat itself.

"Hasn't changed a bit," Guthren said while the four bosun's mates stared at their surroundings with evident curiosity.

A small city of low-rise building clusters separated by wide avenues, it was lit and warmed by an artificial sun on the cavern's ceiling. The short, narrow horizon on either side, as it rose along the asteroid's inner diameter, still felt faintly surreal, but Dunmoore ignored it in favor of comparing what her eyes saw with the images stored in her memory.

"They built along the edges. So the city limits are higher up on the wall on both sides."

"Can't go too far. Otherwise, they'll be burned to a crisp by that reactor-fed plasma ball."

Forenza glanced at Guthren over his shoulder.

"There is talk of reducing its size and centering in on the main axis so they can build around the cavern. All that would be needed is a physical axle from end to end, but there are still engineering challenges to work out. Besides, the station's carrying capacity in terms of environmental systems, atmosphere scrubbing, water, and food supplies has an upper limit, and I'd say while they've not yet reached it, we're past the two-thirds mark."

They eventually came to the central plaza with its quasi-pyramidal Kilia Station Principal Management Office at the center and turned left toward several three-story office buildings. One of them bore a small sign that read Commonwealth Consulate by the door.

"Nice. Right at the heart of the action," Guthren commented. "You've got 'em where you can see 'em."

"And they have us where they can see as well."

Forenza ushered the landing party into the consulate lobby and turned to Dunmoore.

"Your escort can stay here while you, the Chief, and I discuss our meeting with Tarrant in my office."

The young petty officer in charge of the bosun's mates briefly came to attention.

"Aye, aye, sir."

Once in Forenza's second-floor office, a room with wall-sized displays instead of windows, they settled into comfortable chairs around a low coffee table. Forenza sat back and crossed his legs, his left ankle resting on his right knee.

"As you might know, Tarrant doesn't keep a place of business as such. Since he runs the station more or less like an autocratic ruler, he pretty much considers the entirety of Kilia his domain."

"The last time we were here, Tarrant buttonholed us at an open-air café just around the corner."

Forenza gave her a knowing nod.

"One of his favorites. This time, we will join him in a private dining room at the back of the restaurant across the plaza. He's intensely curious about your arrival and clearly wishes discussions held behind closed doors. Now, as to which tack you should take, here's what I suggest. I doubt Tarrant knew about the hijacking in advance, let alone supported it after the fact, even in the slightest way possible. Taking *Athena* presents the same level of risk as the slave trade for anyone involved. And though normally, punitive action inside the Zone can't come from either Commonwealth or Shrehari naval units because of the Treaty, he knows both navies operate Q ships in the anti-piracy role. And they don't pull their punches."

"Then, I show up on his doorstep with five warships, the largest fighting formation in the Zone since the war. That must have been quite a wake-up call, whether or not he was in on it."

Forenza let a faint smile of amusement play across his lips.

"From what my sources tell me, it was a shock. I let slip that the Confederacy of the Howling Stars might be responsible for *Athena*'s hijacking, and apparently, that threw him for a loop as well, since he's been hosting them for the last few years. Therefore, I suggest you approach the matter of cooperation as if Tarrant and, through him, Kilia, are aggrieved parties since the hijacking imperils Kilia's operations and possibly even its freedom. I don't know how your last discussion with him went, but I'm going to assume he held the upper hand. So this time, you must lean on him rather than the other way around."

Dunmoore chuckled. "That won't be a problem. Back then, I was operating undercover and couldn't let my ship's true identity come out. Now, my superiors expect me to use my formation's obvious strength and firepower as a simple message from the Commonwealth government — don't mess with us."

"Good." Forenza's communicator chimed. He retrieved it and glanced at the screen. "Tarrant is playing his little games again. He's advanced our meeting time to five minutes from now. Clearly, he knew when you arrived and where you are at the moment. It's his way of exercising power as Kilia's supreme ruler. Would you like a cup of coffee before we head over and arrive fashionably late?"

"Certainly."

"And you, Chief?"

"Sure."

Forenza stood and walked over to a sideboard where an insulated jug and three small cups on a tray waited. He carefully poured, then brought the tray over and placed it on the table.

"Please help yourselves."

They chatted about inconsequential things while enjoying the rich, thick brew, catching up on the unclassified portions of their lives since they last parted company. Once Dunmoore put down her empty cup — she was the last to finish — Forenza glanced at the time.

"Fifteen minutes should do it." He stood. "Shall we?"

Dunmoore felt vaguely ridiculous as they crossed the plaza in precise formation — the petty officer and a bosun's mate in the lead. Then she, flanked by Guthren and Forenza, and finally the other two bosun's mates. But she knew there were dozens of eyes on them, watching and evaluating. They couldn't help but notice the grim determination on their faces and the equally grim blasters on their hips.

The mirror-like restaurant door slid aside silently at their approach even though the window display indicated it was closed. They entered a vast space with chairs, tables, and decorations but with no living beings other than two obvious human bodyguards by a door at the far end. Stocky, wearing tight clothes that outlined bulging muscles, both sported shaved heads and goatees and wore blasters in cutaway holsters at the hip.

As soon as Dunmoore and her escort entered, one of the men held up his hand.

"Mister Tarrant will only see Consul Forenza and Captain Dunmoore. Everyone else, out. And no guns either."

Dunmoore stared at him in silence for several heartbeats.

"Does that mean Enoc Tarrant is alone in the backroom?"

"That's none of your business. You want to see Mister Tarrant, you play the game by his rules."

"Petty Officer Ruad."

"Sir."

"Scan the room and tell me how many life signs you detect."

"Yes, sir." Ruad pulled out his sensor.

"You can't use that in here." The goon took one step forward and reached out to snatch the sensor from Ruad's hand.

Dunmoore pulled out her blaster and pointed it at the man's head.

"One more twitch, and Tarrant will be looking for a replacement. Now, who's with him in there?"

After a moment, the other man said, "His counselor, Mister Hagen, and two guards."

"That wasn't so difficult. I'll be taking Consul Forenza, Chief Petty Officer Guthren, and two of *my* guards in with me, and we will keep our weapons. Now step aside before I order you thrown out."

"No," the first goon replied. "We have our orders."

"And I've just countermanded them." Dunmoore's tone was icy enough to make hell freeze over.

She holstered her weapon and walked past him without another glance, Guthren, Forenza, and two of the bosun's mates on her heels. The other man simply shrugged, as if he figured Tarrant wasn't paying him enough to fight off the Navy at odds of three to one and stepped aside.

The private dining room door opened, and Dunmoore walked through without breaking stride. Inside, she found what she expected — Tarrant and his consigliere seated at a round table facing the entrance, with the guards standing a few paces behind them. They'd been watching the scene from the main room on a wall display, which now showed the two goons staring at her back.

"I can't say your hospitality has improved since my last visit, Mister Tarrant. A shame because the facilities are better than I remember."

— Sixteen —

Dunmoore took the chair in front of him while Guthren and Forenza sat on either side of her. The bosun's mates assumed a parade rest position across from Tarrant's guards and stared at them with hard eyes.

The man himself — bald, with a solid build, swarthy complexion, and craggy face — seemed unchanged except for a few more lines around eyes and mouth. He studied her intently for several seconds.

"Considering the quality of guests who show up unbidden." He gestured at the display. "If I didn't know better, I'd think you were trying to provoke my men into doing something rash that would justify military action against Kilia."

"I was merely teaching them that hired thugs should be more polite toward senior Navy officers whose command could make Kilia vanish in a cloud of rubble with one broadside."

"At gunpoint? Hardly diplomatic, especially with the Commonwealth consul present."

"It's a language all sentient beings understand, even if they're blessed with room temperature IQs."

"Do we know each other, Captain?" His eyes briefly rested on Guthren. "You and your chief seem awfully familiar, and I'm rather good at remembering faces. Besides, you said you'd been here before. Surely it wasn't you in command of that Navy task force with the same name as yours which threatened Kilia back during the war."

Dunmoore gave him an amused smile. "That would be Captain Ezekiel Larkin, a good friend of mine. But, of course, that isn't his real name. He wasn't in command, and it certainly wasn't a real task force, but I was aboard the battlecruiser *Iolanthe*, orchestrating everything. And the reason Zeke played acting commodore was simple. A few weeks earlier, you and I met in person at a little coffee shop around the corner from here. Chief Guthren was with me at the time."

Tarrant snapped his fingers and pointed at Dunmoore.

"You were masquerading as the captain of that huge armed freighter. What was your assumed name again?" He frowned in concentration. "O'Donnell, right? Shannon O'Donnell of the privateer *Persephone*. I remember you because of those gloves you wore when everyone else in your party was barehanded. What happened to them?"

"The medicos repaired my hands after the war. I don't know whether I should be impressed or flattered that you recall such details. Yes, you basically evicted us from Kilia, but by doing so, you gave me the opening I needed."

Tarrant tilted his head slightly to one side as he studied her with narrowed eyes.

"Are you telling me the battlecruiser *Iolanthe* and your *Persephone* are the same ship?"

"Of course not. Now, if we're done skipping down memory lane, can we discuss the reason why my government sent a Navy task force into the Protectorate Zone despite the provisions in the Treaty of Ulufan making it out-of-bounds for military units?"

He let out a soft grunt.

"If you're still a captain more than a decade later, I guess peace hasn't been your thing."

She gave him a wintry smile.

"The Navy put me in stasis after the armistice and decants me whenever they need someone who's ruthless and doesn't give a damn about annoying the rich, powerful, and depraved. So if you plan on lodging a complaint with your bigshot friends on Earth concerning my behavior, don't bother. I'm what you organized crime aficionados call untouchable."

"Noted, not that I'd bother them with tales of a superannuated captain whose ego seems out of control. Now tell me why we're talking."

"Because for once, our interests intersect, as you'll understand in a moment. Pirates hijacked a luxury liner by the name *Athena* at Marengo's heliopause a short time ago. The Commonwealth government chartered *Athena* for a goodwill mission around the Rim Sector. She carries a hundred and twenty VIPs who belong to some of the most connected and wealthy families in the Commonwealth. This, as you no doubt realize, is causing the most severe political crisis on Earth since the war."

Tarrant gave her a dismissive shrug. "So? In what way does that concern me?"

"First, we suspect the hijackers took *Athena* into the Zone so they could escape pursuit by the Navy. It's not much of a jump from Marengo, and they probably didn't think we'd disregard the Treaty of Ulufan for this one. Second, the pirates who seized her — three ships — bear an uncanny resemblance to the Arkanna-built sloop currently docked at Kilia. Since the modifications they did to the standard Commonwealth design are rather distinctive and unique, we're assuming the Confederacy of the Howling Stars is responsible. Oh, they did it on behalf of a person or persons unknown, not on their own account, but that's someone else's problem. My job is finding *Athena* and bringing those aboard back home."

"I'm still not seeing why I should care."

A predatory smile crossed Dunmoore's lips.

"How many of your sketchy suppliers and shippers will approach Kilia if there's a Commonwealth Navy ship carrying out inspections just beyond the range of your weapons? How long will the Confederacy dare stay in these parts if we simply board the ship docked here and take her as a prize? So long as I haven't retrieved *Athena*, the Protectorate Zone is my hunting ground, and provided I avoid annoying the Shrehari, I can pretty much run rampant.

"The relevant laws, unchanged since before the war, allow me to stop and board any vessel I suspect of engaging in activities the Commonwealth considers illegal, such as smuggling, drug running, slavery, or piracy, beyond our sphere and that of the Shrehari Empire. Since I have the Navy's most modern cruiser, three of its most powerful frigates and a corvette at my disposal, I can turn Kilia into an unprofitable wasteland without firing so much as a single shot at you. And along the way, I can clean up a lot of the problematic shipping in these parts while the Shrehari secretly applaud me."

Dunmoore watched as Tarrant's face tightened with anger while she spoke. He knew an unfettered Commonwealth Navy task force under a commander with orders to retrieve a hijacked ship at all costs was more dangerous for Kilia than anything short of its sun going nova.

A sardonic smile lit up her face. "Do you care now, Mister Tarrant?"

"What is it you want from me?" He asked in a low growl.

"The moment I find *Athena* and the people aboard, my task force will leave the Zone, and life can return to normal for you. Help me track them. You can tap a network of informants, connections, and whatnot in these parts. Find me the information I need. Otherwise, I'm dependent on Consul Forenza's diplomatic channels and whatever I can extract from the ship you're hosting — what was its name again? *Vuko*? And its crew after I take it as a prize."

Tarrant reared up, eyes blazing. "You wouldn't dare! This is a free port, neutral in every respect. No one takes prizes here."

A loud snap echoed across the room as Dunmoore struck the table with her open palm. She leaned forward.

"I can do whatever the hell I want in furtherance of my orders, and you cannot stop me. As far as my government is concerned, the importance of bringing those VIPs home safe and sound outweighs any consideration for Kilia's welfare, let alone your precious neutrality, no matter how many friends you have on Earth." She let her words sink in, then continued in a softer tone.

"As I said, your cooperation will ensure my speedy departure. What will it be?"

Tarrant's seemed to chew on his thoughts as he held her eyes.

"Who in *Athena* is so important your government would risk another war?"

"At the head of the list? Sara Lauzier, Secretary General Charles Lauzier's eldest daughter and heir, destined for the highest office in human space."

Tarrant visibly blanched when he parsed her statement.

"You're bluffing again."

Forenza shook his head.

"She's not, Enoc, and Sara Lauzier is just the most notable among a contingent of notables. The Colonial Office itself warned me before Captain Dunmoore arrived."

"If I can't recover Sara Lauzier because you refuse to cooperate, what do you think will happen, Mister Tarrant? Earning the SecGen's rancor is hardly a good business move. But, on the other hand, if your help leads to a rescue, I think you'll find Kilia Station enjoying a special status, at least for a while, because we know that a politician's gratitude sours over time. But his ire? That has an immediate effect on the welfare of its target."

When Tarrant didn't immediately reply, Dunmoore's face hardened.

"This is a one-time offer, Mister Tarrant. Make up your mind and do so now or suffer the consequences, one of which will be placing Kilia under military occupation with my Marines calling the shots. Then, who knows? Maybe Earth will renegotiate the Treaty of Ulufan and annex Kilia. I'm sure the Shrehari wouldn't mind if we give them an acceptable quid pro quo."

Neither Forenza nor Guthren so much as blinked, even though both knew Task Force Luckner's ships, like most in the Fleet, no longer carried Marines except on special missions.

Tarrant raised both hands in a gesture of surrender.

"Okay. I'll give you my full cooperation, Captain. I will send queries through my network when we're done here, and I'll help you seize *Vuko*. He's sketchy, sure, but relatively harmless. Nonetheless, the money I'm making by letting him shift his wares on my station is nothing compared to the damage you can do."

"I'm glad you see things clearly." She glanced at Guthren. "What are your thoughts about boarding that ship, Chief?"

"We let Mister Tarrant's security folks open for us on an excuse involving station business, then I can take an armored boarding party through. The crew is what? Forty or so, none of them equipped to resist the Navy, right?" Guthren turned his gaze on Tarrant.

"Forty-two, actually, but don't underestimate them. They're ex-Fleet, not career outlaws who've never experienced a warship's discipline."

"It won't do them much good against modern combat armor, sir. I'm sure even the strongest among them will surrender when he's staring into the barrel of a scattergun held by someone wearing a tin suit precisely because they've been on the other side of a boarding party operation."

Dunmoore cocked an eyebrow at Tarrant.

"What do you say? How about Chief Guthren and your head of security sit down for a planning session while you speak with your network? I'd like this show up and running without delay."

"Do I have a choice?"

Both Dunmoore and Forenza shook their heads.

"I'm afraid not," the latter said. "This is a case of she who has the firepower makes the rules."

— Seventeen —

Dunmoore, along with Forenza, Tarrant, and Hagen, watched the live video feed from the Confederacy ship's docking arm in the latter's office. She would rather see the view from Chief Guthren's helmet pickup, but since she planned on interrogating the target's captain herself, traveling to and from *Salamanca* several times seemed unappealing. So instead, she'd spent time in the consulate, planning with her staff via a secure channel.

At least Tarrant had accepted his role in the operation and offered her every courtesy, though Dunmoore suspected it was at least in part due to her counting coup on him with the fake Task Force Luckner during the war. Tarrant was the sort who respected strength and cunning.

Guthren, always thinking ahead, had put together a crack platoon of bosun's mates trained in boarding party techniques from *Salamanca*'s crew before he and Dunmoore landed to meet with Tarrant and called them down aboard another of the cruiser's shuttles.

As planned, Tarrant's security personnel, along with his chief harbormaster, took the lead. At the same time, Dunmoore's people hid in the emergency stairwell and the cargo elevator, waiting for an open airlock. Meanwhile, the harbormaster called *Vuko*'s bridge via the docking module's built-in communicator.

"What is it?" A querulous voice demanded.

"I need to speak with your captain in person about a delicate matter that concerns his ship."

"Yeah? Well, he's busy right now, so come back later, okay?"

"I'm afraid it can't wait. If I don't see him now, we will rescind your ship's docking permit, which means you'll have an hour to leave Kilia."

"You can't do that."

"I can, and I will. Your captain knows the rules. When a Kilia Station official issues a demand, it's either obeyed, or we expel the offending parties and ban them for a given period."

Back in Hagen's office, Tarrant turned to Dunmoore.

"You know it'll cost me a lot of goodwill with the Confederacy of the Howling Stars, its financial backers, and anyone else who doesn't like your Navy."

"Still less expensive than my effectively cutting you off with a blockade."

Hagen let out a snort.

"She's right, Enoc. No one who saw her ships can blame you. Besides, I'll put out a statement saying you were coerced — after Captain Dunmoore and her squadron leaves. That will go a long way in regaining any lost goodwill."

Tarrant gave his consigliere an exasperated look. "It'll still cost more than it should."

"Ah, here we go."

Dunmoore nodded at the display, where the ship's main airlock door was slowly retracting into the hull before sliding to one side.

When the opening was clear, the harbormaster stepped inside, followed by his two security guards. One of the crew, a human, met them at the airlock's inside door, then they vanished from sight.

Chief Guthren and his fourteen spacers burst out of the stairwell and the cargo elevator at an unheard signal and ran across the docking module before disappearing inside *Vuko*. Several tense minutes passed, then Dunmoore's communicator chimed. She retrieved it from her pocket and glanced at the display.

"That was Chief Guthren's signal they've taken the ship and secured its crew."

Two boarding party members reappeared shortly afterward, escorting a manacled human male between them — the sloop's captain — trailed by one of the station's security guards.

Tarrant nodded. "He's your man, Captain. We might as well head for the cells now. They'll be there by the time we arrive."

After picking up both Dunmoore and Tarrant's escorts in the lobby of the central administration building, they took a flight of stairs headed downward and crossed a rabbit warren of wide, well-lit corridors carved out of the asteroid with laser drills. The general atmosphere reminded her of Aquilonia Station, and she felt a faint pang of sadness at the memory of those heady days.

Guthren was waiting for them in the cellblock, his helmet visor raised and weapon holstered.

"Sir." He briefly came to attention. "The crew — all of them human — surrendered without a fight. We locked them in an empty cargo compartment guarded by the boarding party, who are also downloading a copy of the ship's computer core. The captain is in one of the interrogation rooms, ready for you. Consul Forenza, Mister Tarrant, and Mister Hagen can watch from the security chief's office if they like. Otherwise, it'll be uncomfortably crowded in there. Besides, I don't think they should be seen in our company at this point."

"We'll be fine watching from behind the scenes, Mister Guthren," Forenza said. "Take your captain to the interrogation room so we can get this done."

Guthren led her past a security station and through armored doors, then along another corridor where one door stood open. They didn't encounter any station security personnel along the way, making Dunmoore suspect Tarrant ordered them somewhere they couldn't see Navy personnel using their facilities.

"Right in that room, Skipper."

Dunmoore stepped in and found the ship's captain sitting at a table, manacled hands fastened to a metal staple at its center. The two spacers assigned as guards stood behind him, helmet visors shut, and scatterguns slung in the ready position.

She sat and studied her prisoner for over a minute, curious about the sort of former Fleet member who'd join a criminal organization to commit illegal acts against his own. Short, graying hair and an equally short white beard framed a square, seamed, craggy face familiar among lifelong spacers. Cold, dark eyes framing an aquiline nose beneath thick black brows stared back at her.

He wore an unadorned, hip-length black leather tunic over black trousers with nothing to indicate his rank, ship, or affiliation. In Dunmoore's estimation, he could be anywhere between forty and sixty, old enough to have seen the worst of the war. And the way he met her eyes, his posture, the set of his jaw, it seemed strangely familiar. Not that she'd met this individual before, but he represented a type she knew well.

"My name is Siobhan Dunmoore, and I command the Commonwealth Navy task force currently in Kilia orbit."

"I know who you are," he replied in a rasping voice, one perhaps damaged by toxic fumes in the heat of battle. "And what you represent."

Dunmoore tilted her head to one side and narrowed her eyes.

"Did we serve together during the war perchance?"

"No, thank the Almighty. A butcher like you?" He made a sound in his throat akin to spitting but without doing so.

"Who are you?"

"I'm under no obligation to reply, so you might as well go frack yourself."

"Here's the deal. Cooperate with me, and I'll not only release you but also your ship and let you transfer the cargo it carries when your contact shows up. Refuse, and you're coming back to the Commonwealth with me, where you'll stand trial on charges of piracy, drug smuggling, and slavery. Your ship will become my prize, and your cargo will be spaced."

He sneered at Dunmoore.

"Bullshit. You have no jurisdiction in the Zone."

"The weight of my guns says otherwise, as the people who run Kilia Station realized. I can do whatever I want in the Zone precisely because Commonwealth law doesn't apply. If I decide on holding drumhead trials for piracy, I'll do so, and once I pronounce a verdict of guilty, I'll space you and your crew without shedding a tear."

"Might makes right?" He scoffed. "You're the Dunmoore I remember."

"So, we did cross paths."

"In a way." He stared at her for a few seconds. "My name is Alan Drex. You murdered my brother in *Stingray*, a thoroughly damned ship if there ever was one."

Dunmoore felt a jolt of electricity course through her body.

"Drex? Good lord, man. He tried to murder me and fell afoul of my security detail. Your brother compromised himself and his honor, not that you'll ever believe a word of the true story."

"Garbage. Your reputation precedes you, Dunmoore. You're a cold-blooded killer. Well, go on, murder another Drex already and be done with it."

She rolled her eyes theatrically.

"I'll say this for the Drex family, you're not particularly smart, are you? It must be genetic. Your brother thought he could murder his captain aboard her own ship while on a battle run inside enemy space and talk his way out of it. As plans go, they aren't much dumber than that. How he ever earned a commission from the ranks, I cannot fathom. But you can escape from this with your life, your ship, and its cargo, which by right I should destroy immediately. Your call." When he simply glared at her in silence, Dunmoore glanced over her shoulder. "Please prepare the interrogation kit, Chief. Mister Drex is obviously offering us his ship as a prize."

"Why am I not surprised you'd do that to a veteran of the Shrehari War, Dunmoore?"

"Oh, so you're a veteran now?" She gave him a skeptical look. "Funny, but from what I've seen, those who served honorably didn't join a criminal organization after hanging up their uniforms. So what were you up to in those days? A little piracy? Some smuggling? And now you're carrying a fake service certificate to con the credulous and help you out of a tight spot with the Navy, right?"

"How dare you?" He gave her a venomous glare. "I finished at the rank of lieutenant commander and captain of a naval transport. Like the rest of my people, I served the Commonwealth honorably both before and during the war. And it tossed me aside after the armistice, like so many veterans who gave up the best years of their lives for humanity's survival."

"I didn't know the Navy released lifers during the reduction in force. It should only have been those who joined for the duration and were surplus to requirements."

A sneer appeared on Drex's face.

"The Fleet didn't RIF me. Oh, no. What it did was worse. It told me I could stay if I reverted to my pre-war rank of chief petty officer, though they'd sweeten it with a promotion to First Class. Sure. Give a man his own ship, watch him serve with honor, then take it away from him. I told them to stuff it where the sun doesn't shine and opted for a pension instead. Then I found myself a ship and the command I'd earned."

"Meaning your commission wasn't permanent. It happened to a lot of people who held brevet rank in the expanded Fleet. Heck, I finished the war as a commodore and found myself a captain again a few weeks after the armistice. As you can see, ten years later and I still don't have my star back. I probably never will, which means I'm on borrowed time. But I didn't join a criminal organization out of spite and don't intend on doing so once I hang up my uniform for the last time."

The sneer grew.

"You're not a commodore, but they didn't kick you all the way down to your pre-war rank. So cry me a river, *Captain* Dunmoore. You'd be surprised how many like me from both the Navy and the Marines put in our papers when we realized what the peacetime Fleet would do with us and joined to form the Confederacy of the Howling Stars. We're mercenaries, by the way, not criminals. We do jobs for hire and don't break the law inside the Commonwealth sphere. Out here? There is no law, which means we can neither be law-abiding nor outlaws."

"Your buddies broke at least half a dozen laws when they hijacked the liner *Athena* at Marengo's heliopause, so don't give a song and dance about not being criminals."

A bark of laugher escaped Drex's throat. "So that's what this is about."

"Yes, and you're going to help me find *Athena*."

— Eighteen —

"I will do no such thing. Go jump into a black hole, you murderous bitch."

Guthren took one step forward.

"You'll show the captain respect, my boy, or I will teach you the sort of lesson you should have learned before the Fleet, in its lack of wisdom, made you a chief petty officer. Of course, since this is a place with no laws, I can smack you around as much as I want."

Dunmoore kept her eyes on Drex, acting as if she didn't hear her coxswain's words.

"Here's the deal. Help me find *Athena*, and you keep your ship, your cargo, and your crew. Refuse, she becomes my prize and you and your people will be my prisoners. Once back in the Commonwealth, I hand you over to Fleet Security, who'll make sure you face a military court for piracy. Then, if the court is merciful, it's life on Parth. If the court is feeling grumpy, it's a firing squad. I'll only make this offer once. Take it or leave it. I don't have time for prevaricators."

Drex didn't react in any noticeable fashion, but then his brother had been a closed book as well. He merely stared at her for a bit before speaking.

"If I betray the Confederacy, I'm a dead man. Not that I could help you, anyway. We work like any big commercial organization — along separate business lines. One division does private military corporation work, another takes care of shipping contracts in the Zone, another — well, you get the idea. I'm in shipping. If the Confederacy took your liner, then the people involved would be part of the PMC division, meaning I don't know where they're hiding."

"What if I told you the passengers are from the highest elite of the Commonwealth political, commercial, and financial worlds and that your colleagues had inside help to take *Athena*, despite the extensive security measures in place?"

Drex cocked an eyebrow.

"Then I'd say well done, chaps. Our leadership must be charging an astronomical fee for the job."

"Whoever commissioned it probably had more than mere ransoms in mind. The nature of the hostages, the way it was done, smacks of politics by other means, and if I'm right, it will come back to haunt your Confederacy of the Howling Stars."

"I'm sure the chief executive and the head of the PMC division took that possibility into consideration. They're veterans of the Fleet, just like my crew and me. They survived the war by learning to evaluate risks." Drex shrugged. "That being said, I still can't help you because I don't know where they went."

"Well, maybe your navigation log will point us at a few likely places."

Drex reared up as far as he could with his hands manacled to the table.

"What do you mean?"

"My boarding party is draining your computer core as we speak. Whatever encryption you may have on your logs won't last long once we run it through our system."

His face lost most of its color. "You can't—"

"I can do whatever I want. You said it yourself. In the Zone, there are no laws. So to whom will you or your employer address their complaint? Now, suppose your ship belonged to Black Nova or any other legitimate corporation, and we were inside the Commonwealth sphere. In that case, I'd be in trouble for violating the computer core without a warrant. But since we're not and moreover, your cargo is the sort that merits a life sentence on Parth, no one will mind."

"I'm a dead man," he rasped. "You killed my brother, and now you've sentenced me to death. What has my family done to earn this?"

"The Confederacy isn't tolerant of errors, I take it? Even though there was no way you could expect the Navy in a port it shouldn't be visiting?"

Drex shook his head. "Even if they let me live, I'll never command another ship thanks to you."

Dunmoore suddenly felt sorry for him. She and Drex shared a particular disappointment with how the Navy treated them after serving honorably during the war.

"In that case, become my informant, and I'll release you under an assumed identity once we're back in the Commonwealth. After that, you're free to pursue a new career."

He seemed to chew on her offer for almost a minute. "What about my ship and crew?"

"The ship is my prize. I'll use her as I see fit, and if she survives this mission, the Navy will sell her. That'll put a bit of money in the pocket of everyone aboard Task Force Luckner's ships." Dunmoore smiled as she brazenly lied. "And the crew? They can spend this cruise in my brig and join you in taking on a new name and a new life inside the Commonwealth, or they can land on Kilia and find their fortunes here. Or I can release you, your crew, and your ship when I leave this system and let you figure out the next steps. It's all the same to me. My sole aim is to retrieve *Athena* and her passengers. Anything else is a distraction, and none of us need the prize money that badly. I suppose you could go full renegade and spend your life running from the Navy, the Shrehari, your lot, and whoever else might want the bounty on your head."

"If my brother was truly trying to kill you, I can't say I blame him. How the hell you became a captain, let alone wore a commodore's star during the war, is beyond me. You're nothing more than a commissioned thug."

"Careful," Guthren said in a tone that brooked no reply.

"Or what? I bet you were a wet-behind-the-ears junior petty officer when the Shrehari invaded."

Dunmoore raised her hand to cut off any further conversation between Guthren, whom she now knew had taken a visceral dislike to Drex, and the latter.

"What will it be? Cooperation and a new life, or one spent evading your employers? I wish I could apologize for putting you in this position, but you made a choice long ago, one which placed you across my path here, today. Karma? Bad luck? The Erinyes getting a hate-on for you?" She shrugged dismissively. "It doesn't change the situation or the choices you face."

"I'll take my chances with the Confederacy's leadership if you don't mind."

"It's your funeral." Dunmoore looked over her shoulder at Guthren. "Space anything in their cargo that's illegal in the Commonwealth, then release the crew. Mister Drex can join them once that's done."

"Aye, aye, sir."

Dunmoore climbed to her feet.

"I won't say it was a pleasure. Seeing an honorable person, serving, or retired, go wrong and figuratively spit on their oath always somehow depresses me."

She turned and left the interrogation room without a backward glance, followed by Guthren and the two spacers, leaving Drex alone to contemplate his future.

They met Forenza, Hagen, and Tarrant in the cellblock's reception room.

"If ever you need a job," the latter said, "come and see me. I can always use another enforcer on my business negotiation team. Does this outcome mean you'll be departing soon?"

She made a noncommittal gesture.

"Probably. I'm still counting on your intelligence network's eyes and ears, though, Mister Tarrant. If Drex was telling the truth, whatever we find in his navigation logs will probably not lead us to our target."

Tarrant raised his hands in surrender.

"I know, I know. If you become unhappy, you'll blockade Kilia."

Dunmoore winked at him.

"Glad we understand each other. My people and I will return to our ship now. You can let Drex go in half an hour, and should he wish to leave the station immediately, he may do so with my blessing."

Tarrant gave her a smirk. "How magnanimous of you."

"Isn't it just?" She raised her hand in a vague salute. "The Commonwealth Navy appreciates your cooperation. Enjoy the rest of your day."

Guthren led them directly to their docking arm, where her shuttle waited, while Forenza returned to the consulate after telling Dunmoore he'd call her later. They settled in, let the airlock cycle through, then the pilot requested that the station release them, which happened with remarkable alacrity.

"While you were twisting Drex's arm," Guthren said once traffic control pushed them away, and the shuttle was moving under its own power, "I received a report from the boarding party over the task force net. First, they successfully copied the computer core. It'll be in the hands of *Salamanca*'s experts for decryption shortly after their shuttle lands, which should be imminent. Then, they planted the subspace tracking devices — three of them — inside Drex's ship, where his crew won't think to look. Each is on a different frequency, so even if they pick up the carrier wave of one, they'll not hear the others. Finally, *Vuko*'s cargo holds contained crates filled with what sensors identified as narcotics, and they were tossed overboard. The rest were more difficult to identify, so in the interests of time, the boarding party let them be."

"Fair enough. We can always make sure a Navy ship intercepts the trader who'll take on *Vuko*'s merchandise. Which means our work here is done."

"And now we wait for someone else to act." He gave her an amused sideways glance. "Something you really enjoy, as I recall, Skipper."

Dunmoore scoffed softly. "Oh, do I ever."

Shortly after boarding *Salamanca*, she called her captains and staff together — those aboard the cruiser in person, the rest virtually — and gave them a rundown of events on Kilia Station. As Dunmoore described how she'd pressured Tarrant and Drex into cooperating, she sensed disapproval from at least two of her captains, Kardas and Bryce.

The former confirmed Dunmoore's impression when she asked, "Wasn't that risky, sir? Granted, we're not in the Commonwealth, but the methods you used could be construed as blackmail, and if either complains to our government, especially Tarrant, there might be repercussions."

"For me, perhaps. But I doubt it. Yes, Tarrant will complain to his friends, and I don't doubt they're powerful or have connections among the powerful. Yet considering our mission, the highest levels of government won't care — provided I bring *Athena* and her passengers back home safe and sound. But then, it's no secret they chose me for this mission in part because I have nothing left to lose."

"With due respect, sir, that isn't the situation for the rest of us. Don't misunderstand me. My fellow captains and I will serve you to the best of our abilities. However, I'd be more comfortable if your methods didn't risk rebounding on us. The Commonwealth has been at peace for almost a decade."

"And you're saying my methods could risk starting another war?" Dunmoore cocked an eyebrow at the younger woman, surprised not only by her words but by her temerity at uttering them publicly. "With whom? The Shrehari? Not a chance."

"That isn't what I meant, sir." Suddenly it seemed to dawn on Kardas she'd overstepped her bounds. "I'm simply not comfortable with the use of certain pressure tactics in peacetime."

Dunmoore nodded.

"Understood, Davina. Yet time, ironically, is our biggest constraint. We can't afford the niceties of a Fleet at peace in resolving what is in effect an act of aggression against the Commonwealth. Again, any responsibility for overstepping the bounds of what our superiors might consider acceptable rests with me and solely with me. That's why the only Commonwealth representatives present when I coerced Tarrant and Drex were Consul Forenza, a senior Colonial Office intelligence operative entirely familiar with tactics of this nature, and Chief Petty Officer Guthren, who's been at my side on and off for almost two decades. Tarrant might complain, but only about me." A faintly mocking smile briefly lit up her face. "Considering my reputation, no one will be surprised, nor will anyone blame you if I've gone rogue in some people's estimation."

She let Kardas squirm for a few seconds under her gaze, then said, "Let's discuss next steps now that we can call on three separate intelligence channels where before arriving here, we had none."

— Nineteen —

"Whenever you drop out of hyperspace, send a query on the Colonial Office's encrypted subspace frequency, and if I have news, I'll reply within, say, six hours. Does that work for you?" Forenza asked over the secure link between *Salamanca* and the consulate.

"Absolutely. And if you could do me a favor, let the Fleet know about the ship which just left with Drex's cargo. I'm sure it merits a full-fledged inspection under the various shipping laws, even if we cleared *Vuko*'s cargo holds of any egregiously illegal stuff."

"I was going to do that anyway, Captain. Just out of curiosity, how will you pursue *Vuko*?"

"One hyperspace jump at a time. I can't allow Drex to see us tail him. And that means our first indication of his heading will be when he drops out of FTL at the heliopause — provided he doesn't find all three subspace beacons we hid in his ship beforehand."

"What are the chances of that?"

"Minimal, unless his communications array is listening to the right frequencies at the right time, which isn't likely. The beacons don't broadcast continuously. Instead, they send out microbursts at random intervals, and the frequencies aren't the sort civilian ships monitor. But he can get lucky. We'll see. At least by using your subspace array network, we'll triangulate his position between jumps a lot more accurately. Please thank the Colonial Office on my behalf." She gave Forenza a wry smile. "Your employers showed more foresight than mine."

"Don't be too harsh on them. The Treaty of Ulufan concentrated on the military aspects of keeping the Protectorate Zone neutral. It said nothing about civilian intelligence gathering and influence activities."

She let out a bark of laughter. "Mostly because the Shrehari couldn't fathom that anyone would let civilians do such things."

"Thankfully. Otherwise, my job would be much harder. Mind you, the odds are ten to one that the crew in that imperial science vessel are *Tai Zohl* and hold ranks equivalent to those in their armed services, so they're skirting the Treaty as well. It makes you wonder why we bothered with this nonsense in the first place."

A shrug. "So grifters on both sides had a chunk of space where they could run their illegal schemes without interference by one navy or the other."

"I think most of those grifters are on our side, sadly. The Shrehari culture isn't one to tolerate much official corruption, especially not under your old friend Brakal's iron-fisted rule." Forenza glanced away for a few seconds. "*Vuko* just advised traffic control it was departing in three hours."

"Finally, thank the Almighty." Dunmoore raised her eyes to the deckhead. "I've been hiding in my quarters for the last thirty hours or so, lest I annoy the crew with my caged she-wolf act.

Did I tell you my staff has a betting pool going on where *Vuko* is headed?"

"No."

"Based on what we extracted from her computer core — and by the way, Drex and his people were incredibly careful with what they recorded. No court would issue a warrant for their arrest based on its contents. I suspect another separate database hidden away where they keep stuff the authorities shouldn't see. As I was saying, from what we found in her logs, she routinely travels between two dozen star systems but visits five more frequently than the rest."

"Which I noted when your Lieutenant Commander Khanjan kindly sent me a copy. I don't have agents in all of them, but I've warned everyone via the subspace network."

"Good, because one or more of those five systems likely is home to a Howler base."

Forenza chuckled. "Is that what you're calling the Confederacy of the Howling Stars? Howlers?"

"Chief Guthren came up with it during my command conference yesterday. It's a bit of genius, if you ask me, deriving an insult from what some would construe as an ominous name."

"Agreed." The amused expression on his face vanished. "Do you honestly think he'll head straight for Howler HQ after what happened here? Wouldn't he be just as likely to go rogue?"

"The odds are better than any other course of action. I wouldn't be surprised if he believes warning his superiors of our presence and intentions will make up for something nobody expected — a Navy boarding party seizing *Vuko* as it was docked with Kilia

Station. And he might well be right. If the Howlers are ex-Fleet, then they'll know there was little Drex could do."

"Especially against a task force commander by the name Dunmoore, who once ran wild in the Zone aboard *Iolanthe*."

"That too. Besides, his crew might not agree with fleeing, and they can easily vote him off the bridge. In any case, if he's leaving in three hours, then we're leaving now."

Forenza cocked a questioning eyebrow. "Not after him?"

"No. I adapted an old wet navy tactic with the original Task Force Luckner during the war called the wolf pack. Individual submersible ships cruised vast areas looking for enemy convoys. When one of them found a target, it would radio back with coordinates, and the other ships in the pack would assemble to strike in unison. We figure he's heading deeper into the Zone, which means he'll drop out of FTL and cross this system's heliopause within a limited arc. I'm spreading my ships around that area of space so, with luck, at least one of them can detect *Vuko*'s subspace trackers and find her. Then, we can determine her heading, assemble, and follow after she goes FTL for an interstellar jump. It would be better if we knew what heading he took from Kilia's hyperlimit because that would narrow down the area of space where he'll drop out at the heliopause. But I don't have time to deploy a ship outward and can't leave one here."

"Let me see what I can do. I'm sure our Shrehari science vessel captain will track *Vuko* in the same way he'll observe your departure. Perhaps I can persuade him to tell me Drex's heading."

She gave him a skeptical look. "You think Retak will cooperate?"

A languid shrug. "He's intelligence, I'm intelligence, we're both here to make sure the Zone remains quiet. He knows your mission and understands the consequences should you fail. Contact me when you emerge at the heliopause, and I should have what you need. And now, I'll let you get Task Force Luckner underway."

"Please accept my gratitude, Consul."

"You saved my life, Captain. That is something I can never fully repay. If we don't see each other again soon, take care and good hunting."

"Thank you. Dunmoore, out." The moment Forenza's face faded from her day cabin's primary display, she touched her communicator. "Flag CIC, this is Dunmoore."

A few seconds later, "Flag CIC, Yun here, sir."

"Make to the task force, execute Plan Wolf Pack. We break out of orbit in fifteen minutes."

"Execute Plan Wolf Pack and break out of orbit in fifteen minutes, aye, sir."

"Dunmoore, out."

**

"Ah, there you are, my dear."

Vitus Amali dropped into a plush chair across from Sara Lauzier without waiting for an invitation. As usual, the latter was alone in the small salon, reading or sampling the ship's entertainment database. Lauzier gave sparingly of herself to

Athena's passengers, though they sought reassurance and leadership, and that mainly, as Amali now understood, because she despised most of them as inferior intellects. That he agreed with her amused him in more ways than one.

"I'm always here between mealtimes when I'm not in my suite nowadays."

"It was merely an expression and," he held up both hands in surrender, "I should remember you hate useless words even more than useless gestures. I'm here to share an observation with you since we can't make out a damn thing beyond our little passenger bubble."

She made an impatient go-ahead gesture.

"You may have noticed we left hyperspace almost six hours ago. Since course changes take no longer than cycling the drives — an hour or so — I would posit we arrived at our destination and are in orbit around a distant world. Which means something should happen any moment now."

"Such as?"

"Being forcibly removed from our pleasant surroundings and taken to a beastly stockade on an alien planet, perhaps?"

"Doubtful. It's easier to keep *Athena* provisioned and ready for the next move than take us in a squadron of shuttles, only to fly us up again. This isn't about turning the idle rich into slaves working alien mines, Vitus. They kidnap ordinary colonists for such jobs. Or use droids. Whoever hired the hijackers wants something from my father, your brother, and a few others with hands on the levers of power. They won't achieve their aims if we're misused as involuntary labor. Their only bargaining point is returning us home intact. Otherwise, our families will cut their losses and erase our names from the records."

Amali gave her a cynical smile. "Always the optimist, aren't you?"

"I'm a realist, just like you, except I don't hide it. In my experience, one gets further by being unrelentingly truthful, even though most would rather hear insincere platitudes because the truth scares people, Vitus."

He raised his glass in salute.

"Clearly seen and succinctly stated. And just so you know, the tier beneath the upper crust on this ship is getting overly restless."

"Then ply them with comforting lies."

**

Just as Rear Admiral Kowalski began wondering about Commodore Holt's daily update, her office display lit with a secure call from another part of Fleet HQ.

"Speak of the devil." She smiled at Holt when his face appeared.

"And here I am."

"What's new?"

"A few things. I just read a report from Consul Forenza, countersigned by Siobhan. She made progress of sorts."

Holt relayed Forenza's report verbatim, and when he finished, Kowalski let out a low whistle.

"Well done, Siobhan. She lost none of her ruthlessness over the years. Having both the Colonial Office's and Tarrant's intelligence networks at her disposal is a major coup, as is tracking a Confederacy of the Howling Stars sloop without its knowledge. This sort of aggressive thinking and forceful action is exactly why the Navy can't afford to lose her, Zeke. How many flag officers these days would have the gumption to coerce a man such as Tarrant, knowing full well he must have friends in high places to survive this long as boss of Kilia Station?"

"Not many, though I daresay if Siobhan were wearing the stars she deserved on her collar right now, she wouldn't act any differently. Mind you, we should find out how much pull Tarrant's friends have because Forenza says Tarrant sent a subspace message to a numbered address inside the Commonwealth." At seeing the surprise in Kowalski's eyes, Holt chuckled. "Yes, the Colonial Office has been reading Tarrant's mail for a while, but without gleaning much of use. He's too canny for that."

"And what did the message say?"

"Siobhan should be relieved of command for threatening him and the trade passing through Kilia. Apparently, his choice of words was rather salty."

"She has that effect on people." Kowalski gave him a knowing smile. "I guess his friends are either inside the government or can call on high-level connections."

"We'll find out soon enough. Our analysts are tracing the numbered address. As for relieving or recalling her, since our only means of communications while she's deep inside the Zone is via the Colonial Office network, and I'm the Fleet's interface with them, it won't happen."

"You would defy an order from Grand Admiral Sampaio himself?"

"Of course not. I'd simply be unable to communicate with Task Force Luckner until she accomplishes the mission." He winked at her. "After all, the Colonial Office surely cannot support a reliable subspace relay network in the same way as the Navy."

"I like the cut of your jib, Commodore."

"You and I both learned well from Siobhan, Admiral."

— Twenty —

The moment Dunmoore shook off the emergence nausea after an almost twelve-hour jump from Kilia to the heliopause, she glanced at Chief Cazano.

"Find the Colonial Office subspace carrier wave and transmit 'Luckner is listening' on the designated frequency and in the code Consul Forenza gave us, please."

"Find the carrier wave and transmit 'Lucker is listening,' aye, sir."

A few minutes passed, then Cazano said, "We received a reply on the frequency and in the expected encryption, sir, an alphanumerical sequence."

"Which I hope is *Vuko*'s heading just before she went FTL." Dunmoore called up the message and studied it. "We really owe the consul a big one. This looks like someone translated it from the Shrehari system to ours because it seems right. Jasmine, please enter the sequence into the navigation system and place the expected emergence area on the tactical display."

Lieutenant Commander Zakaria nodded without turning her head. "Coming right up, Skipper."

Moments later, the holographic display swirled as it reformed to show a red circle hanging in space, just before the shimmering curtain representing the heliopause. Five tiny blue icons — Task Force Luckner's ships — dotted a broad segment on the curtain's far side. One of them, marking *Jan Sobieski,* was almost on top of the circle, so close she would likely pick up *Vuko*'s emergence signature.

"Chief Cazano, please give me a link with the captains, then copy them on Consul Forenza's message."

"Aye, aye, sir."

When the five faced Dunmoore from her command chair's display, she said, "We received a message with *Vuko*'s heading when she jumped at Kilia's hyperlimit. You should have it now. *Jan Sobieski* is closest and will watch the probable emergence zone while the rest of us converge on her. *Vuko* will drop out of FTL in approximately three hours, and we can't afford any hint there might be Navy ships in the area. You will therefore move in two steps. The first will be a two-hour jump at maximum speed, after which we will go sublight and wait for *Jan Sobieski*'s confirmation *Vuko* has gone FTL on an interstellar heading. At that point, we will close the remaining distance to *Jan Sobieski*, regroup and follow."

"Question, sir?" Kardas raised her hand.

"Yes?"

"What if *Vuko* did a dogleg halfway to the heliopause?"

"Then we're out of luck. But the heading we received from the Shrehari works for a passage to the Galadiman system, which has an inhabitable planet with no native sentients but known rogue human settlements. It is also nicely placed relative to the

Commonwealth, the Shrehari Empire, and the Arkanna homeworld. A hub of sorts, you might say, one which *Vuko* regularly visits, according to her navigation log, and Drex didn't strike me as a devious sort. Disenchanted and disgruntled, sure, but right now, chances are he's in a hurry to warn his bosses about us." Dunmoore saw Pushkin grin at her from the operations director station. "Yes, Commander?"

"Sorry, sir, I experienced a surreal moment when you mentioned the Shrehari. Who'd think they would cooperate with the Commonwealth Navy one day?"

"If you'll recall, this isn't the first time."

A light went on in Pushkin's eyes as he remembered *Stingray's* expedition to Miranda and he nodded.

"Point taken, sir. And I'll stop now."

"Thank you, Gregor. Any more questions? No? Then, I will see you when the wolf pack assembles around *Jan Sobieski*. Dunmoore, out."

She climbed to her feet and stretched. "I'll be in my quarters."

"Aye, sir." Pushkin stood as well. "The CIC is mine."

Precisely sixty minutes after *Salamanca* dropped out of hyperspace — the peacetime Fleet-imposed interval to cycle the drives between jumps — a klaxon sounded throughout the ship, followed by the first officer's voice warning them to brace for transition.

Dunmoore, remembering her first wolf pack operation after taking command of Task Force Luckner, felt both elated at one more chance and wistful that this was it. One last chase. One last hurrah.

Then, transition nausea gripped her, and memories of the past receded.

**

"You called it, sir. *Vuko* was on a heading for the Galadiman system when she went FTL."

Did Dunmoore see a newfound glimmer of respect in Commander Kardas' eyes, or was it merely her imagination?

"Excellent news."

Even after the first two-hour jump, Task Force Luckner was still scattered over a vast area and would need another two hours before all ships joined *Jan Sobieski* at her position. Then, an hour to cycle the hyperdrives and the next part of the chase would begin, giving *Vuko* a five-hour head start. But Dunmoore planned on a single jump to Galadiman's heliopause, suspecting Drex would drop out of hyperspace halfway there and cycle his engines, as civilian ships often did because they couldn't manage the Fleet's high standards of maintenance. Of course, the Navy also preferred multiple jumps in peacetime, which reduced the strain on hulls and drives. Still, no one at Fleet HQ would bat an eyelid upon hearing Task Force Luckner covered the distance between Kilia and Galadiman in a single go.

To her mild surprise, none of the captains demurred once she'd reunited her task force and discussed the navigation plan, perhaps because they too were feeling the excitement of the hunt. At least Dunmoore hoped that was the case.

"I'll inform HQ of our intentions via the Colonial Office subspace network when we're done here. If there are no other questions, please sync your navigation plots with that of the flag CIC. Once the last ship finishes cycling her drives, we're off."

**

Commodore Ezekiel Holt poked his head through Rear Admiral Kathryn Kowalski's open office door.

"Got a moment?"

She pointed at the chair in front of her desk. "For you, always. What's up."

Holt sat and crossed his legs.

"News from a regular source and something disquieting from another. First, the expected stuff. Siobhan is tracking the Confederacy of the Howling Stars ship *Vuko* from Kilia to the Galadiman system. She believes the organization established one of its primary hubs there based on *Vuko*'s navigation log. She's operating on the premise this Drex character will try to warn his superiors about Task Force Luckner operating in the Protectorate Zone and her mission to retrieve *Athena*. Since the planet has several renegade human settlements — folks who reject the Commonwealth and its laws — Siobhan may be onto something."

"Let's hope so. And the other bit?"

A frown creased Holt's forehead.

"Our SSB friends are practicing the fine art of controlled leaks again, this time concerning *Athena*."

Kowalski made a face. "Ugh. Nothing good ever comes from their damned leaks. So what are they passing off as the truth now?"

"Their investigation of the hijacking shows Protectorate Zone mercenaries did it at the behest of radical elements espousing immediate sovereignty for Rim Sector colonies and greater freedoms for existing sovereign star systems." When Kowalski cursed under her breath, Holt smiled. "I wasn't aware you knew salty words of that sort, Kathryn."

"This smells of a setup."

"Of course, it does. Mind you, the radical elements exist. They call themselves by various names, depending on their home star system, but believing they acted in concert and hired mercs from the Zone? Yeah, based on what we know, that's a bit far-fetched. For one, even collectively, they're not rich enough to hire a single mercenary ship, let alone three, along with infiltrators. And knowing who was aboard the target would assuredly mean a healthy premium on top of standard rates." Holt shook his head. "I just can't see it. Big money in the Commonwealth is behind the centralists, not the star system sovereignists. Besides, the Rim Sector's wealthiest and most influential would rather attain greater freedom through legal means, so that legitimacy never becomes an issue."

"Then why would the Special Security Bureau be involved in the *Athena* matter?"

Holt grimaced. "Let me count the reasons. Number one — to discredit the sovereignists at the SecGen's orders."

"The SecGen would see his own daughter placed in jeopardy?"

"After two terms in power, Lauzier assuredly has the SSB under his thumb, and he's not the type who hesitates or concerns himself overmuch with ethics, morality, and the law. Power is his god; its pursuit is his life's work and to hell with his eternal soul.

Sara Lauzier is no different, and she's chummy with the SSB director general. If he's involved, then so is she. Reason number two — creating a new piracy threat on the frontier will scare colonists into demanding more protection from a benevolent Earth rather than more independence."

"One incident isn't enough."

"No, but what if this was the first in a series, orchestrated by the SecGen's tame security service?"

She nodded. "Plausible. Keep going."

"Reason number three — to discredit the Fleet. Never mind we can't pursue pirates into the Zone openly, and our Q ships are scattered. The fact we couldn't stop them in the first place will be bad enough publicity." A thoughtful expression crossed Holt's face. "Perhaps the political junket itself was set up to create a crisis along the Rim. Whoever's behind this never figured we'd dispatch a powerful task force so quickly, and to hell with the Treaty. They counted on us dithering and thereby tarnishing our reputation."

A dangerous smile, one which reminded Holt of Siobhan Dunmoore, tugged at Kowalski's lips.

"Unfortunately, they didn't think we might give command of that task force to the one officer who can effect a successful rescue." The smile vanished. "Why leak this now? Surely the SSB are aware we would scrutinize them mercilessly for involvement."

He gave her a shrug.

"They can still achieve their aims. In fact, if Siobhan fails, so much the better. Not only did we — the Fleet — violate the Treaty of Ulufan, but we also couldn't even accomplish the mission, and why? Because we put a superannuated captain, ripe for retirement, in command. Yes, we know she's the best for the job, but the optics, once this is made public, will be terrible. No one cares anymore about the raid on the Shrehari home system a decade ago. People will only see a war hero who couldn't hack it in the peacetime Navy. So I'd say the SSB is sitting pretty right now, and that gave them the impetus to leak word of a politically inspired plot."

"Which means Siobhan must succeed at all costs."

Holt nodded.

"The one advantage we have is our partnership with the Colonial Office and, through it, the ability to communicate with her. They distrust the SSB as much as we do and keep their subspace radio network in the Zone a secret. At this point, considering the Colonial Office probably isn't reading our encrypted mail, you and I and two of my officers tasked with supporting the mission are the only ones who know she's headed for Galadiman. And that's thanks to the Shrehari, by the way. They watched *Vuko* leave Kilia and gave Forenza a heading as she jumped at the hyperlimit. Forenza sent it to Siobhan, who reached the heliopause three hours before *Vuko*."

Kowalski let out a snort. "Who'd figure our former enemies are more trustworthy than parts of our own government."

"Siobhan?"

— Twenty-One —

"Madame Lauzier, your presence is requested." The man, one of the pirates, pressed into service as crew, bowed his head as he filled the door to the small lounge.

"By whom?" Lauzier, whose eyes were on the reader in her lap, didn't bother looking up at him.

"The Commodore, Madame, who wishes to speak with you since you're the most notable person among the passengers."

When Lauzier raised her head, she glanced at a puzzled Amali and gave him a languid shrug.

"Perhaps I'll finally find out what's been going on since these people so rudely interrupted our cruise." She stood and turned toward the strangely deferential pirate. "Let's go."

They met a couple of Lauzier's fellow prisoners along the way. They gave her blank stares as if the sight were beyond their comprehension. But then, Lauzier was increasingly isolated by choice, allowing only Amali and a few others in her presence, and she no longer seemed approachable. It was as if she'd divorced herself from the rest of the junket's participants since *Athena* dropped out of FTL for the last time.

The guest lobby, a broad, well-lit compartment with a wood-paneled reception counter, was where, in better times, live humans greeted new arrivals rather than AI holograms. Wall-sized displays, now dark, covered most of one bulkhead while the main door, which would open when the ship was docked, dominated another. As they entered, Lauzier noticed that the third door, leading to parts of the ship passengers only visited by invitation, stood open, with another armed pirate standing guard. Of the commodore, there was no trace.

Lauzier's guide led her past the guard, through the door, and toward *Athena*'s bridge, which she'd visited several times before the hijacking. But just short of it, the entrance to the captain's quarters stood open, and the pirate ushered her inside. The woman who'd been sitting behind Roy LeDain's desk stood as Lauzier entered.

Tall, thin, middle-aged, she struck Lauzier as the archetype of the icy blond, with pale, shoulder-length hair framing a narrow face that was primarily sharp angles. Intense blue eyes beneath brows that seemed almost white stared back at her with a calculating wariness. She wore a black merchant officer's tunic and trousers, the latter tucked inside knee-high, shiny boots. Her quasi-uniform's sole adornment was a small silver star on her tunic collar.

"You must be the Commodore." Lauzier took a seat without waiting for the mercenary's invitation, eschewing the usual niceties. "I presume you own a name to go with that splendid title and shiny star?"

After a moment of silence during which the woman sat and studied Lauzier, she said, "At one time, yes. But I decided it served no use in this line of business."

"You're ex-Fleet?"

"Like everyone in this organization. We're the ones cut adrift after the war when the Armed Forces returned to a peacetime footing and decided we were surplus to requirements." She shrugged. "It happens after every conflict. I head our private military arm, and for this contract, because of its size and importance, I've taken personal command of the task force."

The Commodore must have seen something in Lauzier's eyes because she added, "I retired as a post captain after several starship commands and senior appointments, so you need not worry about my qualifications. They are impeccable. Shall we discuss the next steps? The contract stipulates I would take orders from you once *Athena* arrives at this rendezvous."

"Is someone in pursuit? Other than the so-called rescue force?"

The Commodore nodded.

"Unfortunately, Captain LeDain sent an emergency message with visuals before we seized his bridge. That message shot up the Navy chain of command like an aviso pushing the upper hyperlimit bands. Fleet HQ formed a task force at Starbase 30 to find this ship and did so in record time. They're even seeking Shrehari permission to enter the Protectorate Zone, as per the relevant articles in the Treaty of Ulufan. The warning I received provided no further details. Since we don't enjoy the luxury of subspace communications between our bases and the Commonwealth, I depend on dispatch runs by our sloops."

A flash of anger crossed Lauzier's patrician face.

"Damn."

"I wouldn't worry too much. The Navy doesn't know where we are, and it will almost certainly take weeks, if not months, to find us, considering peacetime constraints. This operation will be over well before then."

"Let's hope so. The Fleet can't rescue us. It would raise too many questions. Now, my orders. You will remove several passengers from this ship and dispose of them."

The mercenary's pale eyebrows crept up.

"Dispose of? And what, pray tell, does that mean, Madame Lauzier?"

"They're never to be heard from again. How you do it is your problem. The people who hired you will shortly announce they ordered *Athena*'s hijackers to execute prisoners if Earth doesn't issue a proclamation announcing Rim Sector colonies will unconditionally attain independence within the year."

"The government won't do that."

"Of course not. But our rescue will be nicely timed so that only the people who aren't on the list I'm about to give you go home. And that is the only explanation you'll hear. The contract stipulated no questions asked."

She inclined her head with what Lauzier deemed as proper deference.

"Of course, Madame, but if you'll permit me a final one?"

Lauzier made a hand gesture indicating she could ask.

"May we sell the people on the list as indentured workers deep inside the Zone where they'll never escape nor meet any honest human trader?"

A faint sneer appeared on Lauzier's face.

"Squeamish, are you?"

"I'd rather not waste the opportunity for extra profits. This is an unforgiving business with tight margins, and it would please me to see the useless drones surrounding you finally do honest work for the first time in their lives."

"Just be sure they're never heard from again; that's all I want. Now, if you'll call up the passenger manifest, I will point out those you will remove one at a time, every twelve hours, starting today and in the order I tell you."

Half an hour later, the same mercenary escorted Sara Lauzier back to her lounge in the passenger section, where she was joined by Amali, who closed the door behind them.

"So, what was that about?"

"From what the chief pirate told me, we are bargaining chips in a radical attempt at blackmailing Earth on behalf of colonial sovereignists in the Rim Sector. My father should have received their demands for an immediate path to independence by now along with the threat that the pirates will execute us one by one if the Commonwealth government drags its feet."

Amali lost every bit of color in his face.

"Oh lord. This is a nightmare. Will you tell the others?"

"And cause immediate panic? No."

"I disagree."

She gave him a contemptuous look. "And I don't care."

The door to the lounge opened, and two armed pirates entered, heading straight for Amali. He understood immediately and turned crazed eyes on Lauzier.

"Help me!" The words came out as a croak.

The sheer terror writ large on his face was answered by a faint, almost imperceptible look of detached amusement on hers.

"I'm afraid I can't do that, Vitus."

The pirates seized him by the arms, and one of them pressed a spray syringe against his neck. Within moments, Amali was nothing more than a barely conscious automaton, capable of walking with help and not much else.

As the guards took him away, Lauzier murmured, "Always keep your friends close and your enemies closer. Your brother will now be in my debt forever."

And by having one of her seemingly closest confidants go first, suspicions hinting at her involvement would be muted. Besides, Vitus Amali was tiresome as only a younger, perpetually dissatisfied brother of the most powerful CEO in the Commonwealth could be.

**

When Holt, via a secure comlink, finished briefing Kowalski on the hijackers' demands, dutifully transmitted from the SecGen's office to his own by a counterintelligence mole, the latter sat back with a thoughtful expression.

"I still smell a setup, but at least things are moving again. Any idea how those demands were received?"

"With a fair amount of anger and not a bit of badly hidden panic. Lauzier can't bend, of course, not even for his daughter, but I can promise you if she dies, he'll make sure the Rim Sector colonies stay under Home World rule forever."

"See, that's the sort of thing which makes me think this isn't what it seems. There's more at play here, I'm sure of it."

"Your instincts are good, Kathryn, just like Siobhan's, and I agree, there has to be more." Holt tapped the desktop with his fingers, eyes on Kowalski as he let his thoughts roam free. She stared back, lips pressed together. "We already figure the hijacking is a way of discrediting the sovereignists and the Navy. What if executing passengers isn't about making Earth bend to the colonies' demands but Lauzier getting inconvenient members of the Commonwealth elite out of the way to help his daughter's bid for the Senate and soon after that, the top job?"

"Charles Lauzier?" She sounded dubious. "He's ruthless and amoral, but his being involved in this is too risky. Sara Lauzier on the other hand? Why not. I've always figured her as a controlled psychopath, and we know she's in tight with the SSB — on her father's behalf, of course, but still. Sara has boundless ambitions and even fewer scruples than Charles. Or rather, where he has residual scruples, she has none whatsoever."

"Let's hope Siobhan finds *Athena* before the ranks of the elite are thinned out, no matter who is running this increasingly bizarre show." Holt raised his hand as he glanced to one side. "Hold on. One of my desk officers just forwarded an 'urgent, operational' I should read while you're on the link."

After a few moments, he looked up at Kowalski again.

"Another SSB leak, this one hinting that they're preparing a rescue mission because the Navy can't be relied upon."

She took a deep breath.

"Now I know it's a damned setup, Zeke. It can't be anything else. What hostage rescue assets can the SSB deploy?"

"Most certainly more than we know about, but they use private military corporations for their dirty work, so this is probably what they mean. One or two agents controlling a mercenary operation."

"Perhaps we should ask them exactly which system they're targeting for the rescue. If it's Galadiman, we'll find our proof. Not that it'll do us a damn bit of good." Kowalski let out a soft sigh. "The SecGen's minions are untouchable. But let's concentrate on the current mission before we consider the SSB's demise."

"Absolutely, but at this point, there's nothing else we can do. Either *Athena* is where Siobhan expects her, or she isn't. Either someone with the last name Lauzier is setting up the Rim Sector colonies for a fall and targeting a not inconsiderable percentage of the Commonwealth elite for elimination or not. We simply can't tell. All we have is supposition while Siobhan may or may not uncover the truth out there."

A fey smile briefly lit up Kowalski's face.

"She will — don't worry."

— Twenty-Two —

Dunmoore, coffee cup in hand, took the flag CIC's command chair almost precisely five minutes before Task Force Luckner was due to come out of hyperspace at the Galadiman system's heliopause. As usual, one-fourth of her RED One crew — this time Lieutenant Commander Olmos and Chief Petty Officer Second Class Hogan — were on duty.

Commander Pushkin, Chief Petty Officer First Class Guthren, and the rest of RED One showed up moments later, only a few steps behind their commanding officer. As Guthren sat at his usual workstation, he rubbed his hands with the glee of a craft master getting to work.

"I'm feeling good about this, Skipper, really good."

Pushkin gave him an ironic look.

"So, you think Drex didn't pull a dogleg at the halfway mark to head elsewhere, *and* this is where the pirates stashed our target? I should break out a deck of cards and see how lucky you actually are."

"There's no gambling in Task Force Luckner," Dunmoore said absently as she read *Salamanca's* daily status report.

The transition warning from the bridge cut off Pushkin's reply.

When the public address system fell quiet, Guthren gave him a knowing wink.

"Luckier than the poor bastards who'll feel the weight of our broadside in the next twelve hours or so, Commander. Remember, the Skipper is rarely wrong in these matters. She had Drex's measure within moments. He probably knew about the *Athena* hijacking and is dead set on telling his bosses that we're in town, looking for a fight. The bugger wouldn't waste time making a dogleg as if we were watching for his departure vector after crossing the heliopause. Our Drex of bad memory wasn't the most imaginative man in the universe. His brother isn't either, mark my words. Otherwise, he wouldn't have lost his wartime commission during the reduction in force after the armistice, let alone joined the Howlers in a fit of stupidity."

Pushkin grinned at him. "Don't hold back, Chief. Tell us what you think."

The warning klaxon sounded three times at that moment, and everyone in the flag CIC braced themselves for the brief, unpleasant sensation that accompanied transitions to and from hyperspace. But, when it passed, Dunmoore's staff sprang into action without needing orders.

"All ships have emerged and are running silent."

"I'm setting up optical links for the status reports."

"*Salamanca* is looking for Galadiman."

"No traces of *Vuko* or any ship other than ours."

A faint smile appeared on Dunmoore's face. It felt good to be a formation commander with a crack team running her CIC. A few minutes passed, then the status reports appeared on her command chair's virtual display. No issues, as she expected.

"We found Galadiman's current position, sir. I'm preparing the task force navigation plot. I estimate an eleven-hour jump."

Dunmoore nodded at Lieutenant Commander Khanjan. "Excellent. Thank you. Signals, please query the Colonial Office subspace network to see if there's a message for us."

"Already on it, sir," Chief Cazano replied.

"Thanks."

She settled back and composed herself to wait as things proceeded at their own pace. It was the one aspect of formation command she'd never enjoyed overmuch. Finally, Cazano raised her hand.

"A message from Consul Forenza, sir. His agents on Galadiman report significant Confederacy of the Howling Stars activity with the arrival of four ships sailing as a group more than a week ago. They're not sure but based on observations taken from the surface — all four are in low orbit — one of them differs from the others and could be the missing luxury liner. Mister Tarrant's people in the area concur."

Chief Guthren pumped his fist in the air.

"Yes!"

"Reply the following — Task Force Luckner will enter the Galadiman system and expects to begin active rescue operations within eighteen hours of this message's date-time stamp."

**

"Ah, Zeke. Good timing." Kowalski smiled at Holt's image on her display. "We heard back from the Shrehari ambassador just now. His government agrees with Task Force Luckner operating in the Protectorate Zone to rescue *Athena*. It came from *Kho'sahra* Brakal himself, apparently. He also asked why a famed warrior like Dunmoore was stripped of her former rank and remains a captain even today."

"Grand Admiral Sampaio must have loved that."

"I couldn't say. The CNO was a little irked by it, that I did notice."

Holt chuckled. "What is it with these admirals who blame Siobhan for stealing their thunder ten years ago?"

"It's not so much stealing their thunder as it was questioning the entire conduct of the war from her perch at the College. Oh, she did it subtly, but enough of the senior flag officers understood her meaning. Of course, certain truths shouldn't be shouted from the rooftops. It makes people uncomfortable."

"Then the next few weeks will be distressing for a lot of people around here. I just heard from the Colonial Office. Their agents, as well as Tarrant's informants, believe *Athena* is in orbit around Galadiman, and not coincidentally, Task Force Luckner will shortly arrive at the planet's hyperlimit. Siobhan called it."

"As usual. Anything new from the SecGen's office?"

Holt shook his head. "Word about the demands and threats has been forcefully quashed at Lauzier's orders. Whoever blabs will end up in an SSB cell. But I suspect the newsnets' wall of silence on the hijacking is about to crumble. Apparently, the SSB rescue effort is underway, if we can believe the latest whisperings around Geneva, and that's good propaganda for the government."

Kowalski let out a bark of laughter. "And it'll come too late. But do they even know where *Athena* is?"

"Ah, now that's still the question. I don't doubt they have sources in the Zone and among the criminal class we can't tap."

"Just as we do." She chuckled. "Perhaps in the person of Enoc Tarrant, our sources intersect."

"Probably, though he's a smart man and won't allow either the Navy, through Siobhan, or the SSB to find out."

**

"Bridge to the Commodore."

She put down her reader and tapped her communicator. "Commodore here. What is it?"

"*Vuko* just emerged at the hyperlimit. Captain Drex is demanding to speak with the senior executive in the system. He's using our secure frequency and encryption."

After searching her memory for the shipping schedules, she frowned.

"*Vuko* isn't due at Galadiman for at least a month. As far as I remember, she should be on her way to Abaddon."

"Yes, sir. Shall I put him through?"

She repressed a sigh. Drex was competent as a transport captain but didn't have what it took to command a fighting ship, and something about his manner and attitude mildly irritated her. But the board of directors hired him and were happy with his performance at hauling goods across the Zone for transshipping into Commonwealth smuggler hulls.

"Please do."

A few moments later, his face materialized on her day cabin's primary display.

"Commodore." He inclined his head respectfully. "Thank you for taking my call. I came to tell you of a potential problem."

"Then speak, Captain."

As he related events at Kilia Station, her facial muscles tightened, deepening the seams around her eyes, nose, and mouth.

"Dunmoore." The name came out as a hiss. "How is it possible?"

"I'm sorry, sir, but I couldn't do anything about her boarding party storming through the airlock behind station security. Obviously, she either convinced or coerced Enoc Tarrant into helping her. And yes, she has my navigation logs, but not the secret database, so she knows about *Vuko*'s habitual ports of call. However, I visit so many star systems, none will seem more interesting than another. Besides, she left Kilia several hours before I did, so I can't see how she could follow me here."

"You fool." Her voice lashed out with such power that Drex visibly flinched. "Dunmoore perfected commerce raiding tactics during the War. She was waiting for you at Kilia's heliopause and most assuredly spotted your departure vector when you went FTL for Galadiman. You'd have been better heading in another direction and making a dogleg halfway through."

"But that would increase travel time, and I thought the senior officer here should be told about Task Force Luckner as soon as possible."

The Commodore's eyes widened further. "What did you call it? Luckner?"

"Yes," Drex stammered, unnerved by her intensity. "One Reconquista class cruiser, three Voivode class frigates, and an Argo class corvette."

"How is this even possible," she whispered to herself. "Dunmoore turned into a washed-up senior captain after the war, and now she's back in command of a formation bearing that cursed name?"

Then in a louder voice, "You've almost certainly led Dunmoore here. I'm sure of it because I know her."

"They couldn't see me cross the heliopause, sir," he protested. "Not without knowing my departure vector from Kilia Station, and the only one capable of tracking me when I left was a Shrehari science vessel."

"You mean a *Tai Zohl* ship." She frowned. "Is it possible..."

"What I wonder is how the Navy obtained permission to enter the Zone, sir."

"It doesn't matter how. What matters is Dunmoore followed you, and she's at most a few hours behind." A quick frown. "We will discuss your future later. Cycle your hyperdrives as quickly as possible and scram. You should be in the Abaddon system by now, so that's where you're headed. Report to the senior executive there, tell them everything you told me."

"Aye, aye, sir."

"Commodore, out." She cut the link, mind adrift, as she searched for a plan while silently cursing Dunmoore. "Think, Lena, think. This operation is almost over anyhow. Your squadron certainly can't stand against hers."

She understood that if she even hinted at fighting a Navy formation of that strength, her crews would mutiny. They understood only too well the sort of broadside they'd face, having served in just such vessels during the war, perhaps even the very hulls now bearing down on them.

A single missile volley from all five, and it was goodnight. Putting a figurative knife at *Athena*'s throat and negotiating her escape was out of the question. The contract stipulated that the liner be 'rescued' by the same people who hijacked her once those targeted by Lauzier were taken.

No, the only option was letting Dunmoore recover *Athena,* and too bad about the folks on Lauzier's list who were still aboard. Since this reincarnated Task Force Luckner would drop out of FTL in the same area as *Vuko*, her sensor techs would see the emergence signature, even if they were running silent. That would be the signal to remove her people from the liner and leave.

Her sloops were faster than a Reconquista cruiser or a Voivode frigate, and together, they could take on a mere corvette. She would make her escape intact with the primary conditions of the contract fulfilled. And, there was the bonus of three dozen warm bodies for the auction block, people who represented everything she hated about the government that tossed her aside.

The Commodore quickly gave her orders, and even before Dunmoore's ships appeared, she'd already thinned out *Athena*'s mercenary crew, leaving one shuttle attached to the airlock for the remainder. They'd ensure said airlock was easily accessible for Dunmoore's boarding party.

Too bad she couldn't afford to face her nemesis one more time. Dunmoore took what was rightfully hers, precipitating an early and forced retirement after missing the commodore promotion list cut-off for the last time.

Still, cashing out her Fleet pension and stashing it away in various numbered accounts had been a good move. Now, she could thumb her nose at the Navy and not worry about anything, provided she retained anonymity. The Commodore smiled at her reflection in the mirror across from the day cabin desk. Let Dunmoore watch them leave, knowing she couldn't catch up. No need for any taunts or threats. She'd fulfilled her part of the contract and would soon earn a nice bonus.

For a moment, she wondered about warning Lauzier, then dismissed the idea. The latter's reaction upon facing a Navy boarding party would be more believable if it came as a total surprise.

— Twenty-Three —

"All ships present and running silent, sir," Chief Cox announced from the flag CIC's combat systems console. "*Salamanca* is scanning Galadiman's orbitals on passive."

The minutes ticked by while Dunmoore caught her fingers dancing on the command chair's arm several times.

"Yes!" Cox swiveled around. "We have her."

He pointed at the starboard secondary display where an image of *Athena* as she looked fresh out of the slipways was displayed side-by-side with her twin, orbiting a planet.

"No doubt about it, Skipper," Lieutenant Commander Zakaria said as the image of the orbiting *Athena* zoomed in on the name painted on her hyperdrive nacelle. "She's the one, and the ships orbiting around her correspond to the images sent with the distress signal."

"What the hell?" Pushkin pointed at the display. "There's a shuttle undocking from *Athena.*"

"The presumed hijackers are lighting up, sir. Emissions consistent with sublight drives spooling."

"You think they spotted us dropping out of FTL?" Pushkin turned toward Dunmoore. "If *Vuko* made it ahead of us, they might have been scanning this arc of space on the assumption we were following."

"Could be. Any sign of *Vuko*?"

A few seconds passed, then Zakaria shook her head.

"Nothing that *Salamanca* can pick up. None of the ships in orbit currently visible correspond to *Vuko*'s emission signature."

"Let's give it one pass."

Several minutes later, "That shuttle just entered the trailing sloop's hangar bay, Skipper." Then, "Sublight drives flaring. They're breaking out of orbit, leaving *Athena* behind."

"Meaning they definitely spotted us dropping out of hyperspace, which in turn proves *Vuka* got here first and whoever is in command heeded Drex," Pushkin said.

"But how could they know we were in close pursuit?" Lieutenant Commander Zakaria asked. "Surely *Vuko* didn't notice us at Kilia's heliopause."

"Someone on the other side is wise to the Skipper's tactics, sir, the ones she used against Shrehari shipping during the war," Guthren replied. "That's the only explanation."

Dunmoore hesitated for a fraction of a second.

"Chief Cazano, transmit the order up systems. Commander Khanjan, take us to Galadiman at maximum acceleration commensurate with a safe orbital insertion. Our objective is *Athena*."

"What about the pirate sloops?" Pushkin asked.

"We won't catch up no matter what, and our orders are to retrieve *Athena* and her passengers. Track them until they go FTL and note their vector. Not that it'll do much good. If Chief

Guthren is right, whoever commands that squadron will make a dogleg halfway to the heliopause just in case."

Cazano raised her hand. "All ships confirm up systems and are ready to sync navigation with the flag."

"Navigation orders are going out now, Skipper."

"Gregor, warn *Salamanca* that they'll provide the boarding party to secure *Athena*. I want every precaution taken in case the hijackers booby-trapped her."

"Yes, sir. On it."

"And let's scan that liner. I want to know how many life signs are aboard, what her reactors are doing, if she's giving off unusual emissions — everything." Dunmoore stood. "I'll be in my quarters."

**

"Sensors can make out two hundred and twenty-nine distinct life signs," Chief Cox reported.

"But there were two hundred and seventy aboard when she left her last port of call before the hijacking." Pushkin glanced at Dunmoore over his shoulder. "One hundred and twenty passengers and a hundred and fifty crew. That means forty-one people are unaccounted for."

"Either they're dead or were taken off, sir. The sensors can't find any dark spots where that many life signs might be hiding. Other than that, her emissions are normal, her reactors appear to be operating within acceptable parameters, and she's not transmitting anything."

"Thank you."

Dunmoore stroked the control screen embedded in her command chair arm, and moments later, Captain Rydzewski answered.

"Sir?"

"Launch the boarding party."

"Aye, aye, sir."

Task Force Luckner had entered orbit less than half an hour earlier and surrounded *Athena* at a distance sufficient to avoid harm if the worst happened and her antimatter containment fields failed due to sabotage. But, so far, no one aboard acknowledged *Salamanca*'s hails or took notice of five Commonwealth Navy warships orbiting a Protectorate Zone star system where, under the Treaty, they shouldn't be. The handful of other ships in orbit, while no doubt monitoring them with trepidation, were wisely remaining both silent and distant.

Ten minutes passed, then one of the cruiser's shuttles appeared on both the flag CIC's primary display and as a small blue icon in the holographic tactical projection. It approached *Athena* from behind with deliberation, its sensors examining every square centimeter of the liner's hull, looking for hidden airlock release hatches — a boarding party's best friend.

The shuttle finally leveled off abeam of the main starboard passenger airlock used when docking and by the pirate shuttle earlier. Within moments, the speaker came to life with the voice of *Salamanca*'s second officer, who led the boarding party.

"The main airlock is powered up and seems ready to extrude a connecting tube. When the hijackers ran off, they left it live and ready to receive. What are my instructions?"

"Can you sense anything that might indicate a booby trap?" Captain Rydzewski asked.

"No."

Guthren glanced at Dunmoore. "Doesn't mean there aren't any, but if no one's around to run the controls from inside, that's what you'd get after the shuttle docked there buggered off in great haste. The airlock is still primed."

"What would you suggest?"

"Send a boarding droid through without docking."

Rydzewski spoke again, quoting Guthren almost word for word, and they watched the droid, a cylinder just over half a meter tall and a quarter that in diameter come through the shuttle's own airlock and, with a brief burst of its jets, head for *Athena*. Once there, it extruded magnetic clamps and a robotic arm that opened the emergency control panel and manipulated the mechanical release mechanism.

The airlock's outer door opened after an interval just long enough to empty the intermediary compartment of air, then the droid entered, the door closed again, and the compartment repressurized. When the inner door opened, it relayed live video of an empty, though opulent guest lobby. Neither humans nor AI holographs stood behind the reception desk, and the wall displays were dark.

Now on wheels, the droid trundled toward the passenger section and found its entryway barred. The second officer ordered it around then through the open door leading to the crew compartments and the bridge. But it encountered no one.

"All right," Rydzewski said. "You're clear to dock. Take control of the ship, then find its crew. Don't open the passenger section until Niner-Niner arrives."

Dunmoore, whose radio call sign it was, stood.

"And that's my signal to prepare."

Guthren imitated her.

"You mean our signal, Skipper."

"Enjoy dealing with over a hundred scared and probably pissed off scions of Earth's elites." Pushkin grinned at her. "We'll be watching from the safety of your CIC and passing around a tub of popcorn."

"Enjoy the show."

**

In contrast to the boarding party's armored pressure suits, Dunmoore, Guthren, and the two bosun's mates assigned as security wore nothing more than dark blue Navy battledress, holstered sidearms, and the Fleet's sky blue beret with its starburst and anchor insignia.

The ride over in *Salamanca*'s pinnace was brief and, with the boarding party's shuttle undocked and shadowing *Athena* a hundred meters off her starboard beam, they docked at the main airlock. *Salamanca*'s second officer greeted her in the guest lobby with a quick salute which Dunmoore returned.

"Welcome aboard, sir. We are in control of the ship and can sail it home if necessary. As far as we can tell, they locked the crew up with the passengers where they can't access critical systems."

"Lead on, Commander." She gestured at the guest corridor. "You found the coordinates for Sara Lauzier's cabin, I presume?"

"Yes, sir." An amused look crossed his usually serious features. "Not unexpectedly, it's the Commonwealth Suite, also known as Cabin Number One. But based on the live video feed we've been watching, Madame Lauzier is in a nearby lounge, alone, reading. It appears our boarding has gone unnoticed by the inmates."

"Good. That way, they will hopefully not mob us."

Dunmoore had decided she would deal with the passengers via the one they would consider their leader by dint of her parentage and the power she wielded behind the scenes in Geneva.

No one waited on the other side of the armored, airtight door when it opened, but her escort entered first, wary expressions on their faces, hands hovering near their holstered blasters, the second officer on their heels. As they walked down opulent corridors and across luxurious common spaces, startled heads appeared through open doors and followed their progress with wide eyes, though no one called out. Dunmoore could only presume the eerily unexpected appearance of Commonwealth Navy personnel startled them, and they didn't quite believe what they saw.

"In here."

The second officer stopped by a door that opened at his touch. He stepped aside as Dunmoore's escort entered, eyes scanning the lounge and its sole occupant. They took position on either side of the door under the astonished gaze of Sara Lauzier, who stood when Dunmoore and Guthren appeared.

"Madame Lauzier? I'm Captain Siobhan Dunmoore, Commonwealth Navy. I command Task Force Luckner. We've come to bring you and everyone else aboard home." Dunmoore, who'd been observing Lauzier from the moment the door opened, thought she picked up something more than surprise in her gaze. A tinge of annoyance, perhaps? What she didn't notice was relief at being rescued. "The people who hijacked this ship fled shortly after spotting us at the planet's hyperlimit a few hours ago."

After a moment of silence, Lauzier said, "Then I — we — owe you our gratitude."

Her flat tone sounded somehow wrong to Dunmoore's ears.

"Our sensors detected fewer life signs than expected, forty-one less, to be precise. Do you know what happened?"

"The hijackers took them off this ship, obviously. Why I couldn't say."

This time, Dunmoore was sure she spotted a flash of annoyance in Lauzier's eyes.

"Do you know if anyone requires medical care?"

Lauzier shook her head.

"No. Our captors treated us well. The ship's hospitality personnel, who were not confined, took care of our needs. Other than on odd occasions, whoever hijacked *Athena* left us alone."

"My boarding party will release the ship's crew from confinement and, if we're satisfied with their condition, return control of *Athena* back to Captain LeDain. In the meantime, would you be so kind as to reassure your fellow passengers and let them know they're in the Navy's hands now? We will be escorting you back to Starbase 30. From there, 3rd Fleet will make sure you reach Earth safely."

A nod. "I'll speak with them. Thank you, Captain."

"One last question. Did you see any of your captors clearly enough to describe them so we can have an AI draw up their likenesses? From the intelligence I received, many, if not most, are ex-Fleet. Having images would allow us to track down their identities."

Lauzier hesitated long enough to awaken Dunmoore's curiosity.

"They summoned me to the captain's day cabin shortly after we arrived here, where I met a woman who calls herself the Commodore. She claims to be a mercenary and commands the ships that hijacked *Athena*."

"What did this Commodore want?"

"She told me her employers were using us to blackmail the Commonwealth government, and that if it didn't accede to their demands, our lives would be on the line. When she suggested I plead with my father for cooperation via video recording, I refused. And that was it. I wasn't aware she'd removed people from *Athena*, seeing as how we've mostly withdrawn into our own little bubbles. You'd have to ask the others if they noticed anything."

"What can you tell me about this Commodore?"

Lauzier shrugged.

"Not that much. Claims she was a Navy captain, with starship commands and senior staff appointments, before taking forced retirement after the war. In appearance, she's an icy blond — pale skin, shoulder-length platinum hair, cold blue eyes, narrow face. Her voice is clearly in the alto range and a little rough. I'd say she's a few years older than you are, and I got the sense she's bitter at being cast adrift by the peacetime Fleet."

Many Navy officers could fit that description, but Dunmoore could only think of one who knew her tactics well enough to spot Task Force Luckner emerging at the hyperlimit after being warned by Drex.

— Twenty-Four —

Captain Roy LeDain was practically falling over himself, thanking Dunmoore for rescuing them. His crew was complete, minus the five last-minute replacements planted aboard *Athena* by the hijackers, and ready to retake control of their ship.

He provided them with a manifest, and after doing a headcount, the boarding party could identify the thirty-six missing passengers. They subsequently debriefed him and his people for the investigation, a task that took most of the day. Then, Dunmoore turned *Athena* back to LeDain with the caveat that he obeys navigation instructions from the flag CIC in *Salamanca* until they arrive at Starbase 30. Otherwise, she would put a prize crew aboard and temporarily press his ship into the Navy as an auxiliary. Of course, LeDain did not know she couldn't do that in peacetime, but he promised he would faithfully follow her instructions.

Her last task before heading back into Commonwealth space was sending a report via the Colonial Office's subspace relay network. After preparing a draft for discussion, Dunmoore sat down with Pushkin and Guthren to review it.

"Looks good, Skipper," Puskin said once he read it.

"Should I or shouldn't I include my suspicions this Commodore might be Lena Corto?"

"Shame we don't have her image in the database, but how many retired post captains, the sort separated from the Service after the war as surplus to requirements, fit the description Lauzier gave you? If it is Corto, she prepared her escape the moment Drex arrived at Galadiman's hyperlimit and raised the alarm, knowing you would heavily outmatch her squadron. What I don't understand, however, is why not take *Athena* along? Why simply take her own people off and run?"

Dunmoore nodded. "That question has been bothering me as well, along with the matter of those thirty-six passengers taken away at regular intervals. What did maybe-Corto do with them, and why those when they held someone like Sara Lauzier in their grasp?"

"How about you put those questions in your report, Skipper," Guthren suggested. "See what the brains at Fleet HQ come up with. There has to be a lot more going on than we can see right now."

"Good idea. I'll do so. In the meantime, Gregor, if you could see the task force on its way to the hyperlimit, I'd be grateful."

"Will do." He chuckled as he stood. "You know, the more I think about it, the more convinced I am it really is Lena. Who the hell other than a bitter failure like our dear former flag captain would insist on calling herself the Commodore and wear a star on a mercenary's uniform? I've never heard of mercs doing so, especially not when her command is a handful of sloops, something which rates four rings at the most, if not three."

Guthren nodded. "He's right, sir. That fits with the Lena Corto we remember so fondly."

**

"Siobhan found *Athena* and is on her way back. But thirty-six passengers were taken off by the hijackers and are now listed as missing, as are the five crewmembers who infiltrated the ship on their behalf." Holt dropped into a chair facing Kowalski's desk. He fished a data chip from his tunic pocket and placed it on the desktop. "I've classified her report top secret special access, and when you read it, you'll know why. Go on. I'll wait."

Kowalski placed the chip on her desktop reader, and a virtual display popped up with text on its holographic screen. As she read, her face hardened, and after a few minutes, she turned her eyes on Holt.

"You know this Corto character, I presume?"

"Oh, yes. The original Task Force Luckner's flag captain until the day Siobhan got her star and took command, with me inheriting *Iolanthe* and those flag captain duties she didn't assume herself."

"Do you think Siobhan could be onto something?"

He nodded.

"I did a quick check on Corto. She cashed out her pension seven years ago and vanished. There's no trace of her anywhere. And calling herself Commodore while wearing a star is so in character for the woman I remember."

"What do you think of her last section, listing the questions she raises?"

Holt looked up at the ceiling in a theatrical gesture. "Where do I start?"

"How about with the list of those who vanished? Do they have anything in common?"

A slow grin appeared as he turned his eyes back on Kowalski.

"You mean beyond the fact they come from filthy rich clans and are politically connected to a fare thee well?"

She nodded. "Please don't draw this out for your own amusement, Zeke. Siobhan would disapprove."

"No, she wouldn't. She'd set up the chessboard and then utterly destroy me." A wink. "Consider yourself lucky. To her, chess is a blood sport. The disappeared have more than just those characteristics in common. In one way or another, many of them have been critical of Charles Lauzier, his daughter, or other members of that tribe. And they would most certainly oppose Sara's rise to the top job by any means fair or foul. The rest are the sort of relatives their families wouldn't miss, said families being Lauzier supporters."

"And there's our *cui bono*, though it seems far-fetched the Lauziers would make three dozen of their own clique vanish in such a manner."

"From a public perception aspect, it beats assassination."

Kowalski inclined her head. "Good point. Would this Lena Corto terminate civilians at the orders of someone such as Lauzier?"

Holt considered the question for a moment, then slowly shook his head.

"I don't think so. She's not a sociopath, unlike Sara and most of her family. But she's bitter enough to see members of the political elite suffer for the rest of their lives. Otherwise, she would have successfully backstabbed her way to an admiral's stars instead of watching Siobhan take over Task Force Luckner. Or she could have farmed out the executions. Unfortunately, according to our friends in the Colonial Office Intelligence Service, the Confederacy of the Howling Stars, like most organized crime outfits, has a surplus of soulless killers." He gave Kowalski a helpless shrug. "Unless we track down the hijacker ships in question, we'll likely never know."

"Who's notifying the families?"

"The CNI is kicking that one up the chain to the Grand Admiral who will no doubt declare it a job for the SecGen's office and walk away before one of Charles Lauzier's minions can pin it on the Fleet."

"Next item on Siobhan's list — why did the hijackers leave *Athena* behind when they ran? They could have taken her with them and jumped out well before Task Force Luckner entered effective engagement range."

Another shrug.

"Your guess is as good as mine. Perhaps they'd taken the people they needed from among *Athena*'s passengers and didn't want to bother with the rest. Or *Athena* suffered from mechanical issues that prevented her from keeping up with fast-moving sloops. Or Corto panicked when she heard Dunmoore was coming with five warships and left *Athena* behind to slow the task force so she could make her escape."

This time Kowalski let a slow smile play on her lips.

"Or," she drawled, "the mission to help precipitate a political crisis was mostly completed. A rescue by the Navy would do just as well as a rescue by the SSB's mercenaries, especially if Corto took off the folks the Lauziers would rather never see again. No need to stick around or take *Athena* with her."

"If you discuss that hypothesis with the CNO, let alone the Grand Admiral, they'll make you the senior patient at the Armed Forces Psychiatric Institute. But yeah, that's a distinct possibility because it answers Siobhan's questions. And plausibly at that." Holt let out a soft sigh. "Which leaves us with a conundrum. What do we do about it? If we're right, the SSB won't investigate. With *Athena's* return to Commonwealth space, the Fleet's involvement will be over, and we can't officially pursue the matter."

"True. But three dozen of the Commonwealth's leading citizens have vanished at pirate hands inside the Protectorate Zone. I think it gives us an excuse to pursue the matter from that end at least and perhaps wipe out the Confederacy of the Howling Stars and their allies — beings who present an increasing threat to Commonwealth security."

Holt let out an amused snort.

"You actually said that with a straight face. Congratulations. We'll never obtain authorization for a big anti-organized crime campaign in the Zone, Kathryn. Didn't you hear? The Fleet no longer conducts dark and dirty wars beyond the frontiers. They annoy the powers that be who profit from said organized crime, which, in turn, doesn't help promotion prospects. You won't find a single flag officer who'll volunteer to lead such an effort, never mind allow it, and for reasons beyond the letter of the Treaty. Once the current tempest settles, those poor sods taken off *Athena* will be consigned to the memory hole, especially if they were targeted."

Kowalski gave Holt the sort of sweet smile he remembered seeing on Siobhan Dunmoore's lips when the latter was plotting something her superiors might not like.

"The flag officer to lead such an effort already began fighting a dirty little war, though we'll have to put a star or two on her collar and get her an established formation instead of the borrowed ad hoc one she has at the moment."

Holt stared at Kowalski with unfeigned astonishment.

"Did you start happy hour during the morning coffee break?"

"Come on, Zeke. You know I'm right. We simply need to make it happen."

"We? What's this we, oh future chief of naval operations? I'm a terminal commodore tucked away in the darkest corner of Naval Intelligence because the snooping my division does must remain hidden from the government. But please continue, tell me how you plan on making a miracle happen."

"Right now, our Q ships are operating individually and rather haphazardly in the Zone. Sadly, Special Operations Command isn't as aggressive on the naval side since the war ended. General Espinoza would rather send Pathfinder and SOF units into suspected pirate lairs and wipe them out with daggers and small arms fire rather than hunt for their ships. That's what you get when you appoint a Marine Corps four-star as commander. Besides, while controlling each Q ship's individual mission profile from SOCOM HQ works in most places along the frontier, the Protectorate Zone needs a more concerted effort under a flag officer who not only knows the area of operations but is there in person."

"And?"

"I am preparing a proposal to make something like Task Force Luckner a permanent unit that'll help clean up the Zone and keep it clean. Once the idea's been accepted, I'll suggest it comes under the command of one Siobhan Dunmoore. If the powers that be agree, I'll see about getting her star back and perhaps even add a second one right away, since commodores don't hold independent commands these days. You may not know this, but regulations specify officers can skip commodore if they held that rank as a wartime formation commander. Should it all come together, the task force's first mission would be finding the hijackers and wiping them out while recovering the people missing from *Athena*."

Holt cocked an eyebrow at her.

"That sounds like a tall order. So permit me to be skeptical you can pull it off."

Kowalski's sweet smile returned.

"I'm seeing the CNO this afternoon about the first step, creating a permanent formation separate from regular battle groups to deal with the Zone. After Siobhan's stunning success and our growing cooperation with the Colonial Office, who, I'm sure, will be more than happy to help, I think I can sell the idea. Especially under the banner of preventing further high profile attacks. I assume Admiral Lowell knows by now Siobhan pulled it off and is on her way home?"

"Admiral Doxiadis called him right after I delivered the news — minus Siobhan's unanswered questions, which will stay our secret for now. Well, ours and Mikhail Forenza's, since her report went over his network. And he could be the key to finding answers. Your boss and the Grand Admiral should be heading for the Palace of the Stars any moment now so they can brief the SecGen."

"Good. It means he'll be that much more receptive to my idea."

— Twenty-Five —

Secretary General of the Commonwealth Charles Lauzier, who'd been staring out his office window at the shimmering surface of Lake Geneva while Grand Admiral Sampaio spoke, turned around. A tall, lean, severe-looking seventy-five-year-old whose wavy black hair was slowly turning silver, he studied both naval officers with deep-set eyes on either side of a patrician nose.

"That's quite a commendable feat by your task force commander, Admiral, recovering most of our people and the ship so quickly without firing a shot. What was her name again?"

"Dunmoore, sir. Captain Siobhan Dunmoore," Lowell replied, knowing full well Lauzier could recite Sampaio's report almost verbatim and would have remembered.

Lauzier snapped his fingers and pointed at him. "Of course."

He rejoined them around the coffee table and sat, elbows on the antique chair's upholstered arms, hands joined loosely in front of his chin.

"Tell me, Admiral, is this the same Dunmoore who led the raid on the Shrehari home system and escorted me to the armistice talks, the one with whom *Kho'sahra* Brakal spoke after we signed the documents?"

Sampaio nodded. "Yes, sir."

"Why the blazes is such a capable officer still a mere captain? I seem to recall she wore a commodore's star ten years ago."

Lowell glanced at Sampaio as if to say, how about you handle this one, boss?

"Well, sir, after the war, a number of officers were reduced in rank as the Fleet laid up ships and released personnel back to civilian life. Dunmoore, as one of the most junior commodores, reverted to captain since there were no commodore billets available for her. Since then, in the estimation of successive promotion boards, she's not been deemed sufficiently competitive with other captains and never ranked above the cut-off line."

Lauzier let out a snort of derision.

"I'll bet she stepped on a lot of sensitive toes after the armistice, Admiral. A capable officer such as her doesn't go from hero to zero in such a short time. And having carried off the *Athena* rescue, she's still the same competent, hard-charging naval officer I remember. You will please give Captain Dunmoore and her people my personal thanks. What does the Navy call a well done again?"

"A Bravo Zulu, sir."

"Yes. Thank you. And I would ask that you reconsider the Fleet's questionable decision to deny her the promotion she so clearly deserves."

"Unfortunately, sir, an officer can only be considered by a promotion board so many times, and Captain Dunmoore's last chance was a few weeks ago." A hint of embarrassment crept into Sampaio's tone. "She was deemed uncompetitive against her peers again. Her retirement orders will be cut once she turns the Task Force Luckner ships back to their parent formations."

"I've heard a lot of horse shit in my career, Admiral, but I never expected it from a distinguished officer of your caliber." Lauzier held Sampaio's gaze with cold eyes. "I know neither the SecGen nor the Defense Secretary may intervene in promotion decisions below four-star rank unless they consider them injurious to the Commonwealth's security. But I ask you this once, recall the commodore promotion board, find a vacant billet somewhere or create one, and give Dunmoore her due after what she just carried off. I'm sure the regulations give you enough leeway."

Sampaio remained silent for a few seconds, holding the SecGen's cold eyes, then inclined his head.

"I will reconvene the promotion board, sir, and it may judge her competitiveness in light of her most recent accomplishments. Unfortunately, I cannot do more without compromising the promotion system's integrity."

Lauzier, an old pro at shadow sparring with other influential people, remained silent for just the right amount of time.

"I think that ship sailed long ago, Admiral. Now, onto other matters. How will you tackle the growing criminality spilling over the Protectorate Zone's boundaries and into the Commonwealth at an alarming rate? We can't allow liners to be routinely hijacked by political malcontents, rapacious pirates, or even worse, slavers. And on that note, what about the thirty-six missing VIPs? Some of them are personal friends, and their families — all of them among the greatest in the Commonwealth — will demand we do something."

Lowell raised a hand. "If I may?"

Sampaio made a go-ahead gesture.

"I'm meeting with one of my brightest operations directors, Rear Admiral Kathryn Kowalski, this afternoon to discuss that very question, sir. Kowalski, who served under Dunmoore's command for three years during the war, came up with the Task Force Luckner idea and made it happen in record time."

"Then I owe her my gratitude as well." He turned his eyes on Sampaio. "Please let me know how the promotion board turns out and what this Kowalski suggests to secure the Rim Sector from further troubles. As for making the entire incident and its resolution public, my office will handle it — after the families of the missing are notified. Please make sure no one in the Fleet, especially the personnel of Task Force Luckner, speaks about the matter without authorization."

"Of course, sir."

Lauzier stood, followed by both admirals.

"Thank you for coming. Enjoy the rest of your day."

With that, Sampaio and Lowell came to attention, bowed their heads in a formal gesture, since neither wore a beret, pivoted on their heels, and left.

Once in the staff car, where no one, not even the driver up front, could overhear, Sampaio let out a sigh of frustration.

"How dare he impugn the integrity of the promotion system?"

Lowell let out a bitter chuckle.

"He's not wrong, Ben. If Dunmoore hadn't been blackballed over what she published while serving as a professor at the War College, she'd be sitting in Kathryn Kowalski's chair right now. The promotion board finding Dunmoore uncompetitive with her peers had nothing to do with her abilities as a commanding officer, a tactician, and a naval thinker. She is smarter and more capable than three-quarters of the commodores currently serving, two-thirds of the rear admirals and half of the vice admirals."

Sampaio gave the Chief of Naval Operations a stern look.

"I didn't know you were one of her fans, considering your objection to her appointment as commander of Task Force Luckner."

"Only idiots never change their mind, Ben. The way she handled this has proved me wrong, and I'm big enough to admit it. Though we never said so, we both thought of her as the ideal sacrificial goat if the mission failed. Well, that goat turned out to be a tiger." A brief pause. "No, a wolf. The leader of the pack."

"Ah yes, her encore performance of the wartime tactics that made her feared by the Shrehari if we can believe the after-action report she submitted."

"Now you're being totally unfair. The reason she's still a captain is because of her unflinching commitment to the truth, despite the fact said truth made a lot of us feel lacking in tactical and strategic acumen during the war."

"Good Lord, Zeb, when you change sides, you don't do so halfway."

Zebulon Lowell gave his superior a smug grin.

"My only side is, and has always been, the Navy and its welfare."

"So, you think I should reconvene the commodore's promotion board?"

"I think you should follow your sense of fair play and do what's best for the Navy rather than its querulous and sometimes inadequate flag officers."

Sampaio let out a grunt.

"Listen to us. The two most powerful military commanders in the known galaxy, and we're debating the merits of a mere captain whose best before date was long ago."

"For one thing, the Shrehari Deep Space Fleet commander might dispute your first point, and for another, Dunmoore just proved she's still as good as she was, meaning we haven't reached that theoretical best before date yet. Let me listen to Kathryn's proposal about the damned Zone, and we can discuss Lauzier's wish that you hold a special promotion board." Lowell's grin reappeared. "Which isn't strictly necessary to get the result he wants, as you might recall. And think of the propaganda value when we reward the hero of the Raid on Shrehari Prime for her latest feat while neatly forgetting the intervening years when she was persona non-grata in the flag officers' mess."

"Then we get to enjoy fending off that same flag officers' mess for admitting a persona who is still non-grata," Sampaio growled. "Don't stampede me, Zeb. I'm sure Dunmoore used methods that would see her called on the carpet if she'd used them inside the Commonwealth sphere. I still vividly remember the stunt she pulled on Toboso. It caused quite the uproar around here. Governor Dunmoore, Commonwealth Navy, if you please. She wasn't popular with the Colonial Office back then."

"But she is now, according to Jado's counterintelligence division chief, Holt."

"Yes, and Holt is Dunmoore's man. He was her first officer during the Toboso affair and one of her captains when she wore a star."

Lowell chuckled. "You sure know a lot about Dunmoore, Ben. Should I worry?"

"Worry about the next scheme your wunderkind Kowalski has up her sleeve. We can resume this conversation later."

**

"Grab a seat, Kathryn" Lowell nodded at the chairs facing his desk.

"How did it go with the SecGen, sir?"

"As could be expected. He's happy with the outcome of Task Force Luckner's operation, sends Dunmoore and her people a Bravo Zulu, worries about the missing thirty-six, and expresses his gratitude to you for coming up with the scheme. That being said, he'd like us to step up operations in the Rim Sector and beyond, with particular emphasis on the Zone, so hijackings don't happen again, and we suppress the organized crime menace before it gets out of control. And I believe that's what you're here to discuss."

She nodded. "Yes, sir."

Over the following fifteen minutes, Kowalski outlined her plan for a small battle group that wasn't tied to a specific area or starbase. One whose sole mandate was hunting down and destroying all enemies in what she termed the dirty little wars of peace increasingly bedeviling the Commonwealth's borders.

"In essence, you're saying SOCOM isn't doing the job it should by suppressing hostile activities beyond our sphere."

"Not in the Zone, sir. There's too much going on in too big an area for targeted special ops missions, which is their primary focus nowadays."

"A mix of Q ships and regular units, eh?" Lowell rubbed his chin while he absently gazed at the order of battle Kowalski put up on the primary display. "With resupply, maintenance, rest and recreation, and any other support to be provided by the nearest starbase capable of handling a second battle group."

"Yes, sir. For operations in the Zone, that would be Starbase 30. And we can shift the entire formation or parts of it to other theaters of operation as needed."

"SOCOM will resist losing any Q ships, and it would need taking frigates away from regular battle groups, which means the various fleet commanders will make their unhappiness known. But the SecGen wants solutions and won't be pleased if Navy politics stand in the way. So I'll speak with the Grand Admiral, and if he agrees, we'll discuss it at Armed Forces Council."

"When is AFC's next scheduled meeting?"

"In two months, I believe."

"That won't help the folks taken off *Athena* nor prevent the doers from striking again."

Lowell gave her a shrug. "The Grand Admiral will decide whether we convene early."

"Maybe we can send Dunmoore back into the Zone after *Athena* is safely docked at Starbase 30."

He shook his head.

"No. Task Force Luckner disbands once Dunmoore releases *Athena* into 3rd Fleet's care. But I'm sure Naval Intelligence will keep working with the Colonial Office to track down the missing passengers, and when they do find them, SOCOM can send a few Q ships on a raiding mission." Lowell held her eyes. "Was that it?"

Kowalski hesitated. Something in his gaze told her it would be best if she ended the discussion.

"Yes, sir. Thank you for your time."

**

"How did your presentation to the CNO go?" Holt asked, falling into step beside Kowalski. Both were on their way out of the Fleet HQ main building after another long day.

"He seemed interested but figures it'll need a blessing from the Armed Forces Council."

Holt grimaced. "Ouch. AFC is where good ideas go to die before being resurrected as bad ideas."

She smiled at him as the armored glass doors slid aside to let them out.

"Harsh, but fair. Although Admiral Lowell mentioned the SecGen being rather interested in a solution that could stem the tide of lawlessness spilling over our frontier with the Protectorate Zone. Or words to that effect."

"Did you raise the question of who might best command such a formation?"

Kowalski shook her head. "Something in Lowell's eyes told me it wouldn't be a good idea. And no, I couldn't say why. Perhaps something from his meeting with Sampaio and Lauzier still rankled."

— Twenty-Six —

"There you are, Skipper." Chief Petty Officer First Class Kurt Guthren's solid figure filled the flag CIC door.

Siobhan Dunmoore was sitting in the command chair watching Starbase 30's spindle-like shape on the primary display, alone and lost in her thoughts. She'd said her farewells to the captains, except for Rydzewski, the moment they dropped out at Dordogne's hyperlimit and released them back to their regular duties. *Salamanca* alone was escorting *Athena* for the last bit.

Upon hearing Guthren's voice, she turned the chair around and gave him a wan smile.

"What's up?"

"*Salamanca*'s cox'n was wondering whether you should be piped off the ship once we dock."

Dunmoore shook her head.

"No. I've dissolved the task force, as per orders from Fleet HQ, and am only a passenger now. Passengers don't receive honors unless they wear stars on their collars. Besides, it's not like we went into battle together and came through the flames with kill marks on our ship's hull."

"But you accomplished the mission, sir. What did Sun Tzu say again? Wasn't it something to the effect that the supreme art of war is subduing the enemy without fighting?"

She gave him an amused smile.

"Yes. Although part of me can't help but wonder whether it was a little too easy, but I suppose that's no longer any of my concern." Something on the primary display caught her eye, and she pointed. "Is that what I think it is, Chief?"

He scrutinized the ship slowly coming around Dordogne, trailing Starbase 30.

"It sure is. I'd recognize the Furious Faerie anywhere, Skipper. Those were good times. Want me to see if we can drop by for a quick visit?"

"I don't think her captain would be overly thrilled by a pair of plank owners playing tourist. We'd better stick with our memories of times past."

"If you say so. The other thing I came to tell you is that Starbase 30 gave us the same quarters as before until we catch a ship home. No idea when that might be. I'll see that your dunnage is transferred in good order."

"Thanks, Chief. If we're stuck here for a while, we might as well head planetside and visit the vineyards that make this star system famous." She climbed to her feet and looked around the CIC one last time. "It was fun while it lasted, though."

"Oh, aye, Skipper. That it was." They left the CIC and headed aft to their borrowed cabins. "What'll happen with *Athena*?"

"If I were Oliver Harmel, I'd see that starbase engineering checks her systems out while she's re-provisioning, then I'd send her back to Earth pronto. The people aboard can cause the Navy a lot of grief now that they're out of danger and can safely behave like members of the refined elite again."

"True."

They stopped at the door to Dunmoore's quarters, which opened at her touch. Her packed bags waited in the day cabin, neatly lined up by the desk. Nothing else remained that might indicate her temporary occupation. Shifting from ship to shore and back over the years had become so commonplace for her, she barely gave it a second thought. Yet leaving *Salamanca* felt a little less like routine, probably because this had indeed been her last command.

She could always follow Lena Corto's example — become a mercenary 'commodore' and lead a squadron of sloops hijacking liners or transports under the orders of employers who wielded more power than they should within the Commonwealth's political structure.

"Are you okay, Skipper? You kind of froze there for a moment."

Dunmoore turned to Guthren, still standing in the open doorway.

"Just reflecting on life choices — mine, Lena Corto's, Sara Lauzier's."

"Only one out of those three chose wisely, sir."

She was spared from answering by the public address system, calling all hands to docking stations. Then, with a repressed sigh, she picked up the shoulder bag in which she carried her personal electronics and other small items while Guthren went to his cabin.

By the time Dunmoore reached the main starboard airlock, RED One, save Chief Guthren, were waiting. The latter arrived moments later, followed in short order by Captain Rydzewski and his coxswain.

"Sir, it was a pleasure having you in command of Task Force Luckner and aboard this ship." Rydzewski held out his hand. "My cox'n told me you didn't want departure honors."

"I didn't, Piotr. And it's Siobhan, not sir. I haven't enjoyed myself this much in a long time. That flag CIC is a wonder of modernity. Whoever uses it next is in for a treat."

"Aye."

At that moment, the inner airlock door opened with a sigh, revealing an already open outer door and the docking arm's corridor beyond.

"Permission to leave the ship with RED One, Captain?" Dunmoore asked, raising her hand in salute.

Rydzewski returned the gesture. "Granted. Fair winds and following seas."

Once in the starbase proper, Dunmoore glanced at Pushkin.

"I'll go make my manners with Admiral Harmel. As far as I'm concerned, the entire team is stood down, but until we receive our transportation timetable, no one visits the surface."

"Understood, Captain." A lazy grin appeared. "If you don't mind me saying so, I'm getting a distinct sense of déja vu all over again."

"So am I, but this time we won't be sent on an impromptu mission aboard *Salamanca* to rescue the SecGen's daughter."

"No, I suppose not. But I wouldn't mind a cruise in the Furious Faerie so we can look for the missing thirty-six."

"You and I both, Gregor. You and I both."

**

"*Athena* is at Starbase 30, readying for the trip back to Earth. Task Force Luckner Redux is now only a footnote in the Navy's secret operational history. And Siobhan is cooling her heels, waiting for transport," Rear Admiral Kowalski announced when Commodore Holt's face appeared on her office display.

"A little birdie told me the Grand Admiral called a virtual AFC meeting this morning. Is there any truth to that scurrilous rumor?"

"If I told you there's another rumor circulating that the SecGen asked him about new measures to secure the frontier a day or two ago, would that help?"

Holt gave her a mock-exasperated look.

"Admiral, sir, were you ever counseled on your less amusing character traits?"

"Many times, and for my sins, Admiral Lowell is having me draft the Commonwealth Armed Services Organization Order standing up the 101st Battle Group."

"Oh? Do tell."

"The 101st's primary role will be covert operations along the Commonwealth frontiers to eradicate piracy, organized crime, and other illegal activities through targeted strikes everywhere beyond our sphere except the Shrehari Empire."

"Even in the Zone?"

Kowalski nodded.

"The Empire is already doing that. We merely spent the last decade being holier than thou, no doubt at the behest of certain interests, the sort who encouraged our diplomats to create the Protectorate in the first place."

"Hot damn." Holt pumped his fist. "Finally. And before you ask, I'll set up a direct conduit between the Colonial Office's Intelligence Service and the 101st. Now for the big question. Who takes command?"

"That, believe it or not, is still a subject of debate among the Grand Admiral, the CNO, and the Commander SOCOM, who, by the way, is unhappy the 101st will report to Naval Operations instead of Special Ops, at least initially, during the proof-of-concept cruise. They bandied names about, protégés of one four-star flag officer or another, all of them competent but none suitable for this sort of work — they spent the war in conventional units and never experienced the down and dirty stuff. One name was glaringly ignored, not unsurprisingly."

"Figures. Does that mean you attended AFC?"

Kowalski nodded.

"I briefed on the concept and then listened to the debate in case there were questions. When the subject of the battle group commander came up, they forgot I was still there, albeit virtually. So far, no resolution, but I somehow got the impression the SecGen told Admiral Sampaio that Siobhan deserved her star back. In any case, I put together a battle group crest that you might enjoy."

A new image appeared on the display — an eagle clutching an anti-ship missile in each claw, surrounded by a black band with the inscription "101st Battle Group" and "Audaces Fortuna Juvat" in white.

"Hey! I own one almost exactly like that framed and hanging on my wall, except instead of 101st Battle Group, it says Task Force Luckner."

"That's very much by design, Zeke. My plan is making the 101st into Task Force Luckner's spiritual descendant, a formation that'll eschew conventional tactics."

Holt let out a snort of laughter.

"Will the CNO buy it?"

"Why wouldn't he? Though he hasn't said it in so many words, the SecGen wants a force capable of wiping out non-state actors using tactics many would describe as underhanded, just like the old Luckner of proven worth."

A more sober expression replaced Holt's earlier hilarity.

"Many of the SecGen's friends and financiers won't be happy with that. His daughter neither, I suspect."

She shrugged.

"He just experienced the fright of his life and wants to lash out. Let's take advantage of that while we can. By the time this new battle group is in operation, Lauzier and whoever succeeds him won't dare rein it in, at least not publicly. The optics wouldn't be good in the OutWorlds and colonies, not after his office formally confirmed the hijacking and subsequent rescue by a Navy task force that entered the Protectorate Zone. A lot of folks are already roiled up enough because of ugly insinuations that sovereignist movements supposedly use pirates to further their political goals."

"So… A roving battle group with no fixed address. How do you propose handling command and control? The flag officer in charge and his or her staff will live aboard a starship full-time and handle the complete spectrum of tactical and administrative work from there. And if it's heading into the Zone regularly, you can't really use a Reconquista class cruiser with a flag CIC. Too conspicuous. Besides, the Reconquistas configured as flagships assume half of the second and all the third line battle group staff work on a starbase."

Kowalski gave him a mysterious smile.

"Which is entirely true. So, what solution would you recommend, keeping in mind there's only one that answers your questions?"

When he saw mischief dancing in her eyes, a lazy grin appeared on Holt's face.

"You're turning *Iolanthe* into a flagship, aren't you?"

"She's at Starbase 30 right now for replenishment. Within the next few hours, *Iolanthe*'s captain and the Battle Group 30 commander will receive orders to see her fitted with an additional CIC and office suite modules for the battle group staff. And because there will be no base to administer or many of the other responsibilities line battle groups handle, said staff will be much smaller than you might think. Since part of the 3rd Fleet's material depot is housed inside Starbase 30, with the rest on the surface, they hold everything necessary for the job. Oh, and Starbase 30 itself will be the 101st's home port. It's well placed relative to our wildest frontiers."

"Now *I* want command of it!"

"Sorry, my friend. You're barred from any further duties in space, like every other senior Naval Intelligence officer. It's the price of knowing everyone's deepest secrets."

He put on a crestfallen expression.

"I know, so make sure Siobhan gets it."

"One thing at a time. The 101st Battle Group is officially standing up in two weeks. I have that long to convince the CNO it needs a commander with proven experience fighting nasty little wars."

"If you manage it, keep in mind she'll want two specific people as her flag captain and command chief petty officer. So that means two more out-of-sequence promotions, including one for a certain commander who didn't make the cut on his final promotion board appearance."

"Both are already in the works, Zeke. You're not dealing with an amateur HQ bureaucrat here. I not only know where the skeletons are hidden but how to grease the tracks."

Holt smirked. "What a surprise. Maybe the SecGen will help. Perhaps a kind person could put the idea of Siobhan as commander of the solution he wants in his ear. Know anyone in the administration?"

"Perhaps, but so do you."

— Twenty-Seven —

Pushkin popped his head through the open door to Dunmoore's sitting room, a smile on his face.

"*Iolanthe* is now docked at one of the 3rd Fleet Supply Depot's loading arms, Skipper. Looks like they're taking on more than just the usual replenishment load. Chief Guthren is down there chatting with her cox'n to see if he can arrange a tour for RED One. I understand you're not the sort who wallows in auld lang syne, but I know for sure you'd be more than welcome aboard."

"Who's the captain these days?"

The smile broadened into a satisfied grin.

"Trevane Devall. He just took over."

Dunmoore sat up and put away her reader, surprised at hearing the name of her former gunnery and second officer in *Stingray*, as well as Pushkin's former first officer in *Jan Sobieski*.

"Really? I thought he'd be working in the family firm by now, running for elected office like his favorite uncles. So he stayed in the Service after the war."

"Yes, and he evidently joined the only part of the Navy still engaged in combat operations. He went to Q ships straight after

225

leaving *Jan Sobieski* and worked his way up with success if they gave him the premier covert battlecruiser."

"And passed through the War College after my tenure as Dean of Unconventional Warfare ended. Otherwise, I'd remember. Good on him. Yes, I'll visit the old girl with the rest of you, now that I realize her skipper won't look lovingly at the nearest unpressurized airlock earmarked for importunate old captains. When's the tour?"

"It starts when you and I get to the docking arm. Chief Guthren is already assembling the rest of the team."

Dunmoore tossed her reader aside and stood to slip on her Navy blue shipboard uniform tunic with the four gold stripes and executive loop at the collar.

"Is there anyone else in *Iolanthe* we remember from past glories?"

"No idea. Let's visit her and see who we recognize."

They made their way from the habitation decks to the supply depot levels via several corridors and three different lifts, reminding Dunmoore how massive Starbase 30 was. A city in space, with the amenities, food-growing facilities, and environmental systems to sustain over ten thousand humans comfortably, twice that at a pinch, it gave the resident rear admiral more headaches than commanding two dozen warships.

She and Pushkin found RED One chatting among themselves at the base's end of the docking arm, standing to one side so large containers on antigrav pallets could pass. There was no sign of Chief Guthren, however.

Pushkin raised his communicator to his lips.

"The Skipper and I are here."

Within moments, two figures appeared in the docking arm — Guthren and Trevane Devall. Dunmoore watched them dodge an incoming container driven by one of the supply depot's droids, then the latter raised his hand and waved while beaming.

Devall didn't look much older than the image she carried in her memories, even though she'd last seen him a decade ago. But he seemed to exude more gravitas in both the way he moved and held his head, something that probably came naturally to the scion of an aristocratic family like him.

She waved back, remembering the first time they met when she took command of *Stingray*. It had not been an auspicious beginning, but as with Pushkin, she'd developed genuine affection and respect for Devall after that rocky start.

When they reached her, he held out his hand.

"I'm so glad to see you, Captain."

They shook enthusiastically.

"Likewise, Trevane. By the way, since we're both wearing four stripes, it's Siobhan, okay?"

Another grin, this time tinged with mischief. "Yes, Skipper."

"Congratulations on your promotion and appointment in *Iolanthe*." Dunmoore stepped aside and let Devall greet Pushkin.

As Devall led them to his ship, she asked, "What's with the containers?"

"They're giving us a flag CIC and office space for an admiral's staff. Why that is, no one's told me yet. But, since we're not carrying Marines and their dropships, there's an almost obscene amount of extra room aboard."

Pushkin guffawed.

"*Iolanthe* as flagship once again, this time with a permanent establishment? What are the giant brains at Fleet HQ concocting this time?"

"I don't know whether I should be worried."

Pushkin clapped him on the shoulder.

"That depends on the flag officer you'll be babysitting in due course. The Skipper here was low-maintenance, as you might recall. Sadly, few of them are."

Devall nodded.

"I remember, and I suppose kudos are in order, for another win under Task Force Luckner's banner. Word is you extracted the luxury liner we saw a few days ago from pirate claws deep inside the Zone."

"Yep. The Skipper performed her usual magic. It was a real beauty of a bloodless mission." Pushkin grinned at Dunmoore. "And RED One was there to see her in action. Speaking of which, when is *Iolanthe* due for her next readiness evaluation? Since we're already here and in need of transportation, maybe we could combine the useful with the terrifying?"

Devall let out an amused chuckle.

"Attractive as that offer sounds, I'll decline. We're not due until next year, but I'll put in a special request for your team."

"How is the Furious Faerie these days?" Dunmoore asked as they stopped to let another container pass.

"Showing a little age, like any starship after more than a decade in space, but she's still the most powerful thing in the entire Protectorate Zone." The pride in his tone was evident to everyone present.

After the tour, Devall took the officers to the wardroom, and his cox'n took the chiefs to the chiefs' and petty officers' mess for a little libation and a glance at the commemorative, polished wood planks listing the names of those who were the first to crew *Iolanthe*.

"You're wearing the look of a lost soul on your face, Skipper," Pushkin whispered in Dunmoore's ear as the latter studied the wardroom plank on which her name was engraved at the very top of the list.

She touched it with her fingertips.

"I guess Zeke had this made after I left, just like he had the battle honor 'Shrehari Prime' inscribed on her honors plaque." Dunmoore glanced at him with a wry smile. "She and the other Task Force Luckner ships are the only units in the history of the Commonwealth Armed Forces to earn it, and hopefully, they'll stay the only ones."

Pushkin was saved from answering when Devall walked over, two stemless red wine glasses in hand. He offered one to each.

"My predecessor took a generous consignment of wine from a smuggler who was also carrying illegal substances. Since the Navy discontinued prize money for crews, he figured *Iolanthe*'s people should at least get something out of removing another purveyor of banned substances from Commonwealth shipping lanes. All messes received their due. It's as good as the best vintages grown down below us. The Almighty only knows where in the Zone someone is making wine of this quality."

After retrieving his own glass, Devall raised it in salute.

"To the best skippers I ever served under and without whom I'd never have made it this far in the Navy. In fact, I'd probably be working for my uncle the senator on Earth, wading through political muck twenty-four hours a day, three-hundred-and-sixty-five days a year while he grooms me as his successor."

They took a sip, and Dunmoore smiled. "This *is* good stuff."

"How about I see that a bottle or two is delivered to your quarters? A gift from the ship that will bear your name on her plank for as long as she's in commission."

"Don't ask and give her a chance to refuse," Pushkin said. "You remember how she is. Just do it."

Dunmoore scowled at him. "I'm here, you know."

Both Devall and Pushkin burst out laughing, and the latter said, "Just like old times."

When Dunmoore returned to her quarters, she found a bag with *Iolanthe*'s crest by her door. It contained two bottles of red wine bearing a label featuring the Furious Faerie emblem. She couldn't tell how Devall got the package there ahead of her, but strongly suspected Guthren was somehow involved.

**

Two evenings later, Dunmoore invited Pushkin and Devall to dine with her in the starbase wardroom, a way of reciprocating the latter's hospitality and catching up on the last ten years in a more intimate setting. If Devall was embarrassed at outranking one of his former captains and wearing the same rank as the other, it didn't show. He was as gracious, witty, and generous as always.

After retiring to her quarters, Dunmoore had just settled in for another evening with a book when her communicator chimed.

The Starbase 30 Communications Division had just forwarded an encrypted personal message for her from Fleet HQ. She let out a soft sigh. Orders redeploying RED One would come from Caledonia, which meant these were probably her retirement papers.

Dunmoore activated the communicator's virtual display, decrypted the message, and read it — three times. Then she stood, walked over to the sideboard, and poured herself a large serving of Glen Arcturus, a gift from Oliver Harmel, and swallowed a healthy slug. She reveled in the sensation of whiskey burning down her throat and warming her stomach.

After a minute or so, she called Pushkin and Guthren to her quarters, leaving the door to the sitting room open. They arrived together within moments.

"What's up, Skipper?"

Dunmoore nodded at her communicator on the coffee table. "Message from Fleet HQ. Read it."

"Our retirement orders?"

"Read it."

Pushkin picked up the communicator and tilted it so both he and Guthren could see the virtual display. As they scanned the text, their eyes widened, and they glanced at Dunmoore several times while she poured each of them a glass.

"How…" Pushkin accepted his drink and placed the communicator back on the table.

"Not a clue, Gregor, but our career clocks were reset. No need to create our own mercenary outfit."

Guthren, who, as usual, rolled with the punches, raised his glass.

"I propose a toast to congratulate Rear Admiral Siobhan Dunmoore on her promotion and appointment as Flag Officer Commanding the future 101st Battle Group."

"Hear, hear!"

After a sip, she raised her glass again. "And another toast to Captain Gregor Pushkin, the 101st Battle Group's flag captain, and Command Chief Petty Officer Kurt Guthren, the battle group cox'n."

Once they were seated, she looked at each of them in turn.

"Did you notice they backdated our promotions to the last promotion board sittings?"

Pushkin and Guthren nodded.

"That solves an immediate issue since it makes you senior to Trevane."

"Why would that be an issue?"

"Because I suspect that flag CIC and staff workspace going up inside *Iolanthe* is because of her upcoming role as the 101st Battle Group's flagship."

A light came on in Pushkin's eyes. "Oh. When do we put up our new ranks?"

"If you read the message to the end, you might have noticed that it was an advance warning for us, so we're not caught by surprise when the official announcement is made."

"When will that be?"

Dunmoore shrugged.

"Again, not a clue. Things are happening at Fleet HQ we can't even imagine. The orders creating the 101st Battle Group haven't been issued yet, so I expect they'll come first and our appointments second. I think they will rout official notifications through the office of Admiral Zantas, the 3rd Fleet Flag Officer Commanding, even though I'm guessing the 101st won't be part of his command. And that means until they make the official announcements, we keep this to ourselves. Not even the rest of RED One can find out ahead of time."

— Twenty-Eight —

"The notification should be in her hands by now," Kowalski announced when Holt's face appeared on her office display.

"I'd have loved to see her reaction when she read it."

"You can always ask the next time you see her. After a tour with the 101st, she'll be posted here."

Holt chuckled. "You've become her career manager?"

"As I said several weeks ago, we need Siobhan to help stop the Fleet backsliding into what it was before the war — a political plaything for the SecGen, the Senate, and the big financial interests."

"Hah! But you're happy with Lauzier intervening in Siobhan's favor."

"He didn't so much direct Grand Admiral Sampaio to promote her as suggest it would help polish the Fleet's image if the officer who rescued *Athena* was publicly rewarded in a way that corrects the unjustifiable oversights of the past. The Chief of Armed Forces Public Affairs agreed with Lauzier. But your point is noted, though I'm sure you also make use of means that aren't the purest if it helps advance the Fleet's long-term goals."

"Yes, and that makes both of us hypocrites. I see why you plan on Siobhan joining our swamp-dweller family in two or three years — to keep us honest."

"She'll be a hit with the perfumed princes and princesses who haunt the Palace of the Stars."

"More like a holy terror, but I suppose that's your point. When are the formal orders going out?"

"Later today, addressed to Siobhan directly, with copies for Commander 3rd Fleet and Commander, 30th Battle Group directing them to provide the 101st Battle Group with the necessary support. Those will be the easy ones. Corralling the Q ships assigned to the 101st will take a little longer and separating the conventional ships from their current formations even longer than that. Since Starbase 30 will be the 101st's designated homeport, families of crewmembers will have to move from their current locations to Dordogne, which will take the longest. But Siobhan will head into the Zone so she can find *Athena*'s missing thirty-six the moment the Q ships *Gondolier* and *Thespis* join *Iolanthe*. They're the closest of her units. Let Consul Forenza know so he can canvass his agents for potential targets."

**

The following afternoon, Siobhan Dunmoore's communicator buzzed again, and she touched it absently, eyes on her reader.

"Dunmoore here."

"It's Oliver Harmel, Siobhan. I'm calling to offer my congratulations and felicitations on your promotion and appointment as commander of the Fleet's newest battle group and to assure you I'm thrilled that you'll be operating from Starbase 30."

She smiled to herself at the earnestness in Harmel's voice.

"Thank you, Oliver. We'll try to be undemanding, if not always unobtrusive. How is Admiral Zantas reacting at one of his starbases supporting a battle group that answers directly to Naval Operations?"

"I couldn't say," Harmel replied in a diplomatic tone. "But I'm sure the 101st taking the pressure off his forward battle groups with anti-piracy campaigns won't come amiss. That being said, may I invite you for supper in the wardroom, just us two rear admirals, so we can make the youngsters wonder what happened, say eighteen-hundred?"

"Thank you. I accept with pleasure."

"Make sure you're wearing a pair of shiny new stars on your tunic collar.

"Already purchased. See you then.

"Harmel, out."

Dunmoore immediately called Pushkin and Guthren.

"The orders are now public. Put your tunics with your new rank insignia on and call RED One together in my day room right away."

"Wilco."

Within minutes, her team trickled in, all of them staring at the two silver stars on her collar where they last saw the four gold stripes and executive curl of a post captain.

"Blimey," Chief Petty Officer Cox said, blinking his eyes in an exaggerated fashion, "the rumors were right. The Skipper's turned into an über-Skipper."

When they stood facing Dunmoore in a loose half-circle, Pushkin and Guthren entered and joined her in front of the team.

"Folks, the Fleet in its wisdom has stood up the 101st Battle Group, a permanent formation dedicated to prosecuting piracy and organized crime both in the Rim Sector and the Protectorate Zone. For my sins, they appointed me as its first Flag Officer Commanding, with Gregor as my flag captain and Mister Guthren as battle group command coxswain. *Iolanthe,* which you just visited, will be my flagship, and we three will shift over tomorrow morning. Once the Q ships *Gondolier* and *Thespis* join us, we're heading back into the Zone so we can find the people taken off *Athena* and wipe out the hijackers.

"The battle group will be homeported at Starbase 30, though I report directly to Naval Operations on Earth. There's room on my staff for all of you. Perhaps not everyone will be in billets earmarked for lieutenant commanders and chief petty officers second class, but still. However, this is entirely your choice. I would be proud to keep you on my team, but if you'd rather stay with the Readiness Evaluation Division, I will respect that choice, thank you for serving with me, and wish you the best."

No one spoke for a few moments, then Lieutenant Commander Yun shrugged.

"I'm due for a change of scenery, and we can't possibly spend more time away from home in the 101st than with RED One."

Cox jerked his thumb at Yun.

"What the commander said, Admiral. We can have our stuff on Caledonia packed up and shipped out here. Dordogne's not a bad place to settle."

One after the other, they nodded in agreement, even those with families.

"Then I guess it's unanimous. I'll hoist my flag in *Iolanthe* tomorrow. While she finishes provisioning, you'll each sit with Gregor and help him prepare instructions for the Readiness Evaluation Division so they can organize the move of families and personal effects to Dordogne while we're on patrol. Mister Guthren will see that temporary family quarters are available on 3rd Fleet HQ's base for your spouses and children when they arrive.

"Once Gregor and the Chief organize things, further personnel issues will be handled by my N1. So who volunteers for the job, keeping in mind I'll need all staff positions up to and including N6 filled?" She asked, naming the principal staff functions. N1 stood for personnel and administration, N2 for intelligence, N3 for operations, N4, maintenance and logistics, N5, plans and N6, communications.

"I'll take the N4 job, Admiral," Lieutenant Commander Yun said, raising his hand. "Seems like a natural fit."

Lieutenant Commander Olmos gave his colleague a sideways frown, making Yun shrug. "You snooze, you lose, Rod."

"I'll take N3, sir," Zakaria said quickly before anyone else spoke.

"And I N2," Khanjan added, "along with N6, I suppose."

Dunmoore gave each a nod.

"Which leaves N1 for Commander Olmos. Still want to join my staff, Rodrigo? The N1 job comes with the N5 responsibilities as well."

"You always talked about wanting a change from crawling into environmental filter vats, Rod." Pushkin gave Olmos a grin. "This is the right opportunity at the right time."

"What the heck. Sign me up as N1 and N5, Admiral."

Dunmoore nodded again.

"Thank you. And the chiefs? Will you want to stay with your commanders?"

"That would be great, Admiral," Cox said to silent nods from his colleagues, clearly speaking for them.

"Then we have ourselves a battle group staff. Thank you for trusting me enough to come along on this new adventure. I can't guarantee thrills and chills all the time, but it'll surely be more interesting than serving in a regular battle group. One thing, however. Since we'll be putting together a new formation with ships from various commands, I plan on running my own readiness evaluations, so don't toss away your aide memoires just yet."

As she expected, most of them put on mildly amused smiles at the notion of evaluating starship readiness for their own commander rather than on orders from Fleet HQ. It would make for a totally different dynamic. At that moment, her communicator buzzed again. She reached over and picked it up.

"Dunmoore."

"Trevane Devall, Admiral. I just received the fantastic news. Congratulations! When will you be hoisting your flag in *Iolanthe*?"

"How about eight bells in the morning watch tomorrow? I'll be coming aboard with all ten of my staff. You met them the other day. They belonged, until a few minutes ago, to RED One."

"We'll see that everything is prepared for your arrival, sir. The orders came with a battle group crest design. Shall I ask base supply to run off enough for everyone and have them put on for your arrival?"

"Sure." Frowning, Dunmoore searched her incoming messages file and found the fresh orders, along with the crest decreed for her command. "Well, well, well. That does look rather familiar."

She projected it for her staff's benefit.

"The old Task Force Luckner missile-clutching eagle," Pushkin said in a tone of wonder. "Only the formation name was changed. Someone at Fleet HQ really likes us."

Guthren nodded.

"Yup. We sure as hell got friends in strange places."

"I'll send a dozen patches up tonight for you and your staff, Admiral," Devall said. "If there's nothing else, we'll greet you by the entry port with full honors at eight bells in the morning watch."

"Thank you, Trevane. Dunmoore, out."

That evening, Admirals Harmel and Dunmoore renewed their acquaintanceship as equals in a wardroom where every second set of eyes was studying the latter, wondering what sort of redemption she'd undergone.

**

The following day, shortly before oh-eight-hundred, Dunmoore and her staff marched down the docking arm in perfect formation — she leading, with Pushkin and Guthren three paces behind and to either side of her and the other eight in two columns another three paces back. Everyone wore the black and white battle group crest on their shipboard tunic's right shoulder.

An honor guard stood at the far end of the docking arm along with the bosun and a half dozen mates holding silver calls in their hands. Captain Devall, standing in the center of the arm, snapped to attention as Dunmoore approached. She saw that everyone wore the new-old 101st Battle Group crest as well.

"101st Battle Group arriving."

The moment Dunmoore halted in front of Devall, the guard commander, *Iolanthe*'s second officer, called out, "To the Flag Officer Commanding, Rear Admiral Siobhan Dunmoore, present ARMS."

The spacers' hands slapped their carbines' stocks, the bosun's whistles trilled, and Devall raised his hand in a precise parade ground salute. Behind him, a small bundle hanging from the top of a temporary flag post broke open to reveal a rear admiral's flag — a white rectangle with the Navy's starburst and anchor on a blue background in the canton and two silver stars in the middle.

Dunmoore returned the salute and held it until the whistles fell silent. Then, the honor guard was placed at the shoulder arms position, and Devall invited her to inspect them. All the while, Pushkin, Guthren, and the staff remained at attention in the docking arm, watching a ceremonial that dated back to the age of sail, long before humanity left its homeworld for the stars, vaguely aware they might be witnessing history in the making.

— Twenty-Nine —

After the inspection, Devall led Dunmoore into *Iolanthe,* and once the honor guard was dismissed, her staff followed them.

They stopped at what Dunmoore remembered as the door to the VIP suite, which now bore the inscription 'Flag Officer Commanding - RAdm S. Dunmoore.' It opened at her touch, and for a moment, she was transported back in time. Little had changed in what was once hers as commodore. Her bags sat in a neat row in the middle of the day cabin, delivered while she was at breakfast.

"Gregor's is next door — same configuration as yours, just a tad smaller. Chief Guthren's is next to his, again, the same configuration, but smaller. Your staff gets suitable single occupant cabins in the officer and chief petty officer sections. Want to unpack now or visit your CIC?"

"The CIC, please. I have little with me to unpack, not even a rear admiral's service uniform and accouterments, let alone a mess uniform."

"What about your antique clock?"

"It'll be on its way from Caledonia with the rest of my personal possessions once Gregor sends a message to our former outfit, but it won't arrive before we leave on our first cruise." She gestured at the open door. "Shall we?"

"Certainly." Devall took her aft, toward the cavernous midship hangar compartment behind which lay the Marine barracks but stopped at what she remembered as flex space her crew used for extra storage. "We couldn't manage a set up like *Salamanca*'s, with a common conference room separating the ship's CIC with that of the flag, but we're still on the same deck, and you're still within *Iolanthe*'s armored core."

At his touch, the door opened, and Dunmoore entered a space almost identical to the one she'd occupied a short time before in the Reconquista class cruiser, including the same model of command chair occupying its center.

"Nice."

"The supply depot techs did a bang-up job. You have direct and independent access to *Iolanthe*'s sensor feeds, communications array, computer core, databases, and navigation plot. If necessary, such as problems with the gunnery stations in both my CIC and the bridge, you can take control of her combat systems as well."

"Slick."

"That's the beauty of building her from scratch according to the same modular standards as the Voivodes and Reconquistas instead of pressing a merchant ship into service and up-arming it — the 3rd Fleet supply depot carried the required parts in stock. Too bad she's the only one in her class."

"I understand lighter Q ships are in the pipeline though, based on the Voivode class frigate hull. But the speed at which procurement moves nowadays, you and I will be long gone from this business when they're commissioned. Still, the current transports turned Q ships carry a hefty broadside compared to what the bad guys in the Zone and elsewhere use. Nothing beats reconfigured cargo holds stuffed with modular missile launchers for saturation salvos. Between them, *Gondolier* and *Thespis*, who we'll join in a few days, can outshoot *Iolanthe*."

Devall grinned at her. "Now there's a terrifying thought."

"Ah! Nice," Pushkin's voice said from the CIC door. "It gives me yet another eerie bit of déja vu."

"This is basically a Reconquista class flag CIC just like the one in *Salamanca*."

"Then we should feel right at home." Pushkin and the rest of her staff, Guthren included, filed in and wandered around before stopping at familiar-looking workstations.

"Since we're all here, please put out a call to *Gondolier* and *Thespis*. They should have received orders making them part of the 101st and dispatching them to Starbase 30. If they're carrying wartime loads and are provisioned for at least two months in deep space, then I'd rather we rendezvous just short of the Protectorate Zone. No point in putting on extra light-years."

"Will do, Admiral," Pushkin replied. "Any part of the frontier you prefer?"

"What was the most visited port in Drex's log? Abaddon?"

He nodded. "That would be the place — much deeper in the Zone."

"Make it our provisional target until we hear from the Colonial Office." When Devall gave her a strange look, she explained how its intelligence network in the Zone helped recover *Athena*. "I expect we'll be fostering a close relationship between the 101st

and the Colonial Office's network thanks to whoever at Fleet HQ is schmoozing with the head of its Intelligence Service. Right now, our aim is finding those taken off *Athena* and terminating the organization that hijacked her with extreme prejudice."

**

"Siobhan's taken command," Rear Admiral Kowalski announced when Commodore Holt entered her office. "I received a copy of the video made by 3rd Fleet Public Affairs of her flag being hoisted in *Iolanthe*. Want to watch?"

"Of course. I saw her broad pennant lowered in *Iolanthe* back when she stepped down, and this is vindication, even if it doesn't quite make up for the wasted years." He took a chair and turned it to face the primary display. "It should be immensely satisfying."

"Oh, it is. As are the sour faces around HQ. Those attached to the toes she stepped on still haven't forgiven her biting essays about wartime mistakes that prolonged the conflict. You can bet they'll do everything possible to make sure she doesn't receive any high profile assignments once her tour of command is over, let alone a third star."

They watched the brief ceremony in silence, then Holt said, "That was nice. Devall did her proud."

"He did that. Anything new from the SecGen's office on the *Athena* matter?"

"No, though I don't doubt strong words will be exchanged between Lauzier senior and his heir once she's back on Earth, thanks to vague rumors — planted, of course — insinuating the disappearance of the thirty-six conveniently helps Sara's rising ambitions. And I understand the SSB is in a minor uproar at the Navy not only stealing its thunder but finding *Athena* so quickly. There might also be a mole hunt in the offing since other vague rumors hint at the Navy reading the SSB's most private mail. It would explain how we knew we'd find the purloined starship in the Galadiman system."

Kowalski gave him a broad grin.

"Confusion to the enemy — my favorite toast."

He smiled back.

"Disinformation campaigns are among our many jobs, and we do them well. The next steps will be increasingly delicate, however. Sara Lauzier must be led to believe we know what happened, even if you and I aren't entirely sure — yet. Otherwise, as she becomes more powerful, she could present a clear and present danger because of a growing sense of impunity. Her father is probably a highly functioning psychopath, like so many powerful politicians and financiers. But Sara might well prove a real sociopathic piece of work who could precipitate a new civil war if we're right, and she engineered *Athena*'s hijacking for political purposes."

"It's a sad state of affairs when the Fleet is forced to keep dangerous politicians in check."

Holt shrugged.

"The Special Security Bureau won't do so because it uses dangerous politicians or allows itself to be used by them in pursuit of more power. Without a proper federal police force, who's left? Us, and not even all of us, because there are plenty of high-ranking people wearing a uniform who'll prostitute themselves in return for wealth, power, and influence. Let's hope Siobhan's next expedition into the Zone gives us actionable intelligence so we can rope in the delightful Sara Lauzier before she makes more political enemies conveniently vanish at the hands of unidentified pirates while giving colonial independence ambitions the kiss of death."

"If we're right."

He nodded.

"If. But I can feel it in my bones, Kathryn. Before the Navy let me return to space in *Iolanthe*, I was doing this sort of thing when they beached me after the loss of *Shenzen*. And I went back to it after leaving *Iolanthe*. The only difference between the corrupt admirals I investigated then and the corrupt politicians we're looking at now is a matter of scale, both in venality and evil influence. Trust me when I say this. Sara Lauzier is into something that could get her a life sentence on Parth if she were anyone other than the SecGen's favored eldest daughter and heir."

"Fair enough. But it still shouldn't be a naval officer's job. Instead, the Commonwealth needs a true federal police, one with a professional standards branch that investigates malfeasance and corruption across the federal government, politicians included, police forces, and the Fleet."

"No arguments here, but good luck getting the Senate to vote for its creation, let alone a SecGen signing off on the enabling legislation. So many people in this city would find themselves in the crosshairs of your professional standards branch, and they can't allow that to happen."

Kowalski gave him her sweet smile.

"Where there's a will and all that, Zeke. First, we need a core of flag officers with the same vision making their way to the top. You, me, a few others, and Siobhan Dunmoore because we need a fearless, damn the torpedoes type who'll stiffen backbones and terrify the opposition."

**

With their armament hidden, the Q ships *Thespis* and *Gondolier* looked like innocuous, rather worn out bulk carriers in need of maintenance, the sort plying star lanes across the known galaxy. Though smaller than *Iolanthe*, one of the largest warships in the Fleet, they made Voivode class frigates look like corvettes.

Of different designs, both started life as armed commercial ships but were taken into the Fleet during the war. They emerged from their sojourn in a Caledonia shipyard with heavier guns, stronger shields, upgraded reactors and drives, complete combat system control suites, and cargo holds turned into missile launchers capable of overwhelming salvos. Their only true weakness compared to purpose-built warships lay in more lightly armored hulls.

Dunmoore was pleasantly surprised to see a third Q ship, the much smaller *Pinafore*, at the rendezvous along with her larger sisters. A pirate captured during the war, she'd been bought into the Navy and refurbished, though her chief strength lay in her speed, agility, and, like the others, cargo holds filled with modular missile launchers.

"We must have received our orders just after you went FTL at Dordogne's heliopause, Admiral," Lieutenant Commander

Johan Darrell, *Pinafore*'s skipper, said. "Since we were in the general neighborhood, we booted the drives to eleven and arrived here a few hours ago."

"Are you good for a two-month cruise?"

Darrell, a dark-complexioned man in his late thirties with hawk-like features, hooded brown eyes, and short black hair nodded.

"We are, Admiral. And carrying a full wartime load. We haven't fired a shot in anger since our last resupply."

"Excellent. Glad you're with us."

Thespis' captain had been another pleasant surprise — Commander Thorin Sirico, her former combat systems officer in *Iolanthe*, still as piratically debonair as before, though with a few strands of silver in his mustache and goatee.

"I missed your class at the War College by one semester," he'd said the moment they made radio contact. "You left for the Readiness Evaluation Division just as I arrived."

"And how were the irregular warfare classes?"

Sirico had given her a sly grin. "I spent a lot of time running the seminars, Admiral. My course report made a special mention of it, recommending I return as an instructor after my tour of starship command."

"And would you want to do so?"

"Perish the thought."

Dunmoore had never met her third Q ship captain, Commander Adele Leung of *Gondolier*. She was in her early forties with a lean, narrow face, short dark hair, and watchful eyes. But she gave the impression of calm competence. The Fleet would not appoint questionable officers in Q ships — the consequences of a mistake in peacetime could be much worse than most of what a regular warship captain might experience.

"I'm sure you're impatient to find out about our first target. You've heard of the *Athena* hijacking by now, correct?" All three, who'd joined Dunmoore, Devall, and Pushkin in the flag conference room via holographic projection, nodded. "What the official story has so far omitted is that I led the task force which brought *Athena* home. When we reached her, thirty-six of the Commonwealth's leading citizens had been taken off by the abductors aboard three Arkanna-built sloops of human design who fled the moment we appeared at Galadiman's hyperlimit. Our mission is finding those thirty-six and terminate the abductors who belong to a criminal organization made up of Fleet veterans calling themselves the Confederacy of the Howling Stars."

— Thirty —

Dunmoore recounted the Task Force Luckner Redux expedition, what they'd discovered in Drex's computer core and what they learned from the Colonial Office. Her captains' surprise that it had a network of agents and subspace relays was evident. She finished with her suspicions about who led the mercenary squadron.

"We'll begin by visiting the Abaddon system, which, according to the navigation logs of *Vuko*, the Howler ship we boarded, is one of their primary transportation nodes. But before leaving this rendezvous, we'll attempt to contact the Colonial Office consul on Kilia for updates. Lieutenant Commander Khanjan, the battle group's N6, is already working on it."

"Attar Khanjan?" Leung asked with a slight air of surprise.

"Yes? You know him?"

"We served together in *Belisarius* during the war."

"Then you'll be able to renew your acquaintanceship in due course. He also wears the N2 hat and will handle intelligence briefings." When Leung nodded, Dunmoore let her eyes roam around the table. "Once the Colonial Office gives us an update on conditions in the Zone, you'll receive a navigation plot from the flag CIC, and we'll be off. I've been given plenty of latitude in dealing with the Howlers and other criminals we might encounter. And since Commonwealth law doesn't apply in the Zone, I can take whatever actions I deem necessary, provided they're congruent with the Laws of War and the Universal Code of Military Justice. Any questions?"

Contrary to the captains she led on her previous mission, Dunmoore saw nothing less than eagerness in their eyes. Of course, this sort of operation was a Q ship's reason for being, and they'd been in the Zone before, hunting as undercover naval vessels. But it was a double-edged assignment.

While Q ship personnel were almost the only ones facing actual combat nowadays, their missions were classified to the extent that promotions boards wouldn't be aware of details. Thus, they might discount such service as not being a plus compared with those who've never fired a shot in anger since the war and operated under a flag officer's gimlet eyes instead of a distant SOCOM HQ's distracted gaze.

"Will we operate as Navy units or under assumed identities, and what about uniforms?" Devall asked.

"No transponders from the moment we go FTL across the boundary, masking in place, but personnel in uniform unless I say otherwise. I'll take care of any interaction with outsiders if it proves necessary. Captains Devall and Sirico know my methods from firsthand experience. I enjoy creeping up on a target, waving a false flag if necessary, before we strike without warning."

"Oo-rah, Admiral!" Devall pumped his fist in the air at hearing her quote *Iolanthe*'s motto.

She smiled at him. "I figured you might like that. Any other question?"

When they shook their heads in turn, Dunmoore said, "Thank you. Stand by for orders, and welcome to the 101st Battle Group, where fortune favors the bold."

As the holograms vanished, Pushkin, Devall, and Guthren gave her broad grins.

"What?"

"You quoted two mottoes with wartime credentials in the space of ninety seconds," Dunmoore's flag captain said. "I'd say that sets the right tone for the 101st. And you finally got your fondest wish from ten years ago — a squadron of Q ships."

"Let's not turn sentimental." Dunmoore stood. "That was then. This is now. We're hunting rogue members of our own species, not the Shrehari, and humans can be notoriously devious."

When they entered the flag CIC, Lieutenant Commander Khanjan glanced over his shoulder.

"Admiral, we received an intelligence packet from Kilia Station on the Colonial Office net, encrypted, for your eyes only."

"Excellent. Route it to my command chair."

Less than a minute later, she read Forenza's missive on her virtual display, and it confirmed her instincts. Abaddon was the Howlers' true hub, and his agent there spotted more than the usual traffic to and from their planetside lair in the weeks following her recovery of *Athena*.

"I understand you and *Gondolier*'s skipper served together in *Belisarius* during the war, Attar."

"Aye, Admiral."

Did she detect a faint hint of hesitation in his tone?

"Just between my staff and I, is there anything I should be aware of?"

Khanjan shook his head without turning around.

"Nothing worthy of note, sir. She was a solid officer then, though we weren't exactly close. You know how it is. She had her circle of friends and I had mine."

"Understood. Let's send sailing orders for Abaddon out to the battle group. As soon as everyone is synced, execute."

"Aye, aye, Admiral."

**

"Hey, Zeke." Kowalski stopped to let Holt catch up with her on the way to the transit station shortly before the sun was due to kiss the tops of the Jura Mountains boxing in Greater Geneva to the northwest.

"Sorry, I didn't call or visit for a chat in the last few days. Lots happening in my world." He looked around to make sure no indiscreet ears hovered within listening distance. "You heard *Athena* docked upstairs and disgorged her entitled and overly pampered guests."

"Yes."

"Apparently, Sara Lauzier wasn't happy with her father pressuring the Fleet to promote Siobhan for her actions."

"Could she be annoyed because the Navy rescued *Athena* rather than the SSB's tame mercenaries?"

"In part, I suppose. But I think it's more a matter of timing. Perhaps not all those she wanted gone were taken off, and it's possible something else was supposed to happen before the rescue."

Kowalski gave him a curious look. "Such as?"

He shrugged as they resumed walking.

"An incident to further discredit sovereignist movements in the Rim Sector? Another hijacking or kidnapping? A political assassination? At this point, we should consider Sara Lauzier capable of anything in furtherance of her ambitions. She wants the SecGen's job, and she wants it right after her father's successor finishes his or her first term in office."

"Ooh, she's ambitious, no question." Kowalski grimaced. "Sara wants to parlay six years as a senator — I won't say provided she's elected, because that'll happen, no matter what — into the Senate making her SecGen?"

"That's what we hear. I'd say the disappearance of several potential opponents who traveled in *Athena* with her just made the goal more attainable, and she can buy a lot of support from core world senators by espousing a hard line against colonial independence. Plus, there's the whole knowing where the bodies are buried advantage after working closely with the sitting SecGen for almost twelve years. That being said, I sure as hell hope Siobhan's promotion to rear admiral is substantive and can't be undone by anything short of a court-martial."

Kowalski shook her head.

"No fear. Because she held a wartime formation command as a commodore and earned her task force a battle honor in the bargain, she qualified for substantive flag rank and only needed the board's blessing for an out-of-sequence promotion. Sara Lauzier can't do a damn thing about it, even though I wouldn't be surprised if she tried. She enjoys a reputation for vindictiveness."

Holt allowed himself a mild chuckle.

"Imagine her finding out Siobhan's heading deep into the Zone with four Q ships, intent on recovering the missing thirty-six and teaching this Confederacy of the Howling Stars a profound object lesson."

"How about we make sure Sara doesn't? All it takes is her speaking with papa, and we receive recall orders from the Palace of the Stars."

"Ah." He raised a finger. "But is he aware we're using the Colonial Office's clandestine subspace relay network to speak with her? Does he even know about the network? From what I gathered, the Office's Intelligence Service trusts politicians as little as we do and keeps such a low profile that most people at the senior levels of government don't even realize it exists. At this point, the 101st is beyond recall as far as everyone can tell, save for those of us read into the relevant top secret special access codename. But please tell me the CNO hasn't briefed the Grand Admiral, or if he has, that Sampaio hasn't briefed the SecGen on this little expedition."

"Sampaio knows, and he's not telling Lauzier *père*. This is the sort of mission where politicians prefer plausible deniability, so they can appear shocked when word leaks out and immediately chastise a Fleet that looks as if it's turned rogue. But you didn't expect any different, now did you? The Grand Admiral needs to know."

"If I told you the CNI doesn't brief Sampaio on every underhanded thing his people do — and some of them would outrage the average citizen, let alone our esteem senators — would you be shocked?"

She shook her head.

"Of course not. The Grand Admiral needs just as much plausible deniability as the SecGen when it comes to you secret squirrels stashing your illicit nuts. I think Sampaio might not even want to hear the details of Siobhan's wild ride through the Zone, just in case."

**

Once more a passenger in her own flagship while the 101st was in hyperspace, Dunmoore whiled away the hours and days by playing round-robin chess with Pushkin, Devall, and those on the staff brave enough to face her, by reading, and by running simulations for both her people and the flagship's crew.

"Did you ever figure we'd end up almost back where we started, Admiral?" Pushkin asked as he set up the board on Dunmoore's day cabin dining table. "Us playing chess on our way to a fight. You the commanding officer, me your right hand."

"I tried hard not to figure anything in the last five years, Gregor, ever since I understood the toes I stepped on while at the War College were connected to vindictive personalities who felt no compunction about making promotion boards down-rate me."

"It probably didn't help that you were entirely correct in your dissection of why the war dragged on so long."

She gave him a wry smile.

"There's no probably about it. But I suffered from delusions of grandeur. After all, I came up with and led the raid on Shrehari Prime, a tactical maneuver with strategic consequences. Since it resulted in Brakal suing for peace, I thought myself untouchable because I dealt with facts. You understand what that was, right?"

Pushkin nodded.

"Hubris."

"Which, inevitably, led to Nemesis. The ancient Greeks were right about so many things concerning human weaknesses and the consequences thereof."

"But the timeline reset itself before any damage became irreversible, thank the Almighty."

"Considering the circumstances that led us to be aboard this ship at this time, wearing brand spanking new rank insignia, I might as well do so even if I'm not a believer in God, let alone predestination."

He gave her a sly wink.

"Call it luck, then. You were well known for making your own luck during the war, and as with so many of us, peacetime left you at loose ends. The circumstances surrounding *Athena's* hijacking triggered the right chain of events, and your luck returned from wherever it was hiding." He held up both hands, fists clenched. "Your pick."

When she pointed at his right hand, he unclenched it, showing a white pawn.

"Let's see if my luck is sufficient to continue the winning streak I'm on."

— Thirty-One —

"I can think of better things to do with my Saturday evening," Commodore Ezekiel Holt muttered as he and Rear Admiral Kathryn Kowalski climbed out of the self-driving staff car she'd arranged for the ride to the Palace of the Stars' Assembly Hall.

Both were resplendent in gold-trimmed, dark blue Navy mess uniforms with miniature medals on the left breast and gold braid stripes denoting rank on their tunic cuffs — a broad one with the executive loop on top for him, a broad and a narrow one, the latter with the executive curl for her. The Palace, illuminated by countless floodlights, shone like a beacon in the Geneva night beneath a cloudless sky.

"It's not like we have a choice, Zeke. The SecGen specifically asked that the flag officers who dreamed up the *Athena* rescue scheme attend his annual Armed Forces Gala. So put on your best smile and use the time to hone your observation skills. There will be a test Monday morning."

He gave her a quick smirk. "I'm the one who tests people around here, remember?"

Armed sentries from the Terra Regiment, stationed on either side of the Hall's main entrance, presented arms at their approach. As the senior of the two, Kowalski nodded formally in return since neither wore a headdress. Such items often went walkabout in the coatroom at events attended by hundreds of officers, if only by accident, and weren't strictly necessary with mess uniform.

In the lobby, they joined a throng of Navy, Marine Corps, and Army officers making their way up the stairs to the *Salle des Pas Perdus*, an imposing, high-ceilinged gallery. Situated at the heart of the Palace and overlooking the stately Court of Honour around which its main structure was built in the early twentieth-century, not long after World War One, it seemed as ageless as it was venerable.

"I'm always grimly amused by the fact that this place was erected over five hundred years ago to help prevent another murderous war," Holt said in a tone pitched for Kowalski's ears only. "Yet here we are, a species that can't stop fighting among itself unless another species invades, and we'll likely see another dustup in our lifetimes at this rate, perhaps even before you and I retire."

"Something we will try hard to avoid."

Mercifully, the gala didn't feature a reception line, and both made their way to where white-jacketed bartenders handed out champagne flutes filled with the real thing and not some downmarket sparkling wine. Drinks in hand, Kowalski and Holt wandered over to a corner from which they could observe the mass of mess uniform-clad martial brilliance sprinkled with the more sober evening clothes of senators, top government officials, and influential people from the world of commerce, finance, and industry.

Holt nodded at a vice admiral hanging on to every word from ComCorp's Vice President for Government Relations, another member of the Amali clan.

"Even though I should have known better from my time in counterintelligence during the war, I'm still amazed at how many of our fellow flag officers will knowingly or unknowingly sell their souls in exchange for joining the rarefied circles of the elite. That's Guy Olonga speaking with Cristof Amali."

"One of the deputy chiefs in the Procurement Branch. I recognize him. I heard he's a real operator, that one."

"Oh, he's gone beyond mere operator by now. There's a reason Olonga seems so chummy with Cristof. Favoring ComCorp for certain lucrative naval supply contracts gets him a glimpse into the inner circle of those who really run things. But only a glimpse, though he hasn't realized it, not an entry. And yet, he sold his soul for that imaginary ticket. You might be shocked at how many souls are bought and sold during events such as this. Since the end of the war, Fleet HQ has nurtured a growing number of senior officers seeking favor with the powerful and influential, for promotions, for remunerative jobs after retirement, and to become one of the anointed."

Holt took a sip and waved his glass at the crowd.

"Yet few, if any, understand they'll never join the Amalis and the Lauziers and the others who rule the Commonwealth, elites who see obsequious flag officers as tools, to be discarded once their usefulness is exhausted."

"I'm neither shocked nor particularly surprised, Zeke. You're merely confirming what I already suspected or knew."

"At least those at the very top seem to have stopped short of selling out. Sampaio, Lowell, Doxiadis, Espinoza, just to name a few, are as clean as they come. But keep an eye on those who seem overly comfortable or deferential with private sector nabobs tonight. They'll be the ones looking for that golden ticket, and there's enough of them to spread rot at the heart of the Fleet."

Kowalski turned her head and studied him for a few moments.

"You know, I never did ask precisely what sort of work your division did for the CNI, yet I'm beginning to suspect you're our version of internal affairs."

Holt winked at her.

"You may well think so, but I couldn't possibly say. However, if you want to stop this nonsense, get Fleet HQ away from Earth and put it in an environment where interactions with the Amalis and Lauziers of the galaxy can be strictly controlled. Most of our colleagues who step over the line wouldn't do so absent temptations dangled before their eyes and opportunities to act on them. And here comes Admiral Lowell, wondering why we haven't made our manners with the SecGen yet."

Kowalski looked in the same direction as Holt and saw Grand Admiral Sampaio standing with Charles and Sara Lauzier near the center of the gallery, watching them through the space created by Lowell as people moved out of his way. When Holt and Kowalski met his gaze, Lowell slowed his pace. He made a come here gesture, which they obeyed with alacrity, handing their almost empty champagne flutes to a passing attendant.

"Flag officers who aren't mingling stand out from the crowd," Lowell growled in a soft voice when they were within discrete earshot. "And Secretary General Lauzier is wondering why you're playing wallflower in dark corners instead of introducing yourselves."

"Sorry, sir," Kowalski replied. "We were merely getting the lay of the land. This is a first for both of us."

"If you intend to climb further up the ranks, it won't be the last by a long shot. Now smile and pretend you're enjoying this."

"Oh, I am, sir." Holt gave Lowell a lazy grin. "People-watching in this setting is like catnip for a counterintelligence officer."

Conscious that the eyes of the three most powerful people in the Commonwealth government, albeit one of them unofficially, were on them, Kowalski and Holt came to a precise halt and bowed their heads instead of a salute.

Grand Admiral Sampaio gestured at them.

"May I present Rear Admiral Kathryn Kowalski and Commodore Ezekiel Holt, the architects of *Athena*'s rescue? Admiral Kowalski is one of Admiral Lowell's operations directors while Commodore Holt works for the Chief of Naval Intelligence."

Charles Lauzier stuck out his hand and shook with each in turn.

"I offer you my gratitude for helping retrieve Sara and her fellow passengers."

Sara Lauzier acknowledged them with a regal nod.

"So, you're the ones who put Dunmoore on our trail. Well done."

Both Holt and Kowalski noticed Lauzier didn't use their rescuer's new rank and figured it was deliberate.

"How did you put the mission together in such a short time?" She asked, flinty eyes boring into Kowalski's. For reasons she couldn't understand at that moment, the latter knew for sure Sara

Lauzier engineered the hijacking and possessed nothing that anyone with religious inclinations might deem a soul.

"We can't claim much by way of genius, Madame. The conditions were right for a speedy launch. *Athena*'s captain got out a distress signal with images of the hijackers before he was seized. It was picked up by 3rd Fleet and sent to HQ within minutes. That gave us a trail. Admiral Dunmoore had just completed a readiness evaluation on a new cruiser outfitted as a flagship. Both were at Starbase 30, in the right general area for operations in the Zone. Since she knows that part of the galaxy and its less savory denizens best among the senior officers available, she was the natural choice to head the rescue. The rapidity with which Admiral Dunmoore tracked you and the others down proved she was the right choice."

"I see." Sara Lauzier turned her basilisk gaze on Holt.

"And what was your role in this matter?"

"My people provided Admiral Kowalski and Admiral Dunmoore information that allowed Task Force Luckner to proceed with rapidity and precision, Madame." Holt held her flinty eyes and came to the same conclusions as his friend and colleague.

"Earning Dunmoore a two-step promotion in the bargain and, as I understand it, a battle group command."

"Yes, Madame," Lowell said. "The 101st, whose primary role is dealing with the piracy problems spilling out of the Protectorate Zone and threatening our shipping, as you experienced firsthand."

Holt and Kowalski exchanged looks so brief anyone else wouldn't have noticed. But Sara Lauzier did. She fixed first one, then the other with her stare before turning back to Lowell.

"And what is Dunmoore's current mission?"

"Just that, Madame. Seeking out and eliminating any hint of piracy coming from the Zone."

"That's it? Why create a new battle group when existing ones could do the job just as well." Sara Lauzier's tone made it clear she didn't believe the Chief of Naval Operations for a single second.

Charles Lauzier laid his hand on her arm.

"Let's not spoil the evening by debating tactics, my dear. Clearly, Admiral Kowalski and Commodore Holt know their business, which is why you're here, with us, celebrating our Armed Forces instead of worrying whether you're next on the pirates' kill list."

Sara inclined her head with what Kowalski interpreted as forced graciousness.

"Of course, father."

"It was a pleasure meeting you, Admiral, and you, Commodore. Once again, you have my unending thanks for acting so quickly and decisively."

"Sir." Holt and Kowalski briefly came to attention, knowing they'd been dismissed.

"Enjoy the rest of your evening," Grand Admiral Sampaio said, smiling.

"Thank you, sir," Kowalski replied. "With your permission?"

"Carry on."

She led Holt in the direction of the champagne table, sailing through the crowd like a battleship at a naval review. Once they were out of earshot, she glanced at him and spoke in a low tone.

"For some reason, I need to wash a foul taste from my mouth, Zeke."

"Me as well, but that's what gratefulness from those who'd rather not owe anyone gets you."

Kowalski gave Holt a wry smile.

"Like most in this room?"

"Perhaps not most, but many. Of course, in this case, there's probably more than just the uncomfortable gratitude of the elites involved."

"Oh, there's no probably about it, Zeke." She picked up a pair of champagne flutes, handed him one, and raised hers. "Our continued health and that of Siobhan."

— Thirty-Two —

He eyed her while taking a sip, then asked, "Do you think we might fall victim to the unexpected?"

"If like the Mikado after who they named one of our Q ships, she has a little list, then you, me, and Siobhan are on it, along with the people who weren't taken off before the pirates skedaddled. I could see it in her eyes, Zeke, and I'll bet she knows we know. Trust me on this — my finely tuned psychopath detectors don't lie, not after spending all this time at Fleet HQ watching political games."

Holt let out a low chuckle.

"Since I got the same impression as you — not because of psychopath detectors, but because I know her sort — I'd say she and we are now firmly on opposing sides. But I doubt she'll do anything rash. At this point, the sooner everything is forgotten, the better for her."

They fell silent as a vice admiral with what Kowalski privately called a resting jackass face, one that seemed constantly twisted into an unattractive sneer, picked up a champagne flute, then walked over to where they stood.

"Hobnobbing with the top bosses, eh, Holt?" His voice was deep, yet she detected a faintly whiny undertone at odds with his ruddy, rough-hewn features. He glanced at her. "You must be Kowalski, Admiral Lowell's latest prodigy."

"I am, sir."

"Well, don't let shaking the SecGen's hand get to your heads. It won't help with promotion prospects, not that you seem to have problems in that area, Kowalski. I never saw such a young rear admiral as an operations director. The magic of friends in the right places." He turned his gaze on Holt again and studied him through eyes dripping with contempt. "Though I daresay you're in the right niche if several ranks above where you should be."

The man walked away without another word, plowing through the crowd as he made a beeline for one of the private sector nabobs.

"What the hell was that about?" Kowalski asked.

"I suspect a little bird told Vice Admiral Vinq we're looking into his private peccadilloes, and he feels a tad threatened. By the way, I arranged for that little bird, in case you're wondering. Another minor act of psychological warfare against one of our lesser lights."

"So that he overreaches and puts himself in your crosshairs?"

"He's already in our crosshairs. You see, Vinq is the sort who likes cavorting in his birthday suit with partners of barely legal age, though with some, you couldn't tell. He's married and has four children, by the way. That makes him highly susceptible to influence, if not outright pressure. So far, he's done nothing warranting career consequences, let alone arrest, but his proclivities present a threat. I'd rather he stops so we can focus on those who are breaking the law, but that bird chatter has had no other result than cause him to treat me with barely veiled malice." Holt took another sip of his champagne. "I suspect he's also consumed one too many of these already, and he knows I was Siobhan's first officer and then the captain of her flagship and that I remain her friend."

A light came on in Kowalski's eyes.

"Of course. I'd forgotten. Though Siobhan didn't mention any names in her study on the willingness to take risks during the war and the length of the stalemate, I recall hearing rumors Vinq felt personally attacked."

Holt nodded.

"That's the man. He developed a deep hatred for her because, once again, she was entirely right. Vinq was more concerned about damage to his battle group's ships — and thereby his career — than energetically pursuing the enemy. And as one of the deputy chiefs of personnel, he had the necessary influence to kill her chances of promotion. Fortunately, his chances for a fourth star are nil. I've already warned his superiors that there are issues with his off duty behavior that could bring disrepute to the Navy, if not worse. Even his friends in high places will walk away when they find out. He's far from the only one, sadly. It's enough to make you weep that the Vinqs of the galaxy are promoted while better officers aren't."

"Move Fleet HQ away from Earth, and political influence over who gets what will dim." She finished her glass. "And that's all I'm having tonight. Care to mingle?"

"Not particularly. You?"

"Neither, but we'd best spend at least thirty or forty minutes making small talk with the good flag officers, if only because we might need their help one day."

Holt smirked at her.

"Okay. But I want to see what you term good flag officers. Remember — I know about those who are bad although they hide it well."

"We can compare notes on the way back."

**

"Please tell me this is the last time I have to endure the SecGen's Armed Forces Gala," Holt said, settling back in his seat as the staff car moved away from the Assembly Hall's main entrance.

"Make sure you're not promoted again, and you'll be fine. So, are any of my good ones under investigation by your lot? Or can't you say?"

Holt let out a gentle grunt.

"Kudos on your instincts, Kathryn. They're clean as far as we can tell, but a few mistakenly trust the wrong people. Mind you, they'll find out from us in good time, and no, I can't say who."

"Are we agreed that Sara Lauzier wasn't happy about being rescued by Siobhan?"

He nodded.

"No doubt about it, not that our gut feeling counts as sufficient evidence for a covert probe, so don't look at my lot to confirm anything. If Siobhan can find evidence in the Zone linking the SSB with the hijacking, we might have a thread we can pull on. Otherwise…"

"She causes more mayhem on her way up the political ladder." Kowalski let out a sigh. "Charles Lauzier, while a politician with the usual narcissism and lack of empathy, isn't any worse than the rest, not that it's a high bar to cross. How could he raise a daughter like Sara?"

Holt shrugged wearily.

"Our species has been practicing the art of psychiatry for over five hundred years, and the head shrinkers still can't agree whether sociopaths are created by nature or nurture, so your guess is as good as mine."

"That's only because they refuse to admit that other individual traits are probably a result of nature rather than nurture and vice versa, lest they create an ion storm of epic proportions when blindly partisan proponents of one or the other take mortal offense. The mindless mob has ended professional careers for far less."

"Be that as it may. I figure Sara as SecGen down the road will not be good for the Commonwealth — again, if we're right."

"We're right, Zeke. She engineered the *Athena* incident to advance her career by removing potential opposition and pleasing those whose support she needs. Sara is playing the long game. Not the coming election and perhaps not even the one after. Unless she can swing it her way. Which means we can afford to play the long game as well by putting the right people into the right places and preparing our own plans."

"Whoa. Say what? Are you talking of putting us up-and-coming flag officers on a war footing against the up-and-coming future SecGen?"

"Something's going to give in the next ten or fifteen years, the way things are headed. Sara Lauzier is a symptom of the growing dysfunction in the Commonwealth, masked first by the war and then the immediate postwar years. But it's coming back to the fore." Their staff car halted smoothly in front of Kowalski's apartment building, close to the shore of Lake Geneva. "And on that note, enjoy what's left of your weekend. We can talk again on Monday."

She climbed out, and the car sped off again, taking Holt to his quarters on the sprawling base that housed Fleet HQ.

— Thirty-Three —

"Madame Lauzier." Blayne Hersom, Director General of the Special Security Bureau, rose as the SecGen's daughter and closest adviser entered his office. "To what do I owe the pleasure of your visit? Normally, I'm the one seeking an audience with you in the Palace."

Hersom, a lean, tall man in his early seventies with craggy features topped by luxuriant gray hair, exuded the vigor of someone decades younger. He wore an expensive, gray business suit with a high-collared silk shirt, the sort that served as a quasi-uniform among the Commonwealth government's top bureaucrats. And, like his counterparts in other organizations, the sole splashes of color in an otherwise sober appearance were provided by a lapel pin with the SSB's crest, an eagle clutching the scales of justice, a gold watch on his left wrist, and a class ring on his right hand. The latter marked him as a graduate of Earth's Commonwealth University, one of the most prestigious institutions of higher learning in the star system, if not the entirety of human space, although many, especially in the Fleet, attributed a different meaning to its initials.

As Lauzier took a chair across from his desk, he studied her with dispassionate eyes that could unnerve any keen observer thanks to their emptiness. As befit the head of the Commonwealth's shadowy security police, a man who acknowledged no master other than the SecGen himself, he didn't know the meaning of pity, much less that of empathy.

Hersom sat again and leaned forward, elbows on the desktop, and joined his hands, fingertips touching, an expectant air on his face. He was clearly wondering what brought Sara Lauzier to SSB headquarters, a nondescript, high-security, five-story building on Geneva's northern outskirts. His top-floor office enjoyed a magnificent view of the lake and the mountains ringing it, better even than the one enjoyed by humanity's most powerful politician. But she wasn't here for that.

"We may face a bit of a problem with the fallout from our most recent operation."

"How so, Madame? Because Dunmoore retrieved *Athena* ahead of time? She has a habit of showing up unexpectedly where she's not wanted, something the SSB experienced several times during the war."

"You heard they gave her a reprieve from early retirement with a promotion to rear admiral and her own battle group as a result of showing up unexpectedly in the Galadiman system, right?"

He nodded once.

"Of course. Blind luck will derail the most solid planning and meticulous execution, unfortunately. We almost had Dunmoore out of uniform and no longer capable of interfering, thanks to friends in the right places and her own hubris. One week either way," Hersom shrugged, "and she wouldn't have been in the right place to carry out the rescue. Fleet HQ would have appointed a less effective and experienced officer, one who'd still be blundering around the Zone while things unfolded as they should."

"Blind luck and her own friends in the right places — a Rear Admiral Kathryn Kowalski, from Naval Operations, and a Commodore Ezekiel Holt, from Naval Intelligence."

Hersom allowed himself a wintry smile.

"We're quite familiar with both of them. Kowalski is something of a shooting star in the Navy, smarter than ninety-nine percent of flag officers, ambitious, and utterly incorruptible. She made it up the ranks on her own merits. Holt, on the other hand, is something of a cipher. He heads one of the counterintelligence divisions, but what his organization does is more than that. In part, I suppose you could call it an internal affairs branch of sorts. Both served under Dunmoore during the war and are thoroughly loyal to her, making them dangerous."

"I met them at the Armed Forces Gala last Saturday, and my instincts told me they realize the hijacking was a carefully engineered operation and not just a desperate ploy by colonial malcontents. That makes them even more dangerous than you think. But they don't have proof."

When Hersom opened his mouth, she raised a restraining hand.

"More worrisome is Dunmoore and her new 101st Battle Group. Its mission is apparently dedicated to anti-piracy in the Rim Sector, focusing on the Protectorate Zone frontier. When I pressed Admiral Lowell for more, he was suspiciously cagey. My sources inside Fleet HQ can't tell me anything about the 101st because its mission, composition, and patrol routes are hidden behind a top secret special access codename impenetrable even to my father. That can only mean she's inside the Zone, looking for the Confederacy mercenaries and the people taken off *Athena*. If she tracked us down before the operation ran its course — and with extraordinarily little to guide her, by the way — I wouldn't dismiss her chances of finding your hirelings and discovering the truth."

A thoughtful expression crossed Hersom's face.

"I dismiss nothing where Dunmoore's concerned. But she necessarily received help from outside the Fleet because she isn't clairvoyant." His eyes slipped to one side and lost their focus as he parsed the possibilities. "You're aware the Colonial Office has its own intelligence service, right?"

Lauzier nodded.

"One over which the administration should exercise more control, but I've yet to meet a Colonial Secretary who can stand against his own senior bureaucrats."

"One could say the same of the various Defense Secretaries since before the war. Are you also cognizant of the fact the Office established a consulate on Kilia Station for which it didn't obtain Senate approval and whose existence it doesn't advertise?"

A perfectly sculpted eyebrow crept up. "Really? A well kept secret if I wasn't aware of it."

"This consulate is clearly the cover for an intelligence gathering operation. The consul, Mikhail Forenza, was a Colonial Office operative during the war and probably still works for the Intelligence Service. We can take it as a given that he has agents on the main, human-settled Zone worlds." Hersom looked at

Lauzier again. "Now, here's the thing. He knows Dunmoore personally from an incident on Toboso and later when she rescued him along with the passengers and the crew of a tramp freighter after pirates took them in what is now the Zone. Perhaps Forenza has been feeding Dunmoore what his network picked up about the Confederacy of the Howling Stars."

"The Colonial Office and the Fleet working together in secret behind the administration's back?" A frown creased Lauzier's smooth forehead. "That's a disquieting notion."

"Indeed. While the Fleet can't operate in the Zone other than undercover, the Treaty of Ulufan does not prohibit the Colonial Office's activities there. Cooperation between the two in throttling certain activities deemed illegal by our laws could prove costly for many Commonwealth interests."

"And reveal how the SSB has been using mercenaries based in the Zone to conduct extra-judicial operations both within and beyond the Commonwealth sphere."

Hersom inclined his head.

"Just so. Should that come to light, the SecGen — present and future — will lose a powerful tool capable of suppressing dissent in the colonies and OutWorlds."

Lauzier, who was aware Hersom knew all about her ambitions, gave him a wry look.

"Noted. So, how do we deal with this situation? Take Kowalski and Holt off the board since they can't be suborned or otherwise turned?"

A shake of the head.

"No. That would make matters worse and incur Dunmoore's wrath, something we underestimate at our peril. She directly wrecked three major SSB operations during the war, along with several minor ones who became collateral damage when she took out other targets. Remove her friends, and she'll find a way of damaging us again, this time disastrously. That loyalty Kowalski and Holt show toward her? She returns it fully."

"How would she find out you did it?"

"She would. Trust me. There's more going on here than we can fathom right now. If you think Kowalski and Holt smell a rat about *Athena*'s hijacking, then so will Dunmoore. Those well-timed leaks we engineered as part of the operation will make sure the SSB won't be overlooked by any of them considering their known hostility toward the Bureau."

"Probably." She made a face. "In hindsight, those were perhaps a mistake."

"We didn't know then what the outcome would be."

"But you knew about Dunmoore's involvement by the time you released the information."

"True, though the odds of her finding *Athena* before our mercenaries effected a 'rescue' were deemed incredibly small."

"Then I suggest you don't underestimate her again." Lauzier's words, delivered in a casual tone, were belied by an icy glare that could make anyone but Hersom draw back in fear. "Make sure she doesn't find anyone or anything capable of revealing the truth for both our sakes."

"You, Madame, are safe no matter what. Nothing connects you with the hijacking."

"I spoke personally with the woman who calls herself the Commodore. She knows I'm in on it."

A faint smile, the sort capable of freezing methane, appeared on Hersom's lips.

"Perhaps having you speak with her face-to-face was a mistake as well."

"There was no other way of telling her who she must remove from the ship, at what frequency, and how. Communicating that information ahead of time would have been too risky, in case the SSB leaks from places you don't control."

"Touché. But I merely raised the question as a way of pointing out nothing ever works as planned in any given operation, or as the military wisdom goes, no plan survives contact with the enemy. And an enemy like Siobhan Dunmoore will absolutely wreck the best-laid ones. Ask our former foes, the Shrehari, how they feel about her. We were victims of bad timing and faced an officer who acts on the dictum victories result from opportunities clearly seen and swiftly seized. I'll find out what occurred in Kilia. Never fear."

Lauzier gave him a dismissive shrug. "That won't do us much good with the immediate problem."

"True, but then, nothing we do will change what happens in the Zone if that's where Dunmoore is hunting our Confederacy contractors. Pray she destroys their ships with the Commodore aboard. That way, the last one capable of incriminating you will vanish."

"The last one outside this office, you mean."

He inclined his head again, acknowledging her point.

"Other than me, yes. But you and I have an understanding. The consequences if one of us betrays the other will be more than painful."

She made a gesture of acquiescence. "Mutually assured destruction."

"The price for cooperation, Madame. Only a fool in my position trusts ambitious politicians. I suggest we ignore Kowalski, Holt, Dunmoore, and everyone involved. Let them do as they please. Even if they uncover evidence, who will bring it forward? Who will investigate it officially? Who will risk a political crisis like none since the Second Migration War for a mere thirty-six lives?"

"No one."

"Precisely. Let fate decide whether they suffer retribution for meddling in your affairs."

Yet even as he spoke, Hersom thought he saw a murderous glint in Sara Lauzier's eyes. She wasn't the type who forgave an insult or injury, let alone anyone who crossed her. In theory, one of his jobs as head of the SSB was ensuring her sort didn't get near the reins of power after her father left office. But the idea of having a SecGen beholden to his organization in a few years was irresistible.

— Thirty-Four —

"Sara Lauzier visited SSB headquarters this morning." Ezekiel Holt, coffee cup in hand, dropped into the chair facing Kathryn Kowalski's desk. "Yes, we keep a permanent watch on the building, so we're always aware of who goes in and out. You'd think she would choose a less visible method — the area around Geneva is replete with tunnels, including the former Large Hadron Collider, which is now used for long-term storage by the government if you've not yet heard. Or so it claims but checking on that isn't part of my remit."

"Natural arrogance? Or perhaps dear Sara doesn't care who sees her?"

"Or it wasn't her in the staff car we saw entering the building's underground garage, which I doubt." At Kowalski's questioning glance, he said, "Sara Lauzier frequently borrows her father's official means of transportation, and when in Geneva, that's a Terra Shadow from Spirit Luxury Designs. There's only one of that make, model, and color in town, and Charles Lauzier never visits SSB HQ. So it could only be Sara because no one else uses the Shadow besides her and Charles. I'm betting on her overweening sense of entitlement and impunity."

Kowalski cocked a skeptical eyebrow. "You're sure of that?"

"Even her sort has weaknesses we can exploit. It's not because she's without emotions or empathy that she's without blind spots. Sadly, the SSB doesn't have the sort of blind spot that lets us listen to conversations in Blayne Hersom's office. I'll wager she spoke about meeting us on Saturday evening and told him she thought we might not fully believe the hijacking story. Fortunately, Hersom has not only met Siobhan but knows what she's capable of doing — I was present, by the way, though I didn't come face-to-face with him. And yes, it was one of those operations which will remain classified until the end of time, sorry. Suffice to say, if Sara is climbing on her high horse because things didn't go as she wanted, Hersom will talk her back down, lest things that should stay hidden spill over into the public domain."

"Again, assuming we're not dreaming up this whole conspiracy thing."

"Whenever your belief falters, my friend, peruse the list of those taken off *Athena* again. It helps me maintain focus. As I said, many are potential threats to Sara Lauzier assuming the mantle of SecGen in a few years. The rest?" He shrugged. "I could paint a picture of how much Sara's potential supporters would enjoy her engineering the disappearance of inconvenient relatives and business associates. Take Vitus Amali, for example. He and brother Geraldo never agreed on much. However, Geraldo has backed Charles Lauzier's ambitions — for consideration, of course — and wouldn't mind if Vitus dropped into a black hole, so he no longer needs to look over his shoulder all the time."

Kowalski gave him a knowing nod.

"And if Sara hints that she helped engineer Vitus' disappearance, she gains Geraldo's support. Or rather the support of the senators the Amali family owns. Especially if said hint comes with a vague notion that Vitus isn't the only Amali capable of vanishing without a trace."

Holt tapped the side of his nose with an extended index finger.

"Or Geraldo was in on it from the start, which makes him a co-conspirator. Who better to organize a luxury liner from one of his own subsidiaries and put Confederacy mercs passing as replacement crew aboard? I cross-referenced the vanished passengers with people we suspect Geraldo would rather see gone, and guess what? There are enough of them on both Sara and Geraldo's least wanted lists that it cannot be a coincidence. But proving we're right? As much as I place my faith in Siobhan, I doubt she'll uncover anything actionable. The SSB will have compartmentalized the various parts of the operation with only Sara, Hersom, and maybe one or two others who know everything. None of them will talk, nor can we force them into Naval Intelligence interrogation rooms and loosen their tongues with the various methods at our disposal. In effect, the people involved are untouchable, perhaps even if Siobhan brings back irrefutable evidence."

Kowalski made a face at him. "Did you come here to depress me, Zeke?"

"No. I merely want to make you aware of what's happening in Geneva and make sure you realize there will be no straightforward solution. Our operatives are trying to find the SSB's contacts with the Confederacy of the Howling Stars, but it will take time, and success is in no way guaranteed. The only thing in our favor is access to the database of discharged Armed Forces members. It'll allow us to narrow down the list of known and suspected Confederacy members based on law enforcement reports, psych profiles, post-Fleet employment history, etc."

"Did it help you find Lena Corto?"

A wry smile appeared on Holt's lips.

"Sorry. I forgot to tell you. But, no, we couldn't find her whereabouts. Corto cashed out her pension shortly after she retired — involuntarily because she ran out of promotion board chances — seven years ago and essentially vanished. That being said, it's a distinct possibility she's working as a merc in the Zone. Why else would a retired senior officer fall off the sensor grid? There are plenty of legal job opportunities for someone with her pedigree. After all, she has a solid service record even though her ambitions brought her face-to-face with someone more suitable as a raider task force commander. If SOCOM had given Rear Admiral Petras a conventional Q ship instead of *Iolanthe*, the outcome might have been radically different."

"Which outcome? The war's or Corto's career?"

"Both." Holt's communicator buzzed softly, forestalling Kowalski's response. He pulled it from his tunic pocket, activated the virtual display, and read its contents. As he did so, his forehead creased in a frown. "It's from Alexander Rostov, the Director General of the Colonial Office Intelligence Service."

Holt looked up at Kowalski.

"He and I are becoming rather chummy of late. Exchanging data and favors makes both his outfit and Naval Intelligence look good, even though only a few people on either side know about it. Alex says Blayne Hersom called him just now, fishing for information. Specifically, he asked whether Alex's people uncovered more about the hijackers and if he knew what the Navy's new 101st Battle Group was up to in the Zone."

"Sounds like someone's getting worried the Navy might uncover more than it should. Does your friend say what he told Hersom?"

"Words to the effect that his people are still listening and looking and that Alex would share anything they dig up. As for the 101st, Alex recommended Hersom ask the Navy."

Kowalski gave Holt a sardonic smile.

"I'm going to guess the SSB isn't the sort who barters data and favors."

He made a wry face.

"No. Since the SSB director general reports solely to the SecGen, they figure information goes only one way — to them."

"Typical arrogance. One of these days, they'll desperately need friends and find no one willing to help."

A chuckle. "The Hersoms of the galaxy can't conceive of any reason the SSB might need friends, period. That's why they're so popular among the various intelligence and security agencies, never mind star system police forces."

"So, it isn't their blatant disregard for pesky things like the law when they carry out politically driven operations? Funny, that."

He shrugged.

"The SSB isn't the first law enforcement agency to do so. Any organization whose head is appointed through a political process will inevitably become a tool of the politicians to whom they owe fealty. It has been thus since the beginning of time. Hersom is a Lauzier man. Charles made him director general, and Hersom is hoping Sara will ensure he remains so. The massive behind-the-scenes power enjoyed by the SSB director general is a heady drug for anyone, especially for ambitious sociopaths like our friend Blayne. Anything which threatens that power threatens his very existence. I wouldn't be surprised if he taps his contacts in Fleet HQ next, so do me a favor. If anyone so much as wonders about the 101st's mission, let alone our new friendship with the Colonial Office, pass their names on to me. They might be the sort who need a thorough background check, no matter how many stars they wear."

"When you say contacts in Fleet HQ, do you mean willing collaborators or indiscreet individuals with secrets they'd rather keep?"

Holt flashed her an amused grin. "Yes."

Kowalski grimaced. "I see."

"We're no better and no worse than any other government institution. I daresay the SSB has its fair share of such people as well, but if we've suborned any of them, I couldn't say. Not my department."

"We — the Fleet — really spend too many resources watching our own people, don't you think, Zeke?"

He raised both hands in surrender. "You're talking to the converted here, but if not us, then who?"

"I guess there's no one else. Hang on." Holt glanced at his communicator again. "Hersom's already asking around about the 101st. Or rather, one of his minions at the director level is."

"That was fast."

"If you're wondering who, sorry. It's not something I can share. I may not know about SSB members who talk to us, but that doesn't mean we don't use people who pretend they're friends with them so we can pass on disinformation."

"Weren't you an honest warship captain at one point?"

Holt winked at her. "Of a battlecruiser disguised as a bulk carrier operating in places where the regular Navy didn't dare tread. *Maskirovka* and *dezinformatsiya* come as naturally to me as making small talk."

"Ah yes, the fine arts of deception and disinformation. Siobhan's a pretty good practitioner herself."

— Thirty-Five —

"All ships are accounted for, and their emissions are locked up tighter than downtown Marseilles during Fleet Week," Chief Cox reported a few minutes after the 101st Battle Group dropped out of FTL at Abaddon's hyperlimit. "*Iolanthe* is scanning the orbitals in passive mode."

Chief Cazano raised her hand.

"Optical comlinks between *Iolanthe* and the rest of the formation are live, Admiral."

"Thank you."

Dunmoore settled back to study Abaddon's image on the CIC main display. According to Forenza's intelligence package, the planet, hidden away deep inside the Zone, boasted a breathable atmosphere. Yet it seemed dusty enough, where it wasn't frozen over, to make the Commonwealth's premier desert world, Nabhka, look like an oasis.

But if Abaddon were a paradise, colonists seeking a life beyond the reach of interstellar governments would overrun it, and the people who established outposts here wanted to stay as far as possible from honest sentient beings. So it didn't surprise Dunmoore that the Confederacy of the Howling Stars and its non-human associates would make Abaddon one of their hubs and take up residence in a self-proclaimed free port on the surface called Rakka.

"Not the kind of place to raise your kids," Pushkin commented. "Good old Mars seems more welcoming, and it's still being terraformed."

"We're getting our first readings from the orbital scans, Admiral, and my, it's a busy place for an old rock in the middle of nowhere." Lieutenant Commander Zakaria pointed at the starboard secondary display. "First, we have what looks like a full satellite constellation. Considering how sparsely inhabited the place seems, I'll bet many of them are looking outward for intruders like us. That likely means there's a central authority governing Abaddon."

Dunmoore nodded.

"Agreed. Even pirate havens need a governance structure with a boss at the very top, so they keep running profitably."

A guffaw escaped Pushkin's throat.

"Makes me wonder how we would differentiate them from the business-suited pirates running our own governments."

"Cynic."

"Guilty as charged, Admiral. You do recall the definition of a cynic, right?" He grinned at Dunmoore.

"An idealist who's been mugged by reality."

A nod.

"Right. I don't know if everyone in this CIC started off as idealists, but we were definitely all whacked over the head by life."

"Some harder than others," Guthren said in an amused tone.

"If you mean me, Chief, then spot on."

Zakaria cleared her throat softly as a new image appeared on the secondary display.

"That looks suspiciously like a simple defense platform, something with a few missile-filled containers, a reactor, and direct-fire weapons hidden behind armor plating. So far, we can see four of them."

"Simple doesn't always mean ineffective," Lieutenant Commander Khanjan said. "Though against warships like ours, I daresay even two dozen of them opening up at once might be insufficient except at extremely close range. Still, I'm impressed by what we see so far. I didn't expect this many orbitals. Piracy, smuggling, and whatever else they do in the Zone must be rather profitable. Makes you wonder who paid off the diplomats and politicians on both sides during the Treaty negotiations so that this part of space became out-of-bounds for naval vessels."

"Look no further than our Senate, Attar," Pushkin replied. "I'm sure the Empire has its own enterprising plutocrats who are more interested in profits than law, order, or morality."

Guthren gave Dunmoore a knowing grin.

"Your flag captain was definitely whacked harder by reality than the rest of us, Admiral."

"Now, here's where it gets interesting," Zakaria said. "Looks like at least eight Shrehari built hulls, including two that resemble the so-called science vessel passing for a corsair or vice versa we saw orbiting Kilia. Larger than a wartime Ptar, smaller than a Tol. And now, a whole swarm of merchant hulls coming around Abaddon."

"Please put it on the primary display and zoom in."

"Aye, aye, Admiral."

Everyone in the CIC examined the images for several long minutes while the intelligence AI looked for matches in the ship's database.

"Aha." Zakaria pointed at four starships seemingly orbiting as a tight group. "Those look quite familiar."

Dunmoore nodded.

"The Arkanna-built copies of human sloops sold off by the Navy after the war. Do we have the emission signatures of Drex's ship as well as those of the three who fled from Galadiman when we showed up?"

"Yes, we do, Admiral. I made sure we took a copy with us, just in case."

Pushkin winked at her. "What can I say? You're surrounded by one of the best staff teams in the Fleet."

"I am indeed, Gregor."

A red circle appeared around one of the sloops.

"That ship's emissions are an almost exact match for those of Drex's *Vuko*."

"No kidding," Chief Cazano said. "I'm picking up the subspace tracking devices. They're still in operation."

Orange circles appeared around three more. "There was no time to take extensive readings before the ships orbiting Galadiman ran, but these are a close match. Closer than the others of a similar build."

"Okay, thanks. Pass the identification to all ships. Then, Chief Cazano, I'd like to speak with the captains."

"Aye, aye, sir," Zakaria and Cazano replied in unison.

Within moments, four faces appeared on her command chair's virtual display.

"You've received target identification data just now. One, with a high degree of confidence, is the sloop *Vuko* we boarded at Kilia. If he's still around, her captain is a former Navy lieutenant commander promoted from the ranks, Alan Drex. The other three, with a medium degree of confidence, are probably the sloops guarding *Athena* in Galadiman orbit and likely those who hijacked her. I suspect the individual in command of the squadron was also once a Navy officer, based on their reaction when we appeared at Galadiman's hyperlimit.

"I'm sure you've noticed the amount of shipping around Abaddon, including at least eight Shrehari vessels, two of which are suspected Deep Space Fleet or *Tai Zohl*, based on their configuration. The rest might simply be corsairs or armed merchant ships, or they might also serve the Empire. One thing is certain. We cannot afford to clash with them, nor they with us."

She paused while each of the four nodded solemnly.

"My intentions are as follows. We will approach Abaddon running silent and enter geosynchronous orbit above the city of Rakka. Commander Khanjan will prepare a navigation plot that sees the battle group coast toward Abaddon without attracting attention. Hopefully, no one will spot our thrusters firing out here at the hyperlimit. But if anyone does, it'll be one or both of the two larger Shrehari ships. They may call themselves science vessels or whatever else, but if they're not warships like ours, then I'll eat my beret. That means we face naval-grade sensors and naval-grade situational awareness. If they detect us and open a link, I'll do the talking. The one at Kilia even helped us track Alan Drex's ship, and that tells me they probably won't interfere with human-on-human anti-piracy action. After all, keeping the Zone quiet benefits both of our polities. If we make it into orbit undetected, I'll decide on the next steps, based on what else we find circling Abaddon. Are there any questions or comments?"

Dunmoore knew each of her captains was comfortable with improvisation on the spot — it was how Q ships seized opportunities. Timid officers with rigid thinking patterns need not apply. When no one spoke, she smiled.

"In that case, stand by for navigation orders. Let's pay Abaddon a discrete visit."

**

"Please, Commodore. I don't know what I could have done. Enoc Tarrant betrayed us. If you want to lay blame, let it be on him."

After a long wait while he and his advisers debated the next steps, the Confederacy of the Howling Stars senior executive in the Abaddon system, Vice President Jamy Daver, had finally convened a court of inquiry into *Vuko*'s boarding by Commonwealth Navy personnel while docked at Kilia Station. Since she was the most experienced and most senior former Navy officer present, he'd appointed the Commodore as chief inquisitor, directing her to hold the proceedings aboard her flagship, *Mahigan*.

"Tarrant will get his in due course," the Commodore growled, showing her irritation with Drex's faintly plaintive tone. "We're talking about how you led a Navy task force directly to Galadiman where we were conducting one of the most lucrative private military operations in the Confederacy's brief history."

"And from what I understand, you mostly achieved the stated aims, sir."

"But not every one of them, and it cost us."

With Dunmoore securing *Athena* before everyone targeted by Sara Lauzier was removed, and before the designated rescue force could carry out its mission, the Confederacy's mystery employer reduced its payout by a not inconsiderable percentage. And since the contract was illegal, the Confederacy could hardly complain to the Commonwealth agency regulating private military corporations.

"Sir, I can only repeat that while they took a copy of the computer core, they didn't find the secret database. That Dunmoore followed us to Galadiman is just more of her damned luck. She left Kilia several hours before I did. How she could know my heading once I crossed the heliopause is no more than conjecture. My navigation database can only tell her about my most frequent ports of call, and I'll note Abaddon figures more prominently than Galadiman. So do Arkanna and a few others, for that matter."

"But Galadiman is the most conveniently situated for cross-border operations, and Dunmoore knew that because she ran rampant in this part of the galaxy during the war. So I'm well acquainted with her tactics and her way of thinking."

Drex scowled.

"But I'm not, sir. The only thing I know of her is that she murdered my brother in that accursed ship, *Stingray*. I did my duty by warning you of her presence in the Zone as fast as humanly possible. Surely no one can ask more of me. If clairvoyance is a requirement to be captain of a Confederacy of the Howling Stars sloop, then you'll not find a soul who meets it."

Jamy Daver shrugged. "He has a point, Commodore."

Though not part of the court of inquiry, Daver gave himself leave to intervene at will by dint of his position within the organization under the principle of might makes right. And in the Abaddon system, he was might, something even the more established groups, including the one running what passed for a planetary government, acknowledged.

Career pirates were no match for hardened Fleet veterans who saw off the best the Shrehari Empire could muster and didn't give a damn about the niceties of civilized society after said society tossed them aside like so much dirty laundry.

But before she could reply, her communicator — which was sitting on the table, recording the proceedings — gently chimed. She glanced down and frowned.

"What is it?" Daver asked.

"The bridge thinks it briefly caught four sensor ghosts at approximately thirty-five thousand kilometers altitude above the Rakka area."

— Thirty-Six —

Daver sat up and gave her a curious look. "Four? That's awfully specific."

The Commodore nodded.

"I know. We should wrap up this hearing and defer judgment in case those ghosts are naval units running silent. The Almighty knows our former Service does it frighteningly well, and anyone else visiting Abaddon would have no reason to hide."

"The Navy? This deep inside the Zone?"

She grimaced.

"Since Dunmoore appeared in both the Kilia and Galadiman systems so quickly with a full task force despite the Treaty, despite Commonwealth government restrictions, and despite the fact she had no real clue as to our whereabouts, nothing will surprise me."

"All right. We'll end this hearing and set our state at heightened vigilance. But I'd rather we pass judgment now so that Captain Drex can return to his ship and prepare for whatever might have joined us in orbit."

The Commodore briefly gave Daver a hard look, knowing she'd just been told to let Drex off the hook. And in truth, she knew there was no way to avoid the boarding party, not when Tarrant was cooperating with Dunmoore. That he warned her as fast as possible was a factor in his favor, as was the boarding party not finding his hidden database. Besides, if anyone could have tracked Drex, it was Dunmoore, who probably convinced the Shrehari science vessel commander to watch *Vuko*'s departure vector and share it with her once she reached Kilia's heliopause.

"Captain Drex, this court of inquiry has determined that you acted in good faith at all times. Accordingly, you may return to your ship."

The man stood and bowed his head formally.

"Thank you, Commodore." He turned to Daver. "By your leave, sir?"

"Dismissed."

Daver climbed to his feet.

"I'll head home while you hunt for these sensor ghosts. But, if it's the Navy, do remember that discretion is the better part of valor. You did the right thing at Galadiman, even though the mission completion rate wasn't much past eighty percent, and that cost us a slice of the final payment. But losing three ships would have been considerably more expensive. And we are in this for money, not glory, right?"

A flash of resentment briefly lit up her eyes. Daver cautioning her was needless. He'd been a logistics officer, and though he'd retired as a post captain as well, the Confederacy's VP for Abaddon and founding member of the organization never came within a dozen light-years of the fighting during the war.

But he outranked her now, and she would be the first to admit he was a thoroughly competent administrator and businessman, albeit devious, ruthless, and without much of a conscience. Daver would just as easily stab her in the back than give her a performance bonus.

"No worries, Jamy. I'm not the sort who needlessly wastes good hulls."

With that, both exited *Mahigan*'s small conference room. Daver headed for the shuttle deck and she for the bridge. Though the Commodore ran a squadron of ships, none of them had dedicated space for a flag officer, let alone her staff — not that she needed one. As a result, she'd kept command of *Mahigan* while also leading other Confederacy sloops, their numbers varying as necessary, on private military corporation contracts within the Zone. Soon, perhaps once their success with *Athena* became known, she might even carry out missions inside the Commonwealth, cocking a snoot at the Navy that wronged her.

As soon as she entered the bridge, the officer of the watch, who'd been occupying the command chair, stood and stepped aside.

"We haven't found those ghosts yet, sir."

She sat and studied the secondary display where the relevant data waited. Sometimes sensors picked up natural artifacts that bore an eerie resemblance to starships. But was this one of them? Her ship's electronics, while among the best in the Zone, weren't as good as those the Commonwealth Navy fielded — and kept out of civilian hands.

The Confederacy of the Howling Stars was lucky it owned over three dozen human-designed sloops equipped to minimum wartime standards in the first place. Perhaps if their sponsors inside the Commonwealth could divert a few consignments between the factories and the shipyards…

"What was the altitude again? Thirty-five-thousand kilometers? Isn't that just about right for geosynchronous orbit around Abaddon?"

"Aye, Commodore," the officer of the watch replied.

"Then order all ships in the squadron to scan the slice of space above Rakka at that altitude, give or take a thousand klicks. But using passive mode only, so it's not detectable. If visitors are hiding in plain sight, that's a good place to be."

And exactly where someone like Siobhan Dunmoore, of cursed memory, would put her task force — the perfect spot to spring a nasty surprise on unsuspecting ships in orbit *and* the planet's principal settlement. But even if they found naval vessels, what good would it do? Daver was right. Any captain — or commodore — in his or her right mind would flee at the sight of warships. Yes, it was four ghosts against more than seventy ships in orbit. But she knew the sort of Navy captain who operated in the Zone, and although it might not seem so, the math favored a quick departure with no looking back, and the devil take the hindmost.

**

"So far, so good, Admiral," Chief Cox reported without turning around when Dunmoore re-entered the flag CIC after a quick sandwich and a coffee in the wardroom. "No one seems to have noticed us. We're not being pinged, let alone hailed by what passes for traffic control around here."

"But it feels just a bit surreal." Lieutenant Commander Zakaria climbed out of the command chair and stepped aside. "Being able to sneak up on so many ships and orbitals."

"I'll bet they don't remember how good the Navy is at silent running. Many a Shrehari's last thoughts during the war were some form of *where the hell did they come from*." Dunmoore sat and examined a rather crowded tactical projection. "Not that the poor buggers ever mastered the art of making holes in space like we do."

Chief Cox let out a disconsolate grunt.

"Sadly, it might become something of a lost art. As we've seen in every readiness evaluation, crews simply don't practice enough anymore — at least not in the regular Navy. This Q ship bunch, though? Top-notch, Admiral. If I didn't know where to look, I wouldn't even notice their hulls occluding the background stars."

"Let's hope no one below us is doing the same thing."

Yet even as she said those words, Dunmoore wondered whether the ex-Fleet people aboard those Confederacy ships weren't more challenging opponents than the Shrehari because they knew the Navy's tricks intimately.

**

"Holy crap." *Mahigan*'s sensor chief swung around to face the Commodore. "Sir, something is sitting in geosynchronous above Rakka, occluding the background stars, and it's huge. I mean battleship huge. Massive bulk carrier huge."

Her heart skipped a beat at the announcement, but her voice remained the essence of self-control. She knew of one battlecruiser-sized ship who'd made the Zone her hunting ground before it was even known as such.

"Put it on the primary display."

"Whatever that might be," the chief said after complying, "it's way larger than any warship currently fielded by our Navy or the Shrehari. Fleet HQ mothballed everything bigger than the Salamanca class cruisers a few years back, except for replenishment vessels and transports, and what would one of those be doing here, right?"

"Not quite. There is one warship still in active service that fits the bill. See if the AI can build us a three-dimensional schematic of that occlusion. And keep looking for more tangos. I doubt whatever that thing is generated four simultaneous sensor ghosts."

"Aye, aye, sir."

Was it possible? Could that be *Iolanthe*? And why not? A lot of the Fleet's Q ships operated in the Zone. She caught her fingers tapping a disjointed tattoo on her thigh and forcibly stilled her hand. Was she nervous for the first time in years?

"The AI's initial pass is coming through, Commodore."

A sinking feeling tugged at her gut as a three-dimensional rendering replaced Abaddon in the tactical projection dominating the bridge. It could only be *Iolanthe* in her attack configuration. No other ship of that size and shape navigated the star lanes. Suddenly, she knew without a doubt Dunmoore was aboard. This sneaking into orbit undetected reeked of her tactics.

"There are other ships. Find them."

The minutes passed in silence while she fought off a growing sense of peril, nerves taut, muscles almost painfully seized up.

"Sir, you were right. The sensors found three smaller occlusions moving in sync with the larger one. Two are roughly frigate-sized, while the third is approximately the same as a corvette. I'm having the AI build three-dimensional renderings of them as well."

"Get me Vice President Daver's shuttle. I need to speak with him."

"Aye, aye, sir."

Almost a minute passed, then an image materialized on her command chair's virtual display.

"Daver here. What's up? Your ghosts?"

"My ghosts are very real, Jamy. So far, we've made out four ships hiding in geosynchronous above Rakka. One of them is likely the largest warship in commission at this moment, and if I'm right, we're in trouble. Did you ever hear of the battlecruiser disguised as a bulk freighter by the name *Iolanthe*?"

"Not offhand."

"Remember the raid on Shrehari Prime that effectively made the boneheads cry uncle?"

"Yes." A pause. "Tell me this isn't the same *Iolanthe* that led it."

"Task Force Luckner's flagship — the original, mind you, not the one that surprised me at Galadiman."

"Are you saying the Commonwealth Navy's biggest Q ship, along with a few others, is orbiting Abaddon?"

"That's exactly what I'm saying, Jamy." The Commodore repressed a surge of irritation at her superior. "And I'll wager they're here for the people I took off Athena. There's nothing else I can think of that would make the Navy suddenly change its patrolling protocols in the Zone and dispatch four ships to Abaddon. We can't tell what the others are. But believe me. That almost certainly is *Iolanthe* making a hole in space above us, and the last time she operated as part of a formation, it didn't end well for the Shrehari."

"Yet we're not the Shrehari. For one thing, we're not at war with the Commonwealth, and for another, the Navy doesn't attack unidentified ships on spec anymore."

"That doesn't matter to whoever's up there. You hide when you plan on springing a surprise, not when you want to throw your weight around and wave the flag."

"So, what do you propose?"

— Thirty-Seven —

"We run, Jamy. We boot it to the hyperlimit and do a Crazy Ivan jump. It's the only way we'll escape intact."

Another pause. "Aren't you being rather pessimistic?"

"I'm being a realist. This situation is giving me an acute case of déja vu because I've seen a scenario much like it before, during the war, and it involved *Iolanthe* along with several frigates."

Daver chuckled.

"One might almost believe you're suffering from a guilty conscience. Or are you having regrets about your foray into human trafficking, something the Navy thoroughly abhors? I'm fairly sure your bogeyman, Dunmoore, wouldn't hesitate to space you and your crews without even a drumhead court-martial."

"Considering those overfed, over-entitled, useless drones are already on the surface, she'd have a hard time justifying summary execution, even to herself. I know Dunmoore, and she's more scrupulous than most of her detractors would admit. Besides, I'm overjoyed at the notion some of the wealthiest humans alive will finally be put to work. No, I don't regret bringing them here instead of killing them like Sara Lauzier wanted. Long-term suffering will help atone for their misdeeds. A quick death would have been overly merciful."

She shook her head.

"Though I don't rue my own actions, I'm beginning to believe taking this contract was a bad idea. Now that I've thought things over, it's clear the Special Security Bureau hired us at Lauzier's behest, which makes it political as hell. And that means we extract and run until things blow over."

"The Commonwealth government has the Navy tightly leashed and won't let it operate willy-nilly in the Zone — the *Athena* rescue mission was a one-off. An anti-piracy cruise here and there, sure, but an entire squadron coming after you?"

"We're living in Special Operations territory, Jamy. That means the normal rules don't apply out here. But they left us alone until we took the *Athena* contract because we didn't represent a threat to shipping inside the Commonwealth sphere. Yet now, we're marked for termination with extreme prejudice. I'm telling you, that's a Navy Q ship up there, and it can only be *Iolanthe*. She's here for us. There can be no other explanation."

"So, you run. Then what? We're waiting to hear about a new contract for the private military division. If you're in the middle of nowhere, unreachable by subspace radio, we might lose the contract, which means more profits thrown away because we fear the Navy. Let me speak with Galad and see what he thinks. Abaddon has teeth. I doubt the officer in command will want scratch marks on his or her ships' hulls, let alone suffer real damage from orbital defense platforms merely to put you out of business or recover thirty-six people without whom the

Commonwealth is better off. Besides, fleeing is the surest way of suggesting guilt. Our ships are almost indistinguishable from—"

"No, they're not. Did you forget about emission signatures? Dunmoore watched *Vuko* long enough to identify her anywhere. She may not have clean scans on *Mahigan*, *Nashoba*, and *Amarog*, because we booted it out of the Galadiman system fast enough, but she can nail them with a reasonable level of confidence. I'll bet my next contract performance bonus that the ships hiding in geosync have the emission signatures Dunmoore took during the *Athena* business, and they've identified the four ships I just named."

"Alright. I'll ask again. What will you do?" Daver sounded just a tad exasperated.

"Break out of orbit as if things were normal and see what happens. They'll either light up, or they won't. In the latter case, it might prove me paranoid, which should please you. If they light up, I'll simply accelerate and make for the hyperlimit. A big ship like *Iolanthe* won't catch my sloops. She can't put out enough gees."

"And go where?"

Technically, she reported to the Board of Directors, just like Daver, and didn't need his approval on anything other than *Vuko*'s status. But considering the informal power he wielded within the organization as a plank owner, keeping him onside and showing a modicum of deference didn't hurt.

"Cullan, I suppose. If this new contract is what I think it is, we'll be well placed there. I'll take *Vuko* with me if you don't mind. I'd rather Drex not find himself under interrogation again."

"Agreed on both counts. You should find a few more of our ships at Cullan anyway, waiting for orders. And consider *Vuko* attached to your squadron until further notice. Besides, with Dunmoore spacing his illegal cargo at Kilia, it's best we don't parade him in front of our shipping clients for a while."

"I suppose the subspace link between here, there, and Kilia is still operational."

"It is. The local scum knows better than to hunt for our interstellar relays. Please wait until I'm on the ground before doing anything, just in case our hidden visitors are overly trigger happy."

"Of course."

"Daver, out."

"Signals, establish an optical comlink with *Vuko*, *Nashoba*, and *Amarog*. Officer of the watch, prepare a navigation plot that takes us out of orbit once we're on the opposite side of Abaddon from Rakka, then as directly as possible to the hyperlimit."

"Aye, aye, sir."

**

Gregor Pushkin found a preoccupied Dunmoore pacing her day cabin, lost in thought when he arrived for their afternoon game of chess — something to take their minds off the waiting.

"Looks like you're chewing on a problem, Admiral," he said, retrieving the chess set from a sideboard.

"My gut instinct is overactive right now, Gregor. I think someone spotted us."

"How so?"

"No idea. But every one of the crewmembers aboard those Confederacy ships served in the Fleet, so we're not dealing with piratical amateurs whose idea of standing watch is remaining sober. Sneaking into orbit under silent running can generate sensor ghosts, if only because of the extremely close range. Then there's the inevitable fact that our hulls will occlude the background stars, and it only takes a properly programmed sensor covering the right arc of space at the right time. But you know that."

She stopped pacing and watched him set up the board on her dining table.

"And you're a little more antsy than usual." He picked up two pawns, one white, one black. "You won our last game, so it's your pick."

"I'll let you open this time." She took a chair across from him. "Yes, I'm a little antsier. Seventy ships in orbit, at least eight of them Shrehari, along with the orbitals — that's a lot of potential for catastrophic collateral damage. Especially considering how many of the non-Shrehari vessels are legitimate traders and passenger transports."

"No arguments here, sir. The old shoot them to smithereens and let the Almighty sort them out tactic isn't considered acceptable anymore."

Pushkin made the opening move.

"That's the biggest problem with the so-called savage wars of peace, Gregor." Dunmoore picked up a pawn and set it down. "It's not only the whole idiotic doctrine of proportionality our so-called intellectuals — and you know what they're defined as — want to see as the postwar standard. Tip-toeing around the various species of pirates, would-be revolutionaries, organized criminals, and the like never works as either a remedy or a deterrent. And proportionality will always take a backseat to the reality that only bringing a plasma cannon to a knife fight will ensure lasting consequences. As a wise man once said, they put one of ours in the sickbay; we send one of theirs to hell."

Pushkin gave her a strange look.

"Where did that come from?"

"Sorry. I was just channeling a debate I once had with an academic from Sanctum University while at the War College. We were addressing the sort of situation the 101st faces right now. Let's just say the way I demolished his arguments ensured I'd never be welcome at the University in any capacity."

A wry smile creased Pushkin's face.

"You were making friends everywhere back then, weren't you?"

"I think I was becoming more and more frustrated with the general postwar attitude in the Fleet, the government, and in that particular instance, academia. The dawning realization I probably wouldn't get my star back didn't help." Dunmoore shrugged. "Oh, well. That's in the past. However, here, today, I face several decisions, any of which can generate a whole host of second and third-order effects that could resonate for years."

Pushkin moved one of his knights.

"I hear you. It was so much simpler during the war. But I know you'll make the right choices. You always do." When she opened her mouth to protest, he raised a hand and added, "Except, perhaps in matters affecting you personally."

They played on in silence for a few minutes, then he asked, "Any idea what your next move will be? The staff is running a betting pool."

Dunmoore gave him a hard stare.

"Gambling in my flagship?"

"Just a friendly game for bragging rights."

At that moment, Dunmoore's communicator chimed. She picked it up and glanced at the display, then thumb it on.

"Dunmoore here."

"Flag CIC, sir. We intercepted a communication between a Confederacy sloop and a shuttle heading for Rakka, one of the two that left the very same ship in the last half hour. They encrypted the stream with an algorithm that seems derived from the standard Navy codes used at the end of the war. Commander Khanjan and Chief Cazano are working on cracking it right now."

"Isn't that fascinating? And the other shuttle?"

"Headed for *Vuko*," Lieutenant Commander Zakaria replied. "I've marked the sloop in question as a potential command ship."

"Thank you."

"That was it, Admiral."

"Dunmoore, out."

She exchanged a glance with Pushkin.

"Interesting."

"Were you perchance hoping for the Howlers to slowly reveal themselves while we sit here quietly, spying on them? Is that really why you're antsy?"

"I was hoping, and yes, I know hope is not a valid course of action, but we can afford to spend time lurking. If we crack their encryption, perhaps we'll learn something useful." She turned her eyes back on the board. "And I think you've boxed me in. Shall I concede now, or do you want to utter those infamous words, check-mate?"

"I'll take the concession. Best two out of three again?"

"Sure. Until Attar and Chief Cazano decrypt that stream or something else of note happens, you and I have little to do." Dunmoore tipped her king over, and Pushkin reset the board.

After two more games, she stood and bowed her head.

"You beat me two out of three. The universe is in balance once more, *sensei*."

Pushkin let out a guffaw. "The pupil has become the master's equal. That last game was a squeaker."

Dunmoore's communicator chirped again, and she opened a link.

"We decrypted the stream, Admiral. They're using one of the Theta serials from eight years ago as a base — Theta-Three-Seven-One, which was retired long ago. Whoever adapted it didn't go quite far enough to mask its origins, which gave us a way in." Lieutenant Commander Khanjan sounded more excited than she'd ever heard him, even though most wouldn't have noticed. "Sure, it'll foil anyone in the Zone, Shrehari included, but not *Iolanthe*'s sheer computing power and her library of obsolete Theta serials."

"Can you feed it to my day cabin?"

"It's coming right up, sir. I gather Captain Pushkin is with you?"

"He is. We'll watch together now that he's beaten me at chess again."

Khanjan chuckled.

"I feel for you, Admiral. He reminds each of us at least once a week that he's a master."

"And play against you, I'll stay one," Pushkin growled in a voice loud enough to reach Dunmoore's communicator.

"I've queued the stream to your day cabin terminal, sir. So enjoy, because we certainly did."

Pushkin allowed himself an amused snort at Khanjan's tone as he glanced at Dunmoore. "Sounds like we're in for a treat."

— Thirty-Eight —

Dunmoore called up the relevant file and projected it on the primary display while she and Pushkin settled in comfortably.

"Well, I'll be damned. You were right," the latter said after the first twenty seconds. "That's Lena Corto, as I live and breathe. A decade older and twice as sour."

"Notice what she's wearing on her collar?"

Pushkin let out a bark of laughter which echoed from bulkhead to bulkhead.

"That would be the star she thinks you stole from her. She's even nuttier than I remember. Who ever heard of a mercenary commodore?"

As they watched and listened, Pushkin regained his usual sobriety.

"She may have gone off the deep end but figuring out it was *Iolanthe* and a squadron of Q ships hiding in geosync proves there's nothing wrong with her instincts. So, the missing thirty-six are in Rakka. Thank the Almighty they're still alive and within reach. What'll you do now?"

"We know she's heading for Cullan — another star system I visited as *Iolanthe*'s captain — meaning there's no need for pursuit when she breaks out of orbit. So let her think she's made a clean escape by staying in silent running mode until she goes FTL. Afterward, I'll chat with Jamy Daver. You've heard the name before, right?"

Pushkin nodded.

"Apparently, he was a real operator in every negative sense of the word. He ran Starbase 36's supply division like his own private fief before he wangled a promotion to the 3rd Fleet's Logistic staff after Admiral Nagira left. With his reputation, I'm not surprised Daver ended up as an outlaw feeding off every illegal commerce imaginable. But what an intelligence treasure trove that decrypted stream is. Although thinking about it, I can't figure how they thought their link was sufficiently secure when Lena knew we were there, spying on them and waiting."

Dunmoore shrugged.

"Complacency. No one's penetrated their ciphers for years. Neither she nor Daver probably gave it so much as a second thought because they were used to speaking privately around beings who couldn't decrypt a code derived from the best the Navy fielded — eight years ago."

"Yep. That'll screw up anyone. Best we don't even give them so much as a hint that we can read their mail."

"Which is why we'll let Lena take her ships to Cullan unmolested. We can catch up with her after our business here is done. Let's join the others in the CIC and discuss this new development, shall we?"

**

"That's them alright, Admiral. Broken out of orbit when they were on the other side of Abaddon from us. It's almost as if they figured we were sitting above Rakka all this time." Chief Cox gave Dunmoore a knowing grin over his shoulder. "Now that we heard her name, I've recorded *Mahigan*'s signature in the threat database alongside *Vuko*'s and assigned tentatives to *Nashoba* and *Amarog*. Naval Intelligence will be happy with this new information."

"Check their vector, though Lena will either make a dogleg before the heliopause or immediately after crossing it. So long as she heads for Cullan as intended, we can catch up and chat about old times."

"Do you think they faked the entire conversation for our purposes?" Lieutenant Commander Zakaria asked. "As a way of throwing us off."

"I suppose it's possible, but Lena Corto never was much of an actor, and she seemed quite natural speaking with Daver. Him, on the other hand? I wouldn't be too sure. Daver is a confidence artist, a smooth talker who can charm money from a miser, which means he can play any role he has to." Dunmoore shook her head. "But no. I don't think this was a setup. They genuinely didn't consider we might not only intercept their stream but decipher it in short order."

"Bit of a rookie mistake for two veteran Navy officers," Guthren said in a tone tinged with derision.

"Things changed since their day, Chief. We have newer and better tools. Besides, Daver was a logistics specialist whose last assignment aboard a warship predated the Shrehari invasion. After all this time, communication security wouldn't be one of his first thoughts when his organization uses a Navy-derived encryption system. Corto? Well, you remember, right?"

He nodded.

"Overly full of herself. The sort we non-commissioned officers secretly hold in contempt. Point taken, Admiral."

"What are your orders?" Pushkin asked.

"We wait until she's gone FTL, then we'll light up *Iolanthe* — her only, mind you — and I shall speak with Captain Jamy Daver, Commonwealth Navy, retired, about recovering the thirty-six passengers taken off *Athena*. Mind you, I'll probably need to reassure the Shrehari ships in orbit first that we're here on a matter which doesn't involve them, with the full understanding they'll be watching and listening closely to gather as much intelligence as possible."

Pushkin shrugged.

"So long as we don't shoot at each other, it's all part of the Great Game. We've been observing and listening since we arrived and will be giving Naval Intelligence a lot of useful data on the Shrehari as well."

**

"Still nothing, Commodore." The sensor chief sat back in his chair and exhaled. "Either they didn't see us leave, or they're not after us, or what we saw wasn't Commonwealth Navy Q ships."

Lena Corto shook her head.

"They saw us leave all right. Count on it. Which means they're probably after something else, perhaps matters totally unrelated to the *Athena* operation."

Yet even as she spoke, doubt gnawed at Corto's gut. Could she and Daver have missed something? And did it matter at this point? Her squadron was on a heading that pointed deeper into the Zone and not Cullan. They'd drop out of FTL halfway to the heliopause, make a dogleg and jump again, then do so once more after crossing the heliopause. It added almost two days to their trip but would foil even the best wolf pack tactics someone like Dunmoore could muster. Besides, those only worked on complacent commanders or poor sods bound by strict doctrine like the Shrehari.

"There's no way they can catch us now, sir."

"Good. Officer of the watch?"

"Sir?"

"I'll be in my quarters. Once we reach the hyperlimit, confirm the ships are synced and go FTL."

"Aye, aye, sir."

**

"And they're gone."

"Thank you, Chief. Gregor, please ask Captain Devall to power up his ship. Let's see how long it takes for anyone to notice there's an unmarked battlecruiser without a functioning transponder sitting in geosynchronous orbit."

Dunmoore had ordered her four ships to unmask before the last FTL jump, so they arrived at Abaddon in their fighting configuration and not as harmless-looking freighters. Unmasking in front of so many sketchy observers wouldn't have been good for the battle group's continued undercover work.

A few moments later, Chief Cox reported, "*Iolanthe* is live. Her shields are down, but the generators are powered and ready, her combat systems are powered and ready though the gun capacitors aren't charged, and the active sensors are up and running."

"Good. Let's hope our sheer size will deter anyone from doing something stupid. Chief Cazano, try to raise the local Confederacy of the Howling Stars representative on the frequency Lena Corto used."

As pre-arranged, Cazano didn't utter the ship's name or that she was a Navy vessel, mentioning only Dunmoore's name as the one calling, not her rank. Several minutes passed before she received a reply which caused her to give Dunmoore a surprised glance.

"They're not interested in speaking with anyone aboard the unidentified battlecruiser in orbit and recommend we leave this star system forthwith."

Dunmoore had expected a reply of the sort. The Confederacy gained nothing by speaking with her.

Pushkin raised his hand.

"Admiral, *Iolanthe* is receiving multiple calls from the Shrehari, Abaddon Traffic Control, and something that calls itself the Rakka Syndicate, which, if I recall from Mikhail Forenza's briefing package, runs this place. They want to know who we are, how we suddenly appeared, and what we want. Trevane is dealing with them as discussed."

Dunmoore nodded her thanks. Devall would be telling all callers they had business with the Confederacy of the Howling Stars and no one else.

"Chief, put me on with the one who responded."

"It was audio only, sir. I'm connecting your chair's display." A few seconds passed. "You're live."

"This is Siobhan Dunmoore. It's in everyone's best interest if I speak with the senior Confederacy executive on Abaddon. Please put me through now."

"He has no business with you," a gruff voice responded after a long interval. "So piss off, Dunmoore. We remember who and what you are. This isn't a place where you can throw your weight around."

"I don't need to throw my weight around, friend. I only need a rod from God, and your cozy little compound north of downtown Rakka becomes a smoking crater. You're ex-Navy, you understand what a tungsten penetrator can do, and my ship has enough to hammer through Abaddon's crust and turn its habitable zone into lava fields. Give me your top executive, or I'll start with a little demonstration just outside your wire."

"The damned Commonwealth Navy has no business in the Zone, Dunmoore. Go away."

"Who said I was Navy?" Her voice took on that sweet undertone everyone in the CIC knew only too well. "Tell you what, sunshine. I'm going to slice the hyperdrives off one of your ships currently in orbit. Do you think that might entice your boss?"

She glanced at Cox. "Target Tango Five."

"Wait. Hang on, Dunmoore. You can't simply murder forty crewmembers to make a point. They wore Navy blue, just like you."

"This is business, and incentives are part of the negotiating toolkit. Guns, are you locked on?"

"Yes, sir. Ready to slice off hyperdrives at your command."

"Your call, friend. Give me the boss, or I murder forty of yours, no matter what uniform they wore before turning their backs on the Commonwealth. And don't count on your Rakka Syndicate friends for help. Their orbitals will become so much scrap metal the moment my sensors see them powering up, and if you're truly ex-Navy, you understand damn well I'm not bluffing."

Pushkin and Guthren exchanged glances that were half-amused, half-worried. Dunmoore's tone changed from sweet to deadly cold so suddenly, they almost believed she would go through with her threat.

"Wait one."

A few minutes passed, then her virtual display came to life with the face of the man who'd been speaking with Lena Corto a few hours earlier.

"I'm Jamy Daver, the Confederacy of the Howling Stars' Vice President for the Abaddon system. And I know who you are, Siobhan Dunmoore. I'm surprised they gave you rear admiral's stars after all you did. I suppose congratulations are in order."

"That was a fortunate outcome of my rescuing *Athena* from the clutches of your organization."

"Am I supposed to understand what you're talking about?"

"Don't play games with me, Daver. We may not have met, but I'm aware of your reputation. If we'd crossed paths and clashed back during the war, I'd have made sure you never got that fourth stripe."

He cocked an eyebrow as he studied her with mocking eyes.

"What did I ever do to earn your enmity, Admiral?"

"You personally? Nothing. I'm here to finish the job and recover the thirty-six passengers your mercenaries took off *Athena*."

— Thirty-Nine —

"Oh, please. Why would I know anything about these hypothetical abductees? The rumors were right. You lost your bloody mind, Dunmoore. I guess winning the war by yourself really disconnected you from reality."

Dunmoore tilted her head to one side and eyed him like a raptor, studying her prey.

"You're trying my patience, Captain Daver. The ships which hijacked *Athena* broke out of orbit a few hours ago, and Abaddon is a known trafficking hub for sapient beings. This mysterious commodore of yours, which Sara Lauzier described, must surely have landed her captives in Rakka, which means you can tell me where they are."

"And what if the commodore took them with her?"

Dunmoore turned her eyes away from the video pickup.

"Guns, please target the source of this transmission with a penetrator launch and execute on my command."

"You wouldn't dare."

"If you know who I am, then you're aware I will do so without a shred of hesitation."

"Even if it kills the very people you're here to save?"

A cruel smile tugged at Dunmoore's lips.

"Yes, even so. The universe would be better off without them as well as without your lot. But my job is recovering our errant elites. So save your lives by handing them over. Otherwise, my mission report will begin with the words, I regret to inform you even though I'll feel no regrets whatsoever."

Daver stared at her for a bit, then shook his head.

"You're as bloody demented as your reputation makes out. What tells me you won't kill us once I turn over that flock of drones who, as you so eloquently stated, serve no use?"

"My word, Captain Daver. If you know of my reputation, you've surely heard that my word is my bond. Cooperate, and I won't turn Abaddon into a charnel house with only my ship, and the Shrehari left intact. As far as the Treaty of Ulufan goes, so long as I don't target the boneheads, we're good. Besides, we've told the *Tai Zohl* spy ships in orbit I'm here on a family matter which doesn't involve them. They understand these things. Now, what'll it be?"

Daver hesitated for a fraction of a second, then inclined his head.

"Very well. The idea of bringing prisoners back for the slave trade was never part of our procedures, so you're doing us a favor. Give me twelve hours. How do you wish to proceed with the transfer?"

She let out a snort of derisive laughter.

"In a way that ensures you can't play nasty tricks on me. Remember, if they don't make it into my ship safe and sound, I'll scour Abaddon. Propose a plan that doesn't involve my shuttles picking them up from the surface or allowing any of yours within a thousand klicks of my ship."

Daver thought for a moment.

"Shuttles docking halfway to your altitude, then? One of yours and one of mine. The prisoners cross over, and we're done? Once they're in your care, you can scan them for nasties as much as you want. But since I'd rather not find our headquarters compound transformed into a crater for the sake of people our private military arm should have simply spaced at Galadiman, you can rest assured we'll play this honestly."

"Agreed, but I'm not giving you half a day. You have three hours to get that shuttle orbiting at an altitude of eighteen thousand kilometers and make sure your Rakka Syndicate friends stay out of this. Any interference will end Abaddon's status as a hub for the unsavory trade in this part of the Zone." She gave Daver a predatory smile. "After all, I'm not really here because the Treaty forbids the presence of naval forces from either side, and we understand the Commonwealth government is scrupulous about such things. As for the Shrehari, they agree it's best if we hairless apes clean up our own messes and leave them out of it. Not that there's a single Shrehari war veteran who doesn't remember my name."

"This will sound unkind, but you strike me as a little full of yourself, Admiral. Be that as it may, stand by for a prisoner transfer. As soon as we send a shuttle aloft, we'll transmit the requisite identification data. Daver, out."

Pushkin turned to Dunmoore.

"I'll organize a remotely piloted shuttle so we don't risk any crew lives. Daver can't be trusted."

"Oh, I wouldn't worry. Daver understands any tricks will result in a rod from God on his location, and since he's in this for profits, not for glory…" She gave him a wry smile. "By all means, let's use an RPS and subject the thirty-six to intensive scans as they embark, then quarantine them in the Marine barracks. However, I don't trust him a bit. There are ways of organizing delayed retaliation via biological vectors."

"In that case, we'll make them suit up as they climb aboard our shuttle and create an isolation run from the hangar deck to the barracks. If there's nothing else, I'll speak with Trevane right away."

"Thanks, Gregor."

**

"The sensors picked up thirty-six life signs aboard their shuttle, Admiral. So either we're short a passenger or two, or it's an RPS, just like ours."

"And it's only an hour late."

They watched in silence as the two shuttles slowly matched velocities and approached each other. The one belonging to Jamy Daver's organization was a civilian version of an older spacecraft design now withdrawn from service by the Navy. It meant they would experience no issues mating via a transfer tube. And they didn't.

Video feed from *Iolanthe*'s shuttle showed humans in orange jumpsuits entering one-by-one, bewildered looks on their faces. Then, as each appeared, Lieutenant Commander Khanjan matched them with images on file, confirming their identities.

When the last one came through, he glanced at Dunmoore. "And Vitus Amali makes thirty-six."

"Our shuttle is buttoned up and pulling back the mating tube, sir. Theirs is firing thrusters and peeling away."

Dunmoore turned to Cazano.

"Put me through, Chief."

"Yes, sir." Then, "You're on."

"Good day, everyone." At the sound of Dunmoore's voice, the rescuees looked around, panicked. "I'm Rear Admiral Siobhan Dunmoore of the Commonwealth Navy. I command the 101st Battle Group. We're glad to finally retrieve you. You'll be pleased that we recovered *Athena* with the rest of your fellow travelers a few weeks ago. They're safely back with their families by now. As soon as your shuttle is aboard my flagship, we're heading for home. Now, please don the emergency pressure suits you'll find on your seats and seal them. Since we don't know your medical status, you'll be quarantined in the interests of everyone's health. We'll be lodging you in a separate section of the ship, where you'll enjoy every amenity a warship can offer. Once we're away from this place, I will speak with you in person, albeit from behind the quarantine screen."

They watched them examine the pressure suits and then slowly pull them on, some more reluctantly than others. Finally, when several of them didn't seal theirs shut, the voice of *Iolanthe*'s second officer came through the CIC speakers.

"Folks, please seal your suits. Otherwise, we cannot take you aboard. This is for your safety. The ship's hangar deck will not be pressurized when you disembark."

It proved enough to convince the holdouts.

Dunmoore stood.

"I'll be down in the hangar deck control room watching the proceedings, Gregor. Then, as soon as the shuttle is secure and *Iolanthe* ready for departure, execute the navigation plan."

"Aye, aye, Admiral." He grinned at her. "I'm still not tired of calling you that, by the way."

She glanced at Guthren. "You interested in joining me?"

"Sure. It's not every day you see their sort looking like sad sacks."

Pressure-suited crew members met the shuttle on the hangar deck and guided the rescuees to the aft airlock behind which lay the ship's Marine barracks, empty since E Company, 3rd Battalion, Scandia Regiment, disembarked after the armistice. The entire section was isolated from *Iolanthe*'s environmental systems via added filtering modules that would kill viruses or other microorganisms before air and waste products were cycled out. Meals prepared by the main galley would be cycled through the airlock, and any crew entering the section would do so wearing pressure suits until *Iolanthe*'s surgeon determined their passengers weren't deliberately infected with anything nasty. Once their guests vanished, Dunmoore and Guthren returned to the flag CIC.

"We're on a heading for the hyperlimit, aimed at Commonwealth space and definitely not the Cullan system, Admiral," Pushkin reported as he climbed out of the command chair. "The others are conforming to our movements but in silent running mode, save for their sublight drives. That should give watchers in orbit and on the surface something to chew on — there was an entire squadron hiding above Rakka all this time."

"Good. Maybe the gentle beings running piracy, smuggling, and human trafficking operations in the Zone will spend more time looking over their shoulders, wondering who's next. Chief Cazano, can we ping a Colonial Office subspace relay from here with no one noticing? I'd like to send my report before we go FTL."

**

"Siobhan found them on Rakka," Ezekiel Holt said the moment Kowalski answered her secure communicator, "which is where Mikhail Forenza thought they might be held, and forced their captors to hand them over without firing a shot. The thirty-six are now aboard *Iolanthe* and in reasonably good health, considering they spent the last few weeks confined and fearing for their lives. However, just in case the Confederacy of the Howling Stars infected them with a biological agent designed to attack the crew, they're quarantined in the Marine barracks until *Iolanthe*'s doc gives them a clean bill of health."

"That's excellent news."

"The 101st will make a quick detour on the way home. It appears Lena Corto — yes, she's the mysterious commodore — is headed for the Cullan system, where she'll wait in hiding for her next contract. Siobhan plans on either capturing or destroying Corto's squadron as a warning for others."

"Good. We've been overly indulgent with the organized crime groups in the Zone. It's time for some object lessons."

"Do me a favor. So far, you and I are the only ones on Earth who know the 101st has recovered the missing thirty-six. Let's leave it that way until Siobhan docks at Starbase 30 and announces the good news."

She nodded. "There's no point in giving Sara Lauzier extra time to cover her tracks."

"That and I'm running an experiment. If Jamy Daver, the Confederacy's vice president for the Rakka system and a retired Navy captain, decides informing the SSB, or whoever the Bureau uses as an intermediary, is in his best interests, we'll try tracing the communication links with the Colonial Office's help. It might tell us a lot about the SSB's activities in the Rim Sector and the Zone."

"No problems. I've become an old hand at temporarily keeping things from the CNO in the interests of the Service."

"Siobhan and her people will interview each of the rescuees during their trip home and provide me with the recordings at the earliest opportunity. Maybe one of them will know something that points the finger at Sara, but I'm not holding my breath. So far, all we have is a conversation between Corto and Daver implicating her, and that's nowhere near actionable."

"It would have to be someone with a lot of guts and an insane amount of top cover, Zeke. And I doubt that bunch includes an individual who has both. Just the fact Sara felt she could make them disappear speaks to a distinct lack of protection."

He shrugged.

"I don't expect we'll ever uncover the whole truth, but since Sara appears destined for greatness, we'll accumulate every bit we can on her and hope that eventually, her dossier will give the Fleet leverage. The SSB, though, that's another story. Everything we find out about their doings will come in handy sooner rather than later."

**

"We ran tests for every known pathogen that could be used in a biological attack on *Iolanthe* and found nothing. Our guests are healthy and recovering nicely, so I doubt their captors injected them with a bio bomb. Considering how little time they had between the admiral opening communications and the handover, it's unlikely they used something we can't detect after five days of intensive scanning and observation. But I still suggest we keep them confined to the barracks." *Iolanthe*'s chief medical officer, who'd been looking at Captain Devall and Rear Admiral Dunmoore in turn, settled his eyes on the latter. "Oh, and by the way, several of them are becoming rather vocal with demands for greater comforts and especially for an audience with the admiral."

After briefly speaking with the rescuees via holographic projection after *Iolanthe* went FTL and explaining what their lives would look like during the trip to Starbase 30, Dunmoore avoided any contact. She knew they would soon feel well enough to regain their natural sense of entitlement. But, as she'd told Pushkin, gratitude from people of their sort turned sour surprisingly fast. They didn't like owing anyone, let alone a lowly rear admiral whose two stars wouldn't get her past the front door of their private clubs.

"Thank you, Doctor. I'll rescind strict quarantine measures, if only because they need interviewing, so we can understand what happened aboard *Athena* and after they were taken off."

Pushkin chuckled.

"Pity those who demand an audience with Admiral Dunmoore. They rarely enjoy the experience."

"Then so much the better, sir. A few of our guests are genuine pieces of work. I can't help wondering how they survived this long. Now, if there was anything else?"

Dunmoore shook her head.

"No. Thank you, Doctor, and well done to you and your team. Keep monitoring our passengers' health. I'll deal with the rest of our guest issues."

"Better you than me, sir." He stood. "With your permission?"

Dunmoore nodded. "You may return to your normal duties."

— Forty —

"In what order should we conduct the interviews?" Lieutenant Commander Khanjan asked. "I'm not what you could term particularly experienced in these matters."

"Does any part of the intelligence package give us information so we can establish relative positions in the Commonwealth power hierarchy?"

"To a certain extent, sir."

"Then set it up with those who have the most apparent power first, and we'll see if it needs adjusting. We're just as much in the dark on these matters as you are, if truth be told. I don't think we can go terribly wrong by switching a few in the order of march."

"Will you sit in on the interviews?"

Dunmoore allowed herself a wan smile.

"I'll be conducting them. There are a lot of questions I need answered before we report to Fleet HQ again."

"Understood, Admiral. Based on what I read, I suggest you begin with Vitus Amali. He, among them, seems the most highly placed as vice chair of the ComCorp board of directors. The next would be Carl Renzo, spouse of Senator Judy Chu from Arcadia.

Apparently, she pretty much runs the Home World faction in
the Senate despite anything the SecGen may want."

"That's what I hear. Very well. Now that the quarantine's
lifted, we will interview them in the flag conference room one at
a time, starting with Amali and Renzo. The first one right after
lunch today at two bells in the afternoon watch."

Khanjan nodded.

"Will do, sir. No escorts, I presume, just a guide."

"Indeed, seeing as how they're guests and not prisoners. A tray
of non-alcoholic refreshments won't come amiss either."

"I'll see that the wardroom takes care of it."

"And make sure the recorders work. We'll be sending a video
of each interview back to Earth."

**

"Come in, Mister Amali." Dunmoore gestured at the chair
across from her. "Please sit. Help yourself to whatever you want
from the tray."

Vitus Amali didn't immediately enter the flag conference room.
Instead, he stood on the threshold, eyes searching every nook and
cranny before they finally settled on her. His mistrust was
evident, although it fought with equally clear curiosity.

Like the rest of the rescuees, Amali wore simple, dark green
clothes — trousers, collarless shirt, tunic — along with low shoes
produced by *Iolanthe*'s fabricator. They weren't up to his
standards of elegance but still beat orange jumpsuits any day of
the week.

He finally stepped in and cautiously took the indicated chair.

"As I announced this morning, now that we've lifted your quarantine, it behooves us to interview each of you about your experiences from the time *Athena* was captured to the moment you boarded *Iolanthe*. We're recording the interviews for later analysis, hoping the information you provide will help us prevent further hijackings."

"And what if I'd rather not?"

"Then you'd be doing yourself, your fellow passengers, and future victims a disservice, Mister Amali. We interviewed everyone in *Athena*, crew included, and they graciously cooperated."

He gave her a skeptical look. "Even Sara Lauzier?"

She nodded.

"Yes. You expected otherwise?"

Amali gave her a tight shake of the head.

"No. All right, ask away, Admiral."

His story up until Corto's people removed him from *Athena* matched what she'd heard from those who remained aboard. But when it came to the removal itself, he seemed visibly hesitant, as if his recollections of that moment didn't add up.

"What is it, Mister Amali?" She asked in a gentle tone.

"Something Sara said. A few minutes after she came back from meeting the head pirate and was told they would execute us one after the other if Earth didn't cooperate, two thugs entered the private lounge to seize me. Just before they injected me with a knockout drug, I asked her for help, and she said, 'I'm afraid I can't do that, Vitus' in a tone that seemed almost gleeful. Her behavior that day was a bit strange, now that I think back. In any case, I woke up in a large, bare compartment, lying on a thin bedroll. They'd left me in my clothes and shoes but took everything else — jewelry, wallet, reader. Over the next days, they dumped my companions into the compartment one after the other. We had sanitary facilities and were given ration bars three times a day along with bottled water."

Amali rolled his eyes as he sighed.

"Can you imagine? Weeks of nothing but ration bars. Readapting to actual food from your galley is proving a tad — how shall I put this? Uncomfortable. Eventually, we were herded aboard a shuttle, flown planetside, and locked up in a stockade where they gave us orange jumpsuits. I somehow felt they didn't quite know what to do with us, but don't quote me on that. Then, you showed up, they loaded us back aboard the shuttle, and here we are."

Over the following ten minutes, Dunmoore teased out information about the people he'd seen — appearance, weapons, behavior, etc. When he finally fell silent after her last question, he let out another sigh.

"I hope what I've said will be useful in finding these miscreants and the criminals who put them up to it. And now I'd like to ask whether we can move into better quarters. I'm sure a ship this size has plenty of spare cabins with more comforts than the Marine barracks, even though we each have a private compartment."

"I'm sorry, Mister Amali, but no. We can't allow thirty-six civilians to wander around in a warship that's still sailing beyond the Commonwealth sphere. The amenities you're enjoying do not differ from those of *Iolanthe*'s crew, officers included, and you're eating the same food. It won't be for much longer. A week or two, maybe three, then we'll reach Starbase 30, from which you will no doubt be taken home under more luxurious conditions. Thank you for your time. The petty officer in the corridor will take you back to your quarters."

Amali stared at her for a few seconds, then inclined his head.

"Thank you for your courtesy, Admiral. Please enjoy the rest of your day."

The other rescuees had even less to say, though most asked for more comfortable quarters and better catering. However, Dunmoore noted that none ever saw, let alone spoke with Sara Lauzier after the abductions began. It was congruent with her orchestrating the removals when she met with Corto and withdrawing afterward so she could stay in the clear. Hopefully, whoever was reading her reports back on Earth wouldn't shy away from taking a closer look at the SecGen's daughter and decide whether she had reasons for making people disappear.

When the last of them left the conference room, the door to the flag CIC opened, admitting Gregor Pushkin, who'd watched the interviews from his workstation.

"You look ready for a stiff drink, Admiral."

"I'll make do with a cup of coffee, black, no sweetener, and I'll fetch it from the wardroom in a moment." Dunmoore shook her head. "What a bunch. No sense of observation, no self-awareness, but my are they ever concerned with themselves."

"Our esteemed guests normally live in another universe altogether. Ours is rather alien for their pampered sensibilities. I noticed you pointedly didn't tell them we were making a detour to find their hijackers. Any reason?"

She stood and stretched.

"Whatever happens in the Cullan system will be covered by one of our usual top secret special access codenames, so it's best they don't find out. That way, they can't blab to the newsies. Besides, I'd rather only the Confederacy and we know about what happened out here. It makes for fewer political complications back home."

"But what if the Howlers spread the news?"

"After the surprise we pulled at Abaddon, our appearing in the Cullan system unexpectedly will make them rather nervous, something they won't share with potential employers, lest they appear weak. And as a bonus, nervous foes make stupid mistakes. I love taking advantage of those."

"What'll you do if we find Lena?" They left the conference room and took the nearest spiral staircase down one deck.

"Capture or destroy her ships. If we can land the crews on Cullan beforehand and strand them there, so much the better. I'd rather not engage in a wholesale slaughter of Fleet veterans, and we can't take them back for trial because *that* will definitely cause no end of complications. But I'll let Lena believe we'll reduce her and her crews to so much space dust. It might concentrate her mind on the benefits of telling me what happened aboard *Athena* in exchange for their lives. Whoever has been sponsoring our mission at Fleet HQ will surely be pleased if we can find out."

Pushkin chuckled.

"You're becoming rather good at what some would call blackmail backed by threats of unrestrained violence."

She shrugged.

"The dark and dirty little wars of peace are better fought through coercive measures than actual combat. It saves on ships, crews, and ammunition while being more politically palatable for our leaders and the citizenry at large." As they entered the wardroom, she said, "Once we finish our coffee, please see that Attar packages the interview recordings for transmission. I'd like them on the Colonial Office subspace network headed for Earth the moment we drop out of FTL."

"He's already on it, Admiral."

"Did I ever mention how much I enjoy having a flag captain who can anticipate my orders?"

"Yes, but you can say it as often as you like."

**

"Got a few spare hours, Kathryn?"

She grimaced at Holt's image on her office display.

"You know what it's like around here. Ask me for anything but time."

"I see you're familiar with Napoleon Bonaparte's famous saying."

"Siobhan made sure her people spent the time productively by educating themselves when not on watch during long patrols. She gave all of us — officers, chiefs, petty officers, and ratings — a reading list shortly after we limped home from Cimmeria in *Stingray*."

He gave her a knowing smile.

"She did the same thing in *Iolanthe* not long after taking command. I still have it somewhere. I understand those officers who took her recommendations seriously arrived at the War College well prepared. Those who didn't read the classics before or during the course quickly learned to do so. Otherwise, they felt the sharp edge of her wit slashing their egos apart. Now, back to my original question. We received recordings of Siobhan interviewing the thirty-six rescuees. My folks are running the usual analysis on them, but I thought you might be interested in watching a few, such as Vitus Amali and Carl Renzo. We think they were on the removal list because the families of both wanted them gone in exchange for supporting a Sara Lauzier run at the Senate and then the SecGen's chair."

"Nice. I always figured the Amalis as murderous bastards who'd sooner knife you in the back than smile. But why would Judy Chu wish her husband to vanish?"

A cynical smile lit up Holt's face.

"So she regains her marital freedom without losing the money Renzo brought into their union. He's the rich one who funded Chu's career. The new man isn't quite as wealthy, but he is younger, more handsome, and apparently remains sober enough to be a good bed partner in the evenings. With Renzo gone, she inherits and, in return, backs Sara's political rise. And no, it's not actionable evidence, but the theory fits. We're still working on the others, but it's obvious Geraldo Amali has wanted Vitus out of the family business for a long time. Yet because Vitus inherited his block of shares, he can't be dismissed or bought out."

"I'll come over at two. Does that work?"

"It does. Shall I prepare some popcorn?"

"No, but a green tea would be nice."

— Forty-One —

"You know, Admiral, it's almost unfair." Pushkin, who'd been watching the passive sensors pick up Lena Corto's ships one after the other as the 101st Battle Group approached Cullan, running silent from the hyperlimit, glanced at Dunmoore from his workstation. "They don't know we're here, armed to the teeth and without a shred of mercy."

"As a wise man once said, if you're in a fair fight, you screwed up somewhere along the line."

"True."

This time, instead of concentrating in geosynchronous orbit, Dunmoore's ships were coasting toward the planet — a harsh, marginal, sparsely inhabited world — on divergent courses so that they were spread out. That way, no one could escape from view or from incoming fire. Lena Corto wouldn't pull the same trick as at Abaddon.

But was she paranoid enough for enhanced sensor watches hunting ghosts? Corto couldn't know *Iolanthe* intercepted and decrypted her conversation with Daver. Not even he knew.

She would have arrived a day or two earlier thanks to her smaller ships being capable of riding higher interstellar hyperspace bands than a massive warship like *Iolanthe*. But was that enough to relax her people's vigilance? They were ex-Navy and used to staying alert through any sort of tedium.

"The final tally is seven ships, Admiral," Chief Cox reported. "All of a similar design. They're chattering among themselves as if this were a friendly port, not some forsaken rock at the hind end of space. Nothing else in orbit besides a few satellites. Like Captain Pushkin said, it's almost unfair."

The 101st crossed the remaining distance to Cullan without a reaction from the Confederacy ships and assumed a geosynchronous orbit. Once her ships were linked via communication lasers, Dunmoore confirmed they could cover the entire planet, meaning none would escape.

"Chief Cazano, please put me on the frequency used by our targets."

"Aye, aye, sir." A pause. "You may cut through their chatter at your discretion."

"Are we going up systems?"

Dunmoore glanced at Pushkin and shook her head.

"No. I want my voice to come from the ether. Once they're paying attention, we'll stop hiding."

She called up her command chair's virtual display.

"Ships belonging to the Confederacy of the Howling Stars, this is Rear Admiral Siobhan Dunmoore, Commonwealth Navy. Please put your so-called commodore, Lena Corto, on this link. I'd like to give her my terms."

A minute passed, then the display shimmered, and a familiar face appeared, though it seemed to be aging visibly by the second as Corto recognized her old nemesis.

"How the hell—" Corto sounded both outraged and at a loss for words.

"It was simplicity itself, Lena. The problem is, you've always underestimated me and overestimated your own abilities." Dunmoore's voice took on that sweet tone her long-time crew such as Guthren and Pushkin knew only too well. "Which is why I'm wearing a rear admiral's stars, and you're wearing a mercenary's getup. Captain Pushkin, the 101st is to go up systems now, please. Raise shields, power weapons, and activate target acquisition as per fire plan."

"Why are you here?"

"To put you out of business, and as your sensors can now determine, I brought more than enough firepower for the job. By the way, the thirty-six you were intent on trafficking, they're safe and comfortable in *Iolanthe*'s Marine barracks, eager to go home. Jamy Daver figured they weren't worth me turning the Confederacy's ground base on Abaddon into a smoking crater."

An unflattering sneer twisted Corto's face.

"You'd have never done it."

"This is the Zone, where there is no God and no law but that of the mightiest. Oh, I'd have started with a demonstration first, a single kinetic penetrator just outside Rakka. If nothing else, the Syndicate running it would have pressured Daver into cooperation." Dunmoore gave her a sad smile. "And now, I've come for you because you're guilty of piracy, forcible confinement, kidnapping, and attempted human trafficking."

"So, what now? You'll take us prisoner and see that we end up in court? You're hoping for a guilty verdict followed by life on Parth? I can guarantee you no judge will hear our case."

"Why is that?"

Corto hesitated as if she suddenly realized she'd spoken out of turn.

"Let's just say I can reveal things about the *Athena* matter certain people will not want known."

"I see. Well, the fact that you undeniably committed an act of piracy within the Commonwealth sphere is all I need to be the judge, jury, and executioner. Out here, my conducting a drumhead court-martial is legal. Or I could simply blow your ships into their constituent atoms with you aboard. It would save time. Besides, the Navy doesn't pay prize money anymore, so there's no incentive in taking them."

"You're not a butcher, Dunmoore. You don't have it in you to simply murder three hundred Navy veterans."

"I've changed, Lena. I'm no longer so forgiving, but if you're interested in a deal for yourself and your crews, I can offer a way out..."

After a long moment of silence during which Corto's hate-filled eyes were locked with Dunmoore's, she said, "I'm listening."

"Tell me what you know about the *Athena* hijacking, and I'll allow everyone aboard your ships to land on Cullan unharmed with whatever cargo you want, using your shuttles. Then, once your ships are empty, I will destroy them. What happens after is in your hands, but Cullan is reasonably habitable from what I remember, and I'm sure Jamy Daver will eventually send someone looking for you. Information for life. That's what I offer. You know me, Lena. I don't renege on my word."

"Very well. Sara Lauzier, the SecGen's daughter. She was in on it. When we reached Galadiman, I had her brought to Captain

LeDain's day cabin, as per the contract — and before you ask, I don't know who hired us. That was done by others in the Confederacy of the Howling Stars. We went through the passenger manifest while Lauzier told me who to take off, in what order, and at what intervals. She wanted them spaced, but I also have scruples, and she didn't demur when I proposed trafficking them deep into the Zone. Once those on her list were off *Athena*, another part of my organization, posing as specialists for hire by the Commonwealth government, would stage a rescue and take *Athena* home. In other words, it was a contract, nothing more."

Dunmoore nodded to herself. It explained Lauzier's strange reaction when she and her boarding party appeared.

"Did you take everyone on her list?"

Corto shook her head.

"No. We were seven short. You arrived just a bit too early. But since I completed most of the mission, I figured letting you retrieve *Athena* would do, so I ran. There was no point in attempting to fight off an entire task force."

"Pretty much the same situation as now. Give me those seven names, and you just bought yourself a new lease on life. Word to the wise, however. If I catch you or your people engaged in piracy, smuggling, or human trafficking again, I will kill everyone involved without compunction. This was your one freebie. There will not be another. So do yourselves a favor — go home and find legal jobs. Walk away from the Howlers because I'm only getting started. After today, the fact you're Navy veterans will no longer factor in any decision the Fleet makes concerning your future."

"The Fleet? Or Siobhan Dunmoore?"

"Since I'm the Navy's instrument in the Protectorate Zone, there is no difference. I wasn't facetious when I said I've changed, Lena. The years since the end of the war weren't what I'd hoped, and that has transformed me into a rather bitter, cynical person I don't really like. Although I suppose I owe you for my reprieve and subsequent promotion. You and Sara Lauzier. Otherwise, I'd be packing my things while searching for a post-retirement job right now, instead of looking forward to a battle group broadside at your ships, something which will hopefully prove cathartic."

"How much time are you giving us?"

"One hour. Don't bother with sabotage. I meant it when I said we'll destroy them but spare your lives. I give you my word."

Corto nodded. "Okay."

"The names?"

"One moment." Corto glanced away, then, after a brief pause, gave her the list of those who weren't taken off *Athena* in time.

"This is hopefully our last encounter, Lena. I don't wish to see you dead before your time. You were a decent Navy officer who reached the rank of captain on her own merits. But if you don't walk away from the Confederacy of the Howling Stars, I predict you'll no longer be among the living this time next year. Dunmoore, out."

Pushkin let out an amused chuckle.

"Wasn't Lena's reaction something we'll remember over cold beers when we're old, gray, and haunting our local Veterans Association lodge?"

"I didn't know she could turn any paler than she already is, but the Admiral made it happen," Guthren said in a tone of feigned awe.

Dunmoore held up a restraining hand.

"Let's not get too gleeful because it's not over yet. Whatever her faults, Lena Corto isn't incompetent. Nor, I suspect, are her other captains."

Thirty-five minutes passed in quasi-silence, then Chief Cox reported, "Shuttle launch from *Vuko*, sir."

"Drex isn't messing around. So much the better for him."

Over the next quarter of an hour, each ship spat out four shuttles that entered Cullan's atmosphere at steep angles.

"We're no longer reading life signs on the ships, Admiral. So I figure we can — What the hell? They're accelerating and gaining altitude — all seven of them." Then, "Their targeting sensors are active and pinging us."

"*Blyat'*!" Pushkin's hands danced across his workstation as he pulled up the data feed from *Iolanthe*'s CIC. "They turned them into attack drones. I'll wager they set the antimatter containment units to go critical the moment they're within range."

"Signals, make to all ships — we are under attack. Execute fire plan and break out of orbit at maximum rate of acceleration."

Within seconds, *Iolanthe*'s big guns began pumping out streams of plasma aimed at the nearest Confederacy ship, *Mahigan*. Its shields glowed green for a moment, then turned blue for just a heartbeat before assuming a deep purple hue as competing energies clashed. All the while, *Iolanthe*'s sublight drives fired at full military power as she pushed against Cullan's gravity so she could put distance between her and the smaller, faster ship turned doomsday device, one whose return fire was creating its own greenish glow on the Q ship's shields.

With the suddenness everyone remembered from wartime experience, *Mahigan*'s shields failed, and the continuous plasma stream from *Iolanthe* ate through her armored hull plating. Seconds later, a tiny supernova lit up as her antimatter containment failed, vaporizing the sloop and hurling a radiation wave at the Q ship, whose shields gave off a menacing purple aurora.

Iolanthe's guns immediately sought out the next sloop in line, and it too died at the heart of a massive explosion shortly after that but at a greater distance. The battle, such as it was, ended abruptly within minutes, leaving the 101st Battle Group slightly shaken by Lena Corto's brazenness.

"I need a status report from each ship, Gregor."

"At once, sir."

"Should I look for those shuttles, Admiral?" Chief Cox asked. "In case you'd like to repay them."

Dunmoore shook her head.

"No. I gave Corto my word I'd let them live. Besides," she allowed herself a rueful smile, "This is on me. I should have made her swear she wouldn't pull one last stunt, but I didn't.

"Sir, all ships report no substantial damage. Strained shield generators are the worst of it, and they can replace damaged units from their own stocks."

"Good. Commander Khanjan, set the 101st on a course for home."

"Aye, aye, Admiral."

— Forty-Two —

"This better be urgent, Blayne." Sara Lauzier swept into his office like a battleship of yore under a full press of sails and took the chair facing his desk. "I can't visit SSB headquarters too often. Otherwise, people will wonder, and that only creates problems."

He gave her a bitter smile.

"You'll love this. Siobhan Dunmoore made the Confederacy of the Howling Stars hand over the people they took off *Athena*. She apparently threatened a kinetic strike on Abaddon — that's where the Confederacy has one of its hubs and was holding the thirty-six — if they didn't cooperate. Jamy Daver, their top man in Rakka, didn't think Dunmoore was bluffing. She had enough ships in geosynchronous orbit to wipe out the city and its surroundings with a single salvo of penetrators."

Lauzier visibly blanched.

"Damn."

"I hope you didn't do or say anything to those thirty-six which might raise suspicions. So far, no one knows where Dunmoore and her battle group are. The squadron that took *Athena* left before Dunmoore made her presence overtly known, though they suspected she was there, hiding in plain sight. Dunmoore shouldn't figure out where it went, and apparently, her ships departed on a different vector anyway."

"The only one who knows anything is this Commodore person, and you said she fled. Considering how vast the Zone is, we should be okay."

A chuckle.

"I shall be okay either way, Sara. It's you I'm worried about."

She gave him a hard stare.

"If I go down, you go down, Blayne. It's as simple as that. Let's hope Dunmoore doesn't find the Commodore. We can deal with the thirty-six later."

"You mean *you* can deal with them. I'm not doing anything more at this point. Disposing of your potential opponents and of unwanted family members in return for political favors was risky, to begin with. Now that it backfired, bide your time and wait. That's the best I can recommend because the SecGen's chair probably won't be yours in six years at this point. If you can find a fresh source of patience, so much the better because impatience causes errors, some of them fatal. The next twelve years will pass and faster than you might expect."

Her stare turned into a glare.

"I don't need a lecture from you. I need solutions to prevent this from becoming a disaster."

"What is it I should do, other than pretend we're pleased with the outcome and a hearty Bravo Zulu for the Navy?"

"Make sure Dunmoore and her two friends at Fleet HQ, Kowalski and Holt, don't dig any further. Let this become an investigation into sovereignists turned criminals and only that."

Hersom sat back and contemplated her for a few seconds.

"Here's the thing, Sara. Your father made the Grand Admiral give Dunmoore her due. I crossed swords with her during the war, and I'll be among the first to recognize that she's smarter and more ruthless than most flag officers. Holt? He's enjoyed an interesting career so far. But at this moment, he's the flag officer in Naval Intelligence who worries me the most because his division is the one charged with looking inward, investigating misdeeds by the likes of you and me, and prosecuting any sign of official corruption. And he's good at what he does."

"See that he's run over by a truck or something." Lauzier made a dismissive hand gesture. "Accidents happen, even in this town."

"Perhaps, but Holt killed in a traffic accident would seem overly convenient in the eyes of his subordinates, who are frighteningly capable, and especially his friend, Kathryn Kowalski. She's easily the most dangerous of the three because she's navigating the currents and eddies of power not only in Fleet HQ but in Geneva at large as if she were born to it. And she's the CNO's rising star, possibly even a future Grand Admiral. Her dying of an accident at the same time as Holt? Let's just say any fail-safes you and I put in place would pale compared to what those two likely have. As I said, let it be. Allow the *Athena* incident to become a minor footnote in the history of Rim Sector piracy and move on, Sara. Striving for retribution can turn into a deadly vendetta."

"Don't you see how they might become a major impediment, especially if this Kowalski is a potential Grand Admiral?"

"I do, but now is not the time to strike. Go home, let the Fleet do as it will because neither of us can change its course. Welcome the thirty-six as if they were your dearest blood relations, make a big show if you can stomach it, and move on. There will be other opportunities, and even if Holt's counterintelligence specialists build a dossier on the *Athena* incident, nothing can touch you."

When a disturbed and far from reassured Sara Lauzier left SSB headquarters, Hersom called in his operations chief.

"I'm proceeding on the assumption naval counterintelligence traced the communication chain between the Confederacy of the Howling Stars and us at this point. Issue orders to terminate everyone upstream of our people with extreme prejudice. I want existing links between the Confederacy and the SSB eliminated."

"Aren't they too useful for a complete break, sir?"

"They've become a liability for reasons I can't discuss even with you, Dan. Sorry. If we need them again, we'll do so via new channels which can't be linked to the current ones."

Dan bowed his head. "Very well, sir. I'll send out the orders right away."

"And while you're at it, ask your contacts at Fleet HQ if they know the whereabouts of the 101st Battle Group. It seems to have vanished. No one I spoke with knew anything."

When he was once more alone, Hersom turned to face the window, settled back, elbows on the arms of his high-backed executive chair, fingertips touching, and stared out at Lake Geneva shimmering under the bright morning sun. Helping Sara Lauzier with her insane scheme was looking more and more like a tactical mistake. Building new linkages with the Confederacy of the Howling Stars, while annoying, wouldn't be a big deal. No one in that organization knew they were often hired by the Commonwealth's security police via anonymous agents to carry out black ops.

No. What worried Hersom was whether or not Dunmoore found evidence in the Zone that the likes of Holt could use to undermine the SSB either directly or via Sara Lauzier. He shook his head. Dunmoore. If it wasn't for her, the scheme might have worked perfectly, and his hirelings would have 'rescued' *Athena*, giving him complete control over how the rest of the story unfolded. And over dear Sara.

But no. Fate intervened — again. It was enough to make him wonder about the wisdom of terminating Dunmoore with extreme prejudice. Her death wouldn't create quite the same ripples as those of Kowalski and Holt. After all, she was out on the frontier, far from the seat of power, and many in the Fleet weren't pleased with her belated promotion. A least based on what his acquaintances in uniform told him.

Perhaps a warning might be appropriate as a first step. Pity Holt, like every other senior intelligence officer, lived in a residential housing unit on the base, where casual visitors weren't admitted without permission. A laudable precaution in a city teeming with political backstabbers, blackmailers, and other assorted coercion artists, including those who didn't shy from more forceful methods. But it made a subtle approach difficult. So be it.

Several minutes later, Commodore Ezekiel Holt's face appeared on Hersom's office display. Though he showed no reaction at a call from the SSB's director general, he could almost sense curiosity oozing from every pore, even through a secure comlink.

"What can I do for you, Mister Hersom?"

"Join me for a cup of coffee or tea in the Palace of the Stars' Commonwealth Café. How does fifteen hundred hours this afternoon sound?"

Holt nodded.

"I can do that. Fifteen hundred hours it is."

"See you then."

Hersom cut the link and turned his chair to face the lake again.

When he entered the almost empty café a few minutes before three, Hersom found Commodore Holt already seated in one of the private booths by the east-facing, floor-to-ceiling windows, nursing a cup of green tea. Hersom grabbed a coffee at the bar and joined him moments later.

"Thank you for coming, Commodore."

Both men studied each other for a few seconds.

"I'll confess to overwhelming curiosity, Mister Hersom. You're not in the habit of meeting flag officers informally on neutral ground."

"Seeing as how we both serve the Commonwealth, isn't the term neutral ground a bit overwrought? Aren't we on the same side?" Hersom took a sip of coffee. "They do it better here than anywhere else. At least in my opinion."

"Probably, but I've reached my daily caffeine intake limit. So, why am I here?" Holt asked, pointedly ignoring Hersom's questions.

"Did you know this was once called the Serpent Bar, back in the days before the Palace became the seat of humanity's interstellar government? It's a shame the first SecGen changed it. The original name was not only amusing but on point, considering the business transacted in this complex by our honorable elected officials."

Holt raised his tea mug and, before taking a sip, said, "I've studied the Palace's history, among others."

"Good for you. History is a fascinating subject, one whose importance few people understand. Which is why it has a habit of repeating itself, to humanity's detriment. And isn't that the essence of our jobs, yours and mine? Trying to prevent the worst parts of history repeating?"

Another sip.

"Take the growing unrest in the colonies and outer sectors these days, for example. Doesn't that remind you of another dark era, one which saw hundreds of millions dead, whole cities razed, and marginal settlements made uninhabitable? Part of it, of course, is human nature, civilization being merely a thin veneer hiding the primitive beast. But what shatters that veneer is often loss of trust in the institutions that bind our societies. Sometimes, they no longer deserve said trust, or as certain civilizations put it long ago, they lose the mandate of heaven. Sometimes, the people are seized by the madness of a cause and turn on the one thing keeping the beast at bay — our venerable institutions. Yet too often, no matter who's at fault, the end results are disastrous, and that is something you and I, and those alongside whom we serve must prevent."

"Indeed, Mister Hersom. However, we, the protectors of the state, also frequently disagree on what should and shouldn't be done. What's moral or immoral, democratic or tyrannical, right or wrong."

"Oh, absolutely, Commodore. That's why we must find common ground to build a joint vision, one aimed at preserving our institutions and the peace that depends on their smooth functioning. And while doing so, we cannot let the failings and foibles of individuals, perhaps even their misdeeds, stand in our way. On the contrary, we should always take the long view, no matter what obstacles or hiccups occur in the short term. It accrues not only to our advantage but that of society as a whole." He flashed a smile at Holt. "Who indeed wants to be known as the one guilty of needlessly precipitating a crisis?"

Hersom finished his coffee, placed the cup on the table, and stood.

"Thank you for joining me. Enjoy the rest of your day."

— Forty-Three —

"If that wasn't a clear warning to stay away from Sara Lauzier no matter what evidence we uncover, I wouldn't know what it is," Kathryn Kowalski said after Holt recounted his meeting with Blayne Hersom the previous afternoon word for word.

"He's nobody's fool. Our little conversation was clearly an attempt at telling me, and thereby you that pursuing the *Athena* matter after Siobhan recovered it and the passengers wouldn't be in anyone's interests. And he's right insofar as the current political situation is concerned. Let Lauzier believe she won't be called to account and bide our time, even if Siobhan brings back concrete evidence from the 101st's raid in the Cullan system. Her father and his successor can smooth over troubled colonial waters and gain the Commonwealth a bit of breathing space, enough time to figure out how we can dispel the growing clouds of discord."

Kowalski nodded.

"I agree. And I'm surprised Hersom proved to be so rational."

"He's nothing if not clear-headed. Pretty much everything he said made sense. If I weren't such a cynic, I might actually have felt a degree of kinship with him, which was obviously his intent."

"So, what's the conclusion?"

"No different from what I suggested before. Siobhan recovered *Athena* and everyone aboard, and she started the work of scouring the Zone, which means our principal objectives are being achieved. We continue building the dossier on Sara Lauzier for the day she begins her campaign to become SecGen in earnest, identify her backers and build their dossiers as well. Meanwhile, we make sure the 101st Battle Group continues cleaning up our frontiers, which should go a long way in assuaging nervous OutWorlds and colonies and remove that particular irritant from the relationship with Earth."

"Letting Sara get away with it."

Holt nodded.

"If that's what it takes to prevent a crisis. Now is not the time. We, too, must build up our strength so we can give your plan a chance of success, Kathryn. Our turn will come."

"Will you tell the CNI about meeting with Hersom?"

"I have no choice in the matter. Every contact with the SSB gets recorded, especially when it's at such a high level, and yes, I stated my belief Hersom was warning us off Sara Lauzier."

"What was Admiral Doxiadis' reaction?"

"Build a dossier, but let this one go. After all, the plan failed."

Kowalski allowed herself a quick grimace.

"Then she'll look for other ways to dispose of the individuals on her list."

"Not our problem, so long as she doesn't also look for other ways of sowing dissension in the colonies. One of my colleagues has people hunting potential agents provocateurs in the Rim Sector. If they succeed, we'll no doubt uncover linkages to the SSB as well."

"Which means once Siobhan's back in Commonwealth space with the thirty-six, this particular operation is over, and she goes hunting pirates. While we're on that subject, I've been thinking about enhancing the 101st's strike capabilities. The Marine Corps fields Pathfinder companies, one per regiment, whose job is reconnoitering, seizing, and securing beachheads."

Holt nodded.

"Yes. Crazy people who jump out of perfectly good shuttles from low orbit. Although, in fairness, the truly crazy ones are in the 1st Special Forces Regiment. They jump in but not to prepare the way for a regiment. Black ops, creating havoc behind enemy lines, hitting organized crime nodes, terrorists and insurgents, that sort of thing."

"Right. What I was thinking is that the 101st needs a hybrid of the two. A reinforced Pathfinder company embarked in *Iolanthe*, one whose mission is acting as Siobhan's surgical scalpel when rods from God aren't the right solution. Give them a flight of dropships, perhaps a few gunships and some infantry fighting vehicles, organic artillery, and organic combat engineers — a mini battalion group. Lord knows there's enough room for everything three times over. That way, if a mission calls for direct action on the ground, the 101st can deliver them, provide orbital fire support, and extract them when it's done. No matter how good a naval boarding or landing party is, it can never be as good as Marines, especially those from the Special Forces."

"I've heard the idea bandied about during the war, but nothing ever came of it. If memory serves, I think Siobhan even wrote a paper on the subject while she was teaching at the War College, one of her less controversial essays."

A sly smile appeared on Kowalski's face.

"I forwarded a copy with my comments and suggestions to General Espinoza, seeing as how the Marines for this task would come from SOCOM, with Espinoza assigning operational control to the 101st's Flag Officer Commanding."

"Do you think he'll consider it?"

Her smile widened.

"Oh, yes. The idea of projecting Special Forces into the Zone and other parts of the frontier as the ground element of a dedicated naval formation created for that precise purpose, rather than on an ad hoc basis, is like catnip to him and his staff. They've been looking for missions that justify SOCOM's expansion. It hasn't done well in terms of funding and personnel since the war. Suppose the idea I borrowed from Siobhan works. In that case, they can create more of these reinforced Pathfinder companies and assign them the job of rapid reaction force throughout the Commonwealth, embarked in dedicated Q ships and other vessels of sufficient size."

Holt let out a soft chuckle.

"Espinoza will love that. Does it mean the Q ships will return to his command?"

"That's the enticement if he seems hesitant."

"Wait. Didn't you mention something about the 101st going to SOCOM anyway after the current mission is completed?"

"Yes, but so far, it hasn't been made official."

"Sneaky."

Kowalski took a seated bow.

"Why, thank you, kind sir."

"When do you expect an answer?"

"Soon. Espinoza knows as well as I do that our window of opportunity is limited. Once the *Athena* business fades from the consciousness of our superiors and the government, interest in experimenting with Special Forces as part of the 101st will wane quickly."

**

Holt found Blayne Hersom on the restaurant terrace, wine glass in hand, watching the rays of a late afternoon sun dance over Lake Geneva as it kissed the top of the Jura Mountains to the west. He took the other chair, turned it to face in the same direction, and sat.

"I've spent a considerable amount of time reflecting on our previous conversation over the last few days, Mister Hersom."

"Did you, Commodore? I suppose that's a good thing." Hersom's eyes never left the lake. "And what conclusions did you reach?"

"Conclusion, singular. Rear Admiral Dunmoore destroyed the Confederacy of the Howling Stars squadron that hijacked *Athena* a few days ago in the Cullan system. Seven ships in total. That should clip the wings of your tame mercenaries. Tell me, can the SSB's black budget afford replacements from the Arkanna, even at their low, low prices? Because I assume you gave them seed money in the first place. Or will you direct the funds to some other shipyards now that we've zeroed in on the modifications characteristic of those knockoffs and can detect their trace everywhere?

"Anyhow, as far as the Fleet is concerned, the matter has been resolved, or it will be once Siobhan's battle group reaches Starbase 30 and places the last thirty-six of *Athena*'s passengers in civilian hands. You may consider the information she extracted from the Confederacy squadron commander as being memory-holed under so many classification layers that even the Grand Admiral cannot access her report. I believe this meets the intent of our common goals."

Hersom took a sip of his white wine and nodded.

"It does."

"Then do me a favor, from one professional to another. Tell Sara Lauzier the next time she tries something of the sort, she will not escape unscathed. The Fleet's goodwill is as finite as is its patience, and Sara exhausted both. I understand she expects to become SecGen in twelve years, if not six. The last thing she needs is the enmity of the known galaxy's most powerful military force. Imagine what would happen if her true nature — that of a depraved, soulless, calculating sociopath, became common knowledge."

"That's quite the libelous accusation, my dear Commodore. She is an honorable servant of the Commonwealth, trusted by senators, bureaucrats, and the SecGen himself."

Holt didn't immediately reply. Instead, he let a full minute elapse while his eyes rested on the Palace of the Stars, spread out along the far shore.

"One last piece of advice. Don't involve the SSB in any other schemes to support Sara's twisted goals or set yourself against us. It will not end well, that I can guarantee. This was your one and only freebie." Holt climbed to his feet. "Between us students of history, familiarizing yourself with an early twentieth-century event called the Night of the Long Knives can be instructive. Enjoy the rest of your day, Mister Hersom."

Holt turned away, but before he could take two steps, Hersom's voice momentarily stopped him.

"I admire your forthrightness, Commodore, misplaced as it may be. If I were you, I'd always be sure of my audience before speaking. Please give my regards to Admiral Dunmoore the next time you contact her."

For reasons Holt couldn't explain, Hersom's final sentence, spoken in a gentle, almost amused tone, sent an icy shiver up his spine. But he neither replied nor looked back as he walked away.

**

"Message delivered, sir," Holt announced when Admiral Doxiadis gestured at him to enter the office and take a seat. "But I felt a strange vibe from him."

Holt relayed the brief conversation almost verbatim and finished with the eerie feeling he got as he left the restaurant patio.

"Blayne Hersom says nothing that isn't fraught with hidden meaning. Was he threatening you and Siobhan Dunmoore with reprisal for your role in making Sara Lauzier's scheme collapse?" Doxiadis shrugged. "Perhaps. But he also enjoys playing mind games with adversaries, and you threatened him and the SSB quite openly on the Fleet's behalf, something that likely took him by complete surprise."

A wry smile appeared on Holt's lips.

"Us changing the rules of the game unilaterally? There's no doubt I took him by surprise, sir. But at least now he understands we are no longer letting him operate beyond the rule of law with impunity. Oh, and I doubt he was happy that we found out the SSB has been funding the Confederacy of the Howling Stars. But, you know, if we really want to engage in mischief, perhaps anonymously leaking a bit of what we discovered about the SSB to Sara Lauzier might sow dissension between them. You remember the old toast — confusion to the enemy."

"Let me think about it, Zeke. Too much of a good thing can ricochet back on us."

— Forty-Four —

"Oliver! Nice of you to call in person."

"So, did you find them?" Harmel gave her an expectant look. Dunmoore nodded.

"All thirty-six, safe and sound, enjoying the luxury of *Iolanthe*'s Marine barracks. We made a minor detour on the way back and ensured the mercenaries who carried out *Athena*'s hijacking won't do so again. They're still alive but no longer own anything more than a handful of shuttlecraft. That last bit is classified information, by the way, so no sharing with anyone, not even Admiral Zantas, unless HQ clears it."

"Mum's the word." He mimed zipping his lips shut. "I'm calling for a few things. First, you can dock your four ships if you like. There's only one ship in port right now, the civilian yacht that'll take your passengers home. No others are expected for at least two weeks, and I can accommodate a few unexpected arrivals anyhow."

"That's good news. I'd like to give my crews shore leave on the surface after their ships are provisioned."

"Since you'll be the only ones, provisioning will be quick. Second thing, I'd like to invite you, your captains, and your

principal staff officers to join me and my staff for the evening
meal in Starbase 30's wardroom tonight, say eighteen-hundred."

She inclined her head.

"I accept with pleasure."

"Finally, I received a private, encrypted message for you from
Earth. It bears Fleet HQ markers. If you're ready, I can see it's
sent to *Iolanthe* right away."

"Please do so."

"And that was all I had. So welcome home — seeing as how
this is the 101st's home port, and we'll see each other at eighteen-
hundred hours."

"Thanks, Oliver."

"Harmel, out."

Moments later, her communicator chimed — the message
from Earth pushed into her queue by the flag CIC. She entered
her personal decryption key and linked the communicator with
her day cabin display. The Fleet's crossed swords, anchor, and
starburst insignia appeared for a few seconds before fading away,
replaced by the smiling faces of Rear Admiral Kathryn Kowalski
and Commodore Ezekiel Holt, sitting side-by-side at a small
office table.

"Hi Siobhan," the former said. "If you're watching this, you've
arrived home with the rescuees after another successful mission.
I don't know if you figured it out, but Zeke and I were your HQ
controllers for both the *Athena* recovery and this latest one."

"What she means," Holt jerked a thumb at Kowalski, "is she's
responsible for briefly reviving Task Force Luckner, the creation
of the 101st Battle Group, and you finally getting the stars that
should have graced your tunic collar for years by now."

"I couldn't do it without Zeke's almost supernatural counterintelligence skills. He laid a major hex on the SSB. Anyway, congratulations on pulling it off. You haven't lost your touch. Keep in mind there are people here at Fleet HQ who don't like the taste of crow, and I'm afraid you've not made new friends. But the important thing is you're still in uniform, in command of your own battle group, and capable of cleaning up the Rim Sector frontier. As you'll find out when the official messages arrive, the 101st reports to SOCOM now, but the CNO will be assigning your missions. And since I'm the CNO's director for the Rim Sector, they'll be coming from me."

"A few things you should realize," Holt said when Kowalski nodded at him. "You've gained implacable enemies in the persons of Sara Lauzier and SSB Director General Blayne Hersom. Both blame you, along with us two, for ruining their operation. Yes, that would be the same Blayne Hersom you stared down on Raijin's moon, Temar, in the Hecate system long ago. Apparently, our relieving him of political prisoners didn't stunt his career. I don't think either will do something stupid, mainly because we — the Fleet — agreed we wouldn't pursue the matter of Sara Lauzier's involvement in the *Athena* incident. I'm sure you can figure out why. But we will add this to her dossier, and she'll eventually reap the consequences of her acts. In the meantime, your 101st can curtail the SSB's shenanigans in the Zone and make them bleed both resources and funds. We now know they gave the Confederacy of the Howling Stars start-up funding and used the Howlers for various illegal schemes in the Rim Sector and beyond. Consider them your primary target and use extreme prejudice. You have complete freedom of operation."

"We're even working on getting you a reinforced company of Special Forces Marines you can use for surgical strikes. Yes, that's how serious Fleet HQ perceives the growing threat from the Zone and the political unrest it generates." Kowalski gestured at Holt. "You have parting words, I believe?"

"Yes. Although I just said I don't believe either Hersom or Lauzier will do anything stupid, the desire to remove a major irritant on the frontier and teach her quasi-untouchable friends in Geneva a lesson might become overwhelming. Especially since they're the sort who never forgive and never forget. Keep an eye out for potential threats when you step off *Iolanthe*, or better yet, make sure you use bodyguards. And that's it. Hopefully, we'll see each other again at some point, but I'm never getting out of this hellhole, so it'll wait until you join us. Congratulations on a perfect job, and may you rack up many more such victories."

"I second Zeke's sentiments. Until we meet again."

The image faded, leaving Dunmoore to stare at a blank screen. The past had a habit of catching up with her — Blayne Hersom this time. Another whom she'd forced into cooperation by threatening unrestrained violence. And now he headed the fearsome SSB, accountable only to the SecGen whose daughter apparently pulled its strings on Earth. Wonderful.

Once *Iolanthe* was securely docked on one of Starbase 30's arms, Dunmoore watched her passengers leave via the airlock video pickup. She'd debated seeing them off in person, then decided against it. The idea of granting individuals she privately considered useless at best and malignant at worst, the dignity of a flag officer's farewell grated on her sense of self-respect.

Trevane Devall must have felt the same because the officer of the watch saw them over the brow and handed responsibility for their transfer to a lieutenant wearing a Starbase 30 patch on his uniform tunic. The yacht undocked less than thirty minutes later and accelerated for the hyperlimit, leaving Dunmoore with a sense of relief. If she never saw their like again, it would be too soon.

Her cabin door chimed, and she glanced away from the screen. "Enter."

It slid aside, admitting Gregor Pushkin.

"Looks like we need to dust off our old SOCOM badges, Admiral. Orders just came in placing the 101ˢᵗ under its command."

"That was quick. If you're not busy, grab a seat. I received personal mail from Kathryn Kowalski and Zeke Holt."

When Pushkin was ensconced in a chair facing the main display, she re-ran the missive. Once it stopped, he glanced at her over his shoulder.

"Interesting. How did we honest naval officers end up playing dirty politics? Kathryn and Zeke, I can understand. They're stuck on Earth. But you and I?"

She gave him a helpless shrug.

"Comes with working for SOCOM. The 101ˢᵗ was specifically set up to tackle politically sensitive issues on the frontiers and in the Zone. We're just getting started in the fine art of annoying people. Might as well enjoy the ride. This could be the most fun since the war."

"There's no could about it, Admiral."

"Oh, before I forget, our ship captains, you, I, and the four lieutenant commanders are dining with Admiral Harmel and his senior staff officers in the base wardroom at eighteen-hundred tonight. Since Oliver mentioned nothing specific, it'll be in the dress of the day. I think this will be a working dinner, a sort of getting to know us and our needs since we're a lodger unit here and haven't properly met our counterparts yet."

"I'll tell everyone." A frown creased his forehead. "Do you really think this Hersom character might put a hit out on you?"

Dunmoore made a skeptical grimace.

"No idea. He's a psychopath, of course, that I understood when I met him on Temar. It means he'd do it if expedient and in pursuit of his goals."

"What if his goal is getting you out of the way?"

"Then I'll need to be on my guard whenever I'm away from *Iolanthe*."

"That's hardly a way to live."

"It'll pass in time, once Hersom and the other swamp creatures who dislike me face fresh problems caused by different annoyances."

"Still. We need to find you a bodyguard. A shame Vincenzo's not anywhere nearby. He'd take a plasma round for you without even thinking."

Dunmoore held up her hand.

"Let's not go down that rabbit hole. Rear admirals don't go around their home ports with an armed escort."

"And what about shore leave? Or will you stay aboard and spend ten days reading?"

"I hadn't given it any thought if truth be told. On Caledonia, I simply headed south, far away from Sanctum, and found myself a warm, quiet spot where the Navy couldn't track me down."

Pushkin gave her a droll look.

"We realized that after the first few times."

"Post the orders assigning us to SOCOM. Then, chief Guthren can speak with base supply and get enough badges fabricated for those who need them, plus spares. Was there anything else?"

"Other than pleasure at our passengers being outbound, no. Shall Trevane and I wait for you at the main airlock at seventeen-forty-five?"

"Sure."

But the moment Dunmoore reached said airlock at the appointed time, she realized she should have known better. All four of her ship captains, her flag captain, and her four principal staff officers were there, so they would march through Starbase 30 and enter the wardroom as a group. It was Pushkin's doing without a doubt, based on the hoary logic that the larger a flag officer's posse, the more important she was. Tongue in cheek, of course, since he didn't believe it but enjoyed teasing her.

She gave him a stern look, then smiled at the assembled officers.

"Good evening. Thank you for joining me. As Captain Pushkin no doubt mentioned, I think this will be a working dinner, so please get acquainted with Admiral Harmel's staff and that of Starbase 30. Since we've moved in with them, we'll need their goodwill to work effectively, and that goes especially for my staff officers."

"We're going to make best friends tonight, Admiral, don't you fear," Pushkin replied. "And just so you're in the loop, I found out half an hour ago that Admiral Harmel's command chief petty officer will be entertaining Mister Guthren, our coxswains, and our staff chiefs in his mess."

"Good. As important as relations are among senior officers, those among chiefs are even more vital." Her pronouncement elicited wise nods from all present. "Alright. Shall we?"

— Forty-Five —

"Thank you for welcoming us in such a grand style, Oliver."

Dunmoore, Harmel, and their flag captains stopped in front of the wardroom's open doors and shook hands. Their respective staff officers were staying behind for another round of drinks and discussions about how they could best work together.

"My pleasure. I think our teams will get along fine if tonight is anything to judge by. The stories you and your folks related were worth the price of admission alone."

She grinned at him.

"And that's only the unclassified stuff we can talk about."

Harmel glanced at his flag captain.

"Remind me to thank the Almighty that I never faced RED One during my time as a starship captain."

"I'm right there with you, Admiral. It was a pleasure dining with you and your officers." He glanced at Pushkin. "You and I should sit down for coffee tomorrow and hammer out a few protocols, Gregor. Say my office at ten?"

"I'll be there."

Harmel gestured at Dunmoore and Pushkin to exit first and said, "Enjoy the rest of your evening."

They stepped out onto Starbase 30's expansive main Promenade, mostly deserted at this time of the evening. After a final wave, Harmel and his flag captain headed for the personnel lifts leading to the accommodation decks. Dunmoore and Pushkin walked in the other direction, toward the larger lifts connecting the Promenade with the starbase's working levels, docking rings included.

Though Starbase 30, like every other space-based installation and starship, operated twenty-four hours a day, three-hundred-and-sixty-five days a year, it nonetheless felt deserted. The day watch, comprising most of the personnel, and their families, were at home in apartments above the Promenade, leaving the base to the smaller evening and night watches.

A lift cab arrived moments after Pushkin touched the call screen, and they stepped in.

"Destination, please?" An androgynous voice asked in a gentle tone as the doors slid shut behind them.

"Docking Ring One," Pushkin replied.

"Thank you."

They couldn't sense the cab's motion, but the doors opened on a vastly different corridor a few moments later. Though equally wide, this one's lighting was harsher, and it featured utilitarian bulkheads where conduits weren't hidden behind decorative panels and a scuffed deck. Instead, the sole decorations were safety markings, and directional signs. Even the scent was different, with a tang of ozone and lubricants rather than the Promenade's soft aroma of luxurious plant life, pumped in from the arboretum and hydroponic farm.

"That was probably the most productive evening I've ever spent in a wardroom," Pushkin remarked as they stepped off toward *Iolanthe*'s docking arm — One-Alpha, the prime spot, fitting for a battle group flagship. But, if the Promenade had seemed quiet, then Docking Ring One was as still as the proverbial grave, with no signs of human life, let alone activity. Seconds later, Pushkin gave voice to Dunmoore's unspoken observation.

"I guess *Iolanthe* finished replenishing already."

"There's nothing quite like the allure of shore leave to make spacers triple their efforts."

When they were a dozen meters from the starbase end of *Iolanthe*'s docking arm, a spacer in dark blue coveralls and black gloves, the sort worn by Navy maintenance personnel, came through a side door. The patch on his right arm was that of Starbase 30, and the rank insignia on his collar made him a petty officer third class.

Lost in conversation, Dunmoore and Pushkin absently noted his presence and dismissed him as part of the evening watch. Since he wore no headdress, she didn't expect more than a formal nod.

As they were almost within arm's reach and the petty officer still wasn't bracing as expected to acknowledge a rear admiral, Pushkin saw a metallic glint suddenly spring from the man's right fist.

Without conscious thought, he took one big step just as the metallic glint became a dagger aimed upward and placed himself between Dunmoore and the petty officer.

But instead of a warning shout, what came out of Pushkin's mouth sounded more like a strangled yelp of pain. He wrapped his arms around the petty officer and took him to the deck with his sheer weight.

Dunmoore, stunned by the sudden attack, didn't immediately react and stared at the petty officer struggling to climb out from under Pushkin while a thin thread of blood appeared on the gray decking. Then, she backed away, pulled out her communicator, and activated the automated emergency signal, which should bring the spacers standing guard at *Iolanthe*'s brow running toward her along with a patrol from the starbase's military police company. Besides the distress signal, the communicator emitted a loud, piercing siren which drew the attacker's attention.

He finally wriggled out from underneath Pushkin and, with one last glance at Dunmoore, ran away, back to the door from which he'd emerged. Dunmoore watched him go, then went to kneel beside her flag captain and long-time friend. She gently rolled him over and saw the hilt of a dagger protrude from his upper abdomen.

Pushkin looked up at her and croaked, "Out of danger?"

"He's gone."

She hit her communicator's emergency call function again, this time demanding a voice connection with base operations.

"This is Admiral Dunmoore. I need a trauma team at my location now. My flag captain was stabbed in the abdomen. He's bleeding. Docking Ring One, next to docking arm One-Alpha."

Before the operations center could reply, she heard footsteps running through the arm. Seconds later, two spacers, both with blasters in their hands, skidded around the corner and headed for them.

"This is operations. Medevac is on the way, Admiral."

Dunmoore looked up at the men from *Iolanthe*, who'd taken a protective stance on either side of them, eyes searching for the assailant. The senior of the two glanced over his shoulder.

"I've alerted *Iolanthe*'s sickbay, sir. The doc and his team are on the way as well."

She examined Pushkin again and was pleased to see the blood flow remained relatively small. It would stay so as long as the dagger wasn't removed, but only the Almighty knew what sort of pain he was enduring. Dunmoore reached down and took one of his hands in both of hers and held his eyes.

"Help will be here in a few moments, Gregor. Hang on."

"Aye, aye, sir," he replied in a shaky voice. "Hanging on."

Something about the dagger's hilt seemed oddly familiar, but she couldn't place it, and her brain wasn't cooperating in any case.

Iolanthe's chief medical officer and his team, pulling an antigrav stretcher, arrived at the scene first. He knelt beside Pushkin, examined the wound, then scanned him with a medical sensor. After studying the results, he looked up at Dunmoore.

"Is the base hospital alerted?"

She nodded.

"Yes. Medevac is on its way."

"Good. There's a fair bit of trauma. He needs to be in an operating room as soon as possible. The facilities here are better equipped than *Iolanthe*'s sickbay, and they have more surgeons on staff. He's suffering from internal bleeding right now, but we can afford to wait for the medivac, especially if they come with a stasis pod."

"You're the expert, Doctor."

He nodded once, then turned his attention on Pushkin again.

"We'll see you in the best of hands momentarily, Captain. Just hang on a little longer."

"I will. Can't disappoint the admiral." A faint smile briefly lit up his anguished face. "Just wouldn't do, now, would it?"

The same lift Dunmoore took with Pushkin opened and disgorged one of the base's medivac skimmers with three people seated around a long cylinder — the stasis pod. It stopped short of where Pushkin lay, and the riders — a woman wearing a surgeon's badge and two men with medic insignia — jumped off.

"Knife puncture to the upper abdomen," *Iolanthe*'s medical officer said, climbing to his feet. "He has internal bleeding and needs surgery, stat."

She knelt beside Pushkin, examined the wound and took her own sensor readings, then nodded.

"In the stasis pod, he goes. That'll give us time to prepare."

She stood and stepped aside so the medics could put Pushkin on a litter.

Out of the corner of her eyes, Dunmoore saw an entire section of military police — six in all — appear around the docking ring's curvature. They came to a halt within earshot and waited while the medics lifted Pushkin and floated the litter into the stasis pod.

The base surgeon turned to *Iolanthe*'s medical officer.

"I'll let you know when he's in surgery."

And with that, she joined her medics aboard the little ambulance and headed back toward the lift, leaving nothing more than a bloodstain behind.

The MP noncom, a hulking Marine with a face hewn from granite, stepped forward and saluted.

"Admiral Dunmoore? I'm Sergeant Diop. What happened here?"

**

After giving a statement to the MP company's lead investigator, a seasoned chief warrant officer who'd gladly taken it in *Iolanthe*'s flag conference room instead of asking her up to his office, Dunmoore slumped back in her chair, drained of energy. Chief Guthren, who'd hurried back from the base's chiefs' and petty officers' mess, along with everyone else when they heard the news, had been at her side since he arrived.

"You need a shot of Glen Arcturus, Admiral."

"I need way more than a shot, Chief, but that won't change a damned thing. Someone tried to kill me yet failed because Gregor sacrificed himself for my sake. Unfortunately, there's not enough scotch in the universe that'll help right now, so I might as well not start."

"He'll pull through, don't you worry. Captain Pushkin is a fighter, someone who never gives up. Just like you, if I can say so." He let out a tired sigh. "That chief warrant officer was truly shaken by the event, even though he did his best to hide it. Did you notice? An assassin on his starbase? The entire MP company will be running twenty-four-seven until they find answers, poor sods."

"If the attempt was commissioned by who I think, he'll be gone by morning. He's likely wearing a different face already and carrying different, albeit legitimate credentials. Or maybe the petty officer in question was the disguise because he never existed, and the real man is now wearing his original face, which was far from Docking Ring One at the time." Dunmoore forced back a yawn.

"You figure it was either the Confederacy of the Howling Stars or the Special Security Bureau?"

She gave him a wan smile.

"Do you think there's someone else out there looking to take my head?"

"No." Guthren pushed himself upright. "Now, let's see about that shot of Glen Arcturus. Last time I checked, the bottle in your quarters was still three-quarters full."

"Provided you join me."

"Aye, I'll do that with pleasure."

— Forty-Six —

"That Gregor will make a full recovery is the best news I've read in a long time." Holt gave Kowalski a faint smile of relief after reading Dunmoore's report in the latter's office moments after it arrived.

"Yup." She nodded. "The fact he saved his own life by saving hers is one of those mysteries best left to the Almighty. If he hadn't rushed the assassin, the dagger would have gone in just a few centimeters higher and punctured his heart. He wouldn't have survived long enough for medical help. Who do you think commissioned the hit?"

"Hersom, no question about it. That was a professional job. It only failed because the assassin didn't count on Siobhan's flag captain to act like a trained bodyguard. We'll likely never find out. Using a real Pathfinder dagger as the weapon is a nice bit of deflection, though. Plenty of Special Forces operators joined the private sector after the war looking for adventure on a larger salary, and a lot joined the Howlers. The MPs will never find him. He likely came aboard the starbase openly under the guise of an Armed Forces member and left it the same way, then vanished once he was on the ground before the investigation focused on transient personnel. The face picked up by surveillance gear doesn't exist in the security database. So clearly, he wore a disguise at the time. Like I said, professional, which means SSB. Oh, we'll look, but I doubt there's any actionable evidence to find. The locals discovered nothing like usable DNA traces, and even if they had, an SSB assassin would be untraceable."

Holt shrugged.

"All we can do is thank the deity of our choice that Gregor survived and Siobhan's unhurt. He might not make the 101st's next patrol, but that's a minor thing."

"Do you figure they'll try again?"

A grimace.

"Perhaps, but I'm of a mind to warn Hersom the next attempt will cost him personally. If Admiral Doxiadis approves, of course. The attempted assassination of a rear admiral aboard a starbase raises the stakes considerably."

"And shows the Fleet has holes the SSB exploits at will. Granted, a scheme to take Siobhan out was likely concocted before she docked, but considering it occurred less than twelve hours after her unannounced arrival speaks to both good planning and a degree of penetration we did not suspect."

"Don't I know it. My counterintelligence colleague responsible for threats internal to the Fleet will take it as a personal failure, and that means a lot of work ahead ferreting out SSB moles for his people and anyone he can draft."

"So long as your lot doesn't embark on a witch hunt that could cause extensive damage. It would play into the SSB's hands."

"We're not the sort, so don't worry." Holt stood. "I'll let you brief the CNO while I do the same with Doxiadis."

**

"Ah, Admiral." Blayne Hersom looked up as Admiral Jado Doxiadis, Chief of Naval Intelligence, approached his table on the same patio where he'd met Holt. "No uniform today?"

"You don't like my fashion sense, Blayne?" Doxiadis took the other chair, but instead of facing the lake, he stared intently at Hersom.

"Your fashion sense is impeccable. I've just never seen you in civilian during working hours. What's the occasion?"

"I'd rather not make a splash out here where anyone can see, and a four-star admiral's uniform is rather noticeable."

Hersom, who was facing the lake, glanced at Doxiadis.

"Oh? Now I'm intrigued."

"Then stop staring out into nothing and look at me, you despicable, jumped-up bureaucratic weasel."

"What was that?"

Hersom's eyes widened in shock, but he obeyed Doxiadis and turned his chair ninety degrees.

"Listen to me carefully, Blayne. I will only say this once. Do not, ever again, send an assassin after one of ours. Otherwise, I will ensure the SSB is burned to the ground."

"I don't know what you're talking about, and I certainly don't like your tone, Jado."

"The attempted hit on Dunmoore that took out her flag captain — who's doing nicely, by the way, send him flowers, he'll enjoy the irony — that's on the SSB and don't offer me your usual denials. Consider this a formal warning by the Fleet. Should anything happen to Siobhan Dunmoore, you will join her in the Infinite Void. That's a promise, even if Sara Lauzier does something on her own. Consider yourself her guardian. Keep her under control and stay away from the Fleet. We'll be cleaning up the Protectorate Zone and leashing your Howlers, and you'll watch us do it without moving a finger. Otherwise, you might find SSB assets inside the Commonwealth vanish without a trace."

A mocking smile danced across Hersom's lips.

"I never knew you could be so hot-blooded, my friend."

"You tried to murder one of ours. If your assassin had succeeded, we wouldn't be talking right now because our assassin would also have succeeded." Doxiadis stood. "And we are better at using violence than your people. Always a pleasure, Blayne."

**

"Welcome back to the land of the living, Gregor." Dunmoore beamed down at Pushkin as his eyes fluttered open.

"How—how long?" He asked in a dry, raspy voice.

"Five days. Since you came out of surgery, you've been in a medically induced coma to help with the regen therapy. The medicos say you'll make a full recovery, although a centimeter or two higher, and the outcome might have been different." She shook her head. "You fool. Whatever possessed you to jump in front of me and save my life?"

"Instinct?"

"Well, whatever it was, thank you. I owe you a debt I can never repay."

A smile appeared on his drawn features.

"Consider us even, Skipper. You saved my life back when you took command of *Stingray*. If not for you, I'd be dead by now, or just as good as."

"Isn't that a tad dramatic?"

"No." He licked dry lips with an equally dry tongue. "I'd love a drink of water right now."

Dunmoore held up a bulb with a straw.

"Would you like me to do the honors or call a professional?"

"If I can't trust you, who can I trust?"

She gently placed the straw between his lips and tilted the bulb once, twice, three times, then pulled it away.

"Better?"

"Much. So, what happened? I can't remember anything beyond some asshole was about to puncture my admiral."

She recounted every moment, then added a cryptic statement to the effect that friends on Earth would make sure the party responsible never tries again.

"Ah. Zeke and Kathryn, right?"

"Yes."

"Bastards who did this should be nailed against a tree and shot the old-fashioned way, with small steel pellets, repeatedly, until they resemble colanders."

"I'm sure between them, they came up with something workable, though less bloodthirsty."

"Does this mean I can't join you for the next patrol?"

She shook her head.

"We're extending our stay in port, to everyone's delight, so we can take aboard a Marine contingent. By the time that's settled, you'll be released, if not on full duties, then light ones, which don't bar working as flag captain."

"Good. You can't go back into the Zone without me. After this, I deserve a little vicarious vengeance as we wipe out the tools of those fools on Earth."

"Get better, Gregor. The sooner you're back aboard *Iolanthe*, the happier we'll be." She stood. "And before an apologetic nurse tries to tell a rear admiral time's up, I'd better go. I'll be back tomorrow, and every day you're in here. Should I bring the chief next time?"

"Please do. He's another one who helped save me back then."

— Forty-Seven —

"Admiral Dunmoore?"

A stocky, muscular Marine Corps major in a black battledress uniform adorned with gold Pathfinder wings had magically appeared in front of her open day cabin door. The silver and gold embroidered insignia on his beret was that of the 22nd Marine Regiment, a unit with a glorious past that could trace its lineage back to the dawn of the 20th century.

In his mid-thirties, square-faced, with short black hair and deep-set, intelligent blue eyes on either side of an aquiline nose, he bore himself with the sort of self-awareness and confidence Dunmoore recognized as common among Special Forces operators. He raised his hand in a stiff salute.

"That would be me." She climbed to her feet and gave him a formal nod. "And you must be Major Harry Desai, the 221st Pathfinder Squadron's commanding officer. Welcome aboard, and please enter."

She came around her desk, hand outstretched, and they shook. Then Dunmoore gestured at the chairs around her day cabin table.

"Why don't we sit?"

"I came ahead of the squadron with my HQ, sir," Desai said once both were seated comfortably. "The rest will fly up aboard our drop and gunships once my battle captain sorts things out with *Iolanthe*'s first officer."

"Battle captain?"

An amused smile lit up Desai's rough-hewn features.

"Pathfinder Squadrons are new beasts, and the Corps, God bless it, decided we would take our traditions from old Earth cavalry units, hence the name. In one of the pre-Commonwealth armies, the squadron operations officer was called a battle captain and thus, my second-in-command received the title. We're a rather unusual construct. I assume you were briefed on our makeup?"

Dunmoore nodded.

"Three saber troops — the nomenclature being another cavalry tradition, I assume — of thirty Marines and four combat cars each; a fire support troop; a field engineer troop; an aviation troop with twelve dropships and four gunships and a composite logistics troop."

"Got it in one, sir. My complement is two hundred and ten Marines. I understand *Iolanthe*'s barracks can take more than twice that many, though I expect her hangar deck might be a little crowded."

"Actually, she has cargo holds on both sides, aft of the hangar, that were initially part of her Q ship camouflage. They were designed so we could load fake containers to distract curious observers. But we never did so. Instead, when I was her skipper during the war, we turned them into training spaces for my embarked soldiers so they could practice boarding party tactics."

"The Scandians." Desai nodded. "I looked them up when I was given this assignment. Major Tatiana Salminen — I guess she's a lieutenant colonel now — wrote an excellent account of her company's time in *Iolanthe*."

"I read it. She and her people were top-notch. In any case, both holds were modified to take your aviation troop, half in each, by adding hangar deck safety and control measures. You should even be able to take the combat cars off the dropships and park them to one side if they're not needed for a mission."

Desai's smile broadened.

"This sounds better and better."

"I understand your unit was handpicked."

"Yes, sir. The squadron was formed around the 22nd Marine Regiment's Pathfinder Company, which was rated the best in the Corps last year, so being designated as the experimental unit for this new concept is a reward." The pride in Desai's voice was unmistakable. "And it got me my promotion ahead of time since the Corps decided we would be big enough for a major in command with a sergeant major as top kick. He's probably huddled with *Iolanthe*'s coxswain and your command chief petty officer as we speak. Commissioned officer-wise, other than me, I have the battle captain, another captain running the aviation troop, and a senior lieutenant in charge of 'A' Troop. Experienced Pathfinder command sergeants, the best of the best, lead the rest of my troops."

"You've been told that if this concept works, the Corps will be raising more Pathfinder Squadrons?"

Another nod.

"Yes, sir. Rest assured, my Marines and I will make it not only work but shine as a way of winkling pirates out of their lairs in the Zone. This will be the most interesting assignment for any Marine unit since the war."

"Then we're on the same wavelength, Major. But, just out of curiosity, now that the Fleet stripped your regiment of its Pathfinder Company, what happens?"

"They've started reforming it with qualified personnel from elsewhere in the 22nd, and it'll receive priority on the next few courses at the Pathfinder School in Fort Arnhem. Just between you and me, there are probably a few regiments preparing Pathfinder Squadrons in waiting, ready for when the Corps raises additional ones."

"I wouldn't be surprised. This battle group has seen more action in the few weeks since it's been stood up than the rest of the Navy combined."

"Those of us who volunteer to become Pathfinders don't do it because we enjoy garrison duty and endless training exercises, sir. We prefer the real thing, and joining your battle group will probably be more real than anything else nowadays."

An amused smile played on Dunmoore's lips.

"In that respect, you're not much different from my Q ship crews."

"Then we should feel right at home in the 101st, Admiral."

**

"What do you think?" Dunmoore asked Pushkin as they watched the 221st's aircraft land one after the other in *Iolanthe*'s brand new port and starboard hangars on her day cabin display.

"That we might just have the best strike force in the Fleet since the original Task Force Luckner."

"Better. It's all Q ships, as the original should have been, with officers and enlisted personnel who live and breathe irregular warfare."

"We are getting more regular ships in due course, no?"

"Eventually, but for this cruise, it's irregular and special only."

"Any thoughts as to our objective, Admiral?"

She gave him a mysterious smile.

"From what Zeke told me in his latest missive, which arrived just before Major Desai, the Colonial Office Intelligence Service, our trusted ally in the Zone even now that the original reason is gone, will continue pointing out targets of opportunity. Their agent on Galadiman thinks a return visit might help stop a new human trafficking pipeline that sprung up after we retrieved *Athena* on the old principle that lightning never strikes twice in the same spot. So I think we'll snoop around quietly, listen to what the agent has and see if we can't give Major Desai a little workout."

"Sounds like something right up our alley. I'll get the planning cycle in gear." He stood with a faint wince.

"Still a little sore?"

He held out his hand, palm facing down, and wiggled it.

"Sometimes, when I move the wrong way. Oh, I meant to ask ever since I woke up in the base hospital. What happened on Earth after the assassination attempt?"

She flashed him a rueful smile.

"I'm not supposed to know this, but the Chief of Naval Intelligence told Blayne Hersom, Director General of the SSB, that if anything happened to me again, whether it was at SSB hands or someone hired by Sara Lauzier, he would die."

"Meaning Admiral Doxiadis essentially told the SSB we have them in our gun sights." Pushkin nodded, a pleased smile on his face. "And not before time. The bastards are about to discover we're the undisputed masters of the dark and dirty war."

About the Author

Eric Thomson is the pen name of a retired Canadian soldier who served more time in uniform than he expected, both in the Regular Army and the Army Reserve. He spent his Regular Army career in the Infantry and his Reserve service in the Armoured Corps. He worked as an information technology executive for several years before retiring to become a full-time author.

Eric has been a voracious reader of science fiction, military fiction, and history all his life. Several years ago, he put fingers to keyboard and started writing his own military sci-fi, with a definite space opera slant, using many of his own experiences as a soldier for inspiration.

When he is not writing fiction, Eric indulges in his other passions: photography, hiking, and scuba diving, all of which he shares with his wife.

Join Eric Thomson at www.thomsonfiction.ca

Where you will find news about upcoming books and more information about the universe in which his heroes fight for humanity's survival.

Read his blog at www.blog.thomsonfiction.ca

If you enjoyed this book, please consider leaving a review with your favorite online retailer to help others discover it.

Also by Eric Thomson

Siobhan Dunmoore

No Honor in Death (Siobhan Dunmoore Book 1)
The Path of Duty (Siobhan Dunmoore Book 2)
Like Stars in Heaven (Siobhan Dunmoore Book 3)
Victory's Bright Dawn (Siobhan Dunmoore Book 4)
Without Mercy (Siobhan Dunmoore Book 5)
When the Guns Roar (Siobhan Dunmoore Book 6)
A Dark and Dirty War (Siobhan Dunmoore Book 7)
On Stormy Seas (Siobhan Dunmoore Book 8)

Decker's War

Death Comes But Once (Decker's War Book 1)
Cold Comfort (Decker's War Book 2)
Fatal Blade (Decker's War Book 3)
Howling Stars (Decker's War Book 4)
Black Sword (Decker's War Book 5)
No Remorse (Decker's War Book 6)
Hard Strike (Decker's War Book 7)

Constabulary Casefiles

The Warrior's Knife (Constabulary Casefiles #1)
A Colonial Murder (Constabulary Casefiles #2)
The Dirty and the Dead (Constabulary Casefiles #3)
A Peril so Dire (Constabulary Casefiles #4)

Ashes of Empire

Imperial Sunset (Ashes of Empire #1)
Imperial Twilight (Ashes of Empire #2)
Imperial Night (Ashes of Empire #3)
Imperial Echoes (Ashes of Empire #4)
Imperial Ghosts (Ashes of Empire #5)

Ghost Squadron

We Dare (Ghost Squadron No. 1)
Deadly Intent (Ghost Squadron No. 2)
Die Like the Rest (Ghost Squadron No. 3)
Fear No Darkness (Ghost Squadron No. 4)

Printed in Great Britain
by Amazon

46772883R00218